Remnants of Filth

YUWU

1

REMNANTS of FILTH

YUWU

WRITTEN BY
Rou Bao Bu Chi Rou

ILLUSTRATED BY
St

TRANSLATED BY
Yu & Rui

Seven Seas Entertainment

REMNANTS OF FILTH:
YUWU VOL. 1

Published originally under the title of《余污》(Yu Wu)
Author © 肉包不吃肉 (Rou Bao Bu Chi Rou)
U.S. English edition rights under license granted by 北京晋江原创网络科技有限公司 (Beijing Jinjiang Original Network Technology Co., Ltd.)
U.S. English edition copyright © 2023 Seven Seas Entertainment, Inc.
Arranged through JS Agency Co., Ltd
All rights reserved.

Cover and Interior Illustrations by St

No portion of this book may be reproduced or transmitted in any form without written permission from the copyright holders. This is a work of fiction. Names, characters, places, and incidents are the products of the author's imagination or are used fictitiously. Any resemblance to actual events, locales, or persons, living or dead, is entirely coincidental. Any information or opinions expressed by the creators of this book belong to those individual creators and do not necessarily reflect the views of Seven Seas Entertainment or its employees.

Seven Seas press and purchase enquiries can be sent to Marketing Manager Lianne Sentar at press@gomanga.com. Information regarding the distribution and purchase of digital editions is available from Digital Manager CK Russell at digital@gomanga.com.

Seven Seas and the Seven Seas logo are trademarks of Seven Seas Entertainment. All rights reserved.

Follow Seven Seas Entertainment online at sevenseasentertainment.com.

TRANSLATION: Yu, Rui
ADAPTATION: E.M. Candon
SPECIAL THANKS: Aili, Eri
COVER DESIGN: M. A. Lewife
INTERIOR DESIGN & LAYOUT: Clay Gardner
PROOFREADER: Hnä, Stephanie Cohen
COPY EDITOR: Jehanne Bell
EDITOR: Kelly Quinn Chiu
BRAND MANAGER: Lissa Pattillo
PREPRESS TECHNICIAN: Melanie Ujimori, Jules Valera
MANAGING EDITOR: Patrick Macias
EDITOR-IN-CHIEF: Julie Davis
ASSOCIATE PUBLISHER: Adam Arnold
PUBLISHER: Jason DeAngelis

ISBN: 978-1-68579-467-5
Printed in Canada
First Printing: April 2023
10 9 8 7 6 5 4 3 2 1

TABLE OF CONTENTS

陪你弱冠成礼

肉包不吃肉

"I'll keep you company—through youth and into adulthood."

—ROU BAO BU CHI ROU
("MEATBUN DOESN'T EAT MEAT")

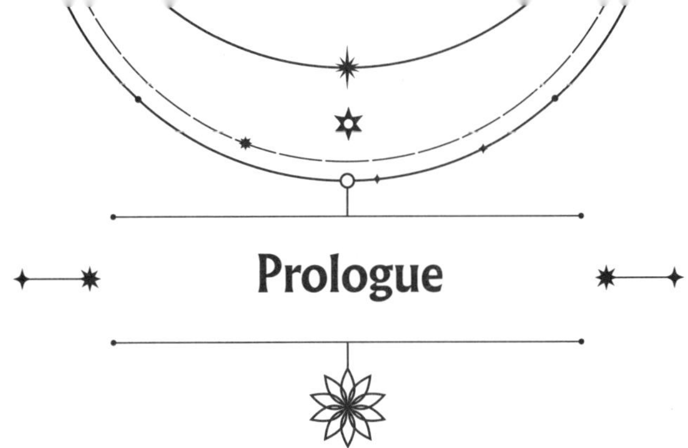

Prologue

CHONGHUA ONCE PRODUCED two young and promising generals as distinct as the Jing and the Wei,[1] as different as water from flame.

The one like water was named Mo Xi. A lifelong bachelor, he had an icy temperament and an ascetic air. The army had a betting pool regarding when General Mo would sacrifice his chastity, and it had long since grown into a fortune that could make any beggar rich overnight. Mo Xi remained a cornerstone of Chonghua's strength.

The one like fire was named Gu Mang. A perfect gentleman, he had a warm personality and smiled often. If he had owed a sack of army wages for every girl he'd kissed, he doubtless would have lost everything he owned ages ago, down to the clothes on his back. Later on, Gu Mang turned his back on Chonghua and became a commander for an enemy nation.

Before Gu Mang turned traitor, there was a day when he was suddenly possessed by a strange whim. Grabbing a little booklet filled with his own writing, he ran to ask Mo Xi to add a few words.

General Mo's hands were full with military paperwork at the time, so he only asked General Gu, "What's in this?"

---

1 *A saying that originates from the visible contrast at the point where the clear Jing River flows into the muddy Wei River. Often used to describe two parties that are sharply divided.*

"All sorts of things," Gu Mang said cheerfully. "Good food, interesting experiences, travel notes, weapon catalogs, and the trifles of life."

Mo Xi accepted the booklet, took up his brush, and dipped it in ink to make his comments.

"I also wrote about you," Gu Mang added with a smile.

Mo Xi's hand stilled as he looked up at Gu Mang. "...What about me?"

"I wrote a little about our past," Gu Mang earnestly replied.

Mo Xi didn't say another word. After staring at Gu Mang for a bit, he lowered those long lashes and expressionlessly inscribed two sharp and icy lines of formal script on the first page.

This book is forbidden. Transgressors will be punished.

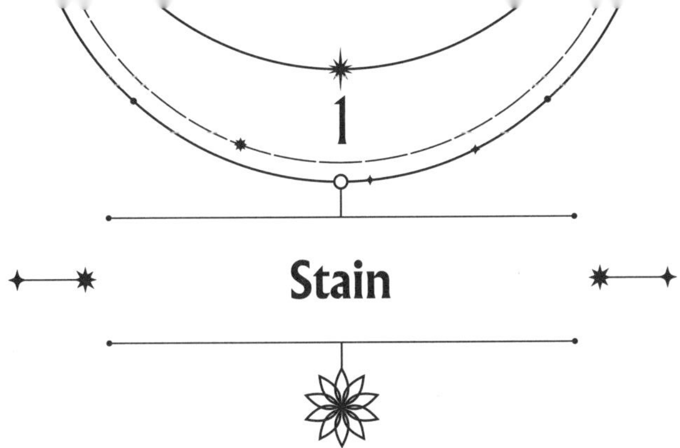

1 Stain

AT DUSK, a light flurry of snow began to fall on Chonghua's border, until it gradually blanketed the ground in a layer of pristine white. The wheels of lumbering carriages and the feet of passersby left uneven trails across the expanse.

The meat pie seller Wang Er-mazi shouted with all his might as his breath puffed out in dense clouds. "Meat pies, meat pies! Fresh out the oven!" He clanged the gong next to his oven as he peddled his goods. "There's nothing thicker than the pies I bake—other than Gu Mang's face! C'mere and get yours quick!"

Everyone who heard snickered to themselves.

This pie stall had been in business for more than a decade, and a few years ago, Wang Er-mazi had sung a different tune indeed. Back then he had crowed, "Look here, look here! General Gu's favorite pies! My dear customers, if you eat them, you'll be just as successful and invincible as General Gu—guaranteed!"

A strikingly outfitted cavalry troop slowly made their way toward him through the swirling snow, headed by a youth who looked to be about seventeen. Luxuriously dressed in brocades and furs, he was the picture of indolence with his handsome and mischievous little face bundled beneath his thick fur collar.

This young man was named Yue Chenqing, and he was the deputy general of the garrison troops. He was possessed of two profoundly formidable talents. The first was being very agreeable—as the ditty went, "What's the point of getting all mad? If I got sick that would be real bad. No one's happy when I'm mad; it's such a pain and makes me sad." Yue Chenqing understood this concept to a tee, and he hardly ever lost his temper. He was the most good-natured young master of them all.

The second talent was making himself comfortable—as comfortable as possible. He never stood if he could sit, nor sat up if he could lie flat. Yue Chenqing's favorite thing to say was, "I'll drink all the wine I've got tonight and mooch off my bros tomorrow." He never deprived himself when it came to enjoying nice things: he downed all his liquor the day he received it and took women to bed without wasting time on talk.

As for patrolling...he'd have his fun, and *then* he'd patrol.

The frontier fortress at the northern pass had many markets like this, most of which sold things like animal hides, herbal medicines, spirit stones, and slaves. These places weren't terribly interesting, but compared to the bitter tedium of army life, they made for a decent way to pass the time.

"I'll take that seven-tailed spirit cat."

"Go buy that guhuo niao tail feather for me too."

"The tumbleweed at that stall looks good. It'll definitely make effective medicine. Get me ten baskets."

As Yue Chenqing walked, he directed the retinue following him to purchase all sorts of goods. Although the members of the retinue felt uneasy seeing him shirk his responsibilities, they couldn't say much to a deputy general.

Over the course of his walk, Yue Chenqing began to feel a little hungry and looked around for something to eat. He suddenly heard Wang Er-mazi shouting in the distance, his raucous voice ringing through the snow.

"Meat pies for sale! Meat pies as thick as Gu Mang's face! C'mere and take a look!"

Upon hearing this sales pitch, a corner of Yue Chenqing's mouth twitched. *Aiya, this guy has the guts to use Gu Mang for his own ends? Doesn't he know that Gu Mang is a taboo subject with our commander, Mo Xi? If Mo Xi heard, we'd all be doomed.*

Yue Chenqing quickly led his horse forward and was about to scold the man when the strong, savory aroma of the meat pies hit him in the face. Just as Yue Chenqing's reprimand reached the tip of his tongue, he swallowed it—along with the drool about to drip down his chin.

The stallkeeper Wang Er-mazi looked up. "Officer, a pastry for you?"

"...I'll have one, I guess."

"All righty!" Wang Er-mazi nimbly grabbed a golden-brown pie from the oven with his tongs and stuffed it into an oilpaper bag, which he passed to the customer before him. "Here you go. Careful not to burn yourself. You gotta eat these pies while they're hot!"

Yue Chenqing accepted the piping hot pie and took a crackling bite. Scalding juice flowed out from the crispy golden-brown pastry as the flavors of wheat dough, ground meat, and crushed peppercorn blossomed on his tongue. Their smoky scents filled the air in an instant, and he swallowed hungrily.

"Tastes as good as it smells," Yue Chenqing couldn't help but exclaim in admiration.

"Doesn't it? Everyone knows my pastries are the best," Wang Er-mazi bragged in delight. "No matter how famous Gu Mang got way back when, he always came to my stall and ate a batch as soon as he returned to the city after a battle!"

Once he was done boasting, he made sure to add, indignantly,

"But if I'd known that Gu asshole would turn out to be a two-faced traitor, I'd have put some poison in those pies and nipped that in the bud for the good of the people!"

"Be careful with that kind of talk," Yue Chenqing said as he chewed. "Also, you'd better change up that slogan of yours."

Wang Er-mazi's eyes widened. "Why's that, Officer?"

"Doesn't matter, just be good and listen to what this officer says." Yue Chenqing took another huge bite of the meat pie, his cheeks bulging. "We'll be going to war with the Liao Kingdom soon, and I'm afraid our troops will be stationed here for a good long time. Watch out. If you keep shouting about Gu Mang all day," he snickered, "you might end up jabbing a certain dignitary right where it hurts."

The dignitary Yue Chenqing spoke of was, of course, their commander: Mo Xi.

Mo Xi, granted the title Xihe-jun by the late emperor, had been born into the prestigious Mo Clan. This clan had produced four such generals, including both of Mo Xi's grandfathers and his father. Having come from such a remarkable lineage, Mo Xi's innate spiritual power was of course extremely potent, and after studying under the cultivation academy's most severe elders, he'd attained the highest rank of general and commanded hundreds of thousands of soldiers.

And he was a mere twenty-seven years old.

Due to his family circumstances, Mo Xi's temperament was as cold and sharp as a knife's edge, and he was ever decisive and determined. His father had often warned him, "Overindulgence will blunt your blades, so do your work and ignore the maids." Thus Mo Xi was assiduously ascetic and self-disciplined, wholly free from corruption. One could have said that he'd lived twenty-seven years without ever making a single major mistake.

Except for Gu Mang.

For Mo Xi, Gu Mang was like ink on paper or mud in snow, the suggestive smear of blood left upon the pristine white of a gentleman's bedsheets.

He was the stain on Mo Xi's life.

After nightfall, a clarion melody pierced the skies in the barracks of the frontier fortress. The opera singer's voice was languid and slow as it drifted, ghostlike, across the frost.

"Rain falls soft over Yuchi Pavilion; sun shines down on Jinni Hall. Let wine and music flow for all; mean although their lives may seem, matters of ants are not so small..."

The soldier guarding the deputy general's tent looked left and right, the very image of a startled quail. At the sight of a tall, black-clothed silhouette approaching, he couldn't help but pale and lift the tent flap in panic. "Uh-oh! Bad news!" he cried.

"What's up?" Inside the tent, Yue Chenqing yawned atop the general's seat of honor and opened his eyes, propping his chin on his hand.

"Aiya! Look at the time! Deputy General, you should hurry and go on patrol—stop watching this show."

"What's the rush?" Yue Chenqing said lazily. "There'll be plenty of time after I'm done." Then he turned to the performers in the tent. "Don't just stand there, keep singing."

The music floated up into the clouds, the singer's voice like a faint silken ribbon drawn out high and long. "In that shade will a kingdom rise, a lifetime's work etched in his eyes. Qi Xuan's teachings only partly gleaned; when will the east wind wake me from this dream?"[2]

---

2 From *A Tale of Nanke*, an opera by Tang Xianzu.

"Aiya, my dear Deputy General Yue, my good deputy general, please stop their singing," the personal guard said anxiously. "What on earth is all this?"

"Life is brutish and short, so we should find our joys where we can." Yue Chenqing happily chewed on his fingernail. "Otherwise, our days would be sorely lacking in spice."

"But if Xihe-jun sees a display like this, he'll get angry again..."

"Xihe-jun isn't here, so what are you worried about?" Yue Chenqing chuckled. "Besides, Xihe-jun stalks around looking dour all day long. He doesn't put any effort into cheering himself up. He's a grown man but he still throws a fit if he hears me tell a dirty joke—how exhausting would it be to try and keep him happy?"

"Deputy General." The guard seemed close to tears. "Lower your voice... Please..."

"Hm? Why?"

"Because, because..." The guard's gaze flitted toward the gap in the tent flap. "B-because..." he stammered.

Yue Chenqing sprawled out on the general's seat and even plopped Xihe-jun's silver fur coat on his head. "Did Xihe-jun spook you guys?" he laughed. "Why're you stuttering as soon as you say his name?" Yue Chenqing sighed. "Then again, Xihe-jun sure is something. *He's* the one who wants to live like a monk, but he makes us all suffer in boredom alongside him. Look, in our whole company, there's not even a single female *dog*."

This was true. In all of Chonghua's military, the branch under Xihe-jun had it hardest. Although the troops under his command didn't lack for food or clothing, the man himself was boring and strict, just as Yue Chenqing said. It would have been fine if Xihe-jun merely insisted on personally avoiding carnal pleasures, but he forbade his subordinates from seeking out fun with girls as well.

Yue Chenqing clearly found the situation hilarious—he held back his laughter to sigh with a wholly feigned seriousness. "He's got everything going for him, except for the fact that he's way too controlling. Look, he's an obsessive clean freak overthinker with no hobbies or interests to speak of. What a waste of that handsome face."

The guard looked like he was watching a disaster unfold before his eyes. "Young Master Yue, stop talking..." he blurted out.

But Yue Chenqing didn't stop. In fact, he became even more excited. "Don't you feel pent up, like you're about to burst? Heh, while he's away, I'm gonna take the chance to cut you some slack. Tonight, let's have the brothers go have all the fun they like! We'll open the gates and host a beauty contest by the bonfire! I want to crown the prettiest girl in the nearby villages—"

"You want to crown who?"

A man's low voice cut through from outside. The tent flap lifted with a *swish*, and a tall man walked in, clad in silver armor that flashed like frost.

His uniform was proper and neat over his wide shoulders and slender waist, and his long legs were wrapped in military boots of black leather. His refined and elegant features made an indelible impression as he looked up with icy-sharp eyes. This was none other than the Xihe-jun whom Yue Chenqing had been having fun mocking—Mo Xi.

Why had Mo Xi come back now?!

At first, Yue Chenqing was struck dumb. When he came back to his senses, he shuddered, bundling himself up tighter in the furs. "General Mo." Deputy General Yue put on a show of being pitiful. "Why didn't you tell us you'd be coming back earlyyy—ahh!"

This "ahh" was due to Mo Xi, who, finding his whining unbearably disgusting, chose to summon a sword of spiritual energy and fling it a hair's breadth from Yue Chenqing's cheek.

Having narrowly avoided decapitation, Yue Chenqing scrambled up from the general's seat. "Xihe-jun, how come you're so violent?!" he demanded, pushing his hair out of his face.

"You're questioning me before I've had a chance to question you? Tell me, why are there women among my troops?" Mo Xi shot a glance at the petrified songstresses before turning back to stare at Yue Chenqing. "You brought them here?"

Yue Chenqing initially wanted to keep complaining, but he quailed the instant he met Mo Xi's eyes. "...Don't be like that. I was only listening to a song, okay? A famous song from Lichun. Does Xihe-jun want to hear it too?"

Mo Xi's expression was cold and annoyed. "Obscene music," he said irritably. "Drag them out."

Thankfully, he didn't end that sentence with, "And have them beheaded."

Yue Chenqing went back to whining as he curled up atop the general's seat, the picture of misery. "You're so coldblooded and heartless. I'm going to tell my dad you were mean to me."

Mo Xi glanced at him. "You can also get out."

Yue Chenqing was struck speechless.

After Yue Chenqing left in sulky silence, Mo Xi sat down alone in the tent. Stripping off his black dragon-skin gloves, he pressed pale, slender fingers to his temples and slowly closed his eyes. In the lamplight, he looked almost ill, his complexion sickly and pallid. That, paired with the restrained ruthlessness that always lingered in his eyes, made him look even more worn-down. He looked as if many things weighed on his heart.

Not long ago, he'd received a secret letter from Chonghua's imperial capital of urgent importance—a missive personally written by the current emperor of Chonghua and affixed with a blood seal that only Mo Xi could open. After this letter was delivered, Mo Xi had to read it three times over to be sure he hadn't misunderstood.

Gu Mang was returning to Chonghua.

Even now, the letter was tucked away in Mo Xi's coat, warmed by the heat of his chest, pressed where his heart beat strong and steady. *Gu Mang was returning to Chonghua.* This news was like a thorny bramble caught in his ribs, and it filled him with a prickling pain.

Mo Xi furrowed his brow, striving to suppress his black mood, but in the end, that burning rage still poured out. His eyes snapped open as a long, leather-clad leg kicked out and overturned the table in front of him with a loud crash.

"Aiya, General Mo!" The guard keeping watch outside the tent leaned in through the flap, uneasy with fear. "Please calm yourself. It's only natural to play around at Young Master Yue's age! It's this subordinate who failed to appropriately handle the matter and neglected to stop Young Master Yue from listening to that opera. If you want to punish or blame anyone, you only need say so, but by all means don't make yourself sick..."

Mo Xi whipped around. In the dim light, his eyes were like sparking flame. "Get out."

Silence.

"*No one* is allowed inside without my express permission."

"Yes, sir..."

The tent flap lowered again, leaving a terrifying stillness on either side. The only sounds were the wail of the northern winter's wind, the movements of soldiers in the distance, the soft crunch of snow beneath military boots, and the whinnying of the warhorses in the spirit beast encampment.

Mo Xi turned his head to stare down at the mulberries rolling across the floor. It was as if those berries were the heads that Gu Mang had personally plucked off these past few years.

He wondered how this person—who had committed so many cruel, wicked, and vile acts; who had betrayed his country, comrades, and friends; who had earned an evil reputation, blood debts, and deep hatred—could have the courage to return.

How could Gu Mang have the nerve to *return*?

Mo Xi collected himself. Only after making a great effort to calm his mind did he take out the letter, worn ragged from repeated reading. The emperor had written in his upright, elegant hand:

The Liao Kingdom wishes to declare an armistice. To demonstrate their sincerity, they will escort the traitorous general Gu Mang back to the capital.

Gu Mang is of our Chonghua and once enjoyed our trust. Instead of repaying that trust with loyalty, he turned traitor for his own gain. For the past five years, he has plundered his mother country, ravaged the peace of his native land, slaughtered his former comrades, and forsaken his past friends. Such crimes cannot be pardoned.

In ten days, Gu Mang will return to the city in shame. With the need for vengeance so widespread, we cannot make a decision alone and urgently write to each noble lord for comment.

General Mo, although you are guarding the nation from afar, you are a trusted aide of ours. Therefore, your timely advisement is sincerely requested.

With regards.

Mo Xi stared at the secret missive for a long time, then burst out into mocking laughter. Traces of bitter pain and deep hatred gradually appeared on his face.

Should he be killed, or kept alive for some other use?

At this point, Mo Xi didn't want to care anymore.

He and Gu Mang had their fights and their grudges; they'd talked of their dreams and shared wine from the same bottle. Over the course of being acquainted for more than ten years, from the days of their youth to the unfathomable changes later on, they'd weathered countless hardships together. Gu Mang had been his companion, his rival, his shixiong, his comrade-in-arms—and in the end, Gu Mang became an enemy he was meant to slaughter.

Their relationship had been doomed to fragility since the beginning. After Gu Mang turned traitor, Mo Xi broke off with him completely, turning his back without hesitation on years of friendship. Nowadays, when people spoke of them, they probably all said something like, "General Mo and Gu Mang? They're as incompatible as heaven and earth, water and fire, a saint and a savage. Even love rivals would get angry at the sight of the other, let alone those two fighting on opposite sides of a war. They're sure to be at each other's throats for the rest of their lives!"

Deeply distraught, Mo Xi refused to think on this matter any further. Taking up the brush, he held it poised above the paper. Halfway through the word *execute*, his hand shook. Ink soaked through the silk paper.

The faint sound of a clay xun started up outside of the tent. Some little brat must have been feeling homesick; he filled the entire encampment with melancholy yearning as pale frost dusted the grounds.

Mo Xi fell into a momentary daze, his black eyes flashing with an unreadable light. In the end, he cursed softly and flung down the brush to grab the secret missive. Flames burst from his palm, reducing the letter instantly to ash.

As the ashes danced in the air, Mo Xi exhaled, forming them into a messenger butterfly that could travel a thousand miles.

"This subject once protected and recommended Gu Mang, and thus must bear blame for his treason. As for the trial, this subject should avoid suspicion and abstain from comment." He continued in a measured tone. "Mo Xi of the Northern Frontier Army wishes Your Imperial Majesty well."

He lifted his hand, and the spiritual butterfly swiftly flew off.

He gazed in the direction in which it had disappeared, thinking to himself that, with this, his decade-long entanglement with Gu Mang was finally settled. Gu Mang had murdered so many Chonghua soldiers and broken the hearts of Chonghua's people; now that he had outlived his use and the enemy kingdom was sending him back, the officials of the court would of course rush to take revenge.

But Mo Xi had to stay at the frontier for another two years. It appeared that he wouldn't be able to watch Gu Mang's execution.

Enemies, nemeses, adversaries. These were the final conclusions others would one day draw from their relationship.

His face devoid of expression, Mo Xi thought perhaps no one else would ever know that he and Gu Mang, who appeared to be incompatible, irreconcilable enemies—

Had, in fact, slept with each other.

Perhaps no one would believe it even if he said it out loud. Their ascetic and disciplined General Mo had once pinned Gu Mang to the bed and taken him ruthlessly. This immaculate saint had lost control on top of Gu Mang, sweat dripping down his chest as desire inflamed his eyes.

As for the fearsome warrior Gu Mang, who seemed to have been born from the fires of war? Gu Mang had been fucked to tears in Xihe-jun's bed, parted his soft lips in a plea for Xihe-jun's kiss, and allowed Mo Xi to leave smudged marks across his rugged and muscular body.

They were enemies, separated by a chasm of accumulated hatred only death could resolve. But before this had come to pass, before they had parted ways, these two youths had once been passionately entangled—until love became one with desire. Until they were loath to part.

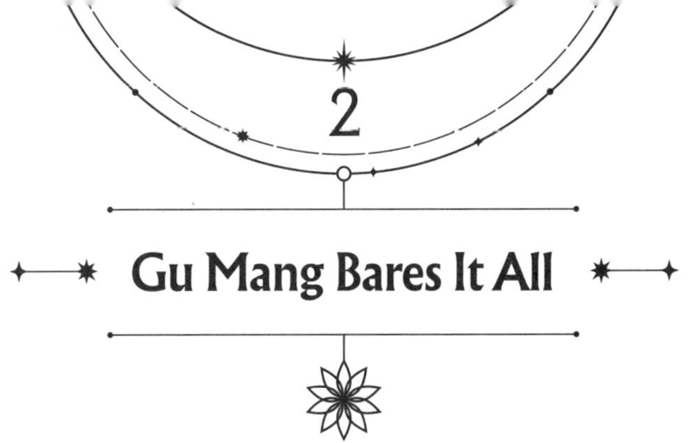

2

Gu Mang Bares It All

NOT LONG AFTER Mo Xi received the secret missive from the capital, the emperor of Chonghua finally announced the news of Gu Mang's return, along with how he would be punished: Wangshu-jun would be granted complete control over him.

The news spread like wildfire across all of Chonghua. Although Mo Xi's army was stationed all the way on the northern frontier, they nevertheless found out a mere three days later.

The Northern Frontier Army exploded. On the surface, they were as solemn and calm as ever, but during breaks between patrols, almost everyone started weighing in. Mo Xi saw it all, and for once, he didn't stop them.

He thought it perfectly normal that these soldiers would feel dissatisfied—after all, the Northern Frontier Army had once been the invincible army of Gu. A healthy majority of the soldiers had once risked their lives alongside Gu Mang. Their feelings about him were extremely complicated. Though their loyalties remained unquestioned, they had once wholeheartedly sworn allegiance to their commander Gu Mang—even though that same Gu Mang had once dubbed them the "Wangba Army."

Seriously—that wasn't a joke. Wangba as in "tortoise," and wangba as in "bastard." Before Mo Xi took over, this army's roster had read like this:

Liu Dazhuang, Soldier of the Wangba Army.

Zhang Dayan, Squad Leader of the Wangba Army.

…

And so on and so forth, bastards all the way down the line.

First on the list had been: *Gu Mang, Commander of the Wangba Army.*

Logically speaking, no one would want to enlist in an army with such a vulgar name, but that concern hadn't borne out. At the time, Gu Mang had been the most illustrious general of Chonghua. Most of the well-known generals were constrained by their own challenges, obligations, or pretensions—but Gu Mang was different. He was slave-born; he had no father or mother, no worries or cares, no ego to lose, nor any fear of death.

If all of Chonghua's noble young masters took off their clothes and stood in a row, Gu Mang might not have been the most muscular, but he definitely would have had the most scars. He had fully deserved the title of Chonghua's "Beast of the Altar."

In those days, Gu Mang's deputy had always reprimanded him at the sight of his wounds. "You're the *commander*—why do you always run to the front? Don't you know how to dodge?"

Gu Mang would smile. His dark eyes were very bright, and his lips looked very soft. His voice was naturally smooth as silk as he cheerfully mollified his angry friend. "My legs are too long; I have no choice but to run fast, no choice at all."

His very presence seemed to bring laughter and sweetness to the battlefield, as though such places could be more than freezing cold and crimson blood.

He remembered every one of his comrade's birthdays, and between battles, he often took the cultivators from his camp to make merry and drink wine in some little village. Sometimes, they'd be met with crafty villagers who charged sky-high prices, but General Gu never got angry; he merely laughed and tossed all his money on the table in order to buy his soldiers wine and meat.

In the end, he'd yell, "Eat up, drink up! You'd better all stuff your faces and eat your fill! You're my precious darlings—if there's not enough money, I'll pay in other ways!"

Gu Mang was a man of his word. He traded fur coats for wine and spirit jades for meat, and once even took off all his military robes and armor and tossed them on the bar in exchange for nü'erhong rice wine,[3] at which point the army thugs started laughing and heckling him, "General Gu, we want beef too. Do you have anything else you could take off?"

By then, he'd already stripped down to a single snow-white robe, but he still laughed and pointed at them. "Just you wait."

"No way! General Gu, you wouldn't really take off your underwear too!"

"That can't be worth very much..."

Gu Mang didn't plan to take off his underwear, but it was true that he didn't have anything left. He bit his lip in thought, and before everyone's amused and shocked expressions, he scooched up to the pretty, widowed proprietress and planted a kiss on her cheek.

The soldiers all stopped talking and stared. Even the widow was stunned speechless, drops of wine plinking off her ladle. It took her a moment to snap back to her senses and start chasing after Gu Mang, ladle held aloft.

"Shameless! You awful flirt!"

Everyone roared with laughter.

---

3 *A rice wine named after a tradition where wine brewed at a daughter's birth is left to age until her wedding, then tasted as part of her dowry.*

Amid the thigh slapping and sympathetic wincing, the widow chased Gu Mang around the entire room. "I'm serious! I'm serious!" Gu Mang cried, begging for mercy as he ran. "You're beautiful! You're beautiful!"

"I know I'm beautiful! You're not bad-looking either, young man! But you're way too fucking shameless! Couldn't you sneak out here alone and kiss me at night? Why'd you have to do it in front of so many people?! Pervert!"

This pervert ran about in utter chaos, yet he made sure to shamelessly shout, "Yes, yes, yes, I'll come over tomorrow night—or I can stay here tonight, as long as you give us another two catties of beef. Please, dear miss."

"Pah! You've already asked me for beef on credit three times since you've been stationed here, and this is the fourth! Every single time, you say you'll come over 'tomorrow night'! Do you think I'm gonna fall for your tricks?!" the widow yelled back, her little fists punching the wooden bar so hard it cracked.

The army ruffians were laughing so hard they were about to fall over. No matter how indignantly the widow spoke, in the end, Gu Mang was still able to use his pretty face and the promise of "coming over tomorrow" to secure another two catties of marinated beef for his brothers.

"General Gu, you sure know how to win people over..."

"Of course I do," Gu Mang said smugly, preening with delight. "I've gone through thousands of beautiful flowers—everyone knows of my exploits."

With a commander like that, it was no wonder a youth in those days grandly declared, "Who cares if they're called the Wangba Army? Even if they were the Jiba Army,[4] I'd enlist in the Cock Army for General Gu!"

---

4 *Jiba,* 鸡巴, *means "cock," which sounds similar to Ji Ba,* 戟罢, *"cease battle."*

His friend standing next to him turned up his nose. "Aiya, you read your classics in vain, I see. How vulgar."

"How would *you* make it elegant?"

"If you're going to go with the Jiba Army, why not call it the Ji Ba Army? Ji Ba as in 'cease battle.'"

"What a good name!" the youth exclaimed in admiration. "I like it."

"No way—I just made that up. Who would like a name like Ji Ba? Wouldn't you find it embarrassing? Go ahead and try it if you don't believe me. Even a dog would get mad at you if you called it that."

The youth laughed. "Never say never. Just because something doesn't exist now doesn't mean it won't in the future. If even an imperial army can be named Wangba, I don't think it's impossible that something else might be called Ji Ba in the future."

Fortunately, Gu Mang didn't hear this discussion—otherwise, he might have slapped the table with a triumphant yell and changed his title to "Gu Mang, Commander of the Ji Ba Army," thereby making all his subordinates suffer alongside him.

Amid the cruelty of war, only a little madman like Gu Mang would be inspired to joke around. In addition to dubbing his troops the Wangba Army, he also personally crafted their flag, creatively cutting a tortoise out of a jade-green banner, complete with a very realistic little tail. He cast a spell on the flag, and with every incense time that passed, the tortoise roared, "Wangba, Wangba, Chonghua's pride, a mighty name known far and wide!"

In short, it was extremely embarrassing.

The first time Gu Mang rode out to battle with this flag, the enemy general nearly laughed himself into an early grave. Nevertheless, before the day was out, Gu Mang's Wangba Army had reduced the hundred-thousand-strong opposing army to a sobbing mess.

Gu Mang fought many more battles after that one, both large and small, and came away victorious every time.

As a result, during the years that Gu Mang was a general, the enemies of Chonghua would pale at the glimpse of a tortoise's tail. The sight they dreaded most was, perhaps, that of a little tortoise flag raised up over the smoke of the battlefield as General Gu rode out, cleared his throat, and introduced himself with absolute seriousness:

"This humble one is Gu Mang, General of the Wangba Army. I'm here to learn from your honorable selves."

Failing to defeat this young cultivator was shameful enough. Even worse was having to snivel through one's report to one's emperor: "Wahh, this subordinate is truly incompetent and failed to defeat the Wangba Army!"

It was the stuff of nightmares.

As for Chonghua's soldiers, although Gu Mang was outrageous and mischievous, his charisma was unsurpassed. Many people revered him in those days, and some even took his nonsense "shitty names keep you safe" mantra as gospel. In accordance with the trend, many babies born during that time had the misfortune of being given "shitty names":

Chu "Strong Root" Genzhuang.

Xue "Iron Pillar" Tiezhu.

Jiang "Aching Balls" Dantong.

When Mo Xi took over the Wangba Army, the first thing he did was change its ridiculous name. He would never allow for his entry on the military roster to become "Mo Xi, General of the Wangba Army." Absolutely not!

And so the Wangba Army was renamed the Northern Frontier Army and assigned to Mo Xi's command. The dark humor that had stood up to spilled blood and the smoke of war crumbled away, much like Gu Mang's glorious reputation.

Those little tortoises that had shouted and yelled "Wangba, Wangba, Chonghua's pride, a mighty name known far and wide" were like an absurd and fleeting joke. They were never seen on the vast battlefields again.

The army's existence became a solemn one. There were no more flowers or nectar; no one who would strive to memorize any of the lowly soldiers' names; no one to take the men out to make merry; no one to buy them cheap wine with the clothes off his back. Battle regained its absolute and pitiless severity.

An eternal winter had arrived.

Although most of the Northern Frontier Army hated Gu Mang nowadays, perhaps that past was the reason they couldn't feel quite the same way ordinary civilians did when they spoke of him.

This was especially true of those old soldiers who'd fought in the Wangba Army with General Gu. Every time they said his name, a hint of something unreadable rose in their eyes.

"Ah, I really, really didn't expect him to end up like this."

"Everyone knows of Wangshu-jun's cruelty. I'm afraid it's an awful sign that His Imperial Majesty is letting Wangshu-jun deal with him."

"He'll definitely die a horrible death..."

A man of ambition wasn't necessarily disliked, but a traitor was certain to be universally reviled. Only when these veterans of the Wangba Army gathered did they murmur about things that had nothing to do with hatred.

As the night wore on, some of the ones who were getting on in years finally lost all enthusiasm. "Ah, what a good man he was... If only certain things hadn't gone the way they had, then he wouldn't have—"

"Shh! Be quiet! The nerve, to mention such things—do you want to die?!"

The old soldier shook himself out of his reverie with a yelp. As he realized what he'd nearly let slip, the drunken sparkle in his eyes vanished, and he couldn't help but shudder.

The other soldiers continued chiding him. "Now we're working under General Mo, and Gu Mang is the person he hates most in the world. It's not as if you don't know his temper—if he heard you, none of us would live to see morning!"

"Ah, you're right, silly me, getting confused as soon as I start drinking..."

The soldiers sitting around the firepit fell silent and stared blankly into the flames, each of them lost in their own thoughts. After a long time, someone else sighed and said, "But everyone changes, I suppose. All we can say is that this is General Gu's fate."

"How many years has it been? Why are you still calling him General Gu?"

"Oh, right, I meant Gu Mang."

It was a still night at the frontier fortress. The bonfire crackled, bursting with a stream of golden sparks more dazzling than the stars.

The tipsy old soldier lay on the ground with his head pillowed on his arms. He gazed up at the starry sky and the twinkling Ziwei Star,[5] the jut of his throat bobbing as he muttered a few words no one else could hear. "Ah, to be honest, it was only because of Gu Mang that I enlisted. I once even drank with him around a fire. He didn't put on any airs, either. Back then...back then, as I watched him laugh, I thought—if one day I could die for him in battle, it would be a good way to go. Who could've known he would end up..."

---

5 *The Ziwei Star, or Polaris as it is known in Western astronomy, is considered the celestial equivalent of the emperor.*

Meeting such a fate.

Gone are the birds, discarded lies the bow.[6]

After making use of Gu Mang, the enemy nation was offering him as part of a gift of peace and giving him back to Chonghua. This man had lived through many turns of fortune and seen much of the world's beauty, but a single wrong move had left him a traitor. What was done was done; there was no going back.

Was this what it meant to reap what you sow? To be the architect of your own destruction?

Returning to the topic at hand—although Gu Mang had come into a cruel fate, he had only himself to blame. It satisfied the people to see him unwanted by either side. For a while, almost everyone in Chonghua eagerly awaited Gu Mang's end.

Whether he was to be beheaded, given death by a thousand cuts, boiled alive, hacked to pieces, or drawn and quartered—even a little girl who had just learned to speak could lisp sycophantically after the adults, "We can't go easy on that disgwaceful pighead."

Thus, Gu Mang, General Gu, Chonghua's former heroic commander, Mo Xi's archenemy—the legendary man who had once been praised as the Beast of the Altar—had so pathetically become a "disgwaceful pighead."

---

6 *A line from* Records of the Grand Historian: Clan of Gou Jian, King of Yue *by Sima Qian. Refers to the desolate fates of those who have outlasted their use.*

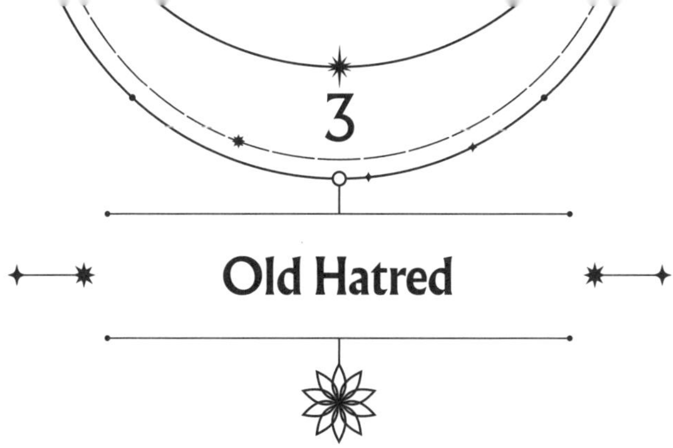

3

Old Hatred

IN THE BLINK OF AN EYE, the Northern Frontier Army had spent two years guarding the border.

A hundred thousand troops set up camp for the night by the Fushui River. After one more long day of travel, they would return home in glory. The soldiers cooked their meals, fed their horses, and washed their clothes as a rosy sunset glimmered over the river's surface. The light shone down on the spirit beasts lying down by the river and the men bathing in the shallows.

"Yo, help me scrub my back. We'll be going home tomorrow, and if I show up covered in mud, my mom's gonna curse me right to death."

"Ge, you gotta help me shave later. I can't get it right on my own."

"Vain, stinky brat—three years of marching and I've never seen you care about your looks. Be honest, are you in a rush to go home and see that girl of yours?"

A group was chattering happily in the shallow waters, heckling each other as they tidied their appearances, their eyes filled with an unstoppable sweetness.

Clad in robes from their mothers' hands, the subjects of those yearning dreams[7]—these faraway sons were returning home. They

---

7 *From the Tang dynasty poems "Song of the Faraway Son" by Meng Jiao and "Four Songs of Longxi II" by Chen Tao.*

would carry out their duties as they ought to, whether it was honoring their parents or marrying a wife; all of them had futures to look forward to.

Mo Xi was likely the only person in the whole army who had no such hopes. His parents were dead, and he had no wives. The entire capital of Chonghua longed for his return, but in a city ablaze with lights, not a single lamp was lit for him alone.

Thus Mo Xi's manner was as aloof as ever, his pale lips pursed beneath that handsomely defined nose. Even though the battle fires of the past few years had gone out, their dying embers remained in his dark eyes. This made him seem all the more ruthless and repressed, as if he'd walked right out of a snowy night—as if what constricted him wasn't his armored silver belt or his leather military boots but rather rule and regulation.

"Xihe-jun, once we get back to the city, you can see Princess Mengze again." Yue Chenqing had finished bathing and was walking up from the riverbank. When he saw Mo Xi, he beamed. "You know what they say about distance making the heart grow—"

"If you want me to kick you back into the river, go ahead and keep talking."

Yue Chenqing shut up and gave Mo Xi a reverential bow. "General Mo, I get the feeling you'll attain enlightenment in this lifetime."

Ignoring him, Mo Xi stood on the riverbank and gazed at the distant mountains. He knew that just beyond these peaks lay Chonghua's imperial capital, which he had not seen in a long time. After a year of battles and another two guarding the frontier, he had spent a thousand days and nights away from home. It was true that he didn't know how Princess Mengze was doing.

And as for Gu Mang...

Mo Xi's eyes darkened.

Two years ago, Gu Mang had been sent back to the capital as a gift from the Liao Kingdom preceding peace talks. Somehow, he had kicked up a huge ruckus as soon as he arrived.

"Ha ha ha, after the city gates opened and the procession came in, what we saw of the renowned General Gu left us totally speechless."

"It was really something! I'll never forget that sight!"

Mo Xi still wasn't clear as to what they had seen. Although he had certainly heard tell of the situation where he had been stationed, it had all been fragmented snippets of passing conversations. Besides, the soldiers revered him to the point that the talkative ones shut up as soon as he appeared and greeted him with utmost propriety, performing obeisance and addressing him as "General Mo."

Mo Xi couldn't say anything to that. He could only nod, stand there for a moment, and coolly walk away. Naturally, when he returned to his tent, what awaited him would be a sleepless night of melancholy, staring at the tent poles as they swayed noisily in the wind.

Yue Chenqing had mumbled some things within earshot a few times, but what he said couldn't be trusted, since his stories changed with each telling. Mo Xi was very reserved and would never have asked of his own volition, so even now, he didn't know what exactly had become of Gu Mang.

He only knew that Gu Mang was alive.

That was enough.

Everyone said Gu Mang was Mo Xi's archenemy. There was a rumor in Chonghua that went as follows: If the traitor Gu Mang were to be defeated someday, the best end for him would be to take a sword to his neck, because at least that meant he'd die quickly. Second best would be to be captured and brought back to Chonghua, because at least then he'd die successfully. The worst possible conclusion for him would be to end up in Mo Xi's hands in the thick of battle—because that was an end that did not bear imagining.

It was said that Mo Xi had prepared three hundred and sixty-five methods of torture, such that he could try a new one on Gu Mang every day for an entire year; these would ensure that Gu Mang suffered a life worse than the death he would be denied.

Yue Chenqing had smilingly told this rumor to Xihe-jun himself, hoping to get a laugh. To his surprise, Mo Xi didn't find it the least bit funny. Instead, he closed his eyes for a moment, then scoffed. "You think I would treat him like that?"

"Um, it was just a joke..."

But Mo Xi entirely ignored Yue Chenqing's explanation. He'd been jabbed where it hurt. In that tent empty of outsiders, in that overflowing madness and obsession, he raged, "Don't be foolish. *He* chose this end, but now he's saying I forced him to it, that I'd take it out on him, that I would make him live a life worse than death..."

Mo Xi's eyes flashed red as he snapped, "Which one of us has been made to suffer a life worse than death—doesn't he know?!"

Yue Chenqing was rendered speechless, and he vowed not to mention it again. It looked like he had been right. Xihe-jun had been betrayed by his best friend, so even though he still appeared cool and collected from without, within, he had been driven to the edge. One more step and he'd lose his mind.

It was true that Mo Xi despised Gu Mang, so much so that he wanted to personally tear open his rib cage and see for himself whether Gu Mang's blood was cold, whether his heart was black—he truly couldn't say if he felt something else as well, separate from that bone-deep hatred.

He'd known Gu Mang for half his life. Far too much had happened in that time.

Gu Mang was once a slave. He wasn't cruel by nature. He was only too focused on making a name for himself, and too blindly devoted to upholding the code of brotherhood. Unfortunately, the entirety of the Nine Provinces valued bloodline above all else. Even though the old emperor had taken pity on Gu Mang on account of his talents and made an exception to grant him the rank of general, after that emperor passed, his successor hadn't looked kindly upon the lowborn Gu Mang.

He grew jealous of Gu Mang, doubted him, and stripped him of his authority.

He even crossed a line Gu Mang couldn't possibly endure.

Mo Xi had watched Gu Mang fall into the abyss with his own eyes.

Mo Xi tried to persuade Gu Mang as a close friend, then argued with Gu Mang as a comrade. They were both assigned to the Bureau of Military Affairs at the time, and Gu Mang was in low spirits and rarely came to work.

Once, when Mo Xi found him, he was listening to music and drinking wine in a brothel, his head pillowed on a dancer's soft thighs. At the sight of Mo Xi, he closed those eyes that flickered with stars and flashed him a mirthless smile. "Xihe-jun, you've come."

Nearly insane with fury, Mo Xi threw open the door and strode into the room. Amid astonished cries, he slapped Gu Mang across the face. "Do you want to rot like this for the rest of your fucking life?"

Gu Mang was drunk. He grinned as he looped his arms around Mo Xi's neck and crooned, "Yes, noble Mo-gongzi; would you like to rot with me?"

"Fuck off!"

Gu Mang burst into laughter. "It doesn't matter. After all, you're a noble, and I'm a slave. I know you think I'm filth. I know that no matter how hard my army strives, how much blood is spilled or how many of us die, we're still meaningless in His Imperial Majesty's eyes. It's our fault that we weren't worthy of learning cultivation in the first place, yet somehow, despite our birth, we still dared to try."

After that, the emperor had dispatched Gu Mang from the capital, but Gu Mang never returned to report on his mission. People thought he must have died in some accident; many of his maiden admirers even cried for him.

For a long time, no news of his death reached Chonghua—until one day, a military report came swift from the front lines, saying Gu Mang had been seen in the Liao Kingdom's battle formations.

Gu Mang had defected.

The scandal burned through Chonghua like wildfire, setting everyone's temper ablaze. Only Mo Xi's heart seemed to freeze over.

He hadn't believed it.

Not until he saw it for himself, over the misty waters of Dongting Lake, where ships and water demons clashed to kill. The Liao Kingdom's tactics felt so familiar that they shattered Mo Xi's composure. He had seen these monstrously fearless strategies countless times before—on the sand tables Gu Mang had once pored over, and during every one of the Wangba Army's glorious battles.

Mo Xi told the commander in charge of the attack that they needed to call the barrier masters and switch to defensive tactics. They had to commit to total retreat and discontinue the fight; if they didn't, the whole vanguard would be buried at the bottom of the lake by the end of the day.

"I know how he fights."

But the commander ignored him. "Who does Gu Mang think he is? Could a slave-born brat defeat a pure-blooded descendant of the gods such as I?!"

The grizzled, white-bearded noble's expression was full of arrogance; he didn't think much of Gu Mang at all.

And so the fires of war blazed without end.

The imperial army that had weathered a hundred battles unscathed under Gu Mang suffered their first complete and utter defeat before the Liao Kingdom's warships. Boats powered by spiritual energy exploded one after another while water demons burst out of the lake to tear cultivators apart. Fire stained the sky; blood dyed the water. Amid the wails of crushing defeat, Mo Xi mounted a sword by himself and flew to the Liao Kingdom's command ship.

The inferno raged on, black smoke spiraling endlessly upward. The Liao Kingdom was a country that cultivated demonic magic, and the spells their cultivators used were savage and cruel. A crowd of hundreds struck forward to kill Mo Xi—

"Hold it."

A familiar voice called out, and a figure sauntered out from the dark cabin.

They met again.

Gu Mang had grown more tanned, and his physique was more toned, but those eyes of his hadn't changed: black and bright, as if they could see through all the world's machinations. His torso was bare, his slim and well-muscled waist bound with layers of bandages, and he wore a black coat draped over his shoulders, a bloodstained ribbon tied around his forehead—he had pulled it off the dead body of an imperial soldier of Chonghua.

Gu Mang leaned carelessly against the ship railing, narrowing his eyes as he looked ahead at Mo Xi. Then he grinned. "Xihe-jun, it's been a long time."

The wind blew in coppery gusts.

The war reports provided by scouts and the strategy at play in the battle of Dongting Lake both suggested that the Liao Kingdom's newest general was none other than Chonghua's former Beast of the Altar. Although Mo Xi hadn't said anything, he had still refused to believe it.

He thought, surely, Gu Mang couldn't be so awful. Despite all that had happened, the Liao Kingdom was evil, a deeply cruel nation that revered only war. Gu Mang might have left Chonghua, but no matter what, he wouldn't have gone to Liao Kingdom territory. Mo Xi thought that a person's nature never changed, so he'd refused to believe anything before he saw the man himself. But now...

Mo Xi closed his eyes, swallowing thickly. After a long time, he only managed two words. "Gu Mang..."

"Hm?"

Mo Xi's voice was low, on the verge of shaking. "So you've truly stooped so low."

Gu Mang laughed in the blazing firelight, the wisps of black hair that framed his face fluttering slightly. He spread his hands with an almost flamboyant air. "What's wrong with this?"

Mo Xi said nothing.

"I think it's great. The Liao Kingdom values talent. Although it's not righteous to cultivate with black magic, everyone's treated quite fairly."

As Gu Mang spoke, he pointed at the gold-edged blue ribbon on his forehead.

"No matter how much of my life I devoted to your honorable country, no matter how many merits I achieved, I could never dream of attaining this kind of pure-blooded nobles' ribbon—all on account of my birth." Gu Mang smiled. "But that's not true in Liao."

"That's the merit ribbon," Mo Xi snarled. "It belongs solely to the descendants of the martyred heroes. Take it off!"

Gu Mang touched the bloodstained ribbon with interest. "Is it? This was worn by a cultivator who looked pretty young. I cut off his head and saw this ribbon was quite well-made. It'd be wasted on a corpse, so I took it for fun. What? Do you want one too?" His lips curled in a malicious smile. "You should have one of your own. Why are you trying to take mine?"

Mo Xi was practically incandescent with rage. "Take it *off*!"

"Xihe-jun." Gu Mang's voice was syrupy sweet, but his tone was laced with danger. "You're alone and surrounded, so where are your manners? You really think I wouldn't have the heart to kill you just because of our shared past?"

A black dagger wreathed in dark mist appeared in his hand.

"Almost all the men of your honored nation's vanguard have died at Dongting Lake today," Gu Mang said. "Mo Xi, even if you're strong, you're still only a deputy general—you couldn't persuade that dumbass old noble commander of yours. Even after so many died, *he* didn't come here to beg for mercy, while you've come to endanger yourself."

Gu Mang smiled at him. "Is it because you want to be buried with the deceased soldiers of Chonghua?"

Mo Xi didn't answer. After a moment of silence, he walked toward Gu Mang. His military boots left tracks through the fresh blood on the deck. "Gu Mang," he finally said. "I know that Chonghua owes you, as do I… You've done too much for me, so I won't fight you today."

"I'd like to see you try," Gu Mang scoffed.

"You asked if I wanted to be buried with the soldiers of Chonghua who died today… If my death will convince you to leave the Liao Kingdom," Mo Xi said, stepping closer, "then yes. My life is yours."

Gu Mang wasn't smiling anymore. He stared, eyes dark. "I really will kill you."

Mo Xi was yet unfazed; he merely glanced at Gu Mang's forehead and the bloodstained blue and gold ribbon. Slowly, he lowered his gaze to Gu Mang's face. "Then kill me. And afterward, remember to turn back."

This was the last time Mo Xi tried to bring Gu Mang back to shore.

A white eagle swooped off the ship's mast, and light flashed from the dagger—

There came a muffled ripping sound. Blood gushed from the wound in spurts.

The cold blade had stabbed into Mo Xi's heart, viciously tearing it apart.

"I did say I would kill you."

The dagger was still buried in Mo Xi's chest. Gu Mang suddenly sneered. "Who do you think you are? What right do you have to lecture me? You think that if you die, I'll feel guilty and turn back? Don't be a fool!"

Head held high, he glanced disdainfully down and sighed. "As a general, as a soldier, and as a person, you can't be too attached to past affections."

As he spoke, he slowly got down on one knee, resting an elbow carelessly on his raised leg as he took hold of the dripping dagger and pulled it out with a squelch. Fresh blood splattered out.

Gu Mang tilted Mo Xi's chin with the tip of the bloody dagger.

"Don't think I didn't know what you were planning. Xihe-jun, you weren't actually reluctant to fight me. You knew you had no chance of victory, so you chose to bet on my conscience with your life."

Blood gradually soaked through Mo Xi's clothes, but at that moment, he didn't feel any pain.

Only cold.

So cold...

He closed his eyes.

No. If I had the choice, I would never have even thought of fighting you.

Light was something you gave me; warmth was something you brought me. All the blood that races through my heart is because of you.

Without you, I wouldn't have made it to today.

"Sorry to disappoint," Gu Mang said blandly. "Mo Xi. If I were you, and I ended up in your situation, I'd prefer to bet on my ability to bring my enemy down with me rather than naively try to persuade my opponent to turn back. We were brothers once—this is the last thing I can teach you."

The final scene Mo Xi remembered before losing consciousness was a Liao Kingdom cultivator swooping in on a sword to say anxiously, "General Gu, reinforcements are coming from the northeast. An army of Mengze's healers, look—"

Mo Xi didn't hear the rest of it. Unable to hold on any longer, he fell forward and collapsed onto the bloodstained deck.

After this bloody battle, Chonghua confirmed that the traitorous general Gu Mang had defected to the Liao Kingdom and was serving the darkest country in the Nine Provinces. The old general had made a grave mistake. The army was devastated; of a vanguard that had been ten thousand strong, fewer than one hundred cultivators returned.

Mo Xi lay unconscious for weeks before waking. Gu Mang had slipped a knife between his ribs, but it hadn't been enough to make him stop and turn back.

He remembered the words Gu Mang had said long ago, before he left the capital...

"Mo Xi, for me, the way up is a dead end. I have nowhere to go—I can only fumble toward hell."

"Gu Mang..."

"That's enough." Gu Mang ordered a jug of wine from the waiter. Breaking the clay seal, he smiled as he poured two cups, one for himself, one for Mo Xi. Gu Mang's eyes twinkled as the cups clinked, sending wine splashing. "Have another drink on me. From now on, your Gu Mang-gege is going to be a bad guy."

At the time, Mo Xi had shaken his head in exasperation, finding him unbearably flippant. Every word out of his mouth sounded so tongue-in-cheek.

Mo Xi had known Gu Mang for many, many years; his heart was so soft that he hesitated to stomp on an ant. How could a sweet child like that become a bad guy?

And what had happened in the end? The subordinates of this "sweet child" had killed Mo Xi's comrades. That "sweet child" himself had almost killed Mo Xi.

"Fortunately, Princess Mengze arrived in time to save you. That dagger was a holy weapon from the Liao Kingdom, tempered with demonic poison. If she had come any later, I'm afraid you would have died. Your wound will scar; you'll need to spend the next few months resting..."

Mo Xi didn't listen to anything else the healer said. He looked down at the bandages wrapped around his chest. The necrosis had been cut away, but something else seemed to have been gouged out of his heart alongside the dead flesh. He felt empty and hurt, dissatisfied and hateful.

It wasn't until much later, when Gu Mang suffered the consequences of his actions and was sent back to his old capital that Mo Xi felt the wound on his chest finally stop bleeding.

But it still ached.

Many years later, the night before the Northern Frontier Army returned to the capital, Mo Xi sat alone and sleepless in his tent, unconsciously wiping slightly damp eyes. He turned his face to the side, faint candlelight streaming through the muslin lampshade to illuminate his sharply defined profile. He closed his eyes.

Without a doubt, he was a loyal subject, and Gu Mang was a traitor. Mo Xi loathed him, and knew he was guilty.

But between his trembling lashes, Mo Xi seemed to see Gu Mang from the past, when they were both at the academy, that smiling face both sweet and mischievous. When he was happy, a sharp little canine would appear, and his eyes would glitter brighter than any star Mo Xi had ever seen. Back then, the sun shone splendidly and the elders droned on, while Gu Mang sprawled out over the desk, sneakily writing picture books starring himself as the male lead, smug and delighted because all the young ladies loved him.

Neither of them had foreseen a future like this.

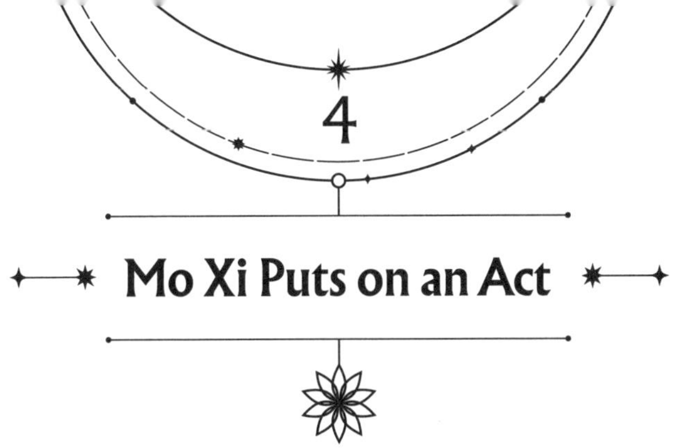

4

Mo Xi Puts on an Act

THE NEXT DAY, the army returned. The whole city bustled with activity as residents of all ages poured out onto the streets as far as the eye could see.

"Northern Frontier Army, welcome back!"

As the procession entered the city, a strange atmosphere spilled forth from both sides of the road. It was as if water had been poured into a pot of sizzling oil, then swiftly capped with a wooden lid to seal all that crackling excitement beneath it.

People lowered their heads respectfully, but they still snuck glances out of the corners of their eyes to peek at the elite army riding past.

Mo Xi wore an imperial army uniform, his steel-toed military boots in their stirrups. Other than his belt and vambraces, which glinted cold silver, he was all in black.

"Ahhh, Xihe-jun is so handsome I can't stand it!"

"I'm dying, I'm dying."

"I think he just looked at me!"

"Ha, stop kidding yourself! How would he have eyes for anyone but Princess Mengze?"

"But he hasn't married the princess yet... He turns thirty this year, and he doesn't have a wife, *or* a betrothed, or even any concubines! Can't I at least fantasize? Seriously!"

As for the officers and soldiers, their expressions were much more cheerful than Mo Xi's as they waved happily at the civilians lining the streets. Yue Chenqing even delightedly accepted flowers from maidens to put in his hair. Only after Mo Xi glanced at him in warning did he sulkily resign himself to holding and sniffing the flowers, all in all looking quite pitiful.

It was a long road from the city gates, and they wouldn't reach the imperial palace for a while yet. Yue Chenqing didn't behave for very long at all before he started twirling his flowers again. He grinned flirtatiously at the onlookers and called out to them as the procession advanced.

"Hey, ladies!"

"Aren't you lovely..."

"This humble one is seeking concubines, food and lodging included."

"Yue Chenqing!" Mo Xi snapped.

Yue Chenqing covered his mouth.

In the sunlight, the Northern Frontier Army's glinting weapons and flashing armor were a magnificent sight as they rode through the capital. They were still Gu Mang's old soldiers, but they could no longer behave as they once had. In the old days, when Gu Mang returned victorious, he had waved and teased from his horse at their head, while the happy, relaxed soldiers behind him had laughed as they accepted wines and desserts from the civilians. But Xihe-jun was their commander now. This man didn't even smile, so no one else dared to let loose.

The slow march from the city gates ended up taking more than an hour. Upon their arrival, the army was greeted with the long and tedious merit ceremony, in which they had to kneel and kowtow and give thanks. It was all terribly irritating. Even when Mo Xi finally made it to the evening feast, he had neither peace nor quiet.

As Yue Chenqing would have said, he found himself obligated to deal with those young mistresses in a manner "chaste yet aloof, reserved yet courteous."

On that note, the first time Yue Chenqing joked about Mo Xi's "chastity," Xihe-jun had made him transcribe *Maidenly Virtues* a hundred times as punishment. Without speaking a word aloud, Xihe-jun had said clearly: *Yue Chenqing, is the problem that you don't know the word "chastity"? Come here, I'll let you learn to your heart's content.*

But no matter how many times Yue Chenqing sniffled through the words "maidenly virtues are boundless; womanly grievances are endless," the joke that Xihe-jun was "chaste yet aloof, reserved yet courteous" still secretly spread throughout the entire army.

Everyone else thought so too. Xihe-jun was already thirty years of age but he still refused to marry, all to wait for Princess Mengze. That much was obvious from the situation at the feast; a crowd of little ladies from noble houses was chattering around Mo Xi, but he wouldn't even look at them.

"Xihe-jun, it's been a long time."

"Xihe-jun, you seem to have lost weight."

"Xihe-jun, what do you think of this pendant I'm wearing today?"

In this group of highborn young ladies, the most provocative was Princess Yanping, the younger sister of Princess Mengze. She had a gorgeous figure despite having only recently come of age, and she gazed around with eyes that overflowed with amorous intent.

She walked toward Mo Xi with a smile, her lips as tender as a juicy berry.

When Yue Chenqing spied this from afar, he didn't bother to swallow his dessert before grabbing a friend he hadn't seen in a while. "Hey. *Hey!*"

"What do you want?"

"Come, look over there!" Yue Chenqing said excitedly.

"Isn't that Princess Yanping and Xihe-jun…? What's interesting about that? Princess Yanping doesn't stand a chance."

"No, no, no. I want you to see the legendary 'chaste yet aloof, reserved yet courteous' Xihe-jun with your own eyes!"

"Aren't you tired of copying *Maidenly Virtues*?" his friend asked.

Yue Chenqing was the sort of person who never learned his lesson. Grinning, he dragged his friend closer to eavesdrop on the general and the princess.

"Brother-in-Law." Still smiling, Princess Yanping came to a stop in front of Mo Xi. Her tone was flirtatious from the instant she opened her mouth.

Mo Xi lowered his lashes, pausing at this form of address, and then *chastely* turned to leave.

Yanping hastily stopped him. "Brother-in-Law, you've been standing here expressionless this whole time, ignoring all the girls. Are you cross that my sister isn't here?"

He paused before replying—*aloof*. "Princess, you're mistaken. I am not yet wed."

"I'm just saying it for fun."

Controlling his temper, Mo Xi was *reserved* in his response. "This is no laughing matter."

"All right, all right, don't get mad. My sister's health hasn't been especially good these past few years. She caught a cold last night. Otherwise, she definitely would have come to see you."

Mo Xi knew Princess Mengze's poor health was inextricably linked to himself, so he *courteously* asked, "How is she?"

"Ha!" Yue Chenqing cackled. "See? I told you so!"

Yue Chenqing's friend felt that he was laughing too loudly.

No matter how noisy the banquet was, there was still a chance he would attract Xihe-jun's attention, and even if Yue Chenqing didn't mind copying those trite passages on womanly conduct, his friend wouldn't be able to take the hit to his pride. He clapped a hand over Yue Chenqing's mouth and dragged him away.

Notwithstanding their departure, Princess Yanping and Mo Xi's conversation continued.

Yanping kept smiling. "After spending two years alone at the frontier, you still think only of my sister? Don't worry, she only had a headache and a fever. It's the same issue, as you know well. She'll be fine with some rest."

Mo Xi said nothing.

"Let's be honest. Given my sister's health, how could she handle Xihe-jun if she didn't recover first?" As Yanping spoke, her admiring gaze swept covetously over Mo Xi's long legs, then lingered on the high bridge of his nose. She sighed. "If my sister doesn't get better, she'll never be able to marry. Are you really going to spend your whole life saving yourself for her?"

Mo Xi remained silent.

"Wouldn't that be an awful shame..."

The princess pressed close to Mo Xi, redolent with powdery sweetness, her dark hair decked in jewels and a rouge-colored peony drawn between her brows. With a smile, she deliberately leaned forward, her pale bosom heaving.

"Why don't you give me a try? I'm all grown up now; I'm no less than her." Yanping tried to wrap her soft arms around his waist. "It's just spending the night together—don't take it too seriously." As she giggled, the pale pink tip of her tongue flicked over her lips ever so briefly. "You'll like it."

That was the end of it.

Don't take it too seriously. This sentence topped the list of sayings Mo Xi hated more than anything. Princess Yanping had not only failed to attract him; she'd jabbed him exactly where he hurt most.

Mo Xi glanced at her, pausing, then said coldly, "Move aside."

"Hey! Y-you—!"

But Mo Xi had already walked away from her with a frown.

Amid the fluttering tassels of Feiyao Terrace, Mo Xi grabbed another liuli glass cup from a servant. Its contents glimmered with an amber hue. His leather-clad legs didn't relax until he strode to the terrace's edge, where he leaned against the red lacquer railing to watch the city lights.

Free of that maddening hall, he caught his breath and took a sip of the berry wine in the cup, the jut of his throat bobbing.

Mo Xi had been subjected to many years of the ladies' "favor," but he still didn't like it, nor was he used to it.

In the past, few people had admired Mo Xi. When he walked the streets, hardly anyone had snuck glances at him. Back then, he had been terribly bad-tempered. How bad, exactly? In comparison, the current Xihe-jun was an absolute sweetheart.

Later, there had been a massive upheaval within his family, and everyone had thought this young master of the Mo Clan was doomed. The other noble cultivators ignored him, and the cultivators of common birth didn't dare approach him.

Only Gu Mang, that lunatic who didn't fear death, was willing to be his comrade. He was the only one who chose to keep that floundering young master company and offer him comfort: *Don't worry, even if you're no longer a noble young master, you'll always be you. There's an ember in your heart, and sooner or later, it will glow. I can see it, and others will too.*

In the end, Mo Xi survived the crisis and escaped from the Mo Clan's shadow. He fought at every frontier, achieving more military merits than even his ancestors. No longer did anyone think of him as the only son of the Mo Clan—they only treated him as the venerated Xihe-jun.

More maidens began to think highly of him.

After Gu Mang defected, the maidens changed their type. They all flocked to admire Mo Xi instead, and some even sighed, "Ah, it's good for men to be a little stuffy—they're more honest that way. At least they won't let us down like Gu Mang."

"Even though Xihe-jun has a bad temper, he tells it like it is. If there's anything he wants to rant about, he'll say it outright. He won't ever put on an act."

A brothel girl once went so far as to smack a table and heroically proclaim with a hand on her hip, "Xihe-jun is the most innocent man I've ever seen! I swear on my honor—if Xihe-jun came to bed me, I'd pay *him* before I'd take his money!"

As it turned out, Xihe-jun really did come the next day. Not to bed her, but to shut down the brothel with a murderous look on his face.

"Seducing shenjun[8]—how shameless. Your punishment is to go become women of good families." After Mo Xi finished shutting down the brothel and berating them ferociously, he left in a rage...

And also left behind a crowd of brothel girls wailing that they'd never again sell their bodies because Xihe-jun had persuaded them to leave the trade, tearfully attesting to the incomparable goodness of Xihe-jun's character.

It made no sense!

People loved to take a person who seemed decent and good and enshrine them in their hearts, pinning all their beautiful fantasies

8 *A polite term of address for a cultivator.*

on that person's shoulders just to bring a little light to themselves. But Mo Xi had no wish to be consecrated as their boring holy idol—he wasn't as perfect as those girls believed.

There were miserably wretched things in his past, things he couldn't speak of to anyone.

But no one understood.

So what Gu Mang had said was right, but it was also wrong.

Mo Xi did indeed throw off the Mo Clan's shadow to shine on his own merit in front of everyone's eyes, but he knew very well that this glory belonged solely to the flawless Xihe-jun of their imaginations. It had nothing to do with that trapped and lonely youth from long ago.

From beginning to end, only Gu Mang had ever walked toward that downtrodden young master, toward that youth with an uncertain future. Only he had ever been sincerely happy to be reunited with his little shidi from the academy, reaching out to him in delight with a little canine peeking from that brilliant smile.

Before the warmth of a bonfire, he'd smiled and said, *It's been a long time, Mo-shidi. Can I sit with you?*

"It's been a long time. Can I sit with you?"

Suddenly, someone behind Mo Xi asked a very similar question. Mo Xi's fingertips shook, the wine in his liuli cup almost spilling.

He turned his head, as if in a dream, and saw, beneath the moonlit blossoms of the foxglove trees, a familiar silhouette calmly watching him on Feiyao Terrace.

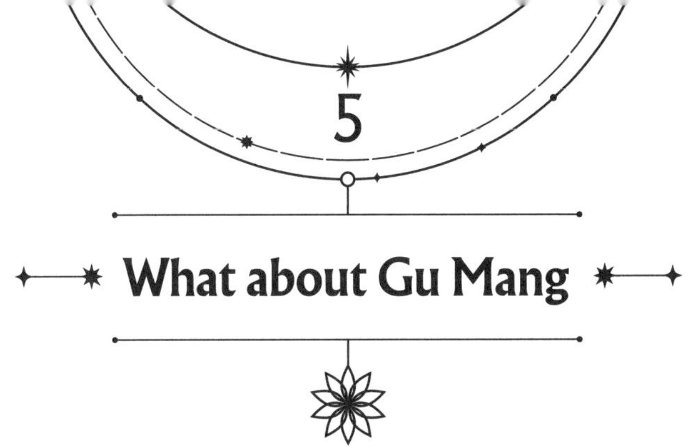

5 What about Gu Mang

But it wasn't Gu Mang—of course it wouldn't be Gu Mang. Mo Xi mocked himself as he came to his senses. What was he thinking?

The speaker was a man with gentle features. He sat in a wooden wheelchair, a white coat draped over his shoulders and a blanket the color of lotus root tucked over his paralyzed legs.

Mo Xi was rather taken aback. "Qingxu Elder?"

Qingxu Elder, Jiang Yexue. He was Yue Chenqing's elder brother.

Jiang Yexue was different from Yue Chenqing, that carefree and silly kid. He had lived a hard and spartan life. His mother had passed away when he was young, and later, because he insisted on marrying the daughter of a criminal, he had been kicked out of the Yue Clan.

At the time, he and his maiden hadn't had much money, so their wedding was very simple. Due to pressure from the Yue Clan, only a few people had persevered to attend—two of whom were Mo Xi and Gu Mang.

Mo Xi had gifted them a small courtyard. Gu Mang stared tongue-tied at the land deed and told Jiang Yexue, "Bro, I'm totally broke, there's no way I can afford to get you one of these." Everyone laughed, and amid the cheer, Gu Mang puffed out his cheeks and played them "Song of Courtship"[9] on his suona.

But the good times didn't last. Jiang Yexue and his wife both joined the military. The battlefield was pitiless, taking first his wife and then his legs.

Mo Xi didn't know how this man had endured. Fortunately, Jiang Yexue was tougher than he looked. In the end, he pulled himself together and secured a position as an elder at the cultivation academy, instructing students in the practice of artificing. But this had angered his father, as the Yue Clan was the most powerful noble family of artificers in Chonghua. Yue Juntian immediately ordered the cultivation academy to oust Jiang Yexue from his position.

"This unfilial son was disowned and no longer shares our surname! How dare he make a living off the Yue Clan's work!"

The headmaster couldn't convince Yue Juntian otherwise and had no choice but to apologetically let Jiang Yexue go.

After watching this take place, Mo Xi had decided to find Jiang Yexue a position at the Bureau of Military Affairs. Yet unexpectedly, the very next day—before Mo Xi could even bring it up—the headmaster of the cultivation academy begged Jiang Yexue to return. This time, no matter how the Yue Clan cried foul, it was no use; the headmaster only said that they had "taken advice from a dear friend."

To this day, the identity of that dear friend was a mystery in Chonghua.

Jiang Yexue and the Yue Clan loathed each other; he rarely ever appeared at these feasts, which was why Mo Xi was so startled to see him.

"What are you doing here?"

---

9 *"Phoenix Seeking Phoenix," a famous love song written by Sima Xiangru for Zhuo Wenjun, with whom the latter eloped.*

"I…" Jiang Yexue said. "I came to see Chenqing."

Yue Chenqing had been young when Jiang Yexue left. Although many of his memories had faded by now, this older brother had never really let go of his little sibling.

Yue Chenqing was unwilling to acknowledge Jiang Yexue as his brother, but in truth, he didn't make trouble for him like his brethren did.

"And to see you." Jiang Yexue smiled. "There was no sign of you anywhere. I thought maybe you couldn't bear the noise, so I came to the terrace to look for you. And as I expected, you're out here standing in the wind."

"If you want to find me, have someone send word. Why come out yourself? It's best not to expose those wounds on your legs to the cold. I'll help you back inside."

"It's nothing. They haven't hurt in a long time," Jiang Yexue said. "I came here to thank you. Chenqing is immature, and I'm grateful to you for taking care of him the past two years."

Mo Xi was silent for a while. "Your brother is still young," he said. "There's nothing wrong with wanting to have some fun. Besides, he's actually made quite a lot of progress these two years at the frontier."

"Is that so?" Jiang Yexue smiled warmly. "He didn't cause any trouble for you?"

A pause. "Only the slightest bit. He was still more help than anything."

Jiang Yexue sighed and nodded. "Good, that's good."

They were quiet for a moment. The breeze rustled through the tassels hanging over Feiyao Terrace, setting them swaying.

"Xihe-jun, you've been gone for a long time," Jiang Yexue said abruptly. "I assume you haven't been able to keep up with many of the happenings in the capital." This man had always been clever, observant, and exceptionally perceptive. "It's too noisy in the hall, and I don't want to return anytime soon. Xihe-jun, if there's anything you want to know, you only need to ask."

"There isn't anything in particular, really," Mo Xi said after a pause. He turned to look at the moon over the capital, the city lights below twinkling like stars. "I don't have any family here."

Jiang Yexue knew that Mo Xi was stiff by nature. He was in no rush, and simply nodded as he looked at him.

Just as he expected, Mo Xi soon cleared his throat to ask a question. "How have you been these past few years?"

Jiang Yexue smiled. "Not bad."

"What about His Imperial Majesty?"

"All has gone well for him."

"Princess Mengze?"

"Safe and sound."

"That's good," Mo Xi said, hesitant.

Jiang Yexue's eyes glimmered with an unreadable light. "Is there anything else you want to know about?"

"No." But a little later, Mo Xi finished the last bit of wine in his cup, gazed at the lustrous night, and finally couldn't help but ask, "What about Gu Mang...? How is he?"

The look in Jiang Yexue's eyes seemed to say, *Ah, after all those twists and turns, you've finally mentioned him.* He said, "Not well, of course."

Mo Xi said nothing for a moment, nodding slightly. His throat was a little dry. "I thought so."

"If you're willing, you should still go visit him. After spending so much time in such an abusive place, he...he's changed a great deal."

Mo Xi blinked in confusion. Frowning, he asked, "Where?"

Jiang Yexue hadn't expected this reaction. He widened his eyes, also dumbfounded. "You don't know?"

"Know what?"

They regarded each other in silence. A great gale of laughter suddenly came from the palace hall. The shadows of drunken men and women were cast against the windows, their silhouettes overlapping chaotically.

Mo Xi had a sudden realization, his eyes flying open. "He couldn't have been—"

"He's spent two years at Luomei Pavilion..." Jiang Yexue hadn't expected Yue Chenqing to keep such important information under wraps, and he was left a little uneasy at having to tell Mo Xi himself.

Mo Xi's face had taken on a sickly pallor.

Luomei Pavilion...

What kind of place was this? It was a land of bliss for the nobles and hell on earth for its prisoners. The people trapped in the pavilion were hollowed out and devoured overnight. The gentle were transfigured beyond recognition, the fierce likewise destroyed. It was a place that shattered the dignity of any slave, where one misfortune led to a lifetime of abuse. Life there was hundreds of times worse than death.

They had actually put Gu Mang there?

They had actually...put him...

Mo Xi swallowed thickly. The first time he tried to speak, nothing came out. Only on the second attempt did he manage anything coherent. "On Wangshu-jun's orders?"

Jiang Yexue paused, then sighed and nodded. "Wangshu-jun hates him. You know this."

Mo Xi was silent, abruptly turning away and looking into the boundless night. He didn't make another sound.

Ever since Gu Mang was sent back to Chonghua two years ago, Mo Xi hadn't thought much about what would become of him.

At the time, he hadn't known what exactly Gu Mang's punishment would be. He'd thought that if Gu Mang were imprisoned, he might go take a look at him, or maybe sneer at and mock him a little. If Gu Mang became an invalid, he wouldn't sympathize; he might even go and make things harder for him.

So many years had passed. Even if they had once shared something soft, the accumulated hatred ran too deep. There was no chance of reconciliation.

The only circumstance under which Mo Xi could imagine amiably sharing a jug of wine with Gu Mang was in a cemetery, with Gu Mang buried in the earth, and himself standing upon it. Then he might talk to the man like he once had, and place a bouquet of red peonies shaped from spiritual energy on his grave.

At least that could afford them a peaceful final farewell.

But Gu Mang had always managed to surprise Mo Xi. Mo Xi hadn't expected that, even now, things would be the same.

Luomei Pavilion.

Those words tormented Mo Xi. He said them again and again in his mind, as if trying to glean the slightest bit of pleasure from them.

But in the end, he realized it was a useless endeavor. They gave him no satisfaction. Instead, he felt only extreme disgust and anger. He didn't know where these feelings were coming from—wasn't karmic retribution supposed to be a cause for celebration?

Mo Xi propped his elbow against the carved railing. He wanted to move his fingers, but they felt far too stiff. He turned to look at Jiang Yexue's face, but he seemed indescribably blurry.

Waves of dizziness ran through him, and pangs of agony twisted his gut.

Gu Mang, sent to Luomei Pavilion.

For two years already.

Mo Xi thought he should burst into wild laughter. That would be the right thing to do; that would be in line with the bone-deep hatred everyone expected of him. At this thought, he really did mechanically move his mouth in an attempt to pry some joy out from within.

But all that came from between his teeth was a hollow scoff.

His vision seemed to flash with an image of that beautiful face he had seen the first time they met. Those smiling black eyes gazed at him in the sunlight. *Nice to meet you, Mo-shidi.*

Then he seemed to see a flash of Gu Mang's dazzling figure from after they enlisted, as he turned to blink at Mo Xi amid a noisy group of his scoundrel buddies. His long and slender eyes, slightly upturned at the ends, curved into tender crescents as he shot him a genuine smile.

He also thought of the sorts of things Gu Mang had said after he became a general.

There were grinning, glib-tongued quips. *C'mere, enlist with Wangba today, and next year you'll be rich off soldier's pay.*

There were furious shouts among mountains of corpses and seas of blood. *Come on, if you've still got a pulse, you better hurry and crawl the fuck up! I'll take you home!*

And then—the time he knelt in the throne room, begging the emperor not to leave his soldiers in a mass grave:

"I want to ask healers to identify their bodies... Please, this isn't meaningless. Every soldier's gravestone should have their name on it. Your Imperial Majesty, I don't want my brothers to wander lost.

"They recognized me as their commander. Whether they're men or ghosts, I have to bring them home. I promised.

"They don't want a lavish funeral. They only want the names they deserved from the beginning."

And that last desperate, tearful howl as he lost control in front of the throne—

"So slaves deserve to die? So slaves don't deserve to be buried?! They shed their blood just the same; they died just the same! They already didn't have parents, and now they don't even have names! How come the Yue Clan, Mo Clan, and Murong Clan's dead are heroes, but when my brothers die, they're thrown in a pit?! Tell me *why*!"

That was the first time Gu Mang had cried in the palace.

He wasn't merely kneeling. He was curled up, hunched over, crouching as he cried.

He'd returned straight from battle; he hadn't even washed away the filth and the blood. His face was covered with traces of soot, and his tears left patchy tracks.

In the throne room, this god of war who always represented hope on the battlefield was beaten back into his original lowly form, like an unidentified corpse.

The palace hall was filled with military and civil officials in solemn and proper attire. Many of them looked disdainfully at this commoner general, whose clothes were tattered and unbearably filthy.

Gu Mang howled, choking back sobs, like a dying beast. "I said I'd take them home... Have some mercy, let me keep my promise..."

But he knew it was useless. In the end, he stopped begging and he stopped crying. Instead, he muttered over and over, his eyes unfocused, almost as if speaking to wandering souls. "I'm sorry, it's my fault. I'm not worthy of being your general. I'm just a slave too..."

As these memories came to mind in bits and pieces, Mo Xi felt a splitting pain in his head. He brought his hand to his brow, covering his face in its shadow. Beneath an expanse of icy chill, his heart was wet and cold.

"Xihe-jun," Jiang Yexue said. "Are you okay?"

No one responded. After a long while, a toneless voice finally floated indifferently out through the shadows. "Yes. Why wouldn't I be."

Jiang Yexue looked at him and sighed. "How long have I known you? Why bother to pretend in front of me?"

The copper bells chimed from the eaves, and long yellow tassels danced in the wind.

"It used to be that the names Mo Xi and Gu Mang were always mentioned in the same breath. You learned cultivation at the academy together, you stepped onto the battlefield together, and you became generals together," Jiang Yexue said. "You remain as distinguished as ever, but he's long since fallen from grace. You had so many years of equal fame, you were dubbed the nation's Twin Jades, and now you're the only one left. I doubt you're truly pleased." Jiang Yexue paused, turning to look at Mo Xi. "Besides, he was once your very best friend."

Mo Xi lowered his long, thick lashes. "I was blind in my youth," he replied after a time.

"But after he defected, you still believed he had some secret. You believed that for a long time."

"My blindness was quite severe." Mo Xi said. He looked at the cup in his hand. A few drops of wine remained, glimmering the color of dusk. He didn't want to continue this conversation any longer. "It's gotten windy. Qingxu Elder, let's return to the hall."

Mo Xi spent the next few days after he learned of Gu Mang's whereabouts in a state of deep irritation. At first, he tried to repress this undesirable emotion, but as time passed, his frustration increased.

Mo Xi knew he'd grown sick in the heart, and only Luomei Pavilion held the cure.

Finally, one night at twilight, a carriage draped in black gauze set out for the northern side of the capital.

Mo Xi sat in the compartment with his eyes closed. Even though the curtains were drawn and he was the only passenger, his posture was perfect. That ridiculously handsome face was completely devoid of expression, terrifyingly stern.

"My lord, we've arrived."

Mo Xi didn't immediately step out, merely pulling the curtain aside and looking out from the darkness.

This hour was the peak of the imperial capital's nighttime revelry. Lit by spiritual energy, two rows of extravagant plum blossom candles burned to augur the coming of spring, illuminating the scarlet inscription board high in the air: LUOMEI PAVILION.

Daybreak's wind blew colder than ice, only to wither so quickly into mud and filth.

Unlike other brothels, most of those on offer at Luomei were prisoners of war. Their spiritual cores had been broken, reducing them to captives and sex slaves.

"My lord, will you be going in?"

Mo Xi glanced toward the pavilion and recognized many of its patrons, all of them spoiled and rich young masters he especially disliked. He furrowed his brow. "Through the back door."

The carriage stopped at the rear of Luomei Pavilion. This was Mo Xi's first time coming to such a place; even though he'd always been the firm and decisive type, a sliver of self-loathing snaked into his heart. Only after repeatedly saying to himself, "This general came to exact revenge," within the carriage compartment did he descend with a stormy expression.

"Go back. You don't have to stay."

After delivering these instructions to his coachman, Mo Xi stood in place and looked over the terrain for a while before leaping elegantly to the roof and noiselessly slipping away under cover of darkness.

He'd studied Luomei Pavilion's layout before coming, so it wasn't hard to locate the area where the courtesans lived. Soon, he arrived at a secluded garden courtyard. He pulled the hood of his cape over his head and stepped through the main entrance like a regular guest, passing door after door of lacquered vermilion.

Priestess of the Flames, Sha Xuerou of Wan Ku

Handmaiden of the Flames, Qin Feng of Wan Ku

Deputy General of the Left Battalion, Tang Zhen of the Liao Kingdom

Official of the Left Battalion, Lin Huarong of Xueyu

Each occupant's country of origin, rank, and name were meticulously inscribed on a little wooden plaque hanging at their door. Everything was labeled clearly, so those clients with grudges against certain enemy nations could find a suitable target for their frustrations.

If a guest came to seek pleasure within, the name on the plaque would turn red; otherwise, it would be black.

At Luomei Pavilion, aside from sincerity, eternity, and those already dead, everything was available for purchase, quietly laid out on intangible shelves for the lords to take at will. With enough money, they could do anything.

These men and women's smiles, charms, bodies, and even each and every one of their lives was clearly priced out.

Mo Xi glanced across the doors, sleeves billowing as he strode past row upon row of corridors. The soundproofing was poor; the cries and moans of passion coming from the rooms were entirely too vivid. His frown grew deeper, and his heartbeat quickened—where was Gu Mang? He'd walked past dozens of rooms, but he still hadn't found that plaque.

He climbed to the second floor to continue his search.

Finally, Mo Xi came to a stop in a secluded corner. Before him was a dark wooden plaque with delicate lettering:

Traitorous Subject, Gu Mang of Chonghua

In the entire pavilion, this was the only one labeled "Chonghua."

Mo Xi's gaze landed on that little plaque with enough weight to crack it. In that moment, a dark flame seemed to ignite in those dark eyes, but its light was swiftly extinguished.

He reached out, then stopped, fingers frozen an inch from the door.

He had realized that the words on Gu Mang's plaque were red.

There was a client inside.

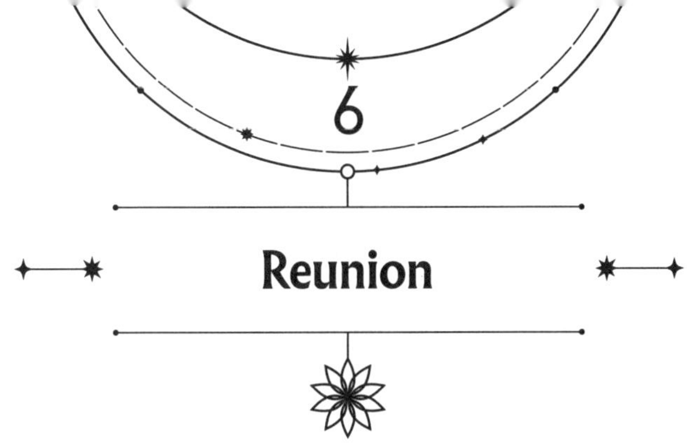

6

Reunion

MO XI'S FURY AND DISGUST blazed to life once more. His face was yet impassive, but his dark eyes hid an inferno of rage.

He felt hatred, but he didn't know whom he was hating. Of course he knew he shouldn't hate the people who came to bed Gu Mang—they were only paying for a night of fun. He shouldn't hate Wangshu-jun, either—*he* was only debasing a guilty subject as ordered.

So he could only hate Gu Mang.

Mo Xi stared at the scarlet text on the plaque, the redness swiftly infecting his eyes like an incurable disease. How familiar this was, like the return of a nightmare.

Many years ago, Mo Xi had returned upon the completion of a mission to hear that, after the new emperor had stripped him of his rank, Gu Mang couldn't pull himself together. Mo Xi was told that Gu Mang was wasting away, drowning his woes in brothels—but he didn't believe it.

Yet when Mo Xi stood panting like a fool in the dim light, when he strode in amid the voices of the women and pushed aside the heavy sandalwood door, he saw that familiar silhouette in the depths of the room.

Only a few months had passed. Gu Mang's face hadn't changed, but he no longer seemed like the same person.

Gu Mang was lying in the bed, surrounded by glinting opulence. Incense burned slowly inside the golden beast-shaped censers, and pale wisps of smoke rose in spirals, the fumes making everything misty and unclear. When Gu Mang heard the door, he opened hazy black eyes to glance at Mo Xi. As though he saw none of the anger and sadness on his old friend's face, he smiled.

Something in Mo Xi's heart seemed to shatter at the sight of that careless smile.

Gu Mang was right, he thought. Pleasure went only skin-deep.

It's just sleeping together. You can do that with anyone. Why take it so seriously? Gu Mang had said to him.

Gu Mang had never been shy about such things. Back in the day, he had been prone to cup Mo Xi's uneasy face as he lay beneath him, smiling as he panted. *Shidi, don't worry, you don't need to be so gentle. Your Gu Mang-gege is tough—you won't break me.*

During the years of their wild entanglement, Gu Mang had been fucked to the point of tears more than once, to the point where he'd mindlessly murmured Mo Xi's name and tearily said, *I love you.*

But he might not have meant it.

That was why Gu Mang could smile as he lay in the brothel, with not a single care for the past.

It was Mo Xi's own fault for being stupid. Like a silly kid, he'd actually believed that words said between the sheets were true.

It's not like it's anything important.

After the new emperor discarded him, Gu Mang refused to pull himself together. Perhaps the emperor's actions and the deaths of his soldiers had shattered his soul, so he wanted to languish in mud for the rest of his life.

In smoke, in wine, in women.

He would drown himself in whatever provided the most vivid illusions, as long as, in those illusions, he was still that young General Gu, who still had his brothers and his passion.

At this moment, in Luomei Pavilion, indistinct sounds of conversation could be heard from inside the room in front of Mo Xi. Feeling faint, he walked to the window at the end of the hallway and gasped for air outside. His slender fingers tightened on the window frame so hard they left a crack in the wooden lattice.

Faithless bitch.

The rims of Mo Xi's eyes were scarlet as he stared out into the night. These blisteringly harsh words had come into his mind unbidden. This was the first time he had ever thought to use such vicious language to describe someone.

Gu Mang, that *bitch*.

Mo Xi had once believed he understood Gu Mang well, that he knew Gu Mang better than anyone else. He had been so stupid, holding Gu Mang in his heart, treating him as the most intimate of friends.

He had been so ignorant. Gu Mang had been clear in his teaching: sleeping together didn't mean anything, and sleeping together multiple times only meant they liked each other's bodies. But Mo Xi still hadn't been able to stop himself from treating Gu Mang like a beloved, never to be betrayed. He was old-fashioned and stubborn when it came to this; no one could change his obstinate temperament.

That was why he'd once believed so firmly in Gu Mang. Even when Gu Mang became the target of a thousand grievances, Mo Xi had stood in the great hall of Chonghua's imperial palace and told everyone: "I, Mo Xi, can swear on my life that Gu Mang would never turn traitor."

But Gu Mang lied to him. Gu Mang betrayed him. Betrayed Mo Xi's trust, again and again. Betrayed his hope, day after day. In the end, Gu Mang personally stabbed Mo Xi in the chest and told him that everything had gone far past the point of return.

Mo Xi had once believed that things couldn't get any worse. He never could have imagined that even now, Gu Mang could still crush his already fractured heart.

Before he came to Luomei Pavilion, Mo Xi had nursed a little bit of hope in his chest. He had hoped Gu Mang was still the same unyielding man whose conscience would never let him bow to the powerful. If that were the case, Mo Xi's heart, which Gu Mang had covered in scars, might have yet felt some measure of relief.

But Gu Mang wouldn't even grant him that slight bit of ease.

Mo Xi felt like the bones in his flesh were shaking, trembling from hatred.

Gu Mang had actually spent these years in Luomei Pavilion, where the slaves were treated worse than livestock...

Mo Xi didn't know whether he should feel satisfaction at a traitor's punishment as Xihe-jun, or anguish over an old friend's ruination as Mo Xi.

The door opened with a *thump.*

Mo Xi tensed instantly, like a falcon sighting prey. Without turning, he was certain the sound had come from Gu Mang's direction.

A man was leaving Gu Mang's room, cursing up a storm. He spat phlegm onto the ground, continuing to swear as he stomped down the stairs. The sharp scent of wine filled the hallway—the departing guest was obviously a drunken alcoholic.

Mo Xi stood frozen in place. Only after a long while, when the scent of wine had dissipated, did he lift his head and close his eyes.

When he slowly opened them again, he was filled with a strange calm. Stepping silently, he made his way back to Gu Mang's door.

He paused, then lifted one black leather military boot and pushed open the carved lacquer door that someone else had closed moments ago.

The room was dark, lit by a single oil lamp, and was still filled with the nauseating scent of alcohol. Mo Xi walked in with his jaw clenched and glanced around, only to find the room empty.

Halfway through his second survey of the room, he heard splashing from behind a screen.

Mo Xi's blood surged fretfully once again. Gu Mang was bathing.

This realization felt like being hit with a rod, the strike making him dizzy. He had suppressed so many emotions—betrayal, disappointment, loathing, hatred—to the point of madness, until his heart was bleeding, the blood rushing up against the current to dye his eyes red. Biting his lip, he forced himself to turn away. His nails had sunk deep into his palms before he managed, barely, to restrain that overflowing fury.

He hadn't realized he would be so angry even now; that his rage had only grown with the passage of time.

Mo Xi sat down at the little round table, closing his eyes to avoid losing control. As he waited for Gu Mang to emerge, he thought: When Gu Mang saw him, what expression would Gu Mang have? When he saw Gu Mang, what should he say?

Mo Xi gritted his teeth and sat in silence for a long time. He didn't even notice when the sound of water stopped; he was too busy hating Gu Mang's lack of dignity.

Only when the room was illuminated by a second lamp did Mo Xi come to his senses. Turning, he saw a young man, clad in only a white robe, standing by the lampstand and quietly looking at him. Mo Xi didn't know how long he had been standing there.

The face was the same as the one in his memories. It was merely a little thinner.

For a moment, neither of them spoke.

The young man stood without making a sound, a magical shackle visible where his robes hung loose at the collar. He was barefoot, his inky black hair unbound and draping obediently down over one shoulder. It set off the thinness and paleness of his face, making his eyes seem extraordinarily bright. His hair was still wet from his bath, and water streamed down his nape to his collarbones, to his chest...disappearing into the shadows beneath his robe and leaving faint smudges of wetness.

Gu Mang.

Gu Mang...

In the terrifying stillness, the sounds of pleasure from the next room over were all the more piercing.

The rims of Mo Xi's eyes were red, and his clenched knuckles were shaking. He stared at the man before him. He swallowed, wanting to say something but rendered mute.

At last, they had met again. Finally, they were reunited.

Mo Xi had thought of so many questions, but he couldn't seem to remember a single one.

All that flashed in his blurry sight was that scene many years ago on the battleship. The blue-and-gold ribbon was askew on Gu Mang's forehead as he lifted Mo Xi's face with that bloody dagger, expression unreadable as he said, *I really will kill you.*

Back then, Mo Xi had thought that might be the end to their story.

Yet now their paths had crossed again. Gu Mang was standing right in front of Mo Xi, his expression serene as he regarded him silently.

To be honest, it was laughable. There was such hatred between them, but in this moment, Mo Xi's first reaction was distress: he had not seen Gu Mang come in, and therefore had missed the look in Gu Mang's eyes when he first caught sight of Mo Xi.

Now Gu Mang seemed serene and undisturbed, as if he were looking at any guest who had entered his room in the past two years. He was devoid of any emotion Mo Xi recognized.

Somehow, it was a peaceful reunion.

The two of them gazed at each other for a while. Then Gu Mang walked over and sat down next to Mo Xi.

Perhaps because Mo Xi had never expected Gu Mang to move so calmly, he unconsciously shifted back, although his face remained impassive. "What..."

Gu Mang retrieved a little bamboo scroll from the table and handed it to him without a word.

Mo Xi didn't know what Gu Mang meant by this, but he took the scroll and opened it under the faint lamplight. When he skimmed through it, his blood boiled then ran cold.

In the end, he closed his eyes and slammed the scroll on the table.

The peace shattered.

"Gu Mang..." Mo Xi stared at him, still restraining himself—but the lava in his eyes surged as his knuckles cracked. "Have you lost your fucking mind?"

Gu Mang said, "You need to choose." His voice was smooth as satin, slightly husky and very deep. Again, he picked up the scroll and passed it to Mo Xi. "Choose something."

"What do you think I came here to do?!"

Gu Mang's vocabulary seemed to have been reduced to only one word: "Choose."

Mo Xi was angry enough to ascend, his chest heaving, his bright black eyes ferocious. The red within their depths grew deeper and deeper; fury, disappointment, hatred, and sorrow all reflected in the bloody crimson of his eyes.

He held that little bamboo scroll for a long time before he flung it back onto the table. The scroll fell open. Luomei Pavilion's prices were meticulously displayed within, from conversation and companionable drinking, to venting rage, abuse, and...and...

Mo Xi looked away.

"If you don't choose, then what should I do?"

Mo Xi was about to lose his mind, but still he endured. In truth, his temper was horribly explosive, but he had become a master at suppressing it. "What do you mean?" he ground out.

Gu Mang looked at him placidly, his eyes like the still waters of an ancient well. "Aren't you here to bed whores?"

Mo Xi's expression froze on his face. He couldn't believe someone had actually said these words to him. He felt a twisting in his gut. "Gu Mang, you..."

"Everyone comes here to do these things," Gu Mang said. "If you haven't, why come?"

He pulled the scroll closer for the third time, picking it up and unfolding it for Mo Xi.

"Choose. Or leave."

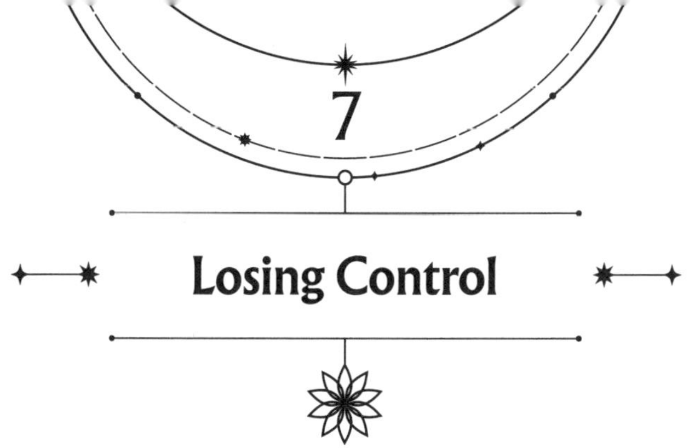

7 Losing Control

If someone had gone back in time and told Mo Xi three days ago, "Xihe-jun, I'll let you in on a secret: Three days from now, you're going to bed a whore," Xihe-jun would have, without a doubt, broken all their teeth and shattered their face.

But now he didn't seem to have any other choice.

In the end, he rapped his knuckles on the line that said *Conversation*. As he chose, his expression was dark, features filled with repressed shadow.

Mo Xi had made his choice.

Gu Mang held his hand out to him.

"What do you want?"

"Give me money."

"You!" Mo Xi was enraged, his eyes red, so much so that he couldn't even articulate his anger. "I—!"

Gu Mang didn't make a sound; he only spread his fingers and waited. He was speaking very little now, not talking unless he had to.

But the General Gu in Xihe-jun's memories spoke often. When he was facing the soldiers on the drill grounds beneath the blazing sun, he always strode about, proud and powerful, pacing back and forth and shouting at them as his skin glistened with sweat like crystal droplets on a panther's fur. He always grinned brilliantly, his black eyes bright and shining, a little canine peeking out.

Mo Xi gave Gu Mang the most valuable unit of currency in Chonghua: a golden cowrie.

Gu Mang didn't thank him. He stood and walked to a shelf, took down a little jar, and carefully put the cowrie shell inside. Then he placed the jar back on the shelf.

Mo Xi watched with cold eyes, his heart filled with complicated emotions: wrath, hatred, resentment, blame—all of it. Looking at Gu Mang's silhouette, he asked in a frigid voice, "How much money have you saved in that jar of yours?"

How many people did you let curse at you, degrade you, trample over you...? How... How many people did you sleep with?

Gu Mang said nothing. He put the jar back and returned to sit in front of Mo Xi. Under the hazy light, Gu Mang's face was difficult to see clearly. Mo Xi couldn't detect any minute expressions on that face—nothing he hadn't already caught.

Gu Mang was too calm, so calm it was unnatural. Had two years of disgrace already ground away the last of his pride?

But Mo Xi hadn't yet made him pay, hadn't even heard him admit his wrongs... How could Gu Mang have cast his body aside so easily, leaving Mo Xi nothing but an empty shell?

"You gave me a gold cowrie."

"...I don't need change."

"I can't afford change," Gu Mang said honestly. With that, he opened the bamboo scroll and again gave it to Mo Xi. "So you can choose some more. You can pick anything from here."

Mo Xi stared at him, speechless. He watched Gu Mang's face, but saw not the slightest hint of humiliated pain. There was only the tranquility with which he asked Mo Xi to choose more services, as if doing so was nothing out of the ordinary.

Mo Xi turned his head, his jaw clenched so tight it was on the verge of cracking. How strange. Shouldn't he have expected this? First, it had been bedding prostitutes; later, it had been treason, as Gu Mang crossed Mo Xi's lines with impunity again and again. Gu Mang had already told him *Don't take sleeping together too seriously* a long time ago. Now he was selling his body in order to stay alive. He had just gone from sleeping with others to being slept with—what was there to be surprised about?

"I don't want to choose." Mo Xi grew more and more irritated, the furor in his chest about to break free. He couldn't endure a second longer—he suddenly got up, his expression bitter as frost. "I'm leaving."

It seemed Gu Mang had never experienced a situation like this. A degree of helplessness finally arose in his eyes; he wanted to say something, but he didn't know what to say.

Mo Xi had already turned away when Gu Mang pulled on his sleeve to stop him.

Mo Xi was at his absolute limit. His anger flickered dangerously, ready to burst into flames at any moment. "What the hell do you want?"

Again, Gu Mang couldn't answer. He turned back to the shelf, picking up the money jar once more. He took out the golden cowrie and quietly returned it to Mo Xi's hands. "Then I'll give this back to you."

Mo Xi stared at him.

"Goodbye."

There were a few heartbeats of dead silence.

With a sudden crash, Mo Xi grabbed that bamboo scroll. Teeth grinding together, he shoved it before Gu Mang's eyes. "How did it feel to spend these past two years here, doing such depraved and unspeakable things? Were you ever satisfied? You can stand the kind of life where someone slaps you and tosses you some money for your troubles?!"

The lava had finally broken free of its confines, those crazed emotions erupting from him all at once.

Mo Xi's pupils flashed scarlet as he panted, but his eyes were filled with tears. "To think you'd offer yourself like this—are you still the same Gu Mang? Look at yourself now—I can't believe I used to be friends with someone like you, fought people for you, even treated you as my...my..."

He couldn't continue. He looked like he had been poisoned by wrath, so angry his lips were quivering. The lamps lit by spiritual energy flickered with the surge of his emotions—they blazed bright and then dim, silhouetting the two as they stood staring at each other.

Mo Xi grabbed Gu Mang by the lapels. Gu Mang had nowhere to hide; all he could do was let his clothes fall into further disarray. They were almost nose-to-nose, their eyes practically touching.

Mo Xi's chest heaved violently. He stared at Gu Mang for a beat in this way, before his gaze fell across Gu Mang's bare shoulder.

It was covered in black and blue welts...

Mo Xi's head rang as if a fuse had blown out. The scarlet rage in his eyes was joined by an emotion he couldn't clearly describe. That emotion made him lash out and seize Gu Mang by the jaw, shoving him against the shelf. His other hand slammed into the wall next to Gu Mang's face, and he pinned him beneath his bulk.

The lamps that had struggled so valiantly finally lost against the spiritual energy exploding from Mo Xi and abruptly went out.

In the darkness, Mo Xi stared at Gu Mang's face from inches away. Those rough, callused fingers dug pitilessly into Gu Mang's cheeks and lips. Even his voice was filled with hate, though it remained low and hoarse. So furious was Mo Xi that he didn't notice the strange color of Gu Mang's irises, nor the flicker of Gu Mang's shock. "To live, to earn a little money, you would do anything, right?"

Mo Xi's tight hold seemed to bring Gu Mang more discomfort than he could bear. His cheeks gradually flushed as he finally reacted and started to struggle in Mo Xi's grip.

But Mo Xi had lost his last hold on rationality. He couldn't see Gu Mang's pain. They were surrounded by so much darkness, a darkness like death. The rooms on either side overflowed with the moaning of women and the panting of men, constantly reminding Mo Xi of where they were, what Gu Mang did here—what the two of them could be doing.

Mo Xi was a little startled by the impulse that flashed through his mind, his scalp prickling.

The woman next door seemed to reach her climax; her gasps came quicker and sharper, the thumping of flesh so clear in the darkness that it could have been right by his ear. Gu Mang's stifled struggles beneath Mo Xi didn't let up in the slightest. They looked to him like shameless attempts at seduction.

Mo Xi's eyes slowly darkened, molten iron bubbling in their depths, terrifyingly scalding—from rage, or from something else.

"Let...go..."

Mo Xi didn't let go. He simply scoffed, a sound devoid of satisfaction, filled with extreme disappointment and hateful jealousy.

When he spoke, it was with bitter hostility—and perhaps some entirely different emotion—his voice searing with sparks, so rough even he found it ridiculous. He bent down to hiss through gritted teeth, right into Gu Mang's ear, "What do you want me to choose? You want me to take you to bed, to fuck you?"

He was answered by silence.

"Haven't I fucked you enough?!"

He'd spoken too impulsively—the sound of the words shocked even his own ears.

Mo Xi almost never said anything like this; he was the sort of person who frowned as soon as Yue Chenqing told bawdy stories. But here, now, he had been driven to the brink, and the words bursting thoughtlessly from his mouth… They were savage, menacing, cruel.

They had lain dormant.

They sounded like despair.

Mo Xi cursed under his breath, punching the shelf without warning. Gu Mang's little coin jar swayed and fell to the floor, where it loudly shattered.

Mo Xi turned toward the sound, his uncomprehending gaze sweeping over the mess. After a moment, he realized something and let go of Gu Mang. He straightened up and turned to look at the floor.

Moonlight spilled through the window. As it turned out, in that little coin jar, there was nothing at all…

Gu Mang hadn't received even one slight, small white cowrie. The jar was empty.

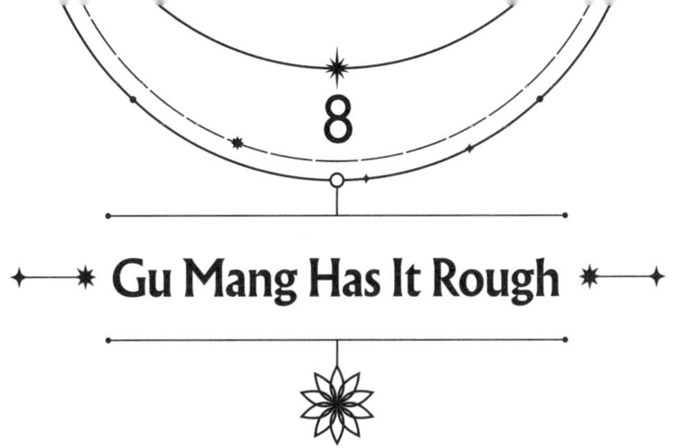

8
Gu Mang Has It Rough

How could this be…? How could it be empty?

It was as if a ladleful of ice had been tossed into boiling water—the roiling waves momentarily ceased, but the thick mist remained.

In this hazy fog, Mo Xi wondered vaguely, *Clearly, clients have come to his room, so why isn't there a single white cowrie in his jar?*

Xihe-jun was strict, stern, and self-restrained, like an indomitable walled city. Nothing could make this fortress light the beacons of warning. Except for Gu Mang.

Ever since the old days, whenever Gu Mang was involved, Mo Xi was prone to losing control, becoming easily enraged, reckless, and impatient—even to the point of losing his composure and ability to think.

Later, when he became a commander, years of ruthless war had sharpened and refined him further. But he still hadn't been able to control this selfish little impulse.

In front of Gu Mang, Mo Xi wasn't the highest-ranked general of Chonghua. He was nothing more than an ordinary young man—one who was less and less able to control himself, and more and more desperate to know how Gu Mang had been these past two years.

Had they disgraced him and then not even paid him for it?

And...how had Gu Mang become so calm, so calm he was almost apathetic? In the face of such a rise in favor and fall into disgrace, could anyone really be so *calm*?

"Waste of money!"

A furious shout came from outside, interrupting Mo Xi's thoughts. The sound of footsteps quickly followed, and a woman cursed as she stalked toward the room.

"He can't do anything right and only fucking knows how to make clients upset! That traitor should've been hanged ages ago! I truly don't understand what compelled Wangshu-jun to spare his shitty life!"

Mo Xi's brow furrowed.

This was the manager of Luomei Pavilion, Madam Qin.

A long time ago, as a gesture of friendship, Wangshu-jun had asked Madam Qin to choose a dozen different beauties to send to Mo Xi's army. But no matter how Madam Qin tried to persuade Mo Xi, and no matter how extravagantly she described these beauties, he had refused to keep the people she sent. More than anything, Mo Xi had made note of that sharp and shrill voice, which was so irritating it made his head hurt.

"He can't cry or smile, can't flirt or fuck. Every time clients leave his room, they end up cursing me out." The woman raged, her shadow already dark on the window paper. "What a total waste of money!"

How could Mo Xi be this unlucky? The news that Xihe-jun was visiting brothels would shake the nation to its core, and word that Xihe-jun had snuck through the back door to visit a brothel would further stupefy all of Chonghua.

And if word got out that Xihe-jun was secretly visiting a brothel to bed his mortal enemy? That would blow the top off Chonghua's capital city.

Mo Xi wrenched Gu Mang's face toward him, his rough breaths brushing Gu Mang's cheeks. "Where can I leave?" he asked, lowering his voice.

Gu Mang coughed, gasping for air. "The words outside will change color when a client's here. She won't come in."

"I'm not a client."

Gu Mang's eyes widened. "Then..."

During the brief span of their conversation, Madam Qin's flickering shadow had reached the doorway. Just as she was about to push open the door, Mo Xi glanced to the side. "Don't tell her I'm here."

The door opened. Nigh simultaneously, Mo Xi let go of Gu Mang and darted behind the decorative screen.

Madam Qin entered, a pipe in her hand. She exhaled through red lips, filling the room with the cloying scent of smoke. Gu Mang couldn't stop himself from sneezing quietly.

"You cough and choke every time I come to your room. I keep hoping you might die." Madam Qin rolled her eyes. "But even though I've kept you for all these years, you sure aren't dead yet."

She sat down at the round table, taking a few more puffs from her water pipe. "Great General Gu, there are only three more days in this month," she said maliciously. "I won't bother comparing you to those who earn thousands of cowries, but even the ugliest and most disagreeable of your brethren can sweet-talk and welcome clients with a smile well enough to earn their keep." She glanced at him. "What about you?"

"...I don't have any money."

"I know you don't!" Madam Qin chewed on her pipe. "You can't do anything right. Your face is acceptable, but you have no other skills."

Gu Mang sneezed softly again.

"Why bother pretending to be frail and pitiful?" Madam Qin was growing angrier, and she raised her voice to berate him. "Look at yourself! What do you have in that rotten jar of yours? Keeping you around only loses me money all year long!"

Gu Mang said nothing.

"Wangshu-jun may have forbidden me from laying a finger on you, but if this continues, I'll kill that dog you keep in the courtyard!"

As soon as Gu Mang heard *kill that dog*, he spoke up. "I did as you said."

"Bullshit. You think I'm stupid?"

"They don't give me money. They tell me I am a..." Gu Mang paused before saying that word aloud, "...traitor."

Mo Xi heard this from behind the screen. Although he couldn't see Gu Mang's expression, Gu Mang's voice was as unmoved as before. He seemed to be expressing something wholly insignificant, without a hint of guilt or shame. To him, the word "traitor" seemed light as a feather.

"Traitors shouldn't earn money," Gu Mang continued. "They say what I do for them is my duty."

Through the gap in the screen, Gu Mang's silhouette was solitary and helpless.

"It's what I owe them."

Madam Qin sputtered. "Yes, indeed, you're a traitor," she said angrily, "but what does this have to do with me? Of course you owe them, but I'm running a brothel, not a charity. Why should I lose money on you?! What's more, those noble clients curse me out every time!

"How many times have I told you to serve those lords? I can't ask for money—*you're* the ones who have to entice them to pay. At least the others can coax *some* coin out of their clients, but you? Great General Gu, can you?"

Gu Mang was silent. After a while, Madam Qin's voice became even sharper, shrill enough to pierce the sky. "What are you glaring at me for? How dare you! Get on your knees!"

Mo Xi assumed Gu Mang wouldn't kneel—or, at least not immediately. But reality once more defied his expectations. Gu Mang didn't seem to care; it was as if he wasn't aggrieved in the slightest. He knelt down in front of the woman.

Mo Xi braced his hand against the icy wall beside him, his ears ringing with rushing blood. Gu Mang actually...

He didn't have time to finish the thought before he heard the crack of a whip. Mo Xi was inarguably a god of war who'd braved great battles, but this sound shocked him to the point of trembling. His pupils contracted as cold sweat beaded on his back.

Through the narrow gaps in the screen, Mo Xi saw Gu Mang kneel in front of Madam Qin. That madwoman stood up, coalesced spiritual energy into her palm, and thrashed Gu Mang savagely on the back with a scarlet whip.

This woman seemed to pour all her pent up resentment over her losses onto Gu Mang. She whipped him hard another twenty or thirty times before coming to a panting stop.

Throughout the process, Gu Mang made not a single sound, not even a muted groan, as if he didn't care about the degradation or the pain.

Once Madam Qin had her fill of beating him, she retracted the spiritual whip. She picked up her pipe again and took a few drags to soothe her heaving chest. "You know that people find traitors even more disgusting than their enemies, right? So you better work harder to flatter them and make them obediently give you their money!"

"Flatter..." Gu Mang echoed, as if trying to understand this word.

"If you don't earn anything next month, not only will the clients beat you, I won't let you off so easily either! You better think about that!"

Madam Qin left in a furious huff.

When Mo Xi emerged, Gu Mang's back was still toward him as he knelt on the floor. His silhouette seemed entirely serene. His collar was open wide, pale skin visible over the hem. Above was his neck, bent like a curl of smoke; below was scarlet, looking like burning embers.

Too much about Gu Mang was unnatural. He seemed too much like a stranger, too quiet, too apathetic toward life or death, humiliation or praise. There were so many questions Mo Xi wanted to ask, but as he stared at the blood still dripping down Gu Mang's back, what came out of his mouth was: "Are all of your wounds...from her?"

"Not all of them." Gu Mang stood up. "When you guys come, most of you beat me."

Mo Xi was speechless.

"She beats me more than anyone." Gu Mang answered without sparing Mo Xi a glance, absorbed in his own business as he walked to the water basin.

Mo Xi was about to reply when he saw Gu Mang shrug off his robe. Gu Mang tossed the bloodstained garment aside and picked up the basin to pour its contents over himself with a thunderous splash.

That back of his seemed to be enchanted—it trapped the invincible General Mo in a nightmare.

In Xihe-jun's memories, when Gu Mang was young, his back had been very pale, his skin like glistening jade fished out of a creek. Later on, when Gu Mang grew up, his back had become straight, broad, and fiercely muscled, like a bowstring pulled taut.

Finally, after they went to war, the harsh elements and scorching sun had slowly burnished Gu Mang's skin the color of honey. When he bathed in the river at dusk, a shrug of his shoulders sent water droplets rolling down his back, like a great army chasing the shifting sand dunes of his shoulder blades. They streamed down in a wild, rugged line—but the path cut off abruptly at his narrow waist, sinking beneath the belt of his uniform pants.

Back then, there had been sparingly few scars on Gu Mang's back. His scars were mostly on his front—for instance, on his chest or abdomen.

But now, in the dim yellow lamplight, the back that Xihe-jun knew so well was unrecognizable, covered in whip scars, knife wounds, and mangled magic burns. It was difficult to locate a single patch of unharmed flesh, not to mention the bloody cuts from the beating moments ago… How much must that have hurt?

But Gu Mang seemed not to care. He indifferently poured cold water over himself to wash the blood away.

Mo Xi's heart was in disarray. He hadn't wanted to say anything, but somehow, he was unable to look away.

He thought of Gu Mang in their academy days, standing with his back to Mo Xi and sighing with exasperation. *Shidi, you work too hard. Can you still move your legs? Come here, get on my back. I'll take you home.*

He thought of Gu Mang on the battlefield, fierce and unyielding, their backs pressed together. *Shidi, don't rush ahead. Stay by my side.*

Mo Xi closed his eyes in silence. In the end, he asked, "Where's your wound salve?"

Gu Mang's eyes were somewhat unfocused, as if he didn't understand what Mo Xi was saying. "Wood…salve?"

"What about bandages?"

"Bandages?"

Mo Xi didn't know whether what he felt right then was anger or hatred, resentment or some other inexplicable pain. "You should at least have a bottle of blood-clotting powder."

Gu Mang stopped moving and turned to look at him. After a few seconds of thought, he finally understood, but he shook his head. "No need. It will heal."

He continued to splash cold water over himself, then haphazardly dried himself with a towel. Finally, he stepped over to the low camphor wood wardrobe, took out a wrinkled robe, and put it on, just like that.

Seeing how thoughtlessly he moved, Mo Xi's frustration roared even louder.

He had seen many prisoners of war. There were those who were unyielding, those who were obedient, those who wanted to die, and those willing to change allegiances.

But Gu Mang was unlike any prisoner he had ever seen. Mo Xi didn't know exactly what the current Gu Mang was like; he sensed not the slightest shred of familiarity, nor the slightest sliver of human emotion.

Gu Mang didn't shed tears, feel shame, show terror, or cast blame. He didn't even seem to feel pain.

After a long pause, Mo Xi asked, "Gu Mang, what exactly are you thinking?" He didn't expect Gu Mang to answer; he only spoke because his chest felt impossibly tight.

But to his surprise, Gu Mang did reply, and his reply was very honest: "I want cowrie shells."

Mo Xi had no words.

"Other people here have them, but I don't. No one's ever given me any."

Mo Xi gazed at him, watching Gu Mang's expression as he spoke. That sense of strangeness intensified.

"Everyone says I shouldn't want them." As Gu Mang talked, he looked toward the fragmented remains of his jar before bending to pick up the shards and put them on the table. He looked as placid as ever, but Mo Xi gradually realized his expression seemed somewhat bewildered, as if there were something Gu Mang didn't understand. Gu Mang turned to look at him. "You're the first person to give me a cowrie shell."

Mo Xi was momentarily silent. "You know very well why I gave it to you," he replied stiffly.

Gu Mang didn't immediately respond, instead continuing to assess Mo Xi. This was the first time since Mo Xi's entrance that Gu Mang had looked at him carefully, without the disinterested blankness he used to appease clients.

Then Gu Mang reached a hand toward him.

"You still want it?" Mo Xi stared down at him. "Didn't you want to give it back to me earlier?"

"I want it."

Mo Xi felt a surge of frustration. In order to stop wasting breath on Gu Mang, in order to avoid getting even angrier, he took out another golden cowrie and passed it to him.

Gu Mang didn't say thank you. He took the shell, holding it in both hands, and lowered his head to inspect it. Then he turned to look at the shattered jar on the table. After some thought, he walked to the bed and dug under the soft mattress until he found a brocade pouch.

Gu Mang was about to open the pouch and put the cowrie shell inside when Mo Xi realized something. He stood up, his heart going cold.

"Hold it."

Gu Mang froze.

"What's that in your hand?" Mo Xi's voice was low and dangerous, each word dripping with threat, as if they would be splintered between his teeth with the slightest exertion of force. "Take it out."

9

Caught Red-Handed

IT WAS AN EXTREMELY well-crafted little pouch, embroidered with a landscape of mountains and rivers, as well as the sun and the moon. A rosy dawn was stitched in golden thread, the winding rivers and mountains in silver, and a red agate pendant hung from the bottom. It was clear at a glance that this item was expensive.

Mo Xi stared at the brocade pouch for a long time, rage boiling in his heart. Slowly, he spat out a few words. "Who gave that to you?"

Gu Mang seemed to have noticed the rancor in his eyes and didn't reply right away. He tucked the pouch back into his robes, against his heart. "Mine," he said, without answering the question.

His? That was absurd. Gu Mang had fallen to such depths, and his jar was completely empty—how could he afford that kind of brocade pouch? Mo Xi was about to laugh from anger. "With what money?"

"I exchanged it."

A pause. "With whom?"

"I exchanged it," he repeated, and that was all.

Mo Xi lost his temper. "What did you exchange for it? What do you have? You—"

He stopped.

Gu Mang lived in a brothel. What kind of people did he meet? What could he give in exchange for this pouch? The answer was self-evident, but Mo Xi was still interrogating him like a fool.

His heart felt as if it had been scraped with sandpaper, painful and itchy. Mo Xi closed his eyes, wanting to soften his voice, but his pale and elegant face couldn't hide the way he clenched his jaw. In the end, as if in defeat, he opened his eyes again, his voice dangerously hoarse. "Why would you want something like that?!"

Gu Mang didn't seem to know what this pouch could be used for either. But he clutched it tight, then stared at Mo Xi, not making a sound.

"Because it's pretty?" Mo Xi asked. "Because you like it? Shouldn't you do something so ridiculous for a *reason*?"

Likely because he couldn't handle Xihe-jun's interrogation, when Gu Mang finally began to speak, it was slowly. "Someone gave it to me..."

"Didn't you say you exchanged something for it? Even now, you'd still lie to me?"

"Someone..." Gu Mang looked as if he wanted to keep talking, but something stopped him. He bit his lower lip, and the end, he again chose silence.

This silence seemed to be the straw that broke Mo Xi's sanity. His gaze was like a sharp knife wrenching open a seashell, suddenly severe. "Continue."

Mo Xi stared at Gu Mang's face. Perhaps due to his extreme anger, or perhaps because the light in the room was too dim, Mo Xi again failed to notice there was something different about Gu Mang's eyes.

"Why did you stop? Is there anything on earth you can't say out loud?" Mo Xi swallowed thickly, each word grinding out between clenched teeth. "Speak. It won't be anything new, no matter how absurd it is. You—"

"Someone was good to me," Gu Mang cut in, unmoving.

It was like a sudden blow. This time it was Mo Xi's turn to be speechless. His throat felt terribly dry.

Someone had been good to Gu Mang? Preposterous... Who would treat a traitor with kindness?

Then Mo Xi remembered: Right, whenever Gu Mang had needed him, he always used smooth talk, teasing and flirting. Now that Gu Mang had fallen on hard times at Luomei Pavilion, it wasn't strange to see him employ silver-tongued lies to entice another person into helping him in his time of need.

But...but...

Mo Xi was so angry his vision flashed dark. For a long time, his mind was stuck on the word *but*, unable to continue.

"Very well... Very well..." Mo Xi stopped, his eyes red with overpowering fury. Only after a long while did he continue, nearly choking on his words. "Gu Mang, Gu Mang...you truly impress me."

Gu Mang didn't make a sound as he leaned against the wall, gazing at Mo Xi's face.

Mo Xi lifted his head; it was as if he was trying to will any wetness from his eyes. He stood there, looking up for a while, before he suddenly brought a hand to his face and burst out laughing. "I really don't know what I was clinging to all these years. I have no idea why I came to see you tonight..."

The more Mo Xi thought about it, the more anger and sorrow filled him. By the end, his voice was shaking. He slammed his fist into the wall beside Gu Mang, scraping his knuckles and leaving gruesome bloodstains behind. As the lamplight flickered between them, Mo Xi pressed Gu Mang against the wall, his face full of hatred, like he was ready to tear the man apart.

Mo Xi clenched his jaw. "General Gu, you truly live a blessed life. Even after rotting so far, you still have someone who treats you kindly. I…"

"Gu Mang!" Madam Qin's shout came like a clap of thunder, echoing from far away. "Zhou-gongzi is here! Hurry up! Change into clean clothes and make the young master nice and comfortable!"

Her voice pulled Mo Xi back to the present. He came to his senses almost immediately; although his chest was still heaving, the uncontrollable rage in his eyes was now restrained.

Mo Xi lowered his head slightly, his ragged breaths rising and falling in Gu Mang's ear. He closed his eyes. When he opened them again, that vicious beast stirring inside its cage had disappeared. Those eyes remained but slightly damp; in the darkness, they shone like morning stars. "Zhou-gongzi? Did he give you the pouch?"

Gu Mang didn't seem to understand Mo Xi's hatred. He continued to gaze at Mo Xi's face, as tranquil as ever, and shook his head.

Zhou-gongzi… Zhou-gongzi. As Mo Xi repeated this name in his heart, he realized this was probably the youngest son of the Zhou Clan. Mo Xi had heard of this young master; among the nobles of the capital, he was regarded as the most brutish piece of trash. What he lacked in competence, he made up for with an unending stream of malicious ideas.

Mo Xi looked toward Gu Mang. Gu Mang's expression hadn't changed, but he was unconsciously rubbing a scar on his arm.

After a few seconds, Mo Xi laughed again, as if tormenting himself. "What's wrong? The person who was good to you doesn't care?"

Without a word, Gu Mang tucked the pouch away.

Mo Xi didn't move. "Is Zhou-gongzi a frequent guest too?" he asked.

Gu Mang nodded.

Mo Xi stared at him, his handsome features seeming to contain some unfathomable emotion. A moment later, he laughed once more. "Before, I thought you had changed. Now I see that you're still the same as ever—you know how to make *anyone* happy." The darkness in his eyes deepened, as though weighed down by the past. "Take care."

Rising from the round table, Mo Xi donned his cloak and strode toward the door.

"You're leaving?"

Mo Xi turned halfway. "I'm leaving," he said, frigid. "I won't stand in the way of your livelihood."

"But I—"

Mo Xi stopped. "What."

"I took your cowrie shell..."

Mo Xi paused. "Think of it as returning your past affections."

Gu Mang knit his brows in confusion. "Past affections..."

Mo Xi felt that Gu Mang was acting very strangely—but he was running out of time. As soon as Zhou-gongzi got upstairs, he wouldn't be able to leave even if he wanted to. Mo Xi glanced at Gu Mang one last time and turned to push open the door.

But at that moment, Gu Mang whispered, "You're rich. You have money. I want to know who you are."

Mo Xi's hand froze inches from the door. He stood stock-still for a long interval before whipping around. "What?"

"You're rich."

"The second part!"

"...You have money."

"After that!"

Gu Mang was confused by this reaction. He sounded hesitant as he repeated himself. "I want...to know...who you are?"

A crash sounded in Mo Xi's ears, like a massive stone falling from a cliff before his eyes. He stopped breathing and stared fiercely into Gu Mang's face, his black-brown pupils shrinking as light flared in the depths of his eyes.

"Gu Mang." His heart had frozen over, but he ground out his words menacingly, "Are you fucking toying with me?"

Gu Mang was confused. "You're the client. You paid, so aren't you supposed to toy with *me*?"

Mo Xi's features were twisted almost beyond recognition. All the strange moments during their conversation flashed through his head like great waves battering his heart, stunning him so thoroughly that for a long time, he couldn't react.

But right then, the door behind them creaked open.

A man's lazy voice came from behind it. "Gu Mang, your Zhou-ge is here to patronize your business. Why haven't you scrambled over to kneel in welcome?"

Mo Xi whipped around, but it was too late.

That little Zhou bastard had swaggered in as he spoke. He looked around the room with bleary eyes, blinking in the low light.

Poor General Mo. He was such a proper person, and now, for the second time in as many hours, he was faced with the same annoying crisis. The last round had gone all right, but this time, he had nowhere to go, nowhere to hide, and was seconds away from being caught red-handed by his own junior.

Mo Xi's head had just been upended by Gu Mang's: *You're rich. You have money. I want to know who you are.* But he couldn't think deeply on it right now, so instead he cursed inwardly and pushed Gu Mang against the wall. He pinned him there with his tall frame, pressing one hand against the wall to neatly obscure both their faces.

Gu Mang's eyes widened within his arms. "You..."

"Hush." Mo Xi lowered his head and lifted Gu Mang's chin. His fingers were rough and forceful as he turned Gu Mang's head and bent down to bring them closer.

Cool, thin lips drew near soft ones, their scalding breaths overlapping.

Mo Xi didn't want to touch this traitor again, so of course he wouldn't actually kiss Gu Mang's mouth. In his effort to create a convincing scene, however, he still pressed very close, so close they were almost nose to nose, their lips almost brushing. The narrow space between them became a wisp of willow catkin, its fluttering drift making Mo Xi's skin tingle.

When Mo Xi had hidden from Madam Qin, he'd thought his luck couldn't get any worse—there was no way anything more vexing could occur. How naive he had been.

Mo Xi caged Gu Mang inside his arms. "Don't make a sound," he rasped.

Gu Mang, trapped beneath him, didn't think much of this situation. All he thought was that Mo Xi was too strong; he bore down on Gu Mang like a mountain and made it hard to breathe. He didn't want to be crushed further, so he instinctively nodded.

"Lean closer."

Gu Mang did as he was told.

Thus, from the doorway, the two looked as if they were kissing with overwhelming passion and desire; as if in the next moment, they would roll into bed, utterly inseparable. This suggestive sight would make most normal people exclaim with shock and instantly turn to leave.

But perverts aren't like normal people.

Zhou-gongzi was taken aback at first. He backed up a few steps and checked the plaque hanging on Gu Mang's door. Rubbing his eyes, he muttered, "The words are black. There shouldn't be a client in here..."

But after the initial shock, this Zhou-gongzi became even more invested. He walked into the room, smiling. "Aiya, this is so embarrassing. It seems like the spell on the plaque doesn't work anymore. I had no idea someone else was in the room."

No response.

"Hey there, you're so skilled. Our Great General Gu is the thorniest problem in all of Luomei Pavilion, but you've got him all pliant in your arms, letting you kiss him however you'd like. Why don't you teach me some of that impressive technique and let me have some fun as well?" He chuckled mischievously. "The more the merrier, right? Let's share."

10

Heart's Fire

MO XI BADLY WANTED to kick Zhou-gongzi to death, but he had to remain anonymous. All he could do was pitch his voice lower and icily snap, "Get lost."

"Hey, what's with that tone?" Zhou-gongzi's friendly overture had been rudely rejected, so after a momentary shock, he turned nasty. "Do you know who I am?"

"Do I care who you are? Don't you see what I'm doing? Hurry up and get lost!"

Gu Mang seemed fascinated by Mo Xi acting the tyrant, and stared unblinkingly into his eyes. They were so close to each other that Gu Mang's direct stare made him uneasy.

"Stop looking at me like that," Mo Xi whispered.

Gu Mang was exceptionally obedient, so he lowered his lashes to stare instead at Mo Xi's pale lips.

Mo Xi was at a loss for words.

When Zhou-gongzi saw the pair still tangled together, paying him no mind at all, he raised his voice to shout angrily. "You're telling *me* to get lost? Why don't you check yourself first!" He ground his teeth. "Your Zhou-ge wants that one to keep him company, so why don't you smarten up and get out of my way? Don't you know where I'm from? *The Bureau of Military Affairs*! I'm friends with

Xihe-jun, General Mo! You scared now? Just wait until I tell on you—he'll break your legs!"

Mo Xi blinked in silence.

Zhou-gongzi was too far gone—and the longer he spoke, the worse he got. "And you, Gu asshole, you little bastard, last time you wouldn't let me kiss you no matter what I said, but you're fine with it now that it's someone else? Everyone says your souls are damaged and your mind's broken—pah! How could you be picky if your mind was broken?"

Mo Xi's heart skipped a beat.

Souls damaged... Mind broken?

He stared at Gu Mang's face up close, all the strangeness from earlier coming back to mind. His ears rang; he felt like he couldn't breathe.

"You're only faking it for some pity! What souls are you missing? How is your mind broken? You're just a bastard! Traitor!"

Gu Mang frowned, wanting to say something.

"Don't move." Even though blood still pounded in Mo Xi's ears, he reacted in time to stop Gu Mang. He closed his eyes, willing himself to remain composed. "Don't move..."

Their mouths were so close that Mo Xi's every whisper sent a gust of heat sweeping over Gu Mang's lips. This sensation startled him. He instinctively tried to struggle free, but Mo Xi's formidable strength kept him restrained with one hand. "Listen to me!" he hissed.

Gu Mang didn't want to listen, but neither could he move. And so, Mo Xi's warmth melded into his lungs only to leave on the next exhale, breaths entwining in the searing heat between them.

Gu Mang's eyes were glued to Mo Xi's face.

Mo Xi swallowed, head spinning as he slowly surfaced from the revelation of Gu Mang's condition. He collected himself with effort and opened his eyes to look at Gu Mang again. Afraid he would make a fuss, he chose his words carefully. "Have I hit you before?"

Momentarily confused, Gu Mang shook his head.

"Has he hit you before?"

Gu Mang nodded.

"Then listen to me and ignore him."

They were too close together, the air from the depths of their lungs tangling between their bodies. Mo Xi deliberately avoided his clear-eyed gaze. "As long as you listen, I'll make him scram."

Another wordless nod.

Seeing the two were still caught in their inseparable embrace, Zhou-gongzi began to feel as if he really had intruded on their intimacy. He became even cruder and more furious, aroused yet frustrated. "What's wrong, Gu Mang? You still won't say anything? What a miracle! You ignore everyone else who comes to your room—so is this man especially handsome? Or is he especially good in bed? Or is it that he's broken our agreement and he secretly paid you, traitorous bastard that you are?"

Zhou-gongzi stepped closer, his ragged breaths smelling of alcohol. "How come a little whore like you wants him to fuck you so bad...?" he mumbled.

Drunk people always sounded a little incoherent, rambling this way and that. After Zhou-gongzi was done taunting Gu Mang, he decided to move on to provoking Mo Xi.

"Hey there, who exactly are you? Why don't you turn around and let your big brother take a look? Judging by your behavior, you must come often." Zhou-gongzi dared to tug unsteadily on Mo Xi's sleeve. "How many times have you had him? How does our Great General Gu feel? Is he hot? Is he tight? Does he make you feel good?"

This Zhou-gongzi had managed to utterly disgust Mo Xi.

Mo Xi's hand whipped out to slap that Zhou asshole square across the face. It was a violent strike; blood spurted from Zhou-gongzi's nose as he crumpled to the floor.

Before Zhou-gongzi could get his bearings, Mo Xi kicked him to the ground, making sure he fell flat on his face at an angle that prevented him from turning.

"I told you to get lost." Sparks flew from Mo Xi's eyes, his teeth tightly gritted. "Don't you fucking get it?"

"You dare to hit me! You actually *dared* to hit me! H-how insubordinate!" Zhou-gongzi wailed. "Wh-wh-who *are* you?! I'll report this to His Imperial Majesty! No! I'll report this to General Mo! I'll report this to my *dad*, I—"

There was a loud clang.

Mo Xi had tossed something before him. One bleary glance was all it took for Zhou-gongzi to break out in a shock of cold sweat. He sobered up a great deal, convulsing with a squeak before going still.

Mo Xi was so repulsed by Zhou-gongzi's earlier crudeness that his expression was yet twisted. "Will you?" he asked menacingly.

"N-no."

"Are you going to visit him again?"

"N-no."

Mo Xi let him go with one last kick. "Get lost! Don't let me see you again."

Zhou-gongzi staggered up and stumbled away, too afraid to even look back.

Mo Xi stood there stonily for a time, letting his anger dissipate. Then he bent down and picked up the command token marked with *Chonghua Bureau of Military Affairs* and fastened it back into the compartment within his sleeve. He turned to glance at Gu Mang, who stood by the wall with his hands behind his back, obediently watching without making a sound.

In the chaos, his initial bewilderment had faded. Mo Xi had wanted to interrogate Gu Mang further, but at the sight of Gu Mang's peaceful face, all he felt was a pain like his heart was being cut apart, a turmoil he couldn't suppress.

There was no point in asking Gu Mang anything more, and Mo Xi had no idea what would happen if he stayed any longer.

Into this silence, Gu Mang suddenly spoke. "He's scared of you."

Mo Xi said nothing.

"You're scared of him too."

Mo Xi seemed deeply insulted by this, turning to shoot him a fierce glare. "Why would I be scared of him?"

"You were scared he would recognize you."

Mo Xi looked at him. His mood was no longer so vicious, though his expression remained displeased. "What does that have to do with you?"

"Did he?"

"No." Mo Xi's voice was cold and stiff.

It was as if the scalding breaths that had brushed against Gu Mang's skin earlier had never existed. "But he saw your token..."

"There's no name on it. Every high-ranking official at the Bureau of Military Affairs has one." Mo Xi glanced at him as he fastened his sleeve compartment. "You did too."

Gu Mang was surprised. "Me?"

His confusion upset Mo Xi. He didn't want to talk to Gu Mang anymore, and he still feared what he would do if he stayed. He pushed open the door and left without a backward glance.

The freezing night wind blew at Mo Xi's face as he stepped into the street outside. He tried to calm himself, but to no avail.

Souls damaged… Mind broken… Ah ha ha… *Mind broken?!*

Wind whipped across his face, the corners of his eyes stinging as if flayed. He'd yearned so long for closure, only to receive such an open ending.

Who had done it! *Who?!*

Had it been the Liao Kingdom? Murong Lian? Or…had it been Gu Mang himself, unable to bear the humiliation, who'd chosen to—

Mo Xi's imagination ran wild. In the end, it was grief, of all things, that suffused him.

Mind broken.

Why did that make his heart ache so much…? Yes, true, Gu Mang had given him friendship and redemption, but Mo Xi had done everything he could to repay him—had nearly sacrificed his life to pull Gu Mang back from the brink! Did Mo Xi owe him anything else? Had he let him down in any other way? Whether Gu Mang's souls were whole or his mind hale, what did that have to do with Mo Xi?

In the empty streets, in the dead of night, Mo Xi stopped walking and took a deep breath.

So many years of obsession, only to receive this *emptiness…*

His hands shook against his will. Without warning, flames blazed from his palms, coalescing into a fireball that smashed explosively into the distant river's surface. Smoke hissed upward from where it struck.

Gu Mang had betrayed him.

Only the heavens knew how dearly he wanted to hear Gu Mang say, *I regretted abandoning, deserting, and lying to you. I cared for you.* Why couldn't he have even that small thing? Why had he received nothing but a mentally impaired madman who had completely forgotten him?! Why?!

Mo Xi closed his eyes, agonized. After so many years, he'd thought he had freed himself of this fixation, but in truth, he had been lying to himself. Gu Mang was too important to him.

That man had taken too many of Mo Xi's firsts: the first time he exorcised demons, the first time he talked for hours around a warm bonfire, the first time he fought shoulder to shoulder...

And that year he turned twenty, on the day he came of age, on that specific night—perhaps he had drunk too much, or perhaps it had never been the wine—that had been the first time he made Gu Mang his.

He still remembered Gu Mang's expression back then. When it came to such matters, Gu Mang cared about his pride. Even though his eyes were teary and his lips were bitten bloody, he endured, insisting that *he* would never leave any flower unplucked.

You're fine! We're both men here, so it's all good as long as we make each other feel good. C'mere, do you want your Gu Mang-gege to teach you how to move?

Gu Mang shouldn't have said such things. At the time, Mo Xi's sanity had already been hanging by a thread. His heart was burning up; he didn't know if the flame of affection behind his ribs would ever go out. He knew he couldn't have done something like this merely because of some wine. No—his actions were born out of searing, passionate desire and deep, undeniable love.

Alas, Gu Mang didn't understand. He only wanted to regain his dignity, and so started babbling all sorts of lewd things. In the end, he personally destroyed what remained of Mo Xi's rational mind.

Later that night, Gu Mang had reached his absolute limit. Lying on his stomach, he began shaking his head and sobbing, begging Mo Xi to be gentler, wailing that—honestly—even if he'd done it with many girls, he'd been lying about having done it with other men, and he'd especially never let another man do *him*. But no matter what he confessed or revealed, or how he beseeched...

Mo Xi could no longer stop himself.

Finally, when he had bullied Gu Mang to the point of tears—until Gu Mang was crying so hard he couldn't quite speak, his eyes red at the corners as he looked at Mo Xi—only then did the desire in Mo Xi's gaze begin to subside.

He stroked Gu Mang's cheek and said, "I'm sorry, does it hurt?"

Gu Mang's lashes were still wet with tears, his face flushed in Mo Xi's palms, his lips quivering. Mo Xi had left him a pathetic sight indeed. Even more pathetically, who would have believed that a crude army thug like Gu Mang, in truth, hadn't even slept with a single girl before?

Faced with Gu Mang's silence, Mo Xi bent down to kiss him again. As their wet lips touched, Gu Mang's tears streamed down into the hair at his temples. Mo Xi caressed his hair, then wordlessly embraced him once more, kissing his teary eyes and taking warmth from the man in his arms.

A young man getting his first taste of carnal desire could never stop himself, no matter how virtuous he was.

Besides, Mo Xi had never really been virtuous. It was only that before Gu Mang, he'd never met someone who could make him lose control.

He had fallen in love with Gu Mang first.

So he had trod carefully all this time. He had never dared to demand Gu Mang's first time; had only ever, with utmost care, passed all his own firsts into Gu Mang's hands. He had stubbornly refused to say how important these were to him, but in his heart, he still nervously hoped Gu Mang would treasure these moments.

But Gu Mang had trampled his heart underfoot.

Yes, it was true that Mo Xi hadn't wanted to stop Chonghua from putting Gu Mang on trial—or even killing him. Mo Xi had even thought that if there ever came a day when Gu Mang had to die, he wanted to be Gu Mang's final judge and final tormentor, to take hold of him with his own hands and crush him into a bloody pulp and grind his bones into dust.

All for the sake of the nation's vengeance.

But if Mo Xi put aside that vengeance, he had to admit that he had never actually wanted to see Gu Mang dead. He had only wanted to obtain a word of truth from his mouth, to receive a single sentence from a sincere heart.

After so long...he...he genuinely only wanted to ask one question: *Gu Mang, when you left Chonghua, when you left...me, did you ever regret it, even a little?*

Only then would these years of love and hatred, gratitude and resentment, come to a conclusion that could allow Mo Xi to breathe, if only barely.

Then he heard those words: *souls damaged, mind broken.*

Gu Mang had forgotten. He would not suffer.

But Mo Xi was damned to an eternity without reprieve.

No one knew Mo Xi had gone to Luomei Pavilion to see Gu Mang, but in the following days, the people of the Bureau of Military Affairs could distinctly sense General Mo's displeasure.

Even though Mo Xi went around looking displeased all the time, and his expression was rarely genial when he spoke to anyone, his moodiness had become even more pronounced. He didn't grow distracted during military councils, but his phrasing grew more curt. When others chattered idly during the meeting, Mo Xi would at once level a dark stare at them even if he didn't cut them off—until the offending individual swallowed their own babble.

This was hardly a problem in itself, but one day, General Mo inexplicably berated the young master of the Zhou Clan for an hour straight, saying he had "slacked off on his martial responsibilities" and was "excessively depraved," even though no one knew what Zhou-gongzi had done wrong.

"Copy the Bureau of Military Affairs' rulebook one hundred times and deliver it to me tomorrow," Mo Xi said. "If you commit another offense, you can call your dad to drag you back home."

Zhou-gongzi obeyed in a fit of terror and left, quaking all over.

Yue Chenqing scooched over to Zhou-gongzi with a nosy look. "Hey, what did you do?"

"I-I don't know..."

"If you didn't do anything wrong, why would that ice-cube face get so angry?" Yue Chenqing glanced around, smiling deviously. "Be honest, are you keeping a stash of portraits of Princess Mengze?"

Zhou-gongzi's face paled, looking as if the heavens were about to strike him down. "Bro, spare me! How could I dare?!"

Yue Chenqing rubbed his chin and looked at Mo Xi in the distance, who was staring down at the sand table with his arms crossed. "That's weird. Then why does he have such a short fuse right now...?"

In the end, Mo Xi with said short fuse couldn't control himself. He pretended not to care for two days, but in the end, he asked his head housekeeper how Gu Mang had been these past two years.

In this day and age, being a housekeeper was no easy task. Those in the position had to excel in both managerial duties and menial tasks, advise the lord and comfort the lady, console the concubines and deal with the young masters' disputes.

Xihe Manor's housekeeper was named Li Wei. All the other housekeepers of other noble lords envied him, as they knew General Mo kept a simple staff and had neither wife nor children nor concubines. It sounded like a blissfully carefree arrangement. Only Li Wei knew how hard it was to work in General Mo's employ...because General Mo would ask questions without the slightest warning.

Sometimes General Mo's questions brewed in his mind for ages until he couldn't stand them anymore. By then, General Mo would have worn his own patience thin, so he would want to know the answer straightaway and would be annoyed if it were even slightly delayed.

In working for this master, Housekeeper Li had to think three steps ahead before he did anything, then four steps ahead when it was done. After all these years, he had more or less honed himself into a prodigy. Whenever Mo Xi was quietly sulking, Housekeeper Li would examine his body language to deduce what General Mo was repressing and roughly how long it would take before he exploded—as well as strategize how he should respond once General Mo did finally combust.

This time was no different.

Mo Xi bit his lip, and said lightly, "Gu Mang..."

Housekeeper Li rushed to answer. "Yes, my lord, Gu Mang is utterly ruined!"

"Was that my question?" Mo Xi said.

Sometimes being too clever wasn't a good thing, so Housekeeper Li obediently shut his mouth.

Mo Xi turned around, eyes indifferent as he gazed at the pot of tea on the stove. It was a long while before he said anything more. Face blank, he asked, "How was he ruined?"

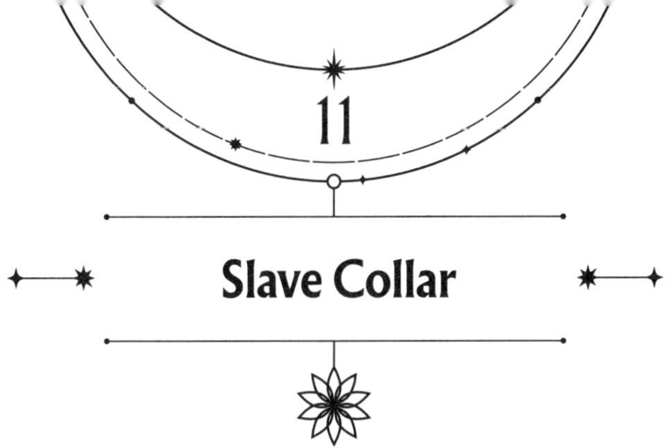

11

Slave Collar

In Li Wei's opinion, working as a housekeeper for a man who never spoke his mind like General Mo was the most exhausting thing in the world.

If time could flow backward, he would have chosen to work for Official Liu with his eighteen concubines instead. It was highly likely that the thoughts of the ruthlessly cold General Mo were more convoluted than all those eighteen concubines' put together.

But time could not flow backward. Li Wei cleared his throat and began again with utmost caution, asking, "My lord, have you visited Gu Mang?"

"...No."

"Oh." Li Wei sighed in relief. "Then it's best you don't."

"Why's that?"

"Um...my lord, how shall I put this? In Gu Mang's current condition, he probably doesn't even know who he is, never mind who you are. According to the healers' diagnoses, in the depths of his mind, he more or less thinks of himself as a strong and mighty male wolf."

Mo Xi's eyes widened. "He thinks he's a...what?"

"A strong and mighty male wolf."

Mo Xi stared. This was without a doubt the wildest sentence he had heard all year.

He rubbed at his temples and collected himself before carefully asking, "Which healer examined him and delivered that diagnosis? Are you sure there's nothing wrong with *their* brain?"

It was rare for Li Wei to see Mo Xi react with so much shock, and he couldn't hold back his snicker. But at the sight of Mo Xi's expression, he quickly and obediently schooled his expression to solemnity.

"My lord, none of us believed it when we heard either. That's why so many nobles went to the prison to settle their debts with Gu Mang when he returned. However, he couldn't even talk like a normal person. It only made everyone angrier." Li Wei paused before continuing. "Then His Imperial Majesty handed him to Wangshu-jun. Wangshu-jun also wanted to pry something out of his mouth. He tried everything, but no matter what, Gu Mang couldn't answer his questions."

Li Wei sighed as he shook his head. "He genuinely didn't understand that he was human."

Mo Xi had to digest this information for a long time before he looked up again, gaze pausing on the little clay teapot steeping hot tea. Steam rose into the air, those tendrils of mist floating about and entwining together.

"I also heard...his souls were damaged." Mo Xi paused. "What happened there?"

Li Wei was stunned. His lord wasn't usually the sort to ask for such news, so how had he learned about this? But he hurried to reply, "They are indeed damaged, but it's not clear what exactly happened. We only know that Gu Mang was already in that state before he returned."

"Already in that state before he returned..." Mo Xi repeated, frowning.

"Mn. When Gu Mang entered the capital, our healers read his pulse. They said his souls, heart vein, and spiritual core all bore traces of recent damage. The people of the Liao Kingdom are definitely responsible—we don't know what secret, shady techniques they employed, but on top of making him think he was a beast, of his three ethereal souls and seven corporeal ones, they somehow removed two of the corporeal."

Mo Xi was still for a while before asking with feigned indifference, "How would losing two souls...affect someone?"

"That depends on which two souls are missing. Shennong Terrace said that of the two souls Gu Mang had lost, the first had to do with memory, and the second was related to mind. Which is to say, he runs into issues in those two areas, but the absence doesn't significantly affect anything else."

Mo Xi lowered his lashes. "I see..." he murmured.

"Yes. Because he lost a soul related to the mind, in the beginning, he had entirely lost the power of speech. Wangshu-jun sent him to Luomei Pavilion, where the overseer trained him for a full two years before he could understand what people were saying or speak enough to get by—if barely." As Li Wei spoke, he let out a heartfelt sigh. "Ah, they used to call him 'Beast of the Altar,' and now he really isn't much different from a wild beast."

This was why everyone had been astonished when Gu Mang was sent back two years ago.

When the city gates had opened and the prison wagon bearing the traitor Gu Mang slowly entered Chonghua, civilians on both sides of the road had seen that General Gu was locked up alongside some wolves. Within the prison wagon with them was a buck, which the wolves proceeded to tear apart, spraying blood everywhere. Gu Mang didn't bother to dodge the spray, instead crouching placidly amid the pack. The wild wolves seemed to treat him like one of their own—a female wolf even dragged one of the buck's legs over to Gu Mang to court his favor.

Gu Mang had reached out and dipped his hand in a little blood. He'd licked at it indifferently but hadn't cared for the taste, and so had lowered his hand again...

Mo Xi listened in silence.

At this point, Li Wei scratched his head. "But, my lord, there's something I don't understand."

Mo Xi's dark brown eyes turned to look at him, impassive. "Hm?"

"Why would the Liao Kingdom go to the effort of destroying two of his souls if they were already going to send him back?"

"Perhaps he knew too much," Mo Xi said. "By extracting those two souls, they could tie up that loose end once and for all."

Li Wei was speechless. "Goodness, how cruel. Can he ever recover?"

Mo Xi shook his head as if many things were weighing on his mind and didn't respond.

Two of Gu Mang's souls had been removed. The only cure was to find and return them to the body. But in all the vast Nine Provinces, who could say where Gu Mang's two souls had gone, or if they still existed?

"I heard Wangshu-jun kept him alive so he could experience suffering worse than death," Li Wei said. "But I also heard he's awfully calm now, and not very interesting. Wangshu-jun seems to have made a miscalculation—oh, right." Li Wei remembered something and turned to Mo Xi. "My lord, have you seen Wangshu-jun since your return?"

Mo Xi shook his head. "No."

Although Wangshu-jun held an important position in the Bureau of Military Affairs, his role was in fact altogether idle and had no attendant obligations. He was highborn and arrogant due to his status; of the three hundred sixty-five days in a year, it was considered quite impressive if he showed up for fifteen.

Mo Xi looked up. "Why are you asking about him all of a sudden?"

"Honestly, these past few years, he's gotten worse and worse," Li Wei said. "If my lord should run into him, don't bother stooping to his level. You know all too well that he's always looking for ways to make trouble for you."

Mo Xi didn't find this the least bit surprising.

In Chonghua there lived three notable gentlemen[10] whose characters exemplified the Buddhist values of virtue, mind, and wisdom. Jiang Yexue's serenity and indifference to public favor had earned him the title of Mind, while Princess Mengze's benevolence and integrity had earned her the title of Virtue.

Conversely, there were three infamous villains who perfectly exemplified the Buddhist poisons of greed, wrath, and ignorance. The one Mo Xi had to deal with most often was Greed. "Greed," of course, referred to one with an avarice for all that pleased, as well as a deep dissatisfaction when that hunger wasn't sated: this was the Wangshu-jun that Li Wei had mentioned.

Wangshu-jun's name was Murong Lian, and he was Gu Mang's former master. In the beginning, it was he who had chosen Gu Mang as one of the study attendants to accompany and look after their young master's needs at the cultivation academy.

Wangshu-jun never could have imagined that this little slave possessed such unbelievable natural talent. Within a few years, Gu Mang's cultivation level had greatly surpassed his master's. Jealousy made Murong Lian hateful, and he constantly picked on Gu Mang,

---

10 君子, *junzi, a term for a person of noble character. In historical settings, it is typically reserved for men.*

beating him, cursing him, and punishing him whenever he experienced the slightest displeasure. Everyone knew he had a cruel temperament, and that his character was incredibly ill-suited to the "mercy" of his given name, Lian.

Let us recall the simplest example:

Once, when Gu Mang was exorcising demons, he came upon a small village. The villagers were plagued by sickness, and out of compassion, Gu Mang used Murong Lian's name to compel the imperial healers to prescribe them medicines. Although this was against the rules, it was an act entirely motivated by kindness. Any other master would only have scolded Gu Mang a bit.

Murong Lian was different. After he learned that Gu Mang had dared use his name to buy imperial medicines, he had launched into a furious flurry of curses. First, he'd given Gu Mang almost eighty hard lashes, then made Gu Mang kneel by the academy walkway for twenty days straight.

At the time, Mo Xi hadn't known Gu Mang very well. They hadn't interacted much, and he normally didn't use that walkway, so he'd known little about it.

That is, until one rainy day when Mo Xi happened to pass by and saw a silhouette. When he walked over to take a look, as it turned out, the person he had noticed was Gu Mang.

Gu Mang was completely soaked, black hair sticking to his freezing cheeks and raindrops streaming down his jaw. He knelt obediently amid the flow of the crowd with his hands around a wooden signboard with six words emblazoned on it in cinnabar: *Slave Impersonates Master, Shameless Beyond Description.*

Mo Xi stopped before him. Crystalline raindrops splashed off his umbrella's paper surface and gathered to flow off the ribs.

Those nearby cast curious glances their way, but when they caught sight of the soaring snake insignia on the young noble's robes, they lowered their heads and kept walking, afraid to look again.

"You..."

It seemed that Gu Mang had become dazed from sitting in the rain. He didn't even realize when an umbrella appeared over his head, nor did he notice that someone had stopped in front of him. When he suddenly heard someone speak from so close, he started, his eyes flicking upward as he woke from his daze.

A confused, soaked face came into Mo Xi's view. There were bloodstains at the corner of the kneeling youth's mouth and whip marks on his cheek. He was chilled to the point of shivering, like a dog that had been thrown out into the mud. Only those black eyes still shone, clear and unclouded.

That pathetic sight, paired with the wooden signboard, was as ridiculous as it was pitiful.

Mo Xi and Gu Mang might not have been close, but Mo Xi knew Gu Mang had requisitioned medicine with a fake identity because he couldn't bear to let a whole village suffer through illness. Thus Mo Xi went to Murong Lian's quarters at the academy and asked him for leniency.

Not only did Murong Lian refuse, he descended into a heated argument with Mo Xi. Finally, he sent for Gu Mang to come before him. In front of Mo Xi, he asked, "Gu Mang, do you know why the insufferably arrogant Mo-gongzi came to me today?"

Water was still streaming down Gu Mang's face. He numbly shook his head.

Murong Lian crooked a finger at Gu Mang, compelling him forward. He caressed Gu Mang's soaking cheek with hands that were terrifyingly pale. Smiling insincerely, he raised his sultry peach blossom eyes, their whites showing below the irises. "He came here for you."

For a moment, Gu Mang was visibly stunned. He turned to glance at the dark-faced Mo Xi, then looked back at Murong Lian. In the end, he carelessly wiped the rainwater on his face and grinned. "Gongzi, are you joking?"

Murong Lian was still smiling. "What do you think?"

No one spoke.

"Your skills grow by the day. If Mo-gongzi hadn't come in the rain solely to ask for mercy on your behalf, I wouldn't even know you had started fooling around with a young master from another family."

"Murong Lian," Mo Xi bit out. "I'm only speaking up for him in the name of justice. Keep those filthy insinuations out of your mouth."

Gu Mang blankly turned to look at Mo Xi. There seemed to be a hint of gratitude in those sea-bright eyes, but while Murong Lian's attention was elsewhere, Gu Mang shook his head slightly at Mo Xi.

Murong Lian shot Mo Xi a glance and snorted as if in threat. Then he turned around and sweetly said to Gu Mang, "Kneel."

Gu Mang did as told, gradually lowering himself all the way down and dipping his head before Murong Lian.

"Take off your upper robe."

"Murong Lian!"

"These are my quarters. Mo-gongzi, no matter how high your rank, you shouldn't be trying to scold me in my own rooms, no?" Murong Lian glanced at Gu Mang once more. "Take it off."

Gu Mang did as he was told. He took off his outer robe, exposing his strong and toned physique, lowering his lashes and saying nothing. Murong Lian slowly looked him over, from the lines of taut muscles to skin that glowed like honey under the lamplight. Murong Lian was very slender, and his eyes raked across Gu Mang's body the same way a perpetually freezing young scion would look over a fine fur pelt—as if he wished for nothing more than to tear off all of Gu Mang's skin and wrap it around himself, to make himself stronger.

Attendants hurried in and brought Murong Lian hot ginger tea. He took a sip and sighed. "Gu Mang, isn't it nice to have a spiritual core? Doesn't it feel good to have so much influence at the cultivation academy? Aren't you so happy you were able to befriend a dignitary like Mo-gongzi?

"I can't imagine who gave you the courage to lie about being Murong-gongzi for the sake of a prescription—and all to save a handful of lowborn villagers." Murong Lian snickered. He set down the teacup with fine-boned hands and suddenly looked up. "Have you forgotten your station from birth?!"

Gu Mang lowered his head even further. "I would not dare."

"Your holy weapon, your clothes, your spiritual core—everything you have today was bestowed upon you by the Murong Clan. You are nothing without Wangshu Manor!"

"Shaozhu[11] is right to reprimand me."

After a long interval, Murong Lian burst out laughing. "But since you're so strong, I obviously can't mistreat you, lest you grow independent and end up serving someone else." He barked out an order to his attendants. "Go get the *young master—*" He drew out each syllable in a tone of extreme ridicule, mocking Gu Mang's presumption in daring to pretend to be the son of the Murong Clan, "—that present I prepared for him so long ago."

The other study attendants of the Murong Clan were also present. One of them, Lu Zhanxing, was Gu Mang's best friend. When he heard that Murong Lian wanted to give Gu Mang this particular

---

11 *The title of the young master and direct heir of a household.*

"present," his expression grew unsightly. He fixed Murong Lian with a gaze that could almost have been described as a glare.

Murong Lian lifted a hand, commanding the attendants to open the box in front of everyone's eyes.

Every attendant paled, and one of them couldn't hold back from crying out:

"It's a slave collar!"

Gu Mang's head snapped up at these words, eyes wide. He stared at the sandalwood tray above his head, seeming numb.

The color had also drained from Mo Xi's face. Only the most disobedient, disagreeable slaves were fitted with a slave collar, which was intended for confinement and punishment. It could never be removed without the leave of the slave's master—much like a dog collar. Though being a slave was the greatest humiliation, being bound with a slave collar was yet another level of disgrace, lowering a man to the point where even other slaves would look down on him.

"Why don't you put it on yourself?" Murong Lian waved a hand. "Do you need me to say please, *Young Master Murong*?"

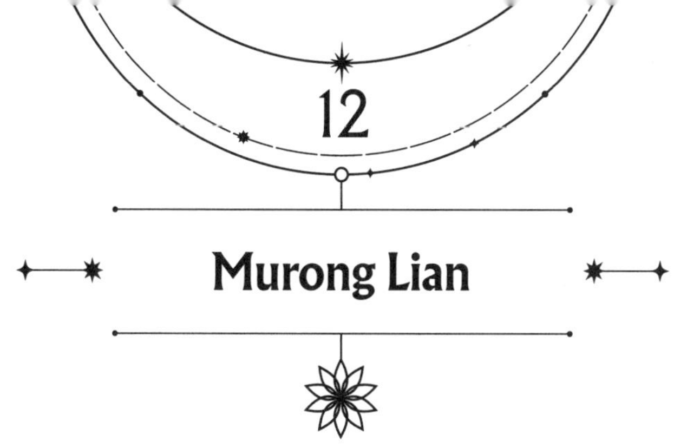

12 Murong Lian

Mo Xi, standing to the side, was furious. "Murong Lian, watch yourself. Without the emperor's permission, a slave collar cannot—"

Halfway through his sentence, Gu Mang cut him off.

"Such a precious gift," Gu Mang said loudly, talking over Mo Xi in a tone that brooked no argument. He reached up and accepted the tray. "Thank you, Shaozhu!"

Amid everyone else's dismay, Gu Mang calmly unfastened the pitch-black collar and looked up, bright-eyed, to where Murong Lian sat on the dais. Those pretty eyes displayed no resentment; rather, they seemed perfectly peaceful.

"Go on," Murong Lian said icily.

Holding his gaze, Gu Mang brought his hands to his neck. Unblinking, he fastened the slave collar around it with a *click*.

"Hey." Gu Mang touched his neck with interest, as if he had discovered a new source of amusement. "It's not too big or too small. It fits just right."

Mo Xi looked at him in disbelief, while among the nearby study attendants, those who were close with Gu Mang were on the verge of tears.

This was Gu Mang's way. Staggering turns of fortune seemed like nothing to him. If the sky fell, he'd probably grin and pull it up to use as a blanket—

"How does it look?"

Lu Zhanxing stared at him.

Murong Lian caressed the corners of his own mouth with pale and slender fingertips. "Wonderful," he said mockingly.

"This one thanks Shaozhu for the gift," Gu Mang earnestly replied.

"It's nothing." Murong Lian's expression was cool and detached. After a moment, he waved a hand. A ball of blue light leapt from his palm, and Gu Mang crumpled to the floor.

Lu Zhanxing couldn't stop himself from crying out, "Gu Mang!"

Several pitch-black cords laced with lightning shot out of the slave collar to tightly bind Gu Mang's arms and torso. The lightning sent him into convulsions; he spasmed on the ground, shaking uncontrollably.

Murong Lian seemed to think this insufficient. He tried a different spell, and the light in his palm turned red. Brambles erupted from the collar, winding around Gu Mang's tanned body. As thorns stabbed into him, blood streamed out...

"Enough!" Mo Xi couldn't stand it anymore, and he gritted his teeth. "Murong Lian, how is this reasonable?!"

"What does the discipline of my own household slave have to do with Mo-gongzi?" Murong Lian said indolently. "He's just a lowly slave. It would be of no consequence even if I beat him to death. Why is Mo-gongzi so concerned?"

"We are in the cultivation academy. By privately collaring an academy disciple with a slave collar, you are plainly holding the academy's rules in contempt. Cease this at once!"

Murong Lian turned to smile at Mo Xi. "Wouldn't it be awfully embarrassing for me to stop because you told me to? Mo-gongzi, you're as arrogant as ever, but if you're asking me for something, I can't be callous." He paused. "However, shouldn't you at least give me some incentive?"

As Murong Lian spoke, he cycled through a few different punishments, grinning all the while. By this point, the slave collar's torments had left Gu Mang in a pool of blood.

Mo Xi grabbed the hand Murong Lian was using to form the sigils and fixed his dark eyes on him. "What do you want?"

"Nothing too important." Murong Lian looked at the hand clamped around his wrist and sneered. "It's only that Mother always complains that I've been lazy in my cultivation studies, that I'm no match for others."

Those sultry peach blossom eyes narrowed. Murong Lian gazed at Mo Xi, expression inscrutable. "I'll do you this favor, so long as you lose to me at the academy's cultivation tournament on New Year's Eve."

Mo Xi turned to look at Gu Mang, only to find him looking back. Gu Mang shook his head slightly, biting his lip.

"I heard that this slave of mine has been quite the help to you on exorcism missions."

Neither of them replied.

"So? Are you willing?"

"Yes," Mo Xi said after a pause. "I give you my word."

Murong Lian laughed as he waved a hand, lifting the punishment spell on the slave collar. Gu Mang collapsed into the puddle of crimson on the floor. Those ever-smiling lips could no longer shape words.

At this, Murong Lian expressed an appropriate amount of satisfaction: "That'll do."

The light of the slave collar went out.

"Just stay there until you stop bleeding," Murong Lian jeered at Gu Mang. "It'll save you from having to do extra laundry. I hope this gift is sufficient to remind you at every moment who you really are." His gaze was like wasp venom. "Remember the filth that is your blood. Remember to whom you belong, to whom you owe your loyalty."

Murong Lian was beyond despicable and beyond insane. Mo Xi had been abjectly disgusted with him for ages now.

What Mo Xi could never understand was why Gu Mang had been so hell-bent on staying at Murong Lian's side despite the cruelty. More than twenty years had passed without the slightest hint of rebellion from him.

Gu Mang was no masochist. He was exceptionally intelligent, fearless, and assertive, which was why Mo Xi found this foolish loyalty absurd. He couldn't even begin to guess what Gu Mang had been thinking, nor did he know what exactly had transpired between Murong Lian and Gu Mang. It was a mystery even to this day.

And now, as Li Wei brought up their old quarrels again, Mo Xi couldn't help but think that his reminder was rather unnecessary. Wangshu-jun had always been wholly vile. How much worse could he get?

He certainly didn't expect that when he finally saw Murong Lian again in person, he would be unpleasantly surprised.

One day, once court matters had concluded, a few young masters suggested going to relax at the new pitch-pot[12] tavern in the eastern part of the city. A new female cultivator was joining in on the fun.

"Xihe-jun, why don't we go together?" she asked.

Mo Xi said, "My apologies."

---

12 *A game involving tossing arrows or sticks into a wine-pot.*

"Another rejection?" The cultivator pursed her lips and mumbled, "I know you have Princess Mengze, but are you so dead set on her that you won't give anyone else a chance?"

Before Mo Xi could reply, Yue Chenqing popped up from behind her. "Heyyyy, Xihe-jun, what do you mean by that?" He patted the cultivator's shoulder. "Let's have some fun together," he said helpfully. "Drink some tea, play a game of pitch-pot. What's wrong with that?"

The others started trying to persuade him as well, smiling.

"Exactly, come with us."

"Pitch-pot is loads of fun."

At that moment, a man's voice came from outside. It sounded like a ghost's, hoarse and wavering, without the slightest trace of warmth. The only emotion it held was scorn. "Idiots pitching at pots. The pastime of imbeciles."

Along with these words came the rustling of footsteps from the darkening hall doors.

Mo Xi turned to see a man holding a gauze umbrella slowly ascend the steps. His was a chilly and aloof silhouette, like a lonely wraith wandering in the evening snow. The man retracted the umbrella to his side, shaking off the snow that had amassed on its surface. He lifted his gaze to sweep it across the people in the hall, then smeared an insincere and mocking smile over his face. "Everyone's here?"

All the juniors of the Bureau of Military Affairs started, each of them performing obeisance. "Wangshu-jun."

"This junior greets Wangshu-shenjun."

It was Murong Lian.

The consummate slacker had finally shown up.

Many years had passed, but when Gu Mang's old master stood before Mo Xi once more, he looked as soft and dainty as ever. Those sultry eyes were long and narrow, curving at the ends like willow shoots. There was cruelty in his charm and coldness in his fragility, and his cheeks were even sharper and more sunken than Mo Xi remembered. His arrogant manner and spiteful haughtiness had also become more pronounced.

Murong Lian's gaze slithered across Mo Xi's face, as if he'd only just noticed him in the crowd. Licking his lips, he smiled. "Oh, Xihe-jun's here too? How uncivilized of me—long time no see."

Yue Chenqing was a brainless loudmouth who could get along with anyone, so he waved at Murong Lian with a grin. "Murong-dage, I haven't seen you in a long time either."

Yue Chenqing may as well have not existed; Murong Lian spared not a glance in his direction.

Yue Chenqing shut his mouth.

After waiting several moments with no response from Mo Xi, Murong Lian flashed another chilling smile. "Xihe-jun, you and I have been apart for a long time. Why don't you seem the least bit happy to see me? That proud and distant character of yours hasn't changed in the slightest."

Mo Xi glanced at him indifferently. "Yet Wangshu-jun has changed a great deal. I presume the affairs of the capital have been a terrible strain; they've caused Wangshu-jun to lose so much weight."

Murong Lian smiled. "Yes. Unlike you, I'm part of His Imperial Majesty's inner circle, and thus must help him shoulder his burdens."

"How moving," Mo Xi said icily.

Xihe-jun versus Wangshu-jun was like thunder against lightning or stone against blade, filling the atmosphere with tension.

Out of all the people in that hall, only the good-natured blockhead Yue Chenqing was willing to speak. He looked at both sides and persevered. "Wangshu-jun, it's so late. What made you decide to take a stroll around the palace?"

"I was just passing by." Murong Lian finally acknowledged him after a beat. "It happens that I am free, and I wanted to invite everyone to come to a gathering at Wangshu Manor..." As he finished, he turned his gaze, bringing with it a slight chill. "...to drink, and so on."

No one dared to dismiss any of Murong Lian's suggestions, least of all the many people in the crowd who wanted to curry favor with him.

"So that's how it is!" they quickly said.

"Obviously it would be impolite to refuse an invitation from Wangshu-jun."

Murong Lian shot a glance at Mo Xi's face. "Xihe-jun, are you coming?"

Mo Xi looked over at Yue Chenqing. Since Yue Chenqing was still young and easily influenced, he thought it would be best for him to keep his distance from Murong Lian.

"Yue Chenqing and I are busy," he said. "We won't be attending tonight."

"Wah, no way! It's so late—how can we be busy?!" Yue Chenqing's eyes flew open. "As if I'd want to discuss military matters with you! I want to go drink at Wangshu Manor..." He ducked behind Murong Lian, looking as if he'd rather be beaten to death than read another imperial military memorial.

Since Yue Chenqing had openly demonstrated where he stood, Mo Xi couldn't force him. All he could do was furrow his brow slightly.

Murong Lian turned, arms behind his back, and gazed at the snow fluttering down outside the hall doors. "On that note, Xihe-jun," he said, "you haven't seen Gu Mang in a long time, have you?"

Mo Xi said nothing.

"I know you hate him. Back when Gu Mang defected, you kept trying to protect him, claiming he would never betray Chonghua." Murong Lian suddenly smiled again. "Later on, when you met him face-to-face in battle and attempted to obtain confirmation from his own mouth, he *wounded* you—and you nearly died."

"Why bother bringing up the past?" Mo Xi asked frostily.

A snicker. "As if you wouldn't remember it so long as I didn't mention it. Xihe-jun, we may not be friends, but it just so happens that Gu Mang deceived, disappointed, and betrayed us both," Murong Lian drawled. "So, even though you're unwilling to admit it, I'm afraid that the one man in the whole world who can understand my hatred and despondency is you and no other."

After this, Murong Lian turned his sickly pale face to the side, his eyes flashing with unreadable light.

"He was my slave all those years ago, and now he's in Luomei Pavilion, under my control." He tilted his head, looking bored. "What about it? Why don't we go take a look?"

Yue Chenqing naively poked his head out from the side. "Hey, Luomei Pavilion? Wangshu-jun, you'd better be joking. We've got maidens in the Bureau of Military Affairs. It wouldn't be appropriate for them to go play at Luomei Pavilion."

The few women cultivators who heard this waved their hands hastily. "We won't be attending—we hope Wangshu-jun has a good time."

Yue Chenqing scratched his head. "Well, even if the girls don't go, Xihe-jun hates brothels more than anything. Why would he go somewhere like that?"

"Oh. That's true." Murong Lian curled his lip. "General Mo is the finest commander of Chonghua, ever pristine and honorable, proper and unwavering. There's no way he could possibly deign to enter an unspeakable house of pleasure. How *filthy*."

Mo Xi made no reply.

"Then what about this?" Murong Lian tilted his neck and stretched tight muscles before continuing. "Luomei Pavilion isn't far from my manor. I'll have Gu Mang brought there straightaway, and we'll let him liven things up for us tonight. General Mo, it'll be my way of giving you..." His lips were wet, his words sinister. "A *warm* welcome home."

13

An Invitation from Murong Lian

"Ah? Only Gu Mang? Wangshu-jun, you should probably get a few more of them," one young master piped up.

The two great noble lords, Xihe and Wangshu, both had reason to hate Gu Mang. Thus the young man didn't hesitate to scoff, "Given Gu Mang's current condition, it'd be impressive if he didn't ruin the mood."

Murong Lian had ignored him at first, his eyes locked on Mo Xi. But when he heard this last, the corners of his lips curved up in a smile. As soon they saw this sign, the juniors striving to ingratiate themselves with him all laughed as well.

"Ha ha, you're right. It's true that Gu Mang wouldn't be enough on his own. Him, attentive? Infuriating's more like it."

"You've given him your patronage before?"

"Everything else aside, he was an infamous manwhore. I was curious and wanted to have some fun, and you know, he—"

Before this young master could finish, he felt a sudden piercing chill at the back of his neck. When he looked around, he found that Mo Xi was staring at him, eyes like frost. That gaze was like a blade in the freezing night, so terrifying that the young master forgot what he had been about to say. He swallowed, breaking out in a cold sweat.

He shivered—what had he said wrong? But before he could think more on it, Mo Xi turned away. That sharp profile had sunk back into cool indifference, without the slightest ripple of disturbance.

It was as if the antipathy in his gaze a moment ago had been no more than the young master's hallucination.

"How funny you are," Murong Lian cut in, the picture of imperious laziness. "Who do you think Gu Mang is? He was once the highest-ranked general of Chonghua, my former slave, and General Mo's shixiong."

Mo Xi didn't respond.

"Even if he doesn't know how to serve anyone attentively, how could we bear to miss his presence at the banquet tonight?" As Murong Lian spoke, his venomous gaze landed on Mo Xi. "Now that General Mo is returned and coming to this little gathering at my manor, how could I be remiss in my duty as the host...to share?"

Mo Xi's eyes darkened with each word Murong Lian spoke. By this point, they resembled black clouds pressing in on city walls[13]—the flames of wrath became an army thousands strong, lying dormant but murderous behind the veil of his lashes.

He did not want to see Gu Mang looking so wretched in front of these people.

But Murong Lian insisted on aiming for Mo Xi's fatal weakness, stabbing each word into his heart.

After this flurry of speech, Murong Lian drew back the corners of his mouth into a chilling smile. "General Mo, your great nemesis—your Gu-shixiong—aren't you curious as to how I've mastered him? Don't you want to see for yourself?"

In the end, the group went.

---

13 *From "Song of the Yanmen Governor," a poem by Li He. The imagery evoked is that of black clouds stirred up by war to overwhelm the skies.*

Wangshu Manor was a magnificent compound situated on the east side of Chonghua. The insignia of the Wangshu bloodline was a bat, and sigils in its likeness glowed year-round above the residence. Within the manor, the staff largely wore deep blue robes with gold trim.

As was custom in Chonghua, pure-blooded nobles wore clothing trimmed in gold, but the underlying base colors were assigned by imperial decree. For example, Xihe Manor's robes were black with gold trim while Yue Manor's were white with gold trim.

At this moment, eight thousand exquisite holy lamps illuminated the sky, exuding an aura of extravagant hedonism. Halfway through the feast, everyone had relaxed; the juniors who had earlier been tense and restrained had grown lively and were milling about, drinking and playing finger-guessing games.

Murong Lian lay in repose on his daybed of xiangfei bamboo, his slender, icy-pale hand wrapped around a slim, silver drinking token as he poked idly at the aromatics in the incense burner.

Within was a type of narcotic fragrance from the Liao Kingdom. It was harmless if smelled from afar, but it filled those nearby with a surge of unbelievable ecstasy. However, the ensuing depression was thrice as strong as that joy. To keep experiencing the ecstasy, the incense had to be inhaled repeatedly and often, which made it an addiction difficult to quit. The late emperor had banned the stuff during his reign.

The sight of Murong Lian's rapturous expression, so hazy amid the smoke that he seemed like an illusion, filled Mo Xi with irritation.

Yue Chenqing was sitting next to him. As he peered at the smoke Murong Lian was inhaling, he found himself curious. He wanted to take a closer look, but Mo Xi stopped him.

"Sit down."

"What *is* that?"

"Ephemera," Mo Xi replied flatly.

Yue Chenqing was shocked. "Ah! As in the Liao Kingdom's ephemera?" He looked over anxiously. "Looks like Wangshu-jun's addiction is serious. No wonder he's so tired today."

"If you so much as think about touching that smoke, your dad will lock you away for years."

"My dad?" Yu Chenqing said. "My dad's not that harsh. At most he'd threaten to string me up and beat me. This stuff about locking someone away is obviously your idea, not his, General Mo."

Before Mo Xi could get angry, Yue Chenqing grinned. "But you don't need to worry. I'm not the least bit interested in that kind of illusory pleasure. I'm so likable, I don't need that ephemera stuff to be happy. There's nothing I can't bounce back from."

Unexpectedly, these last few words fell with perfect accuracy into Murong Lian's ears.

Murong Lian played with the ashes in the golden, beast-shaped censer. The suggestion of a faint, icy sneer slipped through his features. His voice was as indolent as the smoke as he said, "Bounce back? Pfft. Ephemera is worth its weight in gold. With only the Yue Clan's wealth at your disposal, you couldn't smoke it even if you wanted to."

Yue Chenqing didn't want to argue with him. "Yes, Wangshu-jun's bloodline is high and noble," he said nonchalantly. "Your wealth rivals that of the very nation. How could I compare to you?"

Satisfied, Murong Lian turned to Mo Xi. "Xihe-jun, you're sure you won't partake?"

Mo Xi's expression was frigid, which made Murong Lian lean back and laugh. "I nearly forgot. General Mo is in the habit of austerity. He's never cared for extravagance and waste. Ah, looks like this lord is the only individual in Chonghua who can afford to enjoy this Liao Kingdom treasure."

Mo Xi absolutely didn't want to talk to this man any more than necessary. The Murong Lian he remembered had already been the epitome of scum. Who could have imagined that after all these years, he could get even worse?

Murong Lian was proud of his rank as a pure-blooded noble, but he refused to work hard, instead sinking deeper and deeper into the muck. Now he could be described as a mindless wastrel, drowning in drunken dreams.

Li Wei was right: Murong Lian had indeed rotted down to the bone.

"My lord." Just then, the housekeeper of Wangshu Manor stepped in to report to Murong Lian. "The individuals from Luomei Pavilion have been brought as you ordered."

"Oh, excellent. Send them in."

The feast was getting rowdy, and the guests were all a little intoxicated. After the housekeeper received his instructions, he of course complied, clapping for the servants to bring in the best women and men of Luomei Pavilion to liven things up. Mo Xi turned, his pitch-black eyes staring falcon-like toward the door.

The beaded veil tinkled, and several rows of men and women were ushered in by the housekeeper. Each of them had their own charm—some were gaily pretty, some were innocently pure; humble or prideful, reluctant or willing.

Only Gu Mang wasn't there.

"These are the prostitutes sent from Luomei Pavilion. If you gentlemen take a fancy to any of them, feel free to take them out to play," Murong Lian waved a lazy hand. "They're no more than bastards, and it's on me if they die—this lord is treating you tonight.

Now shouldn't you all be singing my praises and tearfully thanking me?"

The crowd jumped to flatter him.

"Wangshu-jun is such a breath of fresh air!"

"He's the emperor's cousin, after all. Anything he wants is only a word away. How enviable!"

The crowd licked Murong Lian's boots and began to noisily drag away the pitiful victims to accompany them in wine and amusement. All at once, the scene of the banquet blurred into debauched chaos.

"Pretty lady, what's your name?"

"C'mere, top up Gege's cup."

Mo Xi's expression grew darker and darker. Though he suffered it for a long while, he finally reached his limit and could listen no longer. But as he made to get up and leave, he heard Murong Lian speak, mirth in his voice: "Xihe-jun, is there no one here who pleases you?"

"You've had too much wine."

"I have not," Murong Lian scoffed. "And Xihe-jun shouldn't be in such a rush to depart. That person you want to see is here—it's just that his temperament is quite strange these days. He gets anxious when he's away from Luomei Pavilion, so he's been standing outside this whole time, refusing to come in." As he spoke, he filled his own cup, downing it in one draught. "If you don't believe me, take a look for yourself."

Mo Xi turned toward the doorway. Just as Murong Lian had claimed, the disjointed swaying of the bead veil revealed a silhouette in the shadows beyond, as if a wary beast were hiding in their depths, looking cautiously outward.

"Do you see?" Murong Lian said. "Why don't we bring him in to have some fun with you?"

When Mo Xi didn't answer, Murong Lian smiled. He stretched, his cheeks flushed red from drink, and shouted, "Hey, everyone, wait a moment!"

"What is it, Wangshu-jun?"

Murong Lian narrowed his eyes, the scorn and malice on his face instantly intensifying. "You're all so poorly behaved," Murong Lian said. "You rushed to take these beauties into your arms, but didn't any of you notice our noble Xihe-jun's lap is still empty?"

Mo Xi was rendered speechless.

Under normal circumstances, no one would dare make such jokes about him. But these young masters were mostly wastrels. A minor wound would make them refuse to step onto the battlefield, and a major injury would make them refuse to leave their sickbed. Few of them had ever worked directly with Mo Xi. Furthermore, they were drunk, so they spoke without a shred of propriety.

"Xihe-jun, the capital isn't like the army," one of them slurred with a grin. "B-beauties are everywhere, and those belonging to Wangshu-jun are the best of the b-best. Why would you d-decline his offer?"

"Even though he's in his most vigorous years, Xihe-jun's always busy with military matters. You ought to relax from time to time."

"Right? General Mo's been to countless battlefields but he's never entered a single veiled bed-canopy. Life is bitter and short, so you should enjoy the present," another snickered.

Yue Chenqing was still relatively sober. When he saw Mo Xi's expression, a sense of dread rose within him. "Come on now," he hurried to cut in. "Why don't you guys shut up already?!"

Mo Xi glanced at him. Against all odds, this kid was the one taking things seriously.

But the next thing he heard out of Yue Chenqing's mouth was:

"If you keep running your mouths like this, when General Mo explodes and starts killing people, I'll be the first to flee!"

Mo Xi glowered wordlessly.

Everyone stared at each other in their addled, half-drunken states, wearing stupid grins.

In this torturous silence, Murong Lian looked sidelong out of his peach blossom eyes, his glance intoxicated yet icy-sharp. "Xihe-jun, even with all these peerless beauties before you, you want neither the women nor the men. Ah, I think—" He smiled maliciously. "The one you yearn for...is actually your enemy, isn't it?"

So saying, he shouted toward the doorway, "Come! Bring the traitor commander Gu Mang for our General Mo!"

14

Xihe-jun the Liar

THE HOUSEKEEPER escorted Gu Mang forward. The iron chain around his neck clanked with each barefoot step he took out of the shadows.

Gu Mang had seemed exceptionally calm the last time they met, as if he didn't feel the slightest unease within his own territory. But now, even though Gu Mang's face was impassive, his muscles were tense, and the keen gaze hidden behind those long lashes was full of wariness as it swept across each face in the crowd.

By chance, those eyes met Mo Xi's. Something shifted in Mo Xi's heart.

He knew his current circumstances were incredibly delicate. If Gu Mang happened to mention their previous meeting at Luomei Pavilion, though Mo Xi wouldn't face any dire consequences, nothing good could come of it.

But although he knew better, some hidden place in his heart secretly howled, hoping Gu Mang would react to him differently than he did to the others, if only by the tiniest bit.

Too bad—Gu Mang disappointed him again.

Gu Mang had no interest in Mo Xi whatsoever; he doubtless saw him as simply another one of his strange clients. His gaze didn't linger on Mo Xi's face for even an instant—he glanced at him swiftly and directly, then carelessly looked away.

Mo Xi stared stormily into his exquisite jade cup on the table and began to fiddle with it, eyes downcast.

"Oh, the illustrious former Beast of the Altar," Murong Lian said with an insincere smile. "Why so anxious, Gu Mang? You've served my family ever since you were young—you're merely visiting an old haunt. What's there to be afraid of? Come." He waved Gu Mang over. "Come here."

Gu Mang slowly stepped forward, eyes falling upon the incense burner in front of Murong Lian. He sneezed, seemingly irritated by the ephemera fumes coming from the censer, and quickly turned to bolt.

Murong Lian hadn't expected him to act out. Once he came to his senses, he shouted sternly, "Grab him!"

Gu Mang's spiritual core had been destroyed, but his martial strength was still formidable. His legs whirled, violently striking a few people nearby. Then, with a push of his hand off the floor, he leapt up like a panther, dodging the servants trying to grab him and landing steadily on the ground.

His movements were as smooth as flowing water; even without the aid of magic, they were breathtakingly powerful.

Gu Mang sent his opponents flying with a kick. Glancing backward, he scratched his cheek, then turned to keep running.

"Well, a starving camel is still larger than a horse. Likewise, the ruined General Gu is still stronger than *these* sorts..." As Murong Lian spoke, he shot a glance at Mo Xi. "Don't you agree, Xihe-jun?"

Mo Xi's arms were crossed as he leaned against the edge of his chair and ignored Murong Lian. Instead, he watched Gu Mang dodging and ducking in the hall. Gu Mang's martial foundation was absurdly good; it took the slaves of Wangshu Manor a great deal of effort to subdue him. By the end, they were all covered in sweat, their noses bruised and faces swollen.

"My lord, we've bound him."

"Look at all of you, panting like oxen. If I didn't know any better, I'd think you were the ones whose spiritual cores had been broken, not him. Idiots!"

The servants hung their heads, swallowing anxiously.

Fortunately, Murong Lian didn't continue to berate them. Instead, he swept his sleeves and said impatiently, "Bring him back."

Gu Mang was once more led to the center of the hall. Because he still refused to obey, they were compelled to bind him tightly with spells as they escorted him to the front of the dais.

"Kneel!"

Gu Mang didn't want to kneel, so someone in the group brutally kicked the back of his knees, and he crumpled to the ground.

His face, neck, abdomen, and knees were tightly bound with black immortal-binding ropes. His expression was confused yet furious, and his originally baggy robes were now gaping open, exposing a broad swath of his pale chest.

Murong Lian stepped down from the bamboo daybed, holding the silver spoon he used to poke the fragrant ash. Bending down, he stared fixedly at Gu Mang. "All of Chonghua falls under the dominion of the Murong name... General, where will you run? Where *can* you run?"

With that, he slapped Gu Mang across the face.

The sound of the strike echoed crisply. Murong Lian hadn't held back in the least, and five marks immediately flushed across Gu Mang's cheek.

His head was smacked to the side. Gu Mang didn't make a sound—but Mo Xi's lashes fluttered slightly.

"I've spent two years teaching you the rules, but you still haven't learned." Murong Lian stood up straight, taking a sniff of the remaining fragrance on the spoon. Then he abruptly turned to look at Mo Xi.

"Ah, Xihe-jun, I heard you handled your army well. When you first took over the Wangba Army that Gu Mang left behind, there were quite a few old soldiers who wanted to rebel, but they were swayed by the oath you swore in front of the troops. Seeing as you're such an expert, why don't you instruct the Wangba Army's former general for me as well? Let him learn obedience too."

Murong Lian waved a hand as he spoke, gesturing for the servants to drag Gu Mang in front of Mo Xi. "Speaking of, he once stabbed General Mo in the chest. An apology...must be offered to General Mo, sooner or later. Now you're the executioner, and he's on your chopping block," Murong Lian said unhurriedly. "You can choose to torture him however you like. Go ahead."

Gu Mang didn't know many complex words. *Executioner, chopping block*—he didn't understand them. But to him, the word *torture* sounded like a stick to a dog terrified of further beatings. He shuddered, eyes widening. From where he lay on the ground, his field of view was limited; he couldn't see Mo Xi standing at an angle behind him. When the two servants at Gu Mang's side moved him, he strove to turn around, but the immortal-binding ropes tightened around his head. The iron chains gagging his mouth were about to dig into his flesh, forcing the breath out of him.

For a moment, all eyes in the room were on Mo Xi and Gu Mang.

Yue Chenqing covered his eyes with his hands and peeked out from behind his fingers. "General Mo, despite the hatred and resentment you share, you *can't* kill him in front of me. I'm just a kid."

Mo Xi said nothing. Slowly, he bent down on one knee, his elbow resting on his kneecap. With his other black-gloved hand, he took hold of Gu Mang's jaw and tilted his face upward.

Gu Mang had been gagged with a chain, and couldn't swear at him. He could only struggle, making the iron clink as he glared.

An inexplicable tremor shook Mo Xi's heart. He didn't understand why a layer of gooseflesh ran down his back at the sight of Gu Mang bound in chains, his clothes in disarray.

Was it the thrill of finally trampling his prey underfoot, of watching it stick out its neck for execution? Fury at his disappointing passivity? Or was it some other emotion?

Mo Xi didn't know, nor did he want to.

His cold black pupils looked down disdainfully. In the flickering light, his field of view was filled with Gu Mang's wretchedness, fierce yet pitiful.

After several long seconds, Mo Xi closed his eyes and got to his feet. "Take him away."

"Hm? What does Xihe-jun mean by this?"

Mo Xi turned his face away. "I'm not interested in him."

Murong Lian smiled. "So that's how it is. And here I thought something had poked Xihe-jun's sore spot, making Xihe-jun upset." As he spoke, he added some powder into the pipe in his hand. He narrowed his eyes and took a deep puff, his fluid gaze darted sidelong again.

"But Xihe-jun is truly admirable. Even after busying yourself with military affairs all these years, you're still as aloof as ever. Of all these men and women, these ill-fated beauties, none of them are worthy of your attention. Let me ask, out of curiosity: what type of divine beauty would it take to catch your eye?"

Mo Xi made no sound, his face darkening.

Realizing that the atmosphere between them was growing more and more strained, Yue Chenqing scratched his head and found himself taking a step in their direction, wanting to interject.

Mo Xi didn't even look at him as he said, "Keep away from it."

A beat. "Oh..."

The drugs had gone to Murong Lian's head. He scoffed. "Does Xihe-jun think a whiff of smoke will make the young Yue-gongzi an addict? Never fear, that is entirely impossible."

"It had better be." Mo Xi's gaze was like a hooked blade on a cold night, piercing through curls of smoky mist to stare at Murong Lian's face.

Perhaps due to the power struggles between aristocratic families, Murong Lian didn't care for the Mo Clan in the least, and he had made things difficult for Mo Xi since they were young. He was constantly trying to ferret out Mo Xi's likes and dislikes, and to gather information that could be used against him. This was far from the first time he had attempted to probe his thoughts by making such insinuations.

Murong Lian laughed and continued doggedly to interrogate Mo Xi in his usual way. "You still haven't answered my question. There are all manner of beauties in my Luomei Pavilion, men and women alike, and more than a hundred in total. Does Xihe-jun truly not care for a single one?"

"You needn't trouble yourself worrying about my personal matters."

Murong Lian took another airy drag, tapping the pitch-black pipe with jade-pale hands as he exhaled a fine cloud of smoke. "Heh, Xihe-jun, why do you restrain yourself so? I know you value your reputation, but as I see it, it's better to enjoy yourself while you can. Those insignificant things, like righteousness and character, are akin to drifting smoke..." He breathed out a dense plume, and an indistinct smile cut through the gray haze. He blew apart those tendrils of fog, his voice languid. "Look, it disperses in an instant."

"Reputation?" Mo Xi asked coldly.

"Xihe-jun keeps his distance from men and women. Why else, if not for your reputation?"

"I'm a clean freak," Mo Xi replied blandly.

Murong Lian didn't respond at once, lowering his lashes and exhaling a thin stream of smoke from between his lips.

They stood facing off for a long while before Murong Lian turned away with a sneer and sunk back down onto his xiangfei daybed. "Prudes...are so boring." As he spoke, he waved a hand, calling for his guests. "Come, everyone, enjoy yourselves to the fullest. Have all the fun you like; don't be modest. If there's a single maiden who's not dead-drunk in someone's arms after tonight's feast, then I'll have to consider you frail and impotent. From now on, Luomei Pavilion will be unable to afford to entertain you."

A family slave approached Murong Lian to ask, somewhat helplessly, "My lord, do...do we take Gu Mang back or keep him here?"

"Keep him here. Why take him away?" Murong Lian smiled. "So Xihe-jun isn't interested; does that mean no one else will play?" As he spoke, he shot a glance at Mo Xi. "Xihe-jun, you truly don't care about him, do you? If you're sure you don't want him, I'm going to let the brothers have their fun."

Seeing that Mo Xi had ignored him once again, Murong Lian grinned, a faint light flashing in his eyes, like shimmering snake scales. "All right." He nodded, pointing at Gu Mang. "This one's too ugly for Xihe-jun's tastes; he doesn't want him. Drag him down and let everyone else enjoy themselves."

The crowd was naturally delighted. The public frowned on degrading ordinary courtesans, but disgracing Gu Mang would be met with praise and applause.

After all, it wasn't *their* fault Gu Mang had decided to be a traitor to Chonghua.

Those intoxicated cultivators surrounded him in an instant, jeering as they imagined the humiliations they'd soon inflict upon him.

Someone noticed Gu Mang seemed to be hungry. He tossed a braised pork hock in front of him. "If you want to eat, then eat."

Gu Mang's bestial instincts were strong. After circling the hock a few times, he was unable to resist his hunger and scooped it up, bringing it to his nose. He first carefully sniffed it, then, finding nothing wrong, opened his mouth to take a tiny bite. As he chewed, he stared at the young masters in front of him, his eyes cautious, yet unwaveringly focused.

Mo Xi watched this scene out of the corner of his eye. His heart felt tight, and he couldn't help turning his face even further away. But no matter which direction he faced, the sounds were inescapable, piercing sharp and shrill through his ears.

"Ha ha ha! General Gu, they said you were a fierce beast, but you actually eat bones from the floor?"

The young masters roared with laughter.

"Didn't you used to be obsessed with cleanliness back in the day? How can you want something that's already been on the floor?"

"General Gu, where's your pride?"

Scorn filled the room to bursting, but Gu Mang didn't notice. He only gnawed intently on that hard-won pork hock. Within seconds, he had picked the bone clean.

He licked his lips and looked up once more, his gaze sweeping across those malevolent, mocking faces and landing on the feast table, laden with plates. It was piled with little towers of braised pork hocks, big and neat and square, the lean meat evenly matched with fat. Each piece of braised pork was covered in thick sauce, rich and aromatic. For a while, Gu Mang stared without making a sound.

"Give," he said suddenly.

This was the first word he had spoken since entering the room. The crowd looked at him as if they had witnessed a habitually silent cat meow, and every one of them began to grow excited.

"Give you what?"

Gu Mang didn't hold back. He looked like a wild beast begging for food. "Give me meat."

The crowd roared with laughter. "Look, he knows how to ask for meat!"

"He can't understand anything else, but he sure knows meat. One hell of a Beast of the Altar, ha ha!"

"You want to eat?" asked one of the young masters sitting on the dais.

Gu Mang nodded.

The young master selected a morsel with jade chopsticks and passed it to him. Gu Mang took it, but just as he was about to bite down, the young master roared with laughter. "A traitorous dog like you wants to eat meat? Keep dreaming!"

As he spoke, spiritual energy flickered at his fingertips, and the piece of braised pork Gu Mang was holding vanished in a cloud of blue-green smoke.

This seemed to startle Gu Mang. For a while, he stared stupidly at his hands, then for another while, he looked back and forth. In the end, he lowered his head to search the floor. Once he had finally made sure, he cocked his head in confusion. "The meat's gone."

At once, the crowd of people in the room began vying to outdo each other to mock him.

"Isn't it easy to get food?"

Someone mixed wine with vinegar, sauce, and grease in a wine cup and passed it to him, snickering. "Come, try some of this. It's a splendid vintage."

Gu Mang had been starved and parched for so long that, even though he didn't trust these people, he still took the wine cup and sniffed it. Finding the smell a little odd, he gave it a cautious lick.

After a moment of stillness, he spat it straight onto that person's face.

The onlookers slapped their thighs as they guffawed, and in their excitement, some started thinking of other ways to disgrace Gu Mang.

The young master who had been sprayed was infuriated by this indignity. He accepted a handkerchief and wiped his face, then grabbed Gu Mang's lapels to slap him hatefully. "Beggars can't be choosers. Go beg in fucking hell."

As soon as Gu Mang was hit, he wanted to fight back. But along with his mind, the Liao Kingdom had destroyed his valiant spiritual energy; he was no match for this cultivator. Those chains restrained him nigh instantly, clanking as he struggled vainly against them. He could do nothing but glare daggers at his opponent.

His eyes really did resemble a wolf's.

"Teach him a lesson! Beat him!"

"Yes! Beat him!"

Who didn't hate Gu Mang? Both Mo Xi and Murong Lian were present tonight, and all these young masters sought to curry favor with the two noble lords. Not a one of them held back a mote with their magic. Offensive spells pelted Gu Mang like rain—as vicious as they could manage without killing him outright.

Gu Mang was soon breathless under the onslaught. He didn't understand why these people hated him so. He wanted to speak, but his mouth was full of blood.

Still unsatisfied, some of the young masters retrieved the wine cup from before, which wasn't fully emptied, and spat into it a few times. Then they grabbed Gu Mang's chin and shouted, "Open up! You better swallow!"

"Drink! If you don't drink it all, you're not leaving tonight!"

This crowd of rich and powerful nobles had surrounded Gu Mang to debase him. Because they wanted to impress Xihe-jun, they strove all the harder to torment him.

Suddenly, they heard a muffled bang from the corner.

The whole group whipped around, only to see that Mo Xi had shot to his feet and tossed his jade cup onto the table. He had been playing with his wine cup in silence all this time, but now he finally looked up, his expression dark as night.

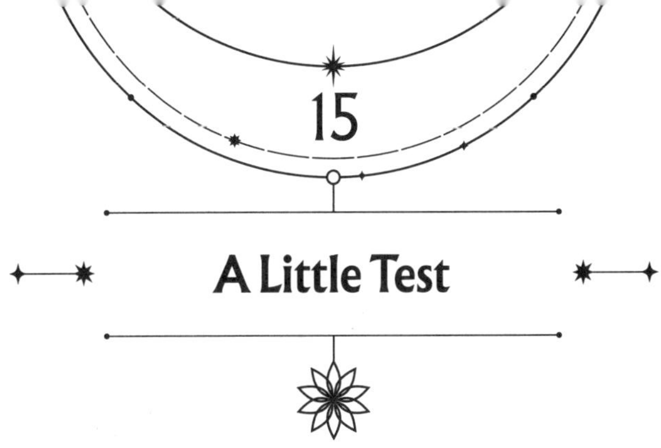

15

A Little Test

"Xi…xihe-jun, what…?"

Mo Xi's teeth-gritted rage was written stark across his pale face, handsome yet frightening. He looked down across the crowd from his full height, but just as that blade-like stare was about to land on Gu Mang, he quickly looked away.

"Xihe-jun…?"

Murong Lian also cast him a sidelong glance. "Oh, Xihe-jun, you were fine a second ago. Why this sudden outburst?"

Mo Xi's expression remained displeased. The sight of Gu Mang surrounded and debased filled him with an all-encompassing hatred he couldn't begin to pin down. If he'd accidentally blurted out a command for the crowd to stop, he would have landed himself in a truly difficult situation.

Fortunately, he had controlled his tongue. He took a moment to gather himself, and when he spoke, it was slowly and through a clenched jaw: "Dignitaries of the court…wine drunk and pleasure-seeking, idling in intoxication. You are all important members of the Bureau of Military Affairs. Yet all you have to perform are these despicable tricks." Each word was clipped with fury. "Where is your decorum?!"

Amid the hush of the crowd, Murong Lian spoke. "Xihe-jun, what do you mean?" He sat up from his sprawling repose. "Gu Mang is a traitor. These lords present are powerful nobles. These nobles are simply playing with a traitor, so where's the lack of decorum? How is this despicable?"

Murong Lian took another drag of ephemera. "Xihe-jun, *you* might be a clean freak, but why should you stop your subordinates from having their fun? Besides, this is Wangshu Manor; Gu Mang belongs to me, and everyone here today is my guest. No matter how high your rank, before you hit a dog, shouldn't you at least look at its owner?"

That speech really did it. Not only had Murong Lian insulted Gu Mang, he had demoted everyone else to the level of dogs.

But as it happened, this crowd was thoroughly drunk, and had they been sober, there was still the fact that Murong Lian was the emperor's cousin. Even if you let them borrow ten times more courage, none of them would have dared say a word of dissent against the powerful Murong Clan.

Mo Xi, however, was immune to such considerations. He stood, arms crossed, and coolly replied, "Murong Lian, the person to whom the members of the Bureau of Military Affairs have sworn loyalty is the emperor of Chonghua, not you. I don't want to hear you describe these important military and government officials as your 'dogs' again." He stared straight into Murong Lian's eyes. "Tread carefully."

"You—!"

Though Mo Xi's words were short and simple, they were extraordinarily heavy, like two swords pointed right at Murong Lian's chest.

The first sword was a reminder: the surname of the most useful and most valuable person in the Chonghua military was Mo. Murong Lian was a military official as well, but his rank wasn't as high as Mo Xi's. In Chonghua, martial law was paramount. If anyone, even a noble, were to truly enrage Mo Xi, they risked swift and immediate punishment.

The second sword was an implication: Murong Lian's behavior had overstepped.

This was even more frightening. It was said that back in the day, Murong Lian's father had participated in a power struggle between di and shu sons.[14] Lucky for him, the late ruler had magnanimously allowed his brothers' heads to remain on their shoulders, but every member of this lesser branch of the Murong Clan was yet anxious. The words "imperial power" were two they dared not touch.

As expected, Murong Lian paled. Only after a spell did he manage to regain his poise.

"Good. Good." The corners of Murong Lian's lips moved, forcing out a mirthless smile. "Mo Xi, you've got guts."

He stared into Mo Xi's eyes, his gaze flitting away, then back again. A moment later, beams of light sprang from his palms with a hiss. A scarlet whip responded to his summons, thrashing through the air and stirring up a haze of dust in its wake.

"I misspoke earlier." Murong Lian paced around Mo Xi, whip in hand, his eyes flashing with jealous light. "Xihe-jun disciplines his subordinates with exacting control. Consider me to be, at last, enlightened. Thus..."

His eyes gleamed with the faint, flashing light of the whip.

"I'll try my hand at disciplining these stupid slaves too!"

His voice echoed in the hall as the bloodred spiritual whip swam out like a snake, pitilessly striking down upon the slaves standing anxiously in the corner.

"Ah—!"

---

14 *Born of the first or official wife, "di" sons are direct heirs in matters of inheritance. "Shu" sons, born of other wives or concubines, are ranked second if at all.*

"My lord, my lord, please calm yourself—"

As Mo Xi heard these cries for mercy, his eyes flickered slightly, then darkened. Though he was a high-ranking noble, the Northern Frontier Army he commanded was a unit of commoners whom Gu Mang had led to prominence with his blood, sweat, and tears. Those cultivators were poor, and most of them were slave-born.

Mo Xi had been friends with Gu Mang early on, and later he had forged deeper bonds with his soldiers through the flames of war. He intimately understood their hardships. This was the reason that, despite his birthright as an aristocrat, Mo Xi had never bedded prostitutes, taken slaves, or disgraced the humble.

After Gu Mang stabbed Mo Xi, the emperor had sought to prevent the rise of any additional traitors once and for all. To this end, he had issued an order to execute the thirty thousand remaining soldiers of the Wangba Army and henceforth ban slaves from learning cultivation.

It was Mo Xi who had dragged his ailing body to kneel for days upon end in the snow, all to ask the emperor not to condemn the army Gu Mang had left behind, not to kill Gu Mang's remaining soldiers, not to strip Chonghua's slaves of their right to cultivate.

"None of the other slaves in that army have ever moved to commit treason. Why, then, does Your Imperial Majesty wish to see thirty thousand heads roll?"

"They haven't betrayed us *yet*, but how does that mean they won't in the future?!" the emperor exclaimed angrily. "Gu Mang led them! They're a horde of traitors in the making! Xihe-jun, do you forget your pain as soon as your wound is healed?!"

Mo Xi's wound was in fact not healed. It still seeped blood beneath the bandages wrapped around his chest.

But he still remembered something Gu Mang had said to him

when they were young. Gu Mang had been sitting on a pile of straw, chomping down on an apple and smiling at Mo Xi.

"Out of all the Nine Provinces and Twenty-Eight Nations, only the five led by Chonghua are willing to let those of us born as slaves cultivate. It would be good if even more allow it in the future. Even though Chonghua's never elevated a slave to officer, as long as the emperor is willing to let us cultivate, there'll always be a chance.

"I want to achieve something. All of us want to achieve something. We only hope the person on the throne will spare us a glance..."

Mo Xi closed his eyes as he spoke. "I ask Your Imperial Majesty to allow me to take responsibility for these thirty thousand slave soldiers."

The emperor burst out laughing. "Let you, a pure-blooded noble, take charge of Gu Mang's army of riffraff? How would you lead them? Would they accept you? Not to mention, how could you promise us those beasts won't target the throne of Chonghua like their former master?!"

Mo Xi stared straight into the emperor's eyes. "I'm willing to take the Vow of Calamity."

The emperor startled. "What did you say?!"

"I will take the Vow of Calamity."

The Vow of Calamity was a grave, unbreakable oath that could only be sworn once. The contract alone took ten years of the oath taker's lifespan. If broken, the heavens would strike them with a calamity, and the oath taker would be annihilated, becoming ashes on the wind. But even if they adhered to their vow for their entire life, those ten years could never be recovered.

Given the ruthlessness of these terms, precious few people on earth would ever take that vow.

But Mo Xi did.

He pledged an oath on ten years of his life, swearing to never let those slave-born soldiers rebel, and swearing that he would be loyal to Chonghua and its emperor for a lifetime.

All so Gu Mang's treason wouldn't result in more innocent bloodshed.

All so Chonghua would continue to allow slaves the right to cultivate.

Almost no one knew about this sacrifice he had made. All they knew was that the emperor was suddenly possessed by a strange whim and handed command of the Wangba Army that Gu Mang left behind to a pure-blooded noble.

When Mo Xi took up his post, the soldiers of the Wangba Army had called him "stepdad" behind his back. They had cursed him for his strictness and indifference, for being an aristocrat who could never understand how the poor suffered.

None of them knew what this noble young master who "didn't understand their suffering" had secretly sacrificed to keep them alive—to ensure those born with Gu Mang's same status wouldn't be condemned to a lifetime of powerlessness from the day they were born.

A decade of his life, an oath for a lifetime.

This "stepdad," whose very heart had been pierced, was imprisoned by his circumstances, unable to please either side. He'd done everything he could. It was just that no one knew.

But Murong Lian did. Because on that day, he had been at the emperor's side.

He had seen with his own eyes how Mo Xi spoke on the slaves' behalf, heard with his own ears when Mo Xi swore the oath and knelt on the ground, forehead in the snow. He knew Mo Xi had compassion for these slaves.

Murong Lian couldn't rage at the empire's general, but now that Mo Xi had displeased him, he struck out cruelly and shamelessly at those helpless slaves until blood flew through the air and wailing filled the room.

Murong Lian threw his head back and laughed, his pale, pretty face distorted by his loathing and addiction. He looked at Mo Xi and said meaningfully, "Slaves will always be slaves; their blood is destined for filth from birth. What chance could they possibly have to achieve anything?"

Nearby, Yue Chenqing was aghast. "Ephemera is no joke," he said softly. "I'm going to tell all my friends that they'd better not smoke it. It was only a little disagreement! Why did Wangshu-jun go so crazy?"

Yet whipping the slaves did not sate Murong Lian. Out of the corner of his eye, he saw Gu Mang standing to the side.

Murong Lian was Gu Mang's former master. For years, he had noticed every detail of his interactions with Mo Xi. Although he had no evidence, he had always felt that something about Mo Xi and Gu Mang's relationship wasn't quite right.

At this thought, a fiendish idea sprouted in Murong Lian's mind. He turned his spiritual whip and sent it sweeping toward the unwitting Gu Mang.

Gu Mang didn't have time to react before the whip had wrapped around his waist. Caught off guard, he was easily jerked before Murong Lian.

Murong Lian grabbed Gu Mang's chin and wrenched his face toward Mo Xi. Those sultry eyes were filled with malice. "C'mere, Gu Mang, look at this man in front of you. Do you recognize him?"

Gu Mang blinked with a bestial wariness.

"It's fine if you've forgotten him. Let me tell you this: Even if you didn't say it back then, I could tell. You might have called me master out loud, but in your heart, you wanted to renounce the Murong family to get on all fours like a dog for this Mo-gongzi."

Mo Xi's expression darkened. "Murong Lian, have you lost your mind?!"

"How have I lost my mind? Today is the day of our long-awaited reunion, but I haven't prepared a present. What about this? I'll test his intentions again. If he still wants to follow you, then I'll consider letting him have his way and relinquishing him. Okay?" Murong Lian looped an arm over Gu Mang's shoulders and leaned against him.

"I've even thought of *how* to test him. Here—"

"Murong Lian!"

Murong Lian had long since been thoroughly intoxicated by the fumes of the ephemera. He brought a finger to his lips and wagged it. "Shh, don't get mad; let me finish. I promise it's very interesting."

As he spoke, he lowered his head. "General Gu," he said, his voice syrupy sweet. "I'm going to give you two choices. Listen up:

"To be honest, I've always been disgusted by your face, and I dearly want to cut it up. But if you can help me..." He drunkenly pointed at Mo Xi. "If you can help me cut off one of his arms..." Smiling, he told Gu Mang in a stage whisper, "I'll spare you."

These words shocked a measure of sobriety into the drunken guests. Their bleary eyes widened in astonishment as they stared at the trio before them.

"What did Wangshu-jun just say...?"

"He wants General Mo's arm?"

Yue Chenqing slapped his forehead, grumbling, "I shouldn't have come." Then he shouted, "Wangshu-jun, Murong-dage! You've had too much ephemera! You're addled! Where do you keep your sobering medicines? I'll go get some for you!"

But Murong Lian didn't acknowledge him. He draped himself over the ignorant Gu Mang, grinning. "So, Gu Mang? Will you do it?"

As Murong Lian finished speaking, the spiritual whip in his hand transformed into a dagger gleaming with cold light. He held it up to Gu Mang's cheek.

"Either get rid of his arm or let me cut up your face. Your mind's broken, isn't it? I really can't wait to see which one you'll choose."

Mo Xi felt a shiver in his heart. Murong Lian wasn't drunk at all.

It was obvious that with Gu Mang's current abilities, even if he took the dagger, he wouldn't be able to touch a hair on Mo Xi's head; there was no danger whatsoever. Murong Lian was merely testing Gu Mang to see if he really had lost his memories, and therefore how much value Mo Xi had in Gu Mang's heart.

"I'll count to three."

The dagger was right at Gu Mang's face. Another inch and it would draw blood. Gu Mang made no sound, turning to look at Murong Lian's dagger nigh indifferently.

"One."

Mo Xi's heartbeat sped up. He wanted more than anything to stop Murong Lian this instant.

But on the other hand...he couldn't help but wonder what exactly Gu Mang would do.

In truth, Mo Xi had his suspicions. He too had considered the possibility that Gu Mang's apparent mental deterioration might be a facade.

If Gu Mang's mind really was broken, running on bestial instinct, then he wouldn't hesitate for a second. If, as Li Wei said, Gu Mang really believed himself to be a wolf, given the choice between self-harm and harming another, he would no doubt choose the latter.

Then why had Gu Mang still not moved to attack?

The atmosphere grew ever more tense.

Murong Lian was smiling, Yue Chenqing was shouting, the crowd was pleading. Smoke wound through the room, making for a surreal and strange scene. Memories of Gu Mang's face rose before Mo Xi's eyes: calm, beaming, concerned, icy.

They swam past in fantastical shapes, like the flashing scales of a massive fish; the light glancing off each scale was a silhouette of Gu Mang from the past, floating up like a dream:

Long time no see, Mo-shidi. Can I sit with you?

Would you like to rot with me?

I really will kill you...

These memories roared past in a torrential flow, surging through Mo Xi's eyes. In the end, they were pierced by Murong Lian's voice, and Mo Xi was hauled back to reality.

Which left only this Gu Mang, still somewhat calm, with only a faint furrow between his brows.

"Two..."

For some reason, Gu Mang still hadn't moved.

Why wasn't he choosing self-defense?! Wasn't he a beast, unable to remember a thing? And that was to say nothing of the ruthlessness he'd heretofore shown Mo Xi. Gu Mang had *stabbed* him, so he should... He should...

"Three!"

"Stop!" Mo Xi reacted instantaneously, sparks of light flashing in his hands as a talisman sigil erupted from his palm and swept toward the dagger Murong Lian had lifted.

It was too late.

The dagger flashed toward Gu Mang's cheek, and blood spurted.

Mo Xi's eyes widened.

16

Suspicion

BLOOD DRIPPED DOWN.

Murong Lian clamped a hand over his arm, but his silk robes were soon soaked through. Scarlet seeped between his fingers. The attendants paled at the sight of it, stuttering, "M-my lord..."

No one had expected that Murong Lian would be the one injured. The crowd in Wangshu Manor erupted.

"Go get medicine! Quick, get the healing powder!"

"Hurry! Tourniquets! Tourniquets!"

Murong Lian's face was ashen. Somehow, in the instant he stabbed down with his dagger, a red lotus sigil had flickered to life at the side of Gu Mang's neck. An explosive flow of spiritual energy swiftly followed as a dozen swords of light lanced toward him. Not only had they jolted the dagger from his hand, they'd thrown him bodily several yards back.

Murong Lian was briefly unable to speak. He bit his lower lip, his face flushing and paling in turns. At length, he collected himself enough to summon a blue light in his palm and more or less stop the bleeding. "Gu Mang!" he shouted, his voice shot through with embarrassment and fury.

In the chaos, Gu Mang had scurried behind a table to hide. He was now rubbing his bare feet together, baring his teeth as he stared at Murong Lian in a manner both extremely wary and extremely innocent. Those swords of light continued to swirl without pause; they completely surrounded him and protected him within the heart of the array.

One of the young masters in the crowd had once gone to Luomei Pavilion to visit Gu Mang. After a moment of thought, he realized what had happened. "Aiya! It's that array!" he cried.

"What array?" Murong Lian said angrily. "If you know something about it, then hurry up and speak!"

"This array... This subordinate also found out by accident... It's a little embarrassing to speak of..."

"Speak!"

Once the young master saw how angry Murong Lian had become, he responded with all due haste. "Wangshu-jun, I answer you with all I know! The array isn't triggered by magic or high-level weapons. However, if you summon an ordinary weapon, or kick or punch Gu Mang, he'll get scared, and a bunch of those light swords will burst from his body. And that's..." Having reached this point, he was somewhat sheepish, but he braced himself to finish. "That's why despite how long Gu Mang's been at Luomei Pavilion, no one can really lay a hand on him."

Murong Lian was still enraged. He glared malevolently at Gu Mang across the table. "What kind of idiotic, ridiculous array is that?!"

That young master shook his head. "Gu Mang used to be a god-damn genius with magic. Who knows how many spells he invented back in the day? Many of them had no purpose other than to make girls giggle. This...might be something he made for fun way back then."

When the young master said this, the rest of the crowd remembered.

To this day, one could find scrolls covered in Gu Mang's randomly scribbled spells within the cultivation academy's libraries. The spells were all for things like instantly warming a cold plate of food, turning yourself into a cat for as long as a stick of incense took to burn, and even conjuring a ball of flame to hold in your arms for warmth in winter. The one most well-known spell was named "I Agree with the General." It was said that when Gu Mang first enlisted, he had liked to skip out on those tedious military meetings. To stop the general from finding out, he'd devised a spell that transformed a piece of wood into his spitting image. This wood would sit there and listen to the general blather while the man it resembled escaped without a trace, haring off on some cheerful adventure or another...

"Come to think of it, that sounds about right."

"Right? It protects against punches and kicks, but it doesn't block magic. It's totally absurd, obviously not a serious protective array."

"That rascal Gu Mang just liked to mess around. But you've really got to hand it to him—that pointless little spell actually did end up protecting him," someone laughed. "Without it, he'd have been fucked to death ages ago. There are tons of people in Chonghua who want him on his back, after all. Too bad no one can break through this array."

Yue Chenqing scratched his head. "Damn, what kind of array is that?" he mumbled. "Array of the Untouchable Flower?"[15]

"Give me a break, Gu Mang the untouchable flower?" Another young master started laughing and quietly quipped at Yue Chenqing. "Why not go ahead and make it a couplet?"

"'Gu Mang the untouchable flower,'" Yue Chenqing repeated, fully invested. "Then what's the second line?"

"'General Mo the faithless philanderer.'"

---

15 高岭之花, *"flower upon a high mountain," an idiom describing aloof, untouchable beauties.*

Yue Chenqing slapped his thigh and burst out laughing. "That's not right at all, but it's still—"

"What are you laughing at?!" Murong Lian cut him off. "You're so undisciplined—see if I don't take it out on your father as punishment!" he snapped in humiliated rage.

"I'm not laughing! How would I dare?" Yue Chenqing hastily replied. "Let me just say that as long as it makes Wangshu-jun happy, you can take whatever you want out on my dad—you can even take my dad out on a date!"

Murong Lian glared at him. Not only had he failed to show off at the feast tonight, he'd suffered wounds to both his flesh and his dignity. He found this very hard to take and turned to bark out, "Where are the attendants?!"

"Awaiting my lord's orders!"

Murong Lian pointed at Gu Mang with a sweep of his sleeves. "Take this stupid pig away. I don't want to see him again. And go get some more sensible and intelligent people from Luomei Pavilion. As for his punishment..."

Murong Lian ground his teeth, shooting a sidelong glance at Mo Xi. For some reason, ever since Mo Xi had seen the array, his expression had been a little strange. His eyes had returned to the side of Gu Mang's neck several times.

"General Mo... Have you nothing to say?"

Mo Xi returned to his senses and looked away from Gu Mang, crossing his arms. "Didn't Wangshu-jun plan to give in and relinquish Gu Mang to my care?" he asked indifferently.

Murong Lian was momentarily startled. Then he said, without an ounce of shame, "I didn't mean it. His Imperial Majesty decreed that I would be the one to punish him. How could he so easily change owners?"

Mo Xi had already known that Murong Lian never kept his promises. The saying "a gentleman's word is worth its weight in gold" was more or less bullshit when it came to this man. Besides, that promise had been farcical from the start. Unless the emperor personally retracted his decree, no one could move to change it.

Mo Xi looked up and met Murong Lian's overbearing gaze. "If that's the case," he said, "Wangshu-jun should deal with his own people. Why bother asking me?"

"As you say." Murong Lian smirked, and turned to give instructions. "Take him away. Give him eighty lashes as a reward, and reduce his food and drink for a month." After a pause, he added another malicious sentence: "If he starves to death, well, whose fault is that?"

Gu Mang was escorted away, and the servants of Wangshu Manor came to clean up the table that had been thrown into disarray. They laid out a few fresh platters of food, allowing the feast to resume.

Amid the murmurs of discussion, only Mo Xi said nothing. When the wine cups and chips for drinking games once more rose around him, he looked up again, staring in the direction Gu Mang had been taken with a complicated expression. In the shadows, where no one else could see, his fingers slowly clenched into a fist.

Mo Xi didn't like to drink and hated being hungover.

But after returning from Wangshu Manor that day, he sat in the empty courtyard of his house and opened a jar of good wine that had been stored for many years. Cup by cup, he drank until the jar was drained. He looked up into the empty sky, where the clouds were clearing after snowfall.

"Li Wei," he said to the housekeeper standing beside him. "How many years have you been with me?"

"Seven years, my lord."

"Seven years..." Mo Xi murmured.

Seven years ago, Mo Xi had pursued the traitorous Gu Mang. After crossing enemy lines, he had been stabbed in the chest and his life had hung by a thread. While Mo Xi lay in bed unconscious, the emperor had ordered Li Wei to go to Xihe Manor to look after him.

So it had already been seven years.

Dissatisfied, Mo Xi wondered why he couldn't let go. Why couldn't he forget?

Drinking so much wine inevitably leads to a degree of inebriation. Mo Xi wanted to remain clear-headed, so when Li Wei moved to top up his cup again, he shook his head. Li Wei complied. Those who were undaunted by beauty and unintoxicated by fine wine were rare. Few men could hold back with ease in the face of desire, but Mo Xi was one of them.

"What do you think about me and Gu Mang?" Mo Xi suddenly asked.

Li Wei startled. "You two aren't...a good match?" he hesitantly replied.

"Why are you talking about matches between two men? Seems you've also had too much." Mo Xi shot a glare at him. "Try again."

Only then did Li Wei react, smiling. "Oh, the relationship between you? Everyone knows it's bad."

"And how was it before?"

"Before..." Li Wei thought this over for a while. "In those days, I hadn't yet had the fortune to be assigned to my lord's side, but I heard that my lord and General Gu were martial brothers at the academy, comrades in the army, and the twin generals of the empire, as well as... Oh, I don't know. To be honest, I can't think of anything else. Some said that you used to be quite familiar with General Gu, and some said it only seemed that way because General Gu was warm to everyone, like sunlight, so perhaps he wasn't truly that close to you. That's about it."

Mo Xi nodded without comment.

Martial brothers, comrades-in-arms, two generals of the empire. This was the impression most people had of Mo Xi and Gu Mang's relationship. It didn't seem to be wrong.

"Then what was it actually?" Li Wei asked curiously.

"Between him and me?" Unexpectedly, Mo Xi smiled very slightly and lowered his long lashes. Something bitter was hidden in that smile. "Hard to say. Can't be said." He paused. "Nor should it be said," he finished slowly.

No one in Chonghua would believe that Gu Mang had been to Mo Xi what a clear spring might be to a traveler dying of thirst.

Before Mo Xi met Gu Mang, he'd had ambition, duty, unyielding willpower, and no fear of hardship, but the most potent sentiment in his heart had, in fact, been hatred.

In Mo Xi's youth, he had treated everyone with earnest sincerity, but what had he received in exchange? His father's death in battle, his mother's betrayal, his uncle's usurpation—and every one of the servants better at taking his uncle's hints than the last. They'd called Mo Xi "young master" to his face, but they'd all acted under his uncle's orders. He'd had to be constantly on guard; there had been no one he could trust.

He didn't know what he had done wrong, to make fate treat him so harshly.

That was when he met Gu Mang.

In those days, Gu Mang had been so kind, so righteous. Although he was a slave, his status as low as dirt, he never resented or criticized anything. When he and Mo Xi first started exorcising demons and monsters together, Mo Xi had been ill-tempered and often rude, but Gu Mang had forgiven it all with a smile—he had always empathized with other people's difficulties, even though he had led such a difficult life himself.

He always strove to breathe in every wisp of kindness in life, and then did all he could to get a little flower to bloom.

That time Gu Mang impersonated Murong Lian to buy medicine, he knew he would be punished—that he might even lose the right to cultivate at the academy—but he had still been determined to do it. And afterward, as he knelt in the cultivation academy's penitence pavilion, Gu Mang hadn't defended himself at all, had only shamelessly said that he felt it would be fun.

But what slave would throw away such a hard-won opportunity to succeed for *fun?*

Clearly Gu Mang had done it because he had seen with his own eyes that this village was plagued by illness year-round.

He had been unable to bear it.

But Gu Mang was so lowly that even if he used the most obliging manner and softest voice to say, "I wanted to save people," he would be met with merciless derision. Even if he carved his chest wide open to reveal the unbearable anguish of his heart, he would still be met with sneers at his passion, doubts of his kindness, mockery of his audacity, and ridicule of his trembling sincerity.

Gu Mang knew all of this, so he didn't argue.

It was said that "In prominence, one should focus on the people; in obscurity, one should focus on oneself."[16] Gu Mang's circumstances were fundamentally bleak and obscure; he was nothing but a slave from Wangshu Manor. But instead of worrying over where he'd get his next meal or how to win the favor of his lord, he took

16 From "Jin Xin I," by Confucian philosopher Mencius.

up the burden of helping the dying and healing the injured—what an audacious fool.

But it was this cockiness of his, that sincere heart overflowing with burning passion, that had pulled Mo Xi, who had lost his faith in humanity, back onto the right path.

"My lord." Li Wei's urging voice broke through his daze. "The night is cold and damp. You should go rest."

Mo Xi didn't immediately respond. His hand was still over his brow, covering his eyes. At the sound of his housekeeper's voice, he turned slightly, and flicked his fingers once, as if to wipe something away. After a several more seconds, he spoke, his voice very low and very soft: "Li Wei."

"I'm here."

"Say..." he muttered. "Could it be that Gu Mang...never lost his memories? That he's only pretending?"

17

Scruffy Beauty

STARTLED, Li Wei asked, "What?"

Mo Xi's head was still bowed. His chiseled features were hidden in the shadow of his hand, and his low voice was slightly nasal as he spoke. "Maybe he still remembers some things. Maybe his mind wasn't wholly damaged. Maybe he's only pretending."

"How could that be?" Li Wei's eyes widened. "Gu Mang's illness was diagnosed by Shennong Terrace, and Chonghua's foremost physician, Imperial Healer Jiang, came to assess him himself. His core's shattered, he's lost two souls, his mind is broken, he thinks he's a *wolf*—"

"Have you ever seen a wolf who would rather allow himself to be hurt than hurt another?!"

Li Wei was shocked stiff. Was he hallucinating? The rims of Xihe-jun's eyes were a little red and wet. "Wh-what brings my lord to say this...?"

Mo Xi closed his eyes. His ire wasn't directed at Li Wei; he simply didn't wish to hear any more about how Gu Mang "didn't remember anything."

"At Wangshu Manor, Murong Lian gave him two options—slice off one of my arms or let his face be cut." Mo Xi turned, gazing out at the shadows of the rustling trees. After a long interval, he murmured, "He chose the latter."

Li Wei stared, speechless.

"Tell me. What kind of wolf would make that decision?"

Li Wei thought, *Tell you? What am I supposed to tell you? Have you seen that temper of yours?! If I said Gu Mang might not have understood Wangshu-jun's question, you'd leap to your feet and kick me to death!*

From that day forward, Mo Xi could only be described as possessed.

Later, when Mo Xi was in a better mood, Li Wei approached him and tactfully tried to explain, "Gu Mang's mind really has deteriorated. There are many words he can't understand, and communicating with him is like communicating with a three-year-old child—any one sentence may have to be repeated multiple times."

However, Mo Xi couldn't relinquish this faint sliver of hope.

In the end, Li Wei had no other choice. "Then, my lord, why don't you go ask Shennong Terrace for confirmation?"

Mo Xi didn't respond right away. Many of those in Shennong Terrace reported to Murong Lian, so he was reluctant to visit.

Li Wei offered another suggestion. "Then you can go to the imperial healers and ask Medicine Master Jiang."

Medicine Master Jiang was aloof and blunt, and Mo Xi's impression of him wasn't especially favorable. But in the end, he couldn't bear the torment in his heart and went to pay him a visit.

Outside the arching eaves of the extravagant Healer's Manor, the attendant anxiously told him, "Xihe-jun, Proprietor Jiang left to collect medicinal supplies."

"When will he return?"

"The proprietor doesn't set dates for his trips, so it may be a few days, or it might be a few months."

"Did he say where he went?"

"When the proprietor goes out to collect ingredients for medicine, he roams the whole nation."

Mo Xi was rendered speechless. As he watched the attendant's head wobble back and forth, he could only nod, turn his horse around, and go back to his manor.

Perhaps his obsession ran too deep. He was preoccupied with Gu Mang all day, and in his sleep that night, Mo Xi dreamed.

In that hazy dream, he somehow returned to a day many years ago, the day when he finally understood his feelings and had to confess without a moment's delay.

It was a silent night in the garrison on the frontier.

Mo Xi was very young, not yet twenty. He wasn't yet the indomitable Xihe-jun, and Gu Mang was still under Murong Lian's control, having not yet made a name for himself.

They had fought a fierce battle against the Liao Kingdom, and many soldiers had died. While Mo Xi was packing up the belongings of his fallen comrades, he stumbled across a love letter. He clutched that unsent letter, staring vacantly at it for a long time.

Mo Xi's family was dogged by misfortune. Since his youth, he had only ever known treachery and deceit, betrayal and manipulation.

This was the first time he had witnessed sincere and passionate love.

The cultivator who had died in battle was a coarse man who hadn't even liked reading books. But amid the fires of war, he had carefully and earnestly written this long letter, word by word. The letter didn't mention the suffering of battle or the merits he'd won, but rather the mole at the tip of the girl's brow and new seedlings planted in a courtyard.

When the flowers bloom splendid next year, I'll play the xiao while Xiao-Yan sings clear.[17]

The poem was clumsy and unpracticed, but it seemed to drip with tenderness.

And somehow, that coarse man was the one who had composed it. When he wrote it, he had truly envisioned singing and making music with the maiden named Xiao-Yan in the flower meadow he planted with his own hands, hadn't he?

But in the end, all that was left was this letter caked in dried blood.

Mo Xi couldn't express what he felt at that moment. He sat on the corner of his bed for a long time, holding the letter.

When the flowers bloom splendid next year, I'll play the xiao while Xiao-Yan sings clear.

If Mo Xi had been the one to die that day, was there anyone he couldn't bear to leave behind?

A familiar figure quickly came to mind, but at first, he didn't take notice of it. Only after a long while did he realize whom he was thinking of—and he was instantly shocked stiff as he broke out into a cold sweat. A blaze seemed to ignite in his chest, lighting up everything within him at once. But at the same time, it seemed like this inferno in his heart had been secretly illuminating him, lapping at him, tormenting him all along.

It was just that he hadn't recognized it before, and so hadn't understood the truth of those suppressed feelings.

He sat there blankly, the wildfire in his heart burning hotter and hotter. Something collapsed, and with a howl, something else rose in its place.

---

17 A variation upon Southern Song dynasty poet Jiang Kui's quatrain "Across the Chuihong Bridge."

From outside the tent there came the sorrowful wailing of cultivators who had lost their brothers. He heard the faint sound of a xun and the soft sigh of the wind.

That thin sheet of paper was still in his hand. Tomorrow, who else would die? Tomorrow, who else's relics of love would end up streaked in bloody filth?

All at once Mo Xi could no longer restrain the impulse in his heart. He tossed the curtain aside and immediately bumped into a healer who had come to treat his wounds. The cultivator started in fright. "Mo-gongzi?"

Mo Xi didn't reply. He strode out of the tent, his footfalls quickening with each step, and tucked the bloodstained letter into the lapels of his robe. He would bring it back and give it to the "Xiao-Yan" mentioned within, but right now, he needed to find someone. He was suddenly in such a rush, as though if he didn't speak today, he would never get another chance; as though death lay waiting before him.

"Mo-gongzi! Mo-gongzi!" The white-robed healer ran out of the barracks after him. "Mo-gongzi, the wound on your arm—"

But Mo Xi ignored him—he didn't care about some insignificant wound. He ran out of the camp, then summoned a spirit horse and galloped ahead.

The freezing wind and early snow blew in his face, and the birds of the garrison twittered behind him. He left all those fragmented sounds in his wake. A burst of passion was growing in his heart, and he wanted to pour it out before Gu Mang, who was on night duty. He could feel his own thumping heartbeat, his emotions burning in a smoky blaze. Even amid the frigid wind and icy snow, his palms were touched with damp.

"Where's Gu Mang?" he breathlessly asked the garrison cultivator as soon as he arrived at the northern barracks, before he even dismounted from his horse. "I'm looking for him. Where is he?"

The cultivator was alarmed by Mo Xi's sudden appearance. "D-does Mo-gongzi have an urgent report?"

"Urgent report? Do I require an urgent report to visit him?" His exhales were scalding steam, his tone becoming more and more impatient.

"Then..." The cultivator trailed off, hesitating as his eyes grazed over Mo Xi's wounded arm. Mo Xi understood what he meant: *Then why aren't you properly resting to heal? Why are you racing across the whole camp in the snow to look for some nameless soldier?*

Mo Xi was too anxious. And too impulsive.

He had just realized something, something extremely important, something that had bothered him for a long time. He had to find Gu Mang. If he couldn't find Gu Mang right this instant, it felt as if all the passion in his heart would boil dry and burn out.

Mo Xi's temperament had always been decisive and firm; the moment he was sure of what he wanted, he had to have it in his hands. On top of that, he was young, and had never experienced the bitterness of love.

He wasn't even considering the consequences; he had no thoughts for propriety or righteousness, or whether he would be rejected.

He didn't know a thing. With his heartfelt sincerity recklessly in tow, Mo Xi arrived outside Gu Mang's tent in a rush. Standing outside it, his fingers trembled slightly, and his blood grew hotter and hotter, his heart beating faster and faster. In the end, he swallowed thickly, took a deep breath, and flung the curtain open.

"Gu Mang—"

A combat cultivator with well-proportioned features turned around. It was Gu Mang's close friend, Lu Zhanxing.

Lu Zhanxing was also one of Murong Lian's study attendants at the academy. He had grown up with Gu Mang, and he had an intractable temperament. He was gnawing on fruit and reading a sword manual when he caught sight of Mo Xi in the doorway. "Mo-gongzi?" He was shocked for a moment. "What are you doing here?"

"Where's Gu Mang?"

"Oh, you're looking for him." Lu Zhanxing took another bite of the juicy pear, then burst into delighted laughter. "How come so many people are looking for him tonight?"

Mo Xi stopped. "Who else was there?"

"Oh, no one, really. A few of our friends, taking him out to the village nearby. You don't know them, Mo-gongzi. I was going to join, but my legs aren't fully healed yet, so I didn't bother..."

As Lu Zhanxing rambled, the anxiety in Mo Xi's heart intensified. He bit his lower lip. "Where did he go?" he asked.

Lu Zhanxing laughed again, ready to answer his question...

But just as Mo Xi was about to dream of the answer he had received back then, he felt a sharp stab—as if his heart was instinctively trying to protect him, stopping him from feeling even greater pain. The heavy darkness fell with inexorable finality, crushing Lu Zhanxing's reply, and the dreamscape scattered like the most insubstantial of windblown dust.

The shadows became even deeper, the dream even darker. There were no more sounds.

In the end, it became nothingness. All returned to silence.

The next day, Mo Xi awoke to the sound of birdsong in the courtyard. He blinked, gradually coming to his senses as though surfacing from the wreckage of a beautiful illusion.

"Gu Mang..."

Mo Xi was trapped in the dreamscape's afterglow. When he lifted a hand, he felt faint warmth in his palms, as well as a thin sheen of sweat. It was as if he could still clearly recall that scorching, youthful emotion, though all that had happened in his dream had already faded.

"My lord." Li Wei saw that he was awake and approached with small, courteous steps, bowing to speak. "Early this morning, Changfeng-jun sent a messenger with some gifts. They're currently being kept in the flower pavilion. My lord, do you wish to accept them?"

"Changfeng-jun?"

After awakening from a depressing dream of the past, even the brilliant and extraordinary Xihe-jun needed some time to gather himself. Only after a long while did he knead his brow and frown slightly as he remembered.

Changfeng-jun was a downtrodden old noble. At present, though he still had his status, it was only in name. Moreover, Changfeng-jun hadn't interacted with other highborn families in many, many years.

Mo Xi was rather grumpy upon waking. He pressed at the protruding veins at his temples. "Why's he sending me gifts all of a sudden?" he asked.

"He didn't say."

Mo Xi was upright and incorruptible to a fault. After a moment of thought, he said, "Then return them. You can say I've accepted the intention, but since it's neither a holiday nor a celebration, I can't accept the gifts."

"Yes."

After Mo Xi washed and dressed, he walked to the flower pavilion to face a scene of true excess: a delivery of eight chests containing treasures of pearls and jade, silky gauze and damask brocade, magical devices and spiritual medicines, and all sorts of other gifts. Upon seeing this, he frowned and summoned the busy Li Wei.

"Is Changfeng-jun in trouble?"

"Eh?" Li Wei looked at him in surprise. "He isn't."

"Then what does he mean by this?"

"Well..." Li Wei thought to himself. Apparently, Changfeng-jun had recently offended quite a few nobles at the cultivation academy because of something to do with his daughter. A few of these nobles were of powerful and prosperous great families. Sending gifts to Xihe-jun was an obvious attempt to test the waters and see if he could get the help of this formidable commander who had recently returned to the city and wasn't yet caught up with events.

But Housekeeper Li was a highly intelligent man. He knew it was best to avoid involving oneself in matters concerning multiple clans. "If my lord doesn't know, then I couldn't possibly know either."

Mo Xi solemnly glanced over the gifts a few more times. He still couldn't figure out the sender's intentions, and so he decided to waste no more time on it. "I'm leaving," he said, adjusting the fall of his sleeves. "I won't be returning at noon. Tell the kitchens there's no need to prepare a meal."

"Oh..." Li Wei replied, unable to stop himself from sneaking a peek at Mo Xi.

These past few days, his lord's behavior had been a bit off.

Ever since he returned from Wangshu Manor, it seemed that as long as there were no courtly nor military matters, he went out every day without fail. Sometimes he was gone for half a day, sometimes for the entire day, sometimes only returning in the dead of night. And he never let his attendants follow.

Given these clues, no matter how you looked at it, it seemed he was having a secret rendezvous with a beautiful paramour...

As soon as this thought came to mind, Li Wei nearly broke out into a cold sweat.

No, no, no! How could it be? How could it be?

First there was Mengze, and then there was Yanping—and that was to say nothing of all the virtuous beauties and scheming seductresses from other illustrious houses. All of them sought to win over the noble, aloof, and icy male idol that was Xihe-jun, but not a one had ever succeeded.

Li Wei thought that if Xihe-jun really was secretly meeting up with a maiden, she had to be a calamitous beauty of prodigious talents.

Expression stormy, Mo Xi took a seat at a tea stand at the corner of a street and asked for a pot of yangxian tea. The tea was promptly brought to him, along with some dried fruits and honey preserves. Mo Xi drank slowly. From time to time, his elegantly shaped eyes peered across the street.

Across the street was the lotus pond in the back courtyard of Luomei Pavilion. A certain scruffy "beauty" had not appeared there for some time.

Starting more than a week ago, Gu Mang had spaced out before this pond almost every day. He stood alone on the floating bridge and did nothing but quietly stare at the fish in the pool below.

His face was vacant, as if blanketed by heavy snow.

At first, Mo Xi didn't understand what was so interesting about these fish—until one day he saw Gu Mang try to grab one. Obviously, he couldn't catch it, so he remained crouched on the shore, blankly watching the ornamental carp shimmer as it swam away. The jut of his throat bobbed as he swallowed, his eyes gradually growing glazed.

Only then did Mo Xi realize that Gu Mang was hungry.

It had been more than ten days since Murong Lian declared that he would reduce Gu Mang's rations for an entire month. So poor Gu Mang wanted to catch a fish to eat...

But for some reason, since the day of that one unsuccessful attempt, Gu Mang hadn't appeared again. Mo Xi came every day, but never again saw him crouching for fish. Today was no different.

Slowly, Mo Xi reached the bottom of the teapot and asked the shopkeeper to bring him a fresh one. He sat there for a long time, but still there was no sign of Gu Mang.

It had been five days since he'd emerged. Could something have happened in Luomei Pavilion?

Despite his indifferent facade, as Mo Xi thought, he grew inwardly anxious. He endured it silently, drinking the last of the yangxian tea in a futile attempt to extinguish the fire in his heart. Finally, he rose to his feet and walked across the street.

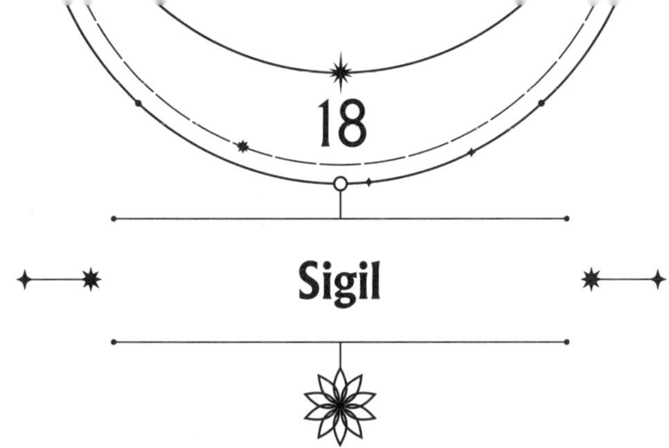

18

Sigil

OUTSIDE LUOMEI PAVILION, a low-ranked cultivator was sweeping the fallen leaves from the foxglove trees off the white jade limestone, broom rustling over the pavers.

Suddenly, a pair of black leather military boots entered his line of sight. The cultivator paused, then looked up with a smile to tactfully turn away the visitor. "Honored customer, it's not yet dark. Our pavilion opens at the hour of xu.[18] How about you return at a later—"

He was still speaking when he caught a clear glimpse of this customer's face. His eyes flew open, and he dropped the broom from pure terror.

"Xi...Xihe-jun?!" the cultivator stammered, stupefied.

Mo Xi's military uniform was neat and proper, his lapels smoothly layered, his collar meticulously arranged. He was the picture of an honorable gentleman. "I'm looking for someone," he said.

The low-ranked cultivator's jaw was about to drop to the floor.

This was Luomei Pavilion, and Xihe-jun was known for his abstinence. *He* was voluntarily coming to a brothel in search of someone? Was the sun about to rise from the west?!

Mo Xi's face was like frost, and his expression grew even more terrifying. "What are you looking at? Am I not allowed to enter?"

---

18 *7:00 to 9:00 p.m.*

"N-n-no. Come, come in." Stammering, the cultivator hastily beckoned him inside. "Who is Xihe-jun looking for?"

Mo Xi paused, then looked away. "Gu Mang," he said expressionlessly.

"Oh! So you're looking for *him*..." The cultivator at once let out a sigh of relief.

Although the idea of Xihe-jun visiting brothels was completely absurd, the idea that he was looking for Gu Mang was reasonable. Given the depth of their mutual hatred, it would be perfectly normal for Xihe-jun to vent himself on Gu Mang if his mood was poor.

Mo Xi followed the cultivator into Luomei Pavilion without a hitch. As they walked, the cultivator told Mo Xi, "Xihe-jun, Gu Mang is in that filthy shack in the back courtyard. When you go in, you should be careful of your clothes—you mustn't get them dirty."

Mo Xi knit his brows. "Why would he be in there?"

"Eh, it's a long story. Wangshu-jun punished him a while ago, right? So we had Gu Mang do hard labor in the courtyard, chopping wood and stuff like that. But a few days ago, he must have been starving, because he snuck into the dining hall in the dead of night and stole some meat buns."

"What then?"

"No one would've noticed if he'd taken one or two, but he had to be a starved ghost about it and eat four whole baskets in one go. He was still chewing with a bun in hand when the cook went to check on things. Of course the cook was displeased, so he rushed over to make him pay. But then..."

Mo Xi glanced at the cultivator's fearful face. "Did the cook try to beat him and set off the sword array?"

"Ah! Right, Xihe-jun, you've seen that array before?"

Mo Xi didn't answer, a hazy shadow flitting through the depths of his gaze. His lashes fluttered, then lowered, hiding his eyes.

"That cook went overboard with all the punching and scolding, so Gu Mang reacted violently. And when the sword array was triggered, the cook didn't have time to dodge, so he ended up cut up and covered in blood." The little cultivator rubbed the goosebumps on the back of his hands. "Aiyo, he got a few hundred wounds—so terrifying."

Mo Xi was silent for a moment. "Is he okay?" he asked.

"Perfectly fine. That sword array isn't too serious. Even though it leaves you with a lot of cuts, the wounds are shallow." He took a breath. "To speak frankly, Xihe-jun doesn't need to worry. That cook is another bastard mongrel who was captured from the Liao Kingdom. If he fights with Gu Mang, well, that's just a dogfight well deserved."

Mo Xi said nothing.

"After that, the madam was furious and locked Gu Mang in the woodshed. We used to give him a cornmeal bun every day, but the madam said we needed to be harsher. Now he only gets one bowl of porridge to let him know the taste of suffering." The cultivator hesitated. "Xihe-jun, how about I get people to bind him before bringing him to you? That array is too dangerous. The cook is still bedridden, bandaged up like a zongzi rice dumpling. He probably won't be able to get out of bed for a few months."

"No need." Mo Xi's face was impassive. "I'll look in on him myself."

Because he wasn't receiving guests while being punished, Gu Mang was staying in the most shameful little shack in Luomei Pavilion.

It was said that "a lone wolf lives in danger." Gu Mang had been molded such that he had a great degree of similarity with wild wolves—he was afraid to be alone and often muttered to himself.

This frightened the other residents of Luomei Pavilion, so they had decided to give him a black dog as a companion.

This black dog was now sitting in front of the doorway of the shack. As soon as it saw a stranger approach, it started barking like mad. Mo Xi's dagger-like gaze quelled it in an instant.

"Xihe-jun, that dog's afraid of you."

Naturally. He had killed so many people—how could a dog hope to face him? Stepping over the stone steps in his boot-clad feet, Mo Xi swept the heavy door-curtain aside in a single movement. His eyes skimmed the dark and narrow room.

Unlike the rest of the extravagantly decorated areas in the pavilion, this room was bare and spartan; it contained only a pile of firewood and a couple of broken pots.

In one dark corner, huddled like a wild beast, was Gu Mang. When he heard someone arrive, his ears twitched, and he lifted his head to look over wordlessly.

"Xihe-jun, be careful," the cultivator hurried to warn. "He's hostile with everyone right now, and he puts up a hell of a fight."

But Mo Xi didn't seem to care, nodding with pure indifference. "You may withdraw."

The cultivator hesitated. Even though Wangshu-jun said he wouldn't care if Gu Mang died, everyone knew he didn't mean it. If Gu Mang really did die, the consequences would be beyond what any of them could pay.

Given how deeply General Mo hated Gu Mang, it was possible that the general would wait until the dead of night to chop him into pieces...

"I want to be alone with him for a while," Mo Xi said.

The cultivator didn't dare say anything else before his dark expression and lowered his head. "Of course."

After the cultivator left, Mo Xi let go of the curtain. The thick and filthy cloth fell behind him, and the room was immediately cast into darkness; not a single candle was lit.

In that darkness, only Gu Mang's limpid eyes still shone.

Mo Xi frowned, suddenly noticing that something was off. What had happened to Gu Mang's eyes?

With a wave of Mo Xi's hand, a flame kindled in his palm. He held the fireball aloft and walked toward those two points of glimmering light.

Gu Mang had been locked up for five days. His mind was already somewhat unstable, to say nothing of how long it had been since he'd seen such blinding light. A low snarl rose from his throat, but when that failed to stop the interloper, he tried to flee like a wounded animal. But he was too weak; he only made it a few steps before he staggered and fell to the ground.

Mo Xi stood before Gu Mang as the firelight finally flooded over his pathetic form. Realizing that escape was hopeless, Gu Mang turned to glare at him.

Sure enough, something was wrong.

During their previous two meetings, between the hazy candlelight and his tumultuous emotions, Mo Xi hadn't actually had a good look at Gu Mang's face. Only now did he realize that Gu Mang's eyes were no longer the same as before.

The always-smiling black eyes he remembered were gone. In their place were a pair of blue irises, gleaming with motes of light in the darkness. They were indubitably the eyes of a white wolf.

Mo Xi was aware that the Liao Kingdom had carried out bestial fusion and tempering on Gu Mang. But when Mo Xi saw the lupine traits that had replaced what he once knew so well with his own eyes, his hands started to shake.

He grabbed Gu Mang's jaw and glared fiercely into those sea-blue eyes.

Who? Who was this?!

Responding to its conjurer's wrath, the flame in his other hand flared more and more violently. Its light burned nearly white, throwing Gu Mang's features into harsh relief while Mo Xi's eyes raked ruthlessly over his body.

Perhaps because this gaze was too searing, too painful, Gu Mang somehow managed to summon a burst of energy and threw off Mo Xi's hand. He staggered a few steps away.

"Stop right there!" Mo Xi snapped.

Mo Xi left the fireball to hover in midair as he clamped a hand around Gu Mang's wrist.

He had moved too aggressively. This time, Gu Mang was truly spooked, and beams of dazzling blue flashed in the dark. The array had been set off again, and dozens of intangible swords of light exploded from Gu Mang's body, each blade flipping around and rushing toward Mo Xi. Blood was about to come spurting forth.

Yet in that fleeting instant, something peculiar happened.

As soon as the sword glares touched Mo Xi, they transformed into glimmering feathers. Slowly, they drifted to the floor...

Gu Mang was immediately stupefied, but it seemed Mo Xi had already known the sword array would be useless against him. With a yank, he dragged the stunned man back toward him and caged him in his arms.

After another moment of astonishment, Gu Mang realized that he was again being restrained by someone's unyielding grip. He began to kick and struggle.

"Stay still!" Mo Xi snarled.

That voice from that close made Gu Mang jerk his head up, only to panic further. He obviously knew that the sword array was his last line of defense. For Gu Mang to lose it was like a lone wolf losing its only weapons, its teeth and claws; he was now at the mercy of others. He had not the slightest ability to resist this man, who was filled with suppressed fury.

"Don't..." Gu Mang finally spoke, shivering.

Chest heaving, Mo Xi looked down at the man in his arms and ground his teeth hatefully. "Don't *what*?"

"Don't..." Gu Mang had once lost the power of speech, and now that he was scared, he spoke slowly and shakily. "Kill me..." Bestial light flashed in those azure eyes. He pleaded so clumsily, so painstakingly. "I..." His lips parted. "I...want to live..."

Mo Xi's heart pounded. As he met those despairing eyes, the scar on his chest seemed to throb sharply.

I do *want to live! What's wrong with wanting to live with a clear conscience?! Mo Xi, do you understand me? Huh?! I can't stand to live like this! I can't bear it! My dreams are filled with the faces of dead men! I can't keep going if I'm sober! Do you know what that pain feels like? The kind that makes you want to die night and day?! You have no idea!*

Before Gu Mang fell from grace, he had once howled at Mo Xi, frantic and broken, his eyes furious as he smashed wine cups and sent blood streaming down his hands.

Mo Xi had understood his pain.

But what could he have done...? Back then, he could do nothing but let Gu Mang drunkenly cry and shout and roar. Nothing but keep him company, waiting for him to slowly recover, waiting for the scars to slowly heal.

After Gu Mang had sobered, he stopped shouting. Yet for some reason, Mo Xi always got the feeling that although Gu Mang was smiling, there was something else behind that smile—something he couldn't clearly see.

Later, the emperor sent Mo Xi away from the capital. Before he left, Gu Mang took him out drinking once more and grinned—that was when he'd said he was going to become a bad guy. At the time, Mo Xi hadn't believed it.

However, by the time he returned, Gu Mang had fallen into a stupor, intoxicated by the illusions offered by brothels until he was completely unrecognizable.

Soon after, he defected.

Gu Mang's wounds had never truly healed. In his heart, each cut lay over another, new wounds covering old scars. He wanted to live. But every day and every night, he also wanted to die. Day in and day out, damned to an eternity without reprieve.

Driven by bestial survival instinct, the blue-eyed Gu Mang whispered sadly, "I want to live..."

Mo Xi closed his eyes. "I won't do anything to you."

The person in his arms was trembling. He'd been badly starved, to the point that his cheeks were sunken and his hair hung limp. He stared at Mo Xi's face. Mo Xi let him stare for a long time, until Gu Mang's trembling came to a stop.

But as soon as Mo Xi moved his arms, Gu Mang's eyes widened once again, darting around with unease. It was like he desired to flee, but also knew that desire was hopeless.

Mo Xi said, "It's me."

Before, Mo Xi had been disappointed, hateful, conflicted, and distraught. But now that he saw Gu Mang frightened and helpless, the turmoil in his heart seemed to quieten, like a momentary pause in a torrential rainstorm. He neither grabbed and interrogated Gu Mang, nor tormented and humiliated him, as he'd imagined he would.

"Do you remember me?" Mo Xi continued after a second. Then, as if he wasn't sure why he persisted: "...It's fine if you don't remember me."

Gu Mang hadn't made a sound. Just as Mo Xi began to grow impatient, Gu Mang said, "I was your whore."

Dead silence.

"Listen up," Mo Xi said in a clipped tone, his temper flaring. "Don't say that word in front of me. I came to see you that day to discuss certain matters. Not...not to..." No matter what, *whore* was a word Mo Xi couldn't say out loud. Mo Xi looked furiously away and snapped, stiff, "Remember, it was to *discuss certain matters*."

"Discuss certain matters..." Gu Mang murmured, finally relaxing ever so slightly. Those eyes, however, remained glued to Mo Xi's face, intent on catching every hint of emotion. He slowly asked, "...But why?"

"What do you mean, *why*?"

"Why did my..." Gu Mang hadn't fully calmed down; he wasn't speaking as serenely and smoothly as he had the night they were reunited. The beatings and starvation had done their work. He could speak only haltingly, one word after another. "My swords... went away. I can't...hit you?"

Mo Xi didn't respond immediately, his expression growing darker and colder.

"Why?" asked Gu Mang again.

Why?

That day at Murong Lian's banquet, someone had lamented that despite the array's intricacies, there was no one left who understood its secrets. That man had been wrong.

On that day, at that banquet, someone in attendance had not only known all of the sword array's secrets, but also why it had been created in the first place: Mo Xi, who'd kept his silence.

Mo Xi stared at Gu Mang's face as he held him with one arm, not letting him move. But his other hand released Gu Mang's jaw and slowly slid down the side of his neck.

Rough fingers came to a stop over the lotus-shaped sigil.

As Mo Xi stared at Gu Mang in silence, caressing his neck, his eyes were very slightly red. As if in the next second, he would viciously bite down on that lotus sigil, tearing through skin and flesh and veins so that Gu Mang would die in his arms. As if that was what it would take to ensure this man never lied to him, betrayed him, or disappointed him again. Only *then* would he behave.

Perhaps because Mo Xi's expression was so fixed, his suppressed emotions so unhinged, Gu Mang grew alarmed. His eyes unfocused and his lips parted as though he were quietly murmuring something.

Mo Xi finally spoke, slow and deep. "You can stop chanting."

Gu Mang flinched.

"No matter what you try, nothing will happen."

Shocked, Gu Mang asked, "You...know?"

"I do." Mo Xi looked away from the lotus, gaze boring slowly and deeply into Gu Mang's clear blue eyes. "Outside of its trigger, if you really wanted it to appear, you could summon it if you only asked for it."

Gu Mang's face instantly paled further, his eyes widening.

Mo Xi's expression was indecipherable, as if a fathomless hatred had sunk into an equally deep fixation and trapped him there within. Gu Mang didn't know what he should do.

"But, if I don't allow it to answer, it won't." Mo Xi paused, the depths of his eyes darkening, his pale lips parting around his slow explanation. "Because it doesn't just obey you. It also obeys me—you are not its only master."

Gu Mang's face grew more and more pallid with every word

Mo Xi said, until it resembled a sheet of flimsy paper. He stared blankly at Mo Xi's face from mere inches away. "Wh-why..."

Mo Xi looked down at him, breath ragged. Despite all his efforts to conceal his emotions, the pain in his eyes could no longer be disguised. His lashes quivered as he swallowed. "Gu Mang." He closed his eyes. "Have you really forgotten everything?"

Gu Mang's eyes widened, those irises clear and blue as seawater reflecting Mo Xi's handsome face. "You... It can't defend me against... you," he muttered, bestial wariness on his face. "Why...does it obey you?"

It was unclear whether Mo Xi's expression was icy or agonized. "Of course it obeys me," he said, each word like frost.

In the stillness that followed, Mo Xi closed his eyes. When they snapped open, it was like lava finally breaking through earth, his pupils a flaming scarlet.

"Of course it obeys me," he said with barely contained fury. "Because your sigil used *my* blood, and your sigil was drawn by *my* hand, because...the one who created this array was never you—it was *me*!"

Gu Mang clearly didn't understand what Mo Xi was saying, but he could understand the anger and heartbreak on the face before him. He stared at this stranger with wide eyes.

This man's expression was unbearably complicated, as if it had accumulated more than a decade of love and hatred, suppressed more than a decade of suffering, and finally exploded with more than a decade of despair.

Mo Xi suddenly raised a hand and tore cruelly at the neat, proper layers of his own collar to expose the side of his bare and slender neck. Mo Xi's gaze was tempered with cold light and coated in icy fire. Every word came from between gritted teeth.

"Do you see it?" The light in his eyes was sharp, but it was also tearful. "This sigil, identical to yours... In your blood! By your hand! It was done for *you*..."

As Mo Xi spoke, he abruptly pushed Gu Mang away, as if he no longer wanted to touch or to look at him.

Mo Xi brought a hand to his brow, the end of his sentence caught within his throat.

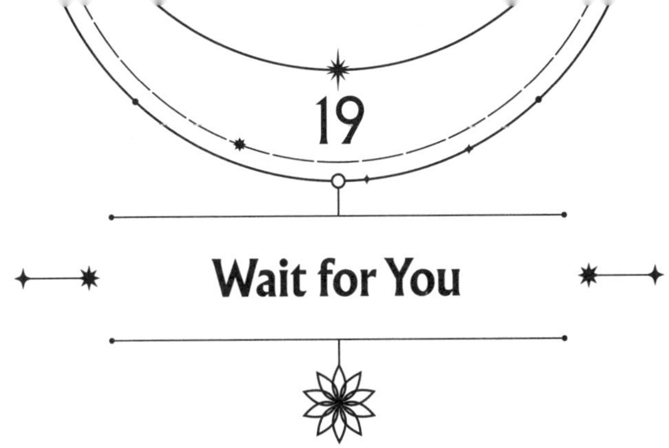

19
Wait for You

GU MANG STARED at the person pacing in front of him, hesitant and wary, lost and confused. At length, he stepped forward and cautiously touched the side of Mo Xi's neck.

Mo Xi jerked his head up, glaring at him through slightly reddened eyes. His breathing was roughened by intense emotion, his lapels gaping slightly. The lotus sigil on his neck rose and fell, throbbing vividly at the artery. While he obviously hadn't undergone demonic tempering, in his current state, he was no different from a beast.

"What are you doing?"

"I..." Gu Mang said in confusion. "But I...don't know you... Why would you have one too...?"

To Mo Xi, this question was a violent stab; his hatred and pride made him cruel. He slapped Gu Mang's hand away, snapping, "I never needed something like this. You're the one who forced me."

Gu Mang looked up at this man, who was on the verge of a breakdown. In that dim woodshed where no one else could see him, in front of Gu Mang, the grown Xihe-jun was as volatile as the youth he had once been.

"Hasn't it always been you?" Mo Xi's chest throbbed, and even the tails of his eyes were red. "It was you who provoked me, you who came to find me..."

For better. For worse.

For richer or poorer, no matter what the future held.

It was you who came to my side with a smile.

"It was you who made me believe..."

That there could be friendship unconcerned with any other pressures, that someone could be good to another person regardless of whether that good would be reciprocated.

That kindness, sincerity, and fiercely unconditional loyalty truly existed.

"It was you who pulled me back from the edge."

Mo Xi really had lost his mind. He had held back and waited for so long, waiting for this day, all to ask Gu Mang for the truth. He'd wanted nothing more than to see what, exactly, was in Gu Mang's heart...

So why had he been denied even the slightest deliverance?

He had been deceived, abandoned, and betrayed.

I like you—a lie; *I'm willing*—a lie; *I won't leave you*—a lie.

Nothing remained but these lotus tattoos on their necks, proof of the things they had shared in their past, proof of how foolish, unreserved, fearless, and unhesitating Mo Xi's sincerity had once been.

Proof that there had once been a youth who hadn't known the trap that was love.

So stupid that he wanted to dig out and offer up his own heart. So stupid that he believed all those promises could come true. So stupid... So stupid that it still hurt, even now.

These overwhelming, intense emotions rang in Mo Xi's ears, and the world swam before his eyes.

As Mo Xi looked at the Gu Mang in front of him, dizzy, his vision steadily darkened at the edges and grew blurry.

He seemed to see the youth who had once stood on the deck of a ship. So close, yet so far; so familiar, yet so unknown. Standing with his back to the sea wind, black robes draped over his shoulders, bandages wrapped around his waist, and a crooked ribbon tied over his brow. He sneered, *I really will kill you.*

Mo Xi grabbed Gu Mang and pressed him against the wall, lost between past and present. "Yes...I knew you would kill me. Haven't you already stabbed me once?" He inhaled. "Why didn't you stab me a second time at Wangshu Manor?!"

He knew he was going mad; he knew he was being absurd. But how could someone who had always rigidly controlled themselves hold back once they exploded?

All Mo Xi had wanted was a single backward glance. An answer, nothing more.

"It was you who gave me faith...and in the end, you were the reason I lost that faith... You said I didn't care about anything, that I had nothing to lose, so it didn't matter..." Mo Xi's voice softened as he choked up. "But when you stepped onto that path, do you know what I lost?!"

Do you know what I lost...? Mo Xi quickly turned aside, lowering his head. Only after recovering for several seconds did he speak again, his words clipped with hatred. "I was never the person who didn't care. It was you. I wish I could—"

He stopped.

Gu Mang had reached out, carefully and hesitantly cupping Mo Xi's face. "Don't... Don't be so sad," he said.

Mo Xi whipped around, meeting those limpid blue eyes that looked like they had been washed with seawater. "I don't know what you're talking about."

"But can you...not be so sad?" Gu Mang said slowly and with difficulty, pausing clumsily on each word. "Don't be sad."

It was as if a molten sword had been plunged into water. Steam hissed as the water boiled, but that crazed heat was instantly quenched. Mo Xi's blood gradually cooled, and reason seeped back in.

Gu Mang gazed at him. "You're not a bad person..." he said slowly, cautiously, lashes trembling. "I don't know you, but you're...not bad... So...don't be sad..."

Mo Xi felt profoundly unwell. Hatred, frustration, ire, and something else he couldn't place—all of it coursed through his heart. He looked at Gu Mang's familiar features, and at those unfamiliar blue eyes.

This same man had once gazed at him with deep black eyes, smiling, and called to him.

Mo Xi. It's fine, don't be sad.

No matter what, we'll always be together. No matter how hard things get, I'll pull through.

Come on, let's go home.

Mo Xi was suddenly overcome with exhaustion. He closed his eyes, near drained, like a dying eagle using the last of its energy to feign strength. "I'm not sad."

It was obvious that Mo Xi hated Gu Mang deeply, hated that he couldn't choke him to death with his own hands—see if he could keep escaping, keep lying, keep leaving him then. Hated that he couldn't watch with his own eyes as Gu Mang's skull shattered and his blood sprayed out, at last bringing an end to all this hope and despair.

Instead, as Gu Mang carefully tried to console him, as Gu Mang asked him not to be sad, Mo Xi found himself thinking of a scene from many, many years ago, when Gu Mang had sat by a blood-splattered trench and summoned his ridiculous little holy weapon—the suona that, after defecting, he had never used again—and played a truly maddening tune.

It had been such a crappy song. Everyone who heard it had covered their ears and cursed, demanding to know what the hell he was playing—was he a wailer at a funeral? Gu Mang had merely flung his head back and laughed, then continued to puff out his cheeks and play "Phoenix Homage."[19] He had played so soulfully, so seriously.

But when Mo Xi had glanced at Gu Mang out of the corner of his eye, he'd seen that his eyes were wet.

Gu Mang cared. He had lied and dissembled for so many years, but Mo Xi knew he cared. So Mo Xi wanted to believe him—to believe that those things in their past weren't all lies.

For this possibility, he was willing to wait.

"Never mind," Mo Xi said after a time. "If you can't remember, then never mind." And finally, in a choked tone, "I misspoke."

After another interval, Mo Xi stood up and carefully fixed his collar, smoothing every last wrinkle to hide that lotus tattoo on his neck. "No matter if you've really forgotten or if you're pretending, I'll wait. I'll wait for a conclusion. I'll wait for you to tell me the truth."

The rims of his eyes and the tip of his nose were yet red.

"You'll...wait for me...?" Gu Mang asked blankly.

"Yes, I'll wait for you. No matter what, I'll wait for you. I'll keep waiting, no matter how long it takes. But remember this: If you lie to me again—if I find out you're still lying to me—I won't be stabbed in the same place twice. I *will* make you live a life worse than death."

It was very quiet in the shed.

Gu Mang lowered his head to think for a while before he spoke again, confused. "What's...a life worse than death?"

---

19 *A cheerful folk piece by Wei Ziyou.*

That bewildered and innocent tone drew Mo Xi's wintry stare, but with the red wetness lingering at the corners of his eyes, his glare seemed less sharp than usual.

Gu Mang felt that gaze and looked up at him. He knew this man had broken his sword array and stripped him of his sharp claws; yet unlike all the others, he hadn't bitten through Gu Mang's neck or degraded him. So he asked, cautiously, "Does a life worse than death...mean...you'll spare me?"

Silence. "No."

"But you didn't kill or beat me."

"I don't beat imbeciles."

Gu Mang didn't say anything, but continued to look at him. Then he moved closer, sniffing.

Mo Xi held a palm up to the tip of Gu Mang's nose to stop him. "What are you doing?"

Gu Mang licked his dry lips. "Remembering you," he said softly.

Remembering him? Remembering what? His face? His scent? Or that he was someone who didn't beat imbeciles?

But Gu Mang didn't explain. He'd more or less lowered his guard—or perhaps it was less that he wanted to lower it and more that his long starvation had stripped him of his strength. He no longer cared about Mo Xi. In any case, the sharp fangs that were his last remaining defenses were useless against this opponent.

Gu Mang slowly ducked his head and curled up in his corner. Those lupine eyes glimmered in the darkness and blinked tiredly. "Thank you," he said. "You're the only one willing to give me a life worse than death."

These words fell to the bottom of Mo Xi's heart; caught off guard, his chest ached. He stood there for a while, looking around the dilapidated little shack, looking at the little mattress with its exposed cotton stuffing and the silhouette curled up in the corner.

Mo Xi closed his eyes tightly, long lashes fluttering.

In the end, he left and got some flatbread and hot soup. He held them out to this man who was on the verge of starvation. "Eat."

Gu Mang quickly came over to sniff the food. He swallowed thickly at the scent before hesitating. "But you didn't bed—"

The moment he said the word *bed*, Mo Xi's expression turned furious, and he wordlessly smacked a flatbread right onto Gu Mang's face.

When Mo Xi returned to his manor, it was already the dead of night.

"My lord, you're back—ah! What happened to you?"

"I'm fine."

"But why are your eyes..." *Red?*

"Flying sand." Mo Xi turned his back on Li Wei and walked to his bedroom without looking back.

He'd spent hours at Luomei Pavilion, but he wasn't remotely sleepy. After tossing and turning in bed to no avail, he draped a black fur coat over his shoulders and stood in the courtyard cloister, looking at the moonlight from the hall. Gu Mang's sickly face was still flashing before his eyes, impossible to escape.

Was his mind actually broken...? When the Liao Kingdom sent him back, had it really been for peace talks, or did they have some other motive?

Mo Xi racked his brain, trying to piece everything together, but no matter how he tried, his train of thought still stopped on those lupine blue eyes.

Thank you. You're the only one willing to give me a life worse than death.

Mo Xi closed his eyes.

It was a long time before he went to Luomei Pavilion to see Gu Mang again.

Firstly, his work started to pile up, and secondly, Luomei Pavilion remained Murong Lian's territory. It would be unwise to go there often.

Only once, when Mo Xi was leading imperial guards on patrol within the city, did he glance at Luomei Pavilion's courtyard. Gu Mang was once again squatting there, looking at the fish, that dirty black dog at his side. Everything was as it had been.

In the blink of an eye, the end of the month arrived. Outside the Bureau of Military Affairs, the first heavy snow of the year fell.

It was an unnaturally cold evening, and most of the members of the bureau had left early to enjoy their time at home. Some young cultivators had taken the opportunity to go back to the city to drink and feast before nightfall.

Mo Xi was preparing to return to his own manor when he heard a timid voice speak in front of his desk. "Xihe-jun, may I… May I ask a favor?"

20 Gu Mang Goes Berserk

THE WOMAN STANDING before him was a very low-ranked cultivator of the Bureau, roughly forty years old and usually the quiet sort.

Somewhat surprised, Mo Xi asked, "What is it?"

"I... I got a message from the academy a moment ago, saying that Changfeng-jun's daughter hit my daughter and injured her. I'm worried and want to go check on her, but I still have a number of files left to sort..." As she spoke, she couldn't hide the embarrassment and anxiety on her face. "I-I've asked many of my colleagues already, but they're all busy. Even Yue-gongzi has plans to go drink at the eastern market with his friends... So I wanted to...see if I could trouble you..."

Mo Xi frowned slightly. He wouldn't mind helping her—but this Changfeng-jun, who had laid low for many years, seemed to be popping up a little too often these days. "Is she badly hurt?"

"They said it was a sprained arm," the cultivator said. "Even though it's not serious, she's been crying nonstop. The elders don't know what to do."

"Then you may go. Be careful on the road."

The cultivator hadn't placed particularly high hopes on this icy commander. She certainly hadn't expected that after asking so many people, the one to help her would be him. She couldn't help but widen her eyes, and a joyous flush appeared on her face.

"Many thanks to Xihe-jun. The baskets for the files are a-all over there..." As she grew excited, she began stammering. "I-I've already sorted most of them. I'm terribly sorry about inconveniencing you with something so trivial..."

"It's no bother. Your daughter comes first."

The cultivator thanked him a few more times before rushing off, leaving Mo Xi by himself in the Bureau of Military Affairs to organize those old scrolls.

Mo Xi was high-ranking and powerful, so he never bothered with trivial tasks like these. Only after he began did he find that it wasn't so easy. There were many files, all of which needed to be organized by year and level. The important ones had to be sealed with a talisman, while the useless ones were to be destroyed. Finding himself a novice at this task, he worked very slowly. By the time the files were mostly sorted, it was already quite late.

One last box remained. The dusty chest held the records of a past bureau cultivator. When Mo Xi glanced at it, he saw a familiar name on the side. He stood still for a moment, his eyes downcast, but he couldn't resist taking out Gu Mang's file. He brushed away the accumulated dust and spread out the pages with care.

A great deal of information was contained within: Gu Mang's family background, slave registry, holy weapon, and favored methods of attack.

Mo Xi read it over, flipping page after page as he stood there unmoving, until he had finished the whole stack from beginning to end. A sheet of silk-paper fell out from the rest of the files.

The yellowed silk was emblazoned with the dignified words, *Cultivation Academy Ethics Examination, Thirty-Third Year.*

Mo Xi was stunned. Was this Gu Mang's final exam from the cultivation academy?

Sure enough, he looked farther down and saw that familiar handwriting, wretchedly messy. The contents rendered Mo Xi speechless.

CULTIVATION ACADEMY ETHICS EXAMINATION, THIRTY-THIRD YEAR

ANSWERING CULTIVATOR: Gu Mang

Q: "One ought to reflect upon oneself every day."[20] The disciple is asked to reflect upon their deficiencies and answer honestly.

A: Personally, I have a money deficiency.

Q: When cultivators of Chonghua exorcise demons, what three things must they avoid? How should they be avoided?

A: One, beware a client who lacks money. Two, beware a client who runs away. Three, beware a client who's running away with the money. How to avoid: It's best to demand a deposit before getting rid of the demons. Never work on credit.

Q: Please list the three kindest and most benevolent elders Chonghua has known since its founding.

A: No idea. But the three most shameless are—

An enraged examiner had burned three holes into whatever followed, so Mo Xi would never learn exactly what names Gu Mang had written.

Mo Xi examined that answer sheet, seeing youth in every brushstroke. He was both amused and depressed, and he stared at it in a daze for a long while, until a clamor rose outside.

"No!"

"Help! Something's happened at Luomei Pavilion!"

Luomei Pavilion? Mo Xi was alarmed. *Gu Mang?!*

The commotion was sudden, and by the time he rushed outside, only two dozen soldiers on night patrol had yet arrived. They had

---

20 *A quote from the first book of* The Analects of Confucius.

arranged themselves into a demon-hunting formation and were now staring at Luomei Pavilion's main gate, which was on the verge of crumbling. The soldiers were covered in cuts and bruises, and the limestone beneath their feet had been crushed to rubble. The surrounding streets fared no better; a number of shops had collapsed, their tiles and bricks scattered and their splintered wood smoking.

The cultivator at the formation's head shouted when he spied Mo Xi. "General Mo!"

"What happened?"

"It's Gu Mang! A burst of extraordinarily potent malevolent qi exploded from his body. He's gone berserk!"

"Where is he?"

"We only injured him. He's gone and hidden within Luomei Pavilion. He doesn't dare rush out to fight again, but neither do we. We're waiting for reinforcements!"

Mo Xi looked toward the creaking gate. Just as he'd been told, a figure was standing in the shadows, eyes glowing faintly in the darkness.

Gu Mang was clearly watching every movement on the street outside.

Mo Xi stared at those lupine eyes. "Isn't his spiritual core shattered?" he asked. "How could he suddenly lash out like this?"

"We don't know!" The head cultivator looked like he was about to cry. "His martial abilities make no damn sense. Ah, we'd be so much better off if we'd chopped off his head at the start instead of letting him bide his time in Luomei Pavilion!"

"He has to be faking it!" another cultivator said angrily. "How could his core be broken, his mind damaged? Did that man we saw seem weak and helpless to you?"

"Exactly! If he really doesn't have spiritual energy, then who gave me this cut on my face?"

"Why did His Imperial Majesty let this dog live?!"

They were still voicing their impassioned objections when they heard the thunder of approaching hoofbeats. Mo Xi turned to see a procession of twelve elite mounted cultivators galloping through the light snow, escorting a carriage engraved in gold.

"Wangshu-jun has arrived!"

The curtain in the gilded carriage was pushed aside as servants prepared a stepping stool, gauze umbrella, and incense burner. Only after a lengthy stretch did a thin, sickly face drift out from within.

"Ooh, how lively." Murong Lian noticed Mo Xi at once. "Xihe-jun's here too."

Mo Xi didn't plan to waste more breath than necessary on him. "Something's happened to Gu Mang."

Murong Lian scoffed. "I am, of course, aware. That's exactly why I've come."

As he spoke, he took a few deliberate steps forward and came to a stop near the red lacquer door of the pavilion. He soundlessly recited an incantation, and blue light blazed from his left hand. "Go. Seize the beast."

Under his command, the blue light transformed into chains and shot toward the door. The door, fully five inches thick, was pierced straight through and fell with a thunderous *boom*. Gu Mang was caught unawares in his hiding spot behind the door and was instantly immobilized by the chains of blue light.

"Return," Murong Lian shouted.

The chains tightened mercilessly. Gu Mang crumpled to his knees amid the sound of clanking metal and was swiftly dragged before Murong Lian.

"No more than a mad dog getting up to no good." A satin slipper embroidered with lunar patterns stretched out and stepped on

Gu Mang's face. "What need is there for General Mo now?" Murong Lian asked lightly.

Gu Mang's eyes were frantic as he struggled against his bonds; his entire body overflowed with spiritual energy, and his teeth gnashed. "Let go—of me..."

"Let go of you?" Murong Lian curled his lip. "Since when do you give me orders?" As he spoke, he tightened his fist. The chains retracted into his hand with a clank, dragging Gu Mang up from the ground as well. Murong Lian grabbed his hair, forcing Gu Mang to look at him.

Two unnaturally pale faces met, their noses almost brushing.

"I am the master, and you are the slave," Murong Lian said. "General Gu, why has a month of starvation still not taught you your lesson?"

"Let go..." Gu Mang choked.

A nearly crazed look flashed across Murong Lian's elegant face. Just as he was about to speak, he saw Gu Mang narrow his eyes. Murong Lian's heart pounded; reacting with a cultivator's instinctive wariness, he immediately released Gu Mang and retreated.

At almost the same time, the brilliant sword array exploded once more from Gu Mang's body. The array this time was far more stunning than before. Every sword of light was taller than a man. The one closest to Murong Lian swiftly broke free from the array and flew directly toward Murong Lian's heart.

"My lord, be careful!"

"Wangshu-jun, watch out!"

The attendants shouted in shock. But though Murong Lian's martial arts were poor, he was vigilant. He flung up a hand, and a wall of ice appeared in front of him. The sword hit the wall, shattering the ice into powdery crystals as Murong Lian ducked to the side.

It was enough to dampen the force of the blow—the sword of light tore a hole in his robe rather than his flesh.

Murong Lian landed on the ground, staring at Gu Mang.

Gu Mang was panting as he yanked Murong Lian's chains off his neck and tossed them rattling to the ground. Then he raised his head, swallowing as his hands curled into fists. A torrential, unceasing flow of spiritual energy burst from beneath his feet, so powerful that the weaker cultivators in the formation at once collapsed to their knees, coughing blood.

The head cultivator paled. "He's about to go berserk again! Hurry—stop him! Back in formation! Prepare to fight!"

But the spiritual energy surrounding Gu Mang was already too great. Not only were the cultivators physically unable to approach, their spells couldn't breach the defense put up by those swords of light.

Just as Gu Mang was about to lose control again, a glowing blue talisman appeared in Murong Lian's hand. He tossed it out with a cry: "Water Demon, rise!"

A chill wind blew, and the shapes of over a dozen blue demons crawled up from the ground, screaming as they rushed Gu Mang's sword array. One water demon was sliced to shreds by the swords of light only to be replaced by another, surging forth one after the next without end. In this way, though they struggled mightily, they steadily pressed near to Gu Mang.

"Take him down!" Murong Lian shouted sharply.

The water demons rose with a shriek, sweeping up wind and snow as they sped toward Gu Mang. Yet with a single gesture, Gu Mang sent a sword glare exploding from his fingertips that demolished a dozen of the apparitions at once.

He lifted his head, those blue eyes staring menacingly at Murong Lian. Then he pelted toward him through the falling snow.

Shocked, Murong Lian instinctively took half a step backward. "What are you doing?!" he demanded.

Gu Mang didn't answer—but the electric-blue phantom image of a lone wolf suddenly soared up from his back.

At the sight of that wolf, Mo Xi roared, "Murong Lian, get back!"

Murong Lian wished to do just that, but a malevolent qi he had never felt before was pinning him in place, rendering him immobile. Gu Mang came ever closer, step by step through the snow. As Murong Lian stared at him, he found himself thinking that Gu Mang was like a wolf king about to deal a killing blow. His hair stood on end before that aura of brutal cold.

"Gu Mang! How dare you! What do you think you're doing?! How dare you!"

Of course Gu Mang dared. He lifted a hand, and several blazing fireballs ignited in his palm to hurtle straight at Murong Lian.

A series of explosions rocked the street as each fireball smashed deep holes into the earth. Broken bricks went flying, leaving the cultivators no choice but to ride the winds and dart into the air to escape his attack.

Murong Lian's expression became even more sinister. His face, ordinarily so pallid and sickly from his dependence on ephemera, flushed with a faint but furious red. He stood in midair, jaw clenched. "You unrepentant bastard..."

Gu Mang reacted to exactly none of Murong Lian's words. With a wave of his hand, flames appeared at all five of his fingertips. "I hit you the first time because you stepped on my head."

Murong Lian stared.

"I'm hitting you now...because I'm hungry."

"Because you're *what*?" Murong Lian asked incredulously.

"You didn't let me eat," Gu Mang said slowly, each word sonorous. "I. Am. *Hungry!*"

Flames blazed to life as Gu Mang waved a hand to cast a spell. Murong Lian's pupils shrank.

In that critical moment, faster than anyone could speak, a sandy barrier burst up from the soil of the road. The ensuing wind bowled Murong Lian over as the barrier blocked the onslaught of Gu Mang's fire.

Murong Lian crawled pathetically upright and coughed, ferociously wiping at the dust on his face. He turned to see Mo Xi standing nearby, controlling the protective barrier.

Murong Lian stared at him and brushed the dirt from his clothes. "You knocked me over on purpose?" he snarled.

"Get behind me. You're no match for him."

Murong Lian's thin lips parted. He was about to reply when he heard an ominous crack—that thick protective wall was crumbling. Amid the falling dirt and sand, a dagger wreathed in black mist broke through the final translucent edge of the barrier and shot directly toward Murong Lian.

That dagger.

Mo Xi's blood ran cold.

That was...that was the same demonic weapon Gu Mang had summoned on that Dongting warship—the Liao Kingdom dagger he'd shoved between Mo Xi's ribs.

But demonic weapons and holy weapons had a crucial similarity: they both required an incantation to be summoned. Gu Mang had lost his memories, so he should also have lost the ability to summon this vicious blade; and besides, his spiritual core had been destroyed. So how—?!

Mo Xi had no time to finish the thought. The dagger struck through his barrier like lightning.

But Mo Xi knew Gu Mang's maneuvers. He turned to shout at Murong Lian, "Duck left!"

Startled, Murong Lian hesitated. That dagger was aimed at his left, so all sense told him to dodge right. Why was Mo Xi telling him to go *left*?

The momentary hesitation cost him his chance. That dagger was indeed shooting toward his left, but at the last second, it streaked right like a cunning snake. In the instant before the dagger pierced Murong Lian's flesh, Mo Xi darted forward and shoved him out of the way.

The dagger sank into his abdomen. Blood spurted into the air.

The crowd paled.

"Xihe-jun!"

"Xihe-jun, are you all right?!"

Mo Xi couldn't hear any of their words. He panted, his hand landing on the dagger's hilt. He yanked it out in one powerful tug, and scarlet splattered onto the ground.

Mo Xi stared into the distance, eyes dark. Amid the flying sand and falling stones, Gu Mang still emanated powerful spiritual energy. Between Gu Mang's bloodthirsty expression and the blade dripping in his hand, a wind from many years ago seemed to blow once more into Mo Xi's ears.

Back then, Gu Mang had told him—

As a general, as a soldier, and as a person, you can't be too attached to past affections.

We were brothers once—this is the last thing I can teach you.

Mo Xi suddenly couldn't hold back his desire to laugh. In the end, his hatred had only deepened. *Ha ha ha!* He'd already risked death at Gu Mang's hand—what was this petty wound compared to that?! Mo Xi gritted his teeth and straightened to his full height. Seething crimson poured from his palms as he stalked toward Gu Mang.

Gu Mang surely sensed the malice rising off him. As Mo Xi drew near, the spiritual energy swirling around Gu Mang exploded once more. But Mo Xi merely brushed away Gu Mang's array of light with a wave of his palm, shattering it with a crash.

The cultivators fighting at his side were astonished.

"Ah! Th-that's beyond terrifying..."

"The Mo Clan bloodline is genuinely insane..."

One of them even started mumbling, "If Xihe-jun's such a good fighter, how did Gu Mang ever manage to stab him through the heart?"

Murong Lian couldn't help but narrow his eyes when he heard that last. He watched the two men face each other with matched hostility, his gaze calculating.

Gu Mang made to attack again, but before he could form another sigil, he heard Mo Xi snap, "Shuairan! Come!"

A crimson snake whip shrieked through the air to answer his call.

Mo Xi's brow creased, his expression predatory. "Gu Mang!" he shouted. "Did you really think I would never raise a hand to you?!"

As Mo Xi's voice rang out, Shuairan shot toward Gu Mang like lightning in a gale. The snake whip tore through the snow, sending sparks in all directions as it struck down without mercy. Gu Mang couldn't dodge in time. The lash bit into his shoulder and drew blood at first touch.

Gu Mang's violence-addled mind seemed to clear at the sight of his injury. He shook his head and involuntarily took a step back.

"Stop right there! Where could you possibly run?" a hoarse voice rasped, and Shuairan thoroughly bound Gu Mang. Mo Xi took his palm off his own wound and wrapped his bloodied fingers around Gu Mang's neck. "Your mind isn't broken at all!" Mo Xi said furiously. "You can still summon that demonic weapon! You remember its incantation, and you fight like you used to—you clearly remember everything!"

Choking, Gu Mang couldn't answer. His pale face gradually flushed red, his fingers scrabbling for purchase on Mo Xi's hand.

Mo Xi ground his teeth. "Speak! Why did you come back to Chonghua?!"

Gu Mang lifted his arms, hands trembling as he covered the fingers Mo Xi had wrapped around his neck. Blue eyes met black. Those black eyes held endless flames, but the blue were wet. Gu Mang couldn't breathe. It was as if he would be strangled to death just like this. "I..."

Mo Xi was infuriated. "Speak!"

The cultivators surrounding them were too terrified to cut in, fear written clear across their faces.

At that moment, the pounding of hoofbeats sounded in the street. "Xihe-jun! Have mercy!" someone cried. "Whoa!"

A palace official had rushed onto the scene. She reined in her spirit horse and leapt off its back to kneel in the snow, her breath fogging white in the freezing air.

"Xihe-jun, please have mercy!" She performed obeisance to both Mo Xi and Murong Lian. "Wangshu-jun, Xihe-jun, His Imperial Majesty has learned of this matter and sent this subordinate to arrest the criminal Gu Mang!"

At that moment, Mo Xi was blind and deaf to any and everything around him. It was thus Murong Lian who turned to ask, "What do you mean? Where would you take him?"

"Wangshu-jun, His Imperial Majesty has ordered me to take Gu Mang to the palace. Upon hearing of this incident, His Imperial

Majesty summoned the best doctors in the nation. Right now, they're waiting in the palace to once again examine Gu Mang."

She glanced at Mo Xi's hand, wrapped around Gu Mang's neck, and hastily added, "This matter is of grave importance. You must not execute him without the emperor's leave!"

21

Have Mercy

Mo Xi didn't spare her a glance. He continued to stare murderously into Gu Mang's eyes.

The official knew Mo Xi's temper was fierce and that he was unpredictably impulsive, so she didn't hold back a cry of warning. "Xihe-jun!"

Still, Mo Xi said nothing, as if he was enduring something with all his might. Only after several long moments did he loosen his grip, letting Gu Mang fall to his knees in the snow. He turned to look at the windblown flurries, and his vision gradually blurred.

The official let out a breath of relief and made obeisance once more. "Many thanks for Xihe-jun's understanding."

Mo Xi stood quiet in the heavy snow, his back to the crowd and his hands clasped behind him.

But as the official moved to help Gu Mang up from where he had fallen in the snow, Mo Xi turned his face, his voice low and muted. "Hold it."

"What is Xihe-jun's command?"

"I will go as well," Mo Xi said.

Startled, the official replied, "Powerful cultivators cannot be present in numbers during Shennong Terrace's examination in case of fluctuations in the flow of spiritual energy. Even if you come, you'll have to wait outside the hall..."

"Very well." Mo Xi still hadn't turned. His tone was terrifyingly stiff, each syllable bitten out. "Then I will wait outside!"

Any further attempt to attempt to dissuade him would have been inappropriate for someone of her station. Thus the official took Gu Mang back toward the palace of Chonghua, Mo Xi following in their wake.

Approximately two hours later, snowy owls were sent out from the palace, urgently summoning every important official to come forth and confer.

It was the dead of night, and this imperial order had pulled almost every high-ranking member of the court from their beds. Elder Yu of Chengtian Terrace had the worst luck: this asshole just so happened to be enjoying the pleasures of a brothel in the northern quarter of the city, and right at the crucial moment, a fat bird crashed through the window-screen.

"Hoot! An order from His Imperial Majesty! An order from His Imperial Majesty!" it shrieked. "Every high-ranked official is requested to come to the throne room at once to discuss Gu Mang's case!"

Elder Yu promptly wilted. "Wasn't his case dealt with ages ago?!" he cursed as he dressed. "How has something come up all of a sudden?!"

"Aiya, Your Excellency, don't be upset." A woman clad in scanty and sensual garb rose from the bed to help him dress. "If His Imperial Majesty has sent an urgent summons, he must have his reasons."

"Reasons, my ass! It's so late—he doesn't give us a moment's rest!"

The woman pressed supple fingers to the elder's lips as she smiled wearily. "Your Excellency shouldn't say such things. The walls have ears."

"What do I have to be scared of? I'm only saying these things to you." Elder Yu rolled his eyes. "The current emperor does what he wants when he wants. This isn't the first time he's hauled us out in the dead of night. He's young and vigorous but doesn't stop to think about our old bones. We can't handle this kind of excitement!"

"Your Excellency, what are you saying?" the woman gently scolded. "You're always so fierce with me—it's more than I can take. Hee hee, if your bones are old, what does that make mine?"

These words couldn't have been any more insincere—Elder Yu had quite obviously just withered. But he ate her words up, chuckling as he pinched her powdered cheek and kissed her nape once more. "I'm off," he said. "Little darling, I'll come see you again tomorrow."

The woman giggled girlishly and saw him out, naturally making a great show of being unwilling to let him go. The moment the door closed, however, her face fell. "Old trash," she spat. "Can't get it up and looks like a damn toad that's taken a dung bath. I sure as hell wouldn't be serving you if you weren't so rich."

She moved briskly behind a screen to bathe herself and change into clean clothes, then sat at the dressing table to redo her makeup.

The woman had been at this brothel for many years and had long since left her youthful beauty behind, but she was good in bed and willing to put up with a great deal. She always did her best to serve her clients no matter how revolting she found them, never letting her honorable guests see any trace of her discomfort. That was why a number of older customers who were getting on in years still flocked to her.

Those younger maidens are so fickle. They don't say anything, but you can see it in their eyes. You're the best, Yu-niang, honest and sincere.

Anytime Elder Yu and his ilk said such things to her, she was secretly cackling.

Yu-niang was neither honest nor sincere. After working in this kind of place for more than a decade, her face had become caked with thick makeup that she could never take off, and she had developed and refined her skills to perfection. With each arched brow and smiling glance, she concealed every hint of her true feelings, even when she was about to die from disgust.

How else could she compete with those tender, supple young bodies?

Yu-niang faced the bronze mirror and carefully traced over the lips that Elder Yu had kissed of their color. She picked up a lip paper and pursed her lips over the small sheet of dark crimson silk as she sat to wait for her second client of the night to push open the door.

She didn't wait long before the rosewood door creaked open.

Yu-niang hastily pasted on her warmest expression, smiling as she looked up to greet her guest. "Gongzi, you..." When she laid eyes on the newcomer's face, she seemed to lose her voice. After a few beats of silence, her vermilion lips parted around a terrible scream.

The man at her door was soaked in blood.

This man was covered in bandages, and his eyes were thoroughly bloodshot. Scarlet drenched his hands, and a sticky eyeball was impaled on a finger of his left hand. He glanced at her. "Don't scream," he rasped.

Then he slowly walked in, lifted his hand to stuff the eyeball into his mouth, and chewed a little before swallowing.

It seemed that for him, eating an eyeball was akin to imbibing a holy medicine: an expression of bliss suffused his face. He licked his lips and slowly turned to look at Yu-niang.

"Get me a pot of tea," he said. When Yu-niang made no move, his tone grew impatient. "Go get me a pot of tea!"

Tea? What tea?

Scared out of her wits, Yu-niang slid from the embroidered bench with a thump, her body convulsing uncontrollably. She wanted to get back up, but her hands and feet were ice-cold, completely unresponsive, incapable of aught but quaking.

She shook for a spell, then let out a mad, bloodcurdling scream and staggered toward the door. "Help! Help me—there's a ghost... A ghost!"

Elder Yu had just left, and as she thought of him now, he really did seem tall, mighty, and fierce. She began to shriek hysterically. "Elder! *Elder Yu!*"

Yu-niang burst through the door with a crash, stumbling as she tried to run out.

Strangely, the eyeball-eating man didn't move a mote, as if he didn't care where she ran off to. Bloodstained lips parted to reveal a mouth of flashing teeth, and he leered cruelly.

"Elder—! *Ahhhh!*"

Yu-niang reached the stairway. When she saw the scene below, her legs gave out. She collapsed heavily, without the strength to rise.

At some point, the entire first floor...all the way to the wooden stairs...had been...covered in corpses...

The only exception was the center of the brothel's hall, where a handful of prostitutes huddled together, terrified out of their wits, their pretty faces awash in tears.

An important official—Elder Yu of Chengtian Terrace—lay dead on one of the tables, two bloody holes where his eyes had once been.

Yu-niang shook her head again and again. "No...no..."

Why hadn't the imperial guards noticed such a terrible event? Why—why hadn't Yu-niang heard any screaming, when she had been only a wall away?

A leisurely voice spoke from behind her, as if its owner had read her mind. "It's not like the nation of Chonghua is the only one with secret techniques. If I don't want anyone to hear me, I have no shortage of methods to employ."

Footsteps echoed.

The man wrapped in bandages stepped out from the shadows, holding a teapot patterned with peonies. Tilting his head back, he poured a good half of it down his throat. He gurgled and swallowed, then carelessly tossed the pot away.

It crashed to the floor and shattered.

"You don't need to be afraid. I won't kill you yet." The man stepped forward and grabbed Yu-niang's hair, yanking her down the wooden stairs to throw her toward the other lucky survivors. Then he pulled up a chair, unhurried, sat down in front of them, and looked them over one by one through bloodshot eyes.

After a long interval, he said, "I want all of you to look at each other's faces. I'll give you an incense time."

With that, he waved a hand from where he sat, and the brothel's doors slammed shut. With another wave, three of the corpses rose from the ground, including Elder Yu's. They limped, stooped and unsteady, toward the middle of the hall.

Among the women, Yu-niang was the only one who could still speak. It seemed the others were so frightened that their souls had fled their bodies. "Wh-what...what...do you..."

"You mean to ask, what do I want with you?" The man spoke for her, then laughed derisively. "Didn't I already say it? I'm giving you an incense time to look at each other's faces."

"But then, then...what?"

"Then what?" The man carelessly stroked his chin, taking a moment to think. It was as if this extremely simple question had stumped him.

At this point, the three corpses had drawn near the women, and the eyeless Elder Yu reached out to take Yu-niang's arm.

"No!" Yu-niang screamed in terror. "Don't touch me! *Don't touch me!*"

"He's scaring you?" the man asked lazily, turning to look at Elder Yu. "Old geezer, you're dead already. How come you haven't stopped groping people?"

Elder Yu looked up and emitted a gurgling noise, as if he were piteously trying to explain something to the man.

The man snorted twice. With a wave of his hand, a burst of black qi swept out to strike Elder Yu in the forehead. The old man went limp and fell to the floor, spasming and convulsing before ultimately melting into a puddle of gore.

"So much babble, so annoying."

The other two corpses seemed to sense something in this; their footsteps became even stiffer, their movements more cautious. In the end, they slowly dragged six chairs over and carefully placed them next to the brothel girls before bowing.

"Please, take a seat," the man said. If it weren't for the fact that he was covered in blood and had just orchestrated this entire evil scene, his tone could have been considered courteous. "What, do you need a hand?"

Though the girls were terrified out of their wits, they could hear what he said—yet they seemed to be frozen. Only after a long while did they muster the strength to clamber upright, shaking with fear. Each of them sat on a chair, unwilling to let either the bandaged man or those two corpses touch them.

"Wh-who...are you?" Yu-niang said, choking up.

"No need to be hasty," the man said. "Once you do as I say and answer a few of my questions, I'll let you know, of course." He thought for a moment. "Oh, right. As a reminder—don't go hoping anyone will come rescue you. I've cast a barrier on the door. No one will find out about this anytime soon."

He slowly turned his head, gazing toward the tightly closed brothel doors. He licked his lips, the red in his eyes deepening, and laughed. "Shall we get started?"

Perhaps Luomei Pavilion had drawn away the imperial guard's attention, or perhaps the bandaged man's secret techniques were as powerful as he claimed. For the time being, just as he said, not a soul knew what was happening in the north quarter of the city.

Chonghua's imperial capital was yet peaceful.

High-level cultivators, each the occupant of a key ministry position, arrived on the imperial steps one after another. Mo Xi had already been waiting outside the throne room for a long time; once Murong Lian arrived, he refused to stand anywhere else, insisting on the spot right next to Mo Xi.

In the wind and snow, Mo Xi's side profile seemed even sharper and more grave. Murong Lian glanced at him, then looked forward again.

"Xihe-jun, have you really waited in this heavy snow all this time?" he murmured mockingly.

Mo Xi made no sound, quietly letting the snow blanket his shoulders. Murong Lian watched for a while, but when it was clear Mo Xi had no plans to respond, he spoke again.

"On that note, let me ask you something: when you lost your temper outside Luomei Pavilion, was it because you realized Gu Mang's mind might not really be damaged?"

Mo Xi closed his eyes, a faint darkness creeping over his face.

But Murong Lian had no tact. He continued without reservation, "Would you really have choked him to death if no one had intervened? From what I know about you, I doubt it."

Mo Xi remained silent.

"The two of you—"

Finally, Mo Xi wheeled around and snapped, "Murong Lian, are you *done*?!"

The snowy night was still, the atmosphere outside the hall solemn. Xihe-jun's outburst frightened every cultivator on the scene. They craned their necks to peer toward the source.

Murong Lian's pride had been dented, and his face flashed green, then pale, in bursts. Right as he opened his mouth to say something, the red lacquer doors opened, and a messenger official emerged to perform obeisance to these important officials.

"Honored shenjun, His Imperial Majesty invites you in."

Murong Lian ground his teeth. "You! Just you wait!" he snarled.

Mo Xi swept furiously forward, the dagger at his waist flashing as he left Murong Lian behind.

22

Fighting Over Him

THE GREAT HALL was filled with candlelight, and the stout coal brazier within burned merrily. Flanking the brazier were a pair of auspicious beast statues that had been enchanted to move. One functioned as a bellows, opening its mouth to shout, "His Imperial Majesty awes the Nine Provinces!" as it made the fire blaze more brightly. The other shouted, "His Imperial Majesty's fortune floods the heavens!" as it opened its mouth wide to inhale the rising smoke into its belly.

Murong Lian had gifted these two bootlicking golden beasts to the emperor, who loved them deeply, but Mo Xi's opinion was that only the mentally impaired could find joy in such garbage. At present, these two bootlickers had just finished their inhale and exhale routine, and they let out twin metallic belches before curling up by the brazier and falling still.

Mo Xi glanced across the palace hall. Almost every Shennong Terrace healer was present. Gu Mang was restrained in the middle of the hall, guarded by the elite cultivators of the palace. Someone had put him under a hypnosis spell, and he was presently unconscious.

The emperor was reclining on the pale yellow cushions of the imperial throne, wearing black robes and the beaded imperial crown. His face was jade-like in its beauty, his features exuding a clear willfulness. He had been resting with his eyes closed, but upon hearing the rustling of robes and hurried footsteps, he opened them and glanced down.

"Everyone's here?"

"Your Imperial Majesty, Elder Yu of Chengtian Terrace has not yet arrived," an official replied.

The emperor scoffed. "The old geezer's getting on in years—not even a snowy owl messenger can wake him. We think it's high time the leadership of Chengtian Terrace goes to someone more worthy."

"Your Imperial Majesty, please calm yourself..."

"Do you think we aren't calm?" The emperor rolled his eyes and sat up straight. With a wave of his pale yellow sleeves, he said, "Gentlemen, take your seats."

"Our thanks to Your Imperial Majesty," the entire hall intoned.

"We understand you're displeased to be called to the palace in the middle of the night. Perhaps you're even secretly cursing our name."

One of the old nobles had barely sat down before this statement made him fall in haste to his knees. "What is Your Imperial Majesty saying?"

"All right, all right, get up. Don't give us that load about emperors needing to set an example for their subjects—it's so annoying. If you want to curse us, then curse away. As long as you don't let us hear it, you can curse to your heart's content."

A few old nobles looked at each other. This youthful emperor of theirs was possessed of a strange and intractable temperament, which to a one they found unfathomable.

Although he manifestly shared sentiments with the conservative senior nobles—to the point that he had removed Chonghua's greatest slave-born general not long after his ascension—his manner was consistently unorthodox, and he approached every situation as if determined to establish a new world order.

"We know you want to get out of here to go back to sleep, mollify your women, and visit your prostitutes," the emperor said wearily. "We will be brief."

They were struck speechless.

This was simply absurd. Did any other emperor in the Nine Provinces and Twenty-Eight Nations behave like this?

"Elder of Shennong Terrace."

"This subject is here!"

"Report on Gu Mang's condition tonight, as well as the results of the examination."

"Understood!" The leader of Shennong Terrace stepped forward, made an obeisance, and relayed his account of how Gu Mang's spiritual energy had suddenly gone berserk. Then he said, "The spiritual core inside Gu Mang has indeed been broken. He has no spiritual energy, but..."

"But what?" the emperor asked.

The healer lowered his head. "We found powerful malevolent qi in his chest."

The emperor mulled this over. "Malevolent qi..."

"Yes. This official has determined that Gu Mang became frenzied due to this malevolent qi. Unfortunately, Chonghua has always followed the righteous path and has no contact with immoral demonic ways, so Shennong Terrace's knowledge of such things is limited. All we can say for certain is that the Liao Kingdom must have done something to Gu Mang's heart; but to acquire further details, I'm afraid we'd..." His expression was harrowed, his voice trailing off.

"You don't need to be afraid," the emperor said. "Just say it, no harm in that."

The healer made further obeisance. "I'm afraid we'd need to wait for Gu Mang to die in order to dissect his heart," he said.

"You mean if we wanted to know what's wrong with him right away, we'd need to kill him right now?"

The healer hesitated. "Yes."

"Useless trash!" the emperor spat.

The Shennong Terrace elder fell to his knees in terror. "Your Imperial Majesty, this official is incompetent..."

"You are indeed! What would we want with a corpse? He's riddled with traces of the Liao Kingdom's magic! So long as he's alive, we can study him. What use is he dead? So we could bury him for the fun of it?"

"Y-Your Imperial Majesty..."

"Find another way!"

"B-but Gu Mang's mind is broken," the Shennong Terrace elder said. "Hardly any traces of those magic techniques remain, and I'm afraid—"

It was then that Murong Lian lazily raised his voice. "Elder, whether Gu Mang is in fact mentally broken is still yet to be determined." He flicked his eyes over to cast Mo Xi a meaningful glance. "Isn't that right, Xihe-jun?"

Mo Xi said nothing.

The elder swallowed with difficulty. It was already terrifying to be called "useless trash" by the emperor, but now Wangshu-jun was interrupting him, and the ruthless killer Xihe-jun had gotten involved too. He felt like he was about to faint.

Only after stuttering for several seconds did the elder manage to speak. "B-but this official has examined him multiple times. Gu Mang truly...truly can't remember anything. His nature is completely bestial. Why...why would Xihe-jun suggest that his mind is intact?"

Mo Xi replied, "Gu Mang was able to summon a demonic weapon."

The Shennong Terrace Elder let out a sigh of relief. "Xihe-jun misunderstands," he said hastily. "Although it is often said that summoning either holy or demonic weapons requires reciting an incantation, that isn't necessarily true. When its owner's emotions are exceptionally strong, or if they're in a very dangerous situation, the weapon may still be summoned, even without the incantation. So that...that does not prove anything."

Mo Xi listened without making a sound. His expression was frosty, but his eyes stared unblinkingly at the unconscious Gu Mang. Mo Xi looked perfectly unruffled—no one had seen that his grip on the sandalwood armrest had left a hairline crack in the wood.

Another noble spoke from among the group. "Your Imperial Majesty, regardless of all else, Gu Mang is simply too dangerous. If not for the timely arrival of the guards today, I'm afraid he would have killed many more people!"

"That's right! Think of the sins he's committed. Why has Your Imperial Majesty continued to extend mercy?! Why not kill him and be done with it?!"

Murong Lian's sort, who believed it was more interesting to keep people alive to torture them, were in the minority. The majority still held to primitive rules: an eye for an eye, a life for a life. Many nobles had blood feuds with Gu Mang, and they couldn't let an opportunity like the one that had presented itself today pass them by.

Cries of "Execute Gu Mang at once!" filled the hall.

The emperor twirled a string of jade beads on his hand—then smashed it down onto the sandalwood table. "What are you yammering on about?" he bellowed.

The crowd fell silent at once.

"What a racket. First the harem won't shut up, and now it's the court's turn. We've got a headache coming on!" The emperor pointed at the Shennong Terrace elder. "You're nothing more than useless trash! If it weren't for Jiang Fuli's refusal to take your position, we would've fired you a thousand times over!"

The Shennong Terrace elder could have cried. His was a difficult and unrewarding position to start; if it weren't for Jiang Fuli's refusal to take his position, he would've begged to resign a thousand times over too.

The emperor cooled down somewhat and abruptly turned to another official. "When is Jiang Fuli coming back?" he asked.

The official fell to his knees. "Your Imperial Majesty, this official is also useless trash. This official doesn't know where Medicine Master Jiang has gone..."

"Enough. You can get up." The emperor waved a hand, impatient. "At least *you're* not useless trash. Jiang Fuli is hard to keep track of. If you don't know, forget it."

The official was close to tears. "Many thanks to Your Imperial Majesty."

The emperor looked up at his crowd of subjects. "If we wanted to kill the traitor Gu Mang, we could have done so two years ago. We obviously have our own reasons for keeping him alive thus far."

It was clear that some nobles still wanted to speak. "Hold your tongues," the emperor warned testily. "Let us finish. We are aware many of your friends and family have had the misfortune of falling by Gu Mang's hand, and that you want to deal with him once and for all. That way, your hatred will be avenged.

"However, aside from retribution, Chonghua wouldn't gain the slightest advantage from that vengeance. So, we will keep Gu Mang alive. Though the marks left on him are too faint for Shennong Terrace to glean any useful information, Jiang Fuli might be able to accomplish what Shennong Terrace cannot. If there's anything

Jiang Fuli cannot accomplish now, he might still be able to in the future. We can wait."

After a moment, he continued, his tone severe. "The memories Gu Mang lost...are useful. The spells on Gu Mang's body...are useful. Gu Mang himself...is *far* more useful alive than dead.

"Chonghua has never cultivated the demonic path and only employs proper techniques to sustain our cultivation. However—if we fail to even try to understand them, if we refuse to make progress or to gain intelligence about the Liao Kingdom..." He sneered. "Then we think, sooner or later, Chonghua will be no match for Liao!"

The emperor wanted to study the demonic path of the Liao Kingdom? An array of different expressions crossed the faces of those gathered.

"But..."

"How can Chonghua dabble in dark magic? Even if we do it to know our enemy, it's still outrageously dangerous."

One of the nobles present was the elder brother of the emperor's favored concubine. Being exceptionally stupid, he couldn't help but ask, "Your Imperial Majesty, if you want to understand the Liao Kingdom's black magic, can't you just take a few more captives? Why does it have to be this one?"

The emperor rolled his eyes. "Because the Liao Kingdom has already poured so much effort into him. He is unique. How hasn't that sheer idiocy of yours killed you yet?"

At that, everyone fell quiet.

After a spell, Murong Lian rose and bowed to the throne. "Since Your Imperial Majesty has explained his reasoning to us," he said, "this subject naturally won't object. It's only that..."

"Speak."

"Today's events demonstrated that the malevolent qi in Gu Mang's body is extremely potent, capable of breaking through the protective barrier outside Luomei Pavilion. It is no longer safe to keep him there." He paused. "If Your Imperial Majesty can trust this subject, why not let me take Gu Mang into the custody of my manor? This subject will keep strict watch over him as atonement for allowing this day's disaster to unfold."

The emperor thought this over, looking weary. "Mn…this could be a solution…"

"Many thanks to Your Imperial Majesty," Murong Lian said. "Then—"

Before he could finish, a low voice interjected.

"No." Mo Xi, who had sat mute with his eyes closed all this time, finally spoke up from his sandalwood chair. He looked up at Wangshu-jun and repeated his objection. "No. You cannot take him away."

At first, the emperor was taken aback. Then he stroked his chin with surprise and interest, looking between Wangshu-jun and Xihe-jun.

Murong Lian stiffened, the corners of his mouth curling into a sneer. "What special insight does Xihe-jun possess? Weren't you the one who thought Gu Mang might still have his memories?"

"I did say that." Mo Xi rose, his height and the expression on his face both intimidating. "So I will take him into custody."

Murong Lian's gaze sharpened. "*Why*, exactly?"

Mo Xi was curt. "Because you can't beat him."

"You!"

Mo Xi turned toward the throne. "Your Imperial Majesty, though Gu Mang has been stripped of much of his power, if he were to go berserk again, he would prove to be as formidable as he was today."

"That sounds reasonable..."

"You're aware of his martial prowess. In terms of one-on-one fighting, few in Chonghua could best him," Mo Xi said, cool and steady. "I ask Your Imperial Majesty to send Gu Mang to Xihe Manor. I will keep him under total control and prevent him from harming Your Imperial Majesty or any other individual in Chonghua ever again."

After a moment, Murong Lian smiled contemptuously. "Xihe-jun uses such pretty language, but are we really supposed to believe that you mean to protect Chonghua and His Imperial Majesty?"

"What are you implying?" Mo Xi asked.

"What am I implying?" Murong Lian tilted his pale face as he narrowed his eyes. "Does Xihe-jun truly not understand what I mean?" He lowered his chin and gestured in Gu Mang's direction. "By taking him in, wouldn't you only be trying to protect *him*?"

"What nonsense is this?" Mo Xi's face instantly darkened. "Gu Mang nearly died at my hand not hours ago—you think I'm *protecting* him?"

"What was that? *Nearly?*" Murong Lian shot him a cool, fluid glance. "He's still alive, isn't he? Besides, right outside this hall, when I asked whether you truly wanted to choke Gu Mang to death with your own hands, did you answer?"

Mo Xi replied with barely suppressed rage, "Why should I tell you?!"

"Whether you wanted to, whether you're willing—yes, why *should* you tell me? Your relationship with him, your private affairs, why *should* they be shared with anyone else? Heh, my fellow gentlemen are quite forgetful, so why don't I give you all a reminder?" Murong Lian's eyes glinted. "All those years ago, didn't Xihe-jun's friendship with General Gu transcend class?"

This proclamation left the crowd not shocked so much as at a loss for words.

Mo Xi and Gu Mang had been inseparably close; everyone knew this. However, it was also common knowledge that Gu Mang had nearly stabbed Mo Xi to death after defecting. Since that stab, their relationship had long since passed the tipping point.

Everyone was embarrassed. Some people laughed awkwardly without agreeing. Someone even said, "Wangshu-jun, that was ages ago. What more is there to say...?"

But Murong Lian seemed to have expected this response. He snorted indolently, the corners of his mouth curving more dangerously. "All right, then I won't speak more on it." He met Mo Xi's gaze again, smirking. "Let me ask Xihe-jun a question: You've always been ascetic and proper, unsullied by houses of pleasure...so, I dare say, what were you after when you secretly visited Luomei Pavilion in search of Gu Mang?"

Mo Xi's heart pounded. So that attendant had indeed reported his visit to Luomei Pavilion to see Gu Mang. But he didn't intend to deny it. Turning his dark eyes away, he said, "For revenge. What else?"

"If it was for revenge, why did you personally offer him water to drink and food to eat?" Murong Lian savored each word as he hissed them out like a venomous snake. "Could it be that seeing your Gu Mang-gege in pain...hurt you?"

If they hadn't been in the palace of Chonghua with the emperor watching mere feet away, Mo Xi would have pelted Murong Lian with a barrage of fireballs. It was entirely possible that Murong Lian's head would have been smashed right off.

"What the hell is wrong with you?" Mo Xi said angrily. "You *followed* me?"

Murong Lian scoffed. "Like I would need to follow you. Luomei Pavilion belongs to me, doesn't it? Moreover, you have only yourself to blame—could it be that you were afraid people would find out?"

As their argument grew heated, one of the nobles tried to intervene. "Let it go. Xihe-jun has always been cold of face but kind of heart. He was just giving some water to someone dying of thirst. Wangshu-jun, why be so aggressive...?"

"Just some water?" Murong Lian's eyes flashed with a chilling light. "Ridiculous. In matters of vengeance, it would be rare enough for someone to resist kicking an already fallen opponent, and here Xihe-jun is offering him *aid in a time of need*. Such depths of moral righteousness have truly opened my eyes."

He bent toward the throne. "Your Imperial Majesty may deny my request to take custody of Gu Mang, but Xihe-jun must not be allowed to take him back to his manor."

It was rare for the emperor to see Mo Xi and Murong Lian argue so heatedly at court. Headache forgotten, he watched with rapt interest. After receiving this request from Murong Lian, he found himself undecided. "Well..." he muttered.

The emperor's hesitation compelled Murong Lian to continue. "Xihe-jun gave Gu Mang water even when he was confined at Luomei Pavilion. If Xihe-jun were to take Gu Mang into his home, who knows what else he would give him?"

These words contained a sly hint of innuendo within their derision. Some of the nobles thought Murong Lian was going too far, and they shot meaningful glances his way in an attempt to get him to shut up.

Visiting male prostitutes didn't raise eyebrows in Chonghua, but actual relationships between men were wholly forbidden. This was especially true for pure-blooded nobles like Mo Xi—the spiritual energy in their lineage was far too precious to waste. The righteous choice for such men was to carry on their bloodline, so Chonghua forbade them from engaging in unseemly affairs.

Furthermore, how could an aloof and noble person like Xihe-jun associate in such a way with filthy, lowborn trash like Gu Mang? The nobles felt this strained belief; they thought that Murong Lian had gotten rather too carried away in his desire to slander his rival.

Only Mo Xi, the victim of slander himself, knew the jab had landed.

"Xihe-jun, you wouldn't want to raise any questions about your allegiance," Murong Lian drawled. "You'd best stop meddling."

After a breath, Mo Xi turned, his expression hostile. He glared at Murong Lian to ask, "And if I refuse?"

23
Prize

MURONG LIAN LAZILY rolled his eyes. Without even turning to look, he smirked and said, "Then Xihe-jun can anticipate further conflict with this lord."

Murong Lian's shift in self-address was a transparent attempt to intimidate Mo Xi with "this lord's" imperial bloodline.

Mo Xi was fully aware of this. His expression grew frostier and his aura more terrifying. There were a few beats of silence in the palace hall, a hush that was broken when Mo Xi next spoke:

"Remember this: Gu Mang carries countless secrets and owes countless blood debts, but because of your selfishness, this incident occurred while he was in your custody." Mo Xi paused, his gaze darkening like ice as it shattered. "I will not let you have him. If Wangshu-jun has more to say, I wait with bated breath."

"You..."

Of these two people, one was a prince of the aristocracy while the other was a general of the military. Their exchanged glance flashed like lightning and disappeared just as quickly.

Murong Lian's face was almost translucent in its pallor, the clenching of his jaw extraordinarily stark against his skin. He ground his teeth for a long moment before barking with laughter.

"Very well! You still dare to claim you're not protecting him? You dare to claim you hate him?" Murong Lian's eyes glinted like poison-feather wine,[21] and his smile tightened on his face. "Mo Xi, haven't you noticed? What you're saying to this lord right now is exactly what Gu Mang said when you were the one floundering, and he was shielding you!"

Mo Xi looked down at Murong Lian calmly, something subtle in his expression.

"To claim that you hate Gu Mang is utterly laughable. If he's handed to you today, sooner or later, calamity will befall Chonghua!"

Unexpectedly, Mo Xi started smiling as well. His smile was almost upsettingly handsome, but his eyes were terribly cold. "How did Gu Mang ever protect me? I only know that he left a scar on my chest that will never fade. I only remember that he tried to kill me. I hate him." Mo Xi spoke evenly, his eyes as clear as fresh-fallen snow. "You say he once protected me. My apologies, Wangshu-jun, but that happened so long ago. This general doesn't remember anymore."

He turned, took a knee before the imperial throne, and lowered his gaze.

"Your Imperial Majesty, none in Chonghua know Gu Mang's spells better than I. Moreover, Wangshu-jun has failed in his supervisory duties, which resulted in today's disaster. I request to be allowed to detain Gu Mang and enforce stricter scrutiny upon him in my manor."

Murong Lian turned. "Mo Xi, you've been working tirelessly to protect him from the moment you returned!" he snapped. "What exactly are you planning?!"

Mo Xi chose not to dignify Murong Lian with any further response.

The emperor thought it over.

Just as he was about to speak, an imperial guard sprinted to the

---

21 *Zhenjiu, wine made poisonous with the touch of the mythological zhen niao's feather.*

door and whispered anxiously to the herald. The herald's expression instantly changed as he hurried deferentially up to the throne. "Your Imperial Majesty, an urgent report from the capital!"

The emperor nearly kicked over the table. "This is the second time tonight! What now?"

The herald's face was drained of color. "There's been a massacre at the Mansion of Beauties in the northern quarter. Almost everyone was killed—i-including Official Yu of Chengtian Terrace..."

"What?!"

The crowd was shocked.

Even the emperor rose shot up from his throne, wide-eyed. "Who is responsible?!"

"N-no one knows... By the time the imperial guard discovered the situation at the mansion, the criminal had escaped. They even l-left a message on the wall..."

"What message?!"

The official was still petrified, and he stammered out his answer. "'Th-this humble one is lonely; sincerely seeking wives.'"

"'This humble one is lonely; sincerely seeking wives'?" The emperor repeated it twice, his temper flaring. "What nonsense! What deranged old bachelor would write this kind of thing and murder a bunch of people? Does he want to kill or does he want women?" He paused, and when he spoke again it was in a still more irritable tone. "Are there no other clues?!"

"N-not yet."

The emperor once more resorted to his favorite catch phrase: "Useless trash!"

He sank back against the throne and collected himself for a while. His lashes fluttered as his attention fell again on Mo Xi and Murong Lian. An idea had popped into his head.

"The matter of Gu Mang will be temporarily set aside." The emperor sat up slowly as he spoke.

This Mansion of Beauties incident had come at an inopportune time, but perhaps it could prove useful. Of the two men fighting in front of the hall for control of Gu Mang, one was a blood relative and the other an important subject. Nothing good could come of refusing either. This case was the perfect opportunity—he could toss the responsibility of decision to a third party.

"An atrocity such as this, within the imperial capital, is an insult that cannot be borne. We command the two of you to go forth and investigate at once. Whosoever catches the culprit first may return to ask us for Gu Mang."

"Your Imperial Majesty intends to make him a prize?" Murong Lian asked.

The emperor glanced at him. "You two are already at each other's throats merely to settle a personal grudge. Or will he not suffice?"

Murong Lian smiled. "He will. However, while I do this for revenge, Xihe-jun's motives are yet unknown."

Mo Xi said nothing.

"Enough, Murong Lian. Xihe-jun has always been a gentleman. Stop throwing around accusations over some petty grievance." The emperor impatiently waved a hand to cut him off, then pointed at Gu Mang, asleep within Shennong Terrace's shield array. "Xihe-jun, we also want to see which of you possesses the greater skill," he said. "If you have no objections, then let it be done."

"I accept," Mo Xi said.

"Then you should get on with it." The emperor spun the beads in his hand. "Whoever wins can take him away."

Thus the still insensible Gu Mang became the incentive for these two noble lords to crack the case. Murong Lian wanted him to suffer, whereas Mo Xi wanted...

Forget it. He didn't know what he ought to do after bringing Gu Mang back to his manor either. Nor, at present, was it something he ought to think about.

Inside the Mansion of Beauties, Mo Xi, clad in a set of black imperial commander robes, stood with his hands clasped behind his back, gazing at the words scrawled on the wall in fresh blood.

At the emperor's command, the healers from Shennong Terrace were handling the corpses that had died tragic deaths within the brothel, while Mo Xi and Murong Lian had accompanied them to investigate the matter and catch the killer.

"Among the dead are fourteen prostitutes, thirty-seven clients, and seven mansion employees." One of the healers was giving Mo Xi the casualty report. "After cross-referencing with the directory, we determined that five prostitutes are missing."

Murong Lian frowned. "Missing?"

"Yes."

"Seeing as everyone in the brothel was killed, and even Official Yu couldn't escape...those five prostitutes can't have gotten away on their own. It's likely that the killer took them away," Murong Lian said thoughtfully. "Why did the killer take those five? Is he really taking women captive to be his wives?"

Mo Xi walked to the side of the bloodstained staircase, where a few healers were handling Elder Yu's corpse. As he approached, they all performed obeisance. "Xihe-jun."

"Mn. What traces of magic remain on Elder Yu's body?"

"Xihe-jun, they are similar but not identical to the black magic spells of the Liao Kingdom. Please come take a look." As the healer spoke, he lifted a corner of the cloth covering the corpse. "Official Yu's eyes have been taken and his heart dug out. The flesh around the wounds has festered with unnatural speed, faster than injuries caused by ordinary weapons. In fact, it seems like..."

"A cannibalistic vengeful ghost," Mo Xi finished with a frown.

"Yes. It does look like the work of a vengeful ghost."

Mo Xi's gaze swept over the evidence of Elder Yu's violent demise. The two hollows of his eyes and the hole in his chest had begun to seep black liquid. But vengeful ghosts were rarely lucid. Writing something like "This humble one is lonely; sincerely seeking wives" didn't seem like the behavior of a vengeful ghost.

As he thought, his gaze slowly traveled down, stopping at the Elder Yu's mutilated chest. "Are the other bodies like this as well?"

The healer flipped through the records and shook his head. "No, only seventeen people had their eyes and hearts dug out."

"Show me the names."

The first one who had died this way was Elder Yu. Mo Xi wasn't familiar with all the names that followed, but those he did know were young masters from influential families.

"The ones who lost their hearts were all cultivators?"

"We can't yet be sure, but that seems to be the case."

A cultivator's heart was where their spiritual core resided, and after hearts, eyes were the strongest source of spiritual energy. When devoured by vengeful ghosts and demons, these organs could serve as potent cultivation amplifiers.

Mo Xi lowered his head, murmuring to himself in thought.

At this moment, an imperial guard pushed open the door. He had been running hard, and despite the cold outside, sweat beaded his forehead. "Xihe-jun! Wang-Wang-Wang—"[22]

22 汪汪汪, *wang wang wang*, is the Chinese onomatopoeia for barking dogs.

Murong Lian flicked his peach blossom eyes to the side, smiling with keen interest. "*Wang wang?* Why are you barking? Are you calling our Xihe-jun a dog?"

The guard swallowed. "Wangshu-jun!"

Murong Lian's smile vanished. "Catch your fucking breath before you speak!"

"Yes sir!" the imperial guard hastily replied. "There's been a new development. After Gu Mang went berserk, the warning barrier at Luomei Pavilion was broken. Just now, when the manager was accounting for the pavilion's occupants, they—they discovered someone missing!"

Murong Lian bristled and grabbed the guard by the lapels. "What happened? They checked three times and said that despite the chaos, no one escaped! How is someone missing now?!"

The guard didn't get a chance to respond before another team rushed over through the snowy night on horseback. As it turned out, they were escorting Madam Qin, manager of Luomei Pavilion. She fell to her knees as soon as she dismounted, shivering on the ground. "Wangshu-jun, this servant deserves death! This servant deserves *death*!"

Murong Lian was about to pass out from pure rage. "If you want to die so badly, do it later! First, tell me clearly: Are you blind or are you stupid? When you took attendance the first three times, you said no one was missing—so how is that now no longer the case?! Explain!"

"Wangshu-jun, please forgive me," she sobbed, "This servant was only counting the prostitutes and courtesans, and she attentively checked on them so many times. They were all present and accounted for, but—but this servant forgot..."

"What did you forget?!"

Madam Qin wailed. "This servant forgot there was a bedridden cook in the kitchen side room!"

"A cook?" Murong Lian was stumped.

"Yes—a month ago, when you punished Gu Mang to confinement and reflection and reduced his meals, he couldn't stand the hunger and went to the kitchen to steal food," Madam Qin cried. "That cook bumped into him, and hit and cursed him. But he set off Gu Mang's sword array and was cut to ribbons."

Everyone was silent.

"The doctor said those wounds required at least a few months of bedrest, so—so at first, I didn't expect that he could possibly do anything. How could I guess that he would sneak out when Gu Mang broke th-the barrier..."

"Useless trash!"

Murong Lian was infuriated. He kicked Madam Qin in the chest and sent her flying into the swirling snow. Pointing at her, he bellowed, "Do you know what manner of disaster you've unleashed?!"

All the servants and prostitutes of Luomei Pavilion were prisoners who harbored deep loathing for Chonghua. Although their cores were destroyed when they entered the pavilion, every country had their arcane secrets. It was said that there had once been a black magic practitioner from the Liao Kingdom who could even repair shattered cores, so a great many barriers were layered around Luomei Pavilion.

No one could have predicted that Gu Mang's rampage would let him break through every single one of those barriers. Moreover, it would have been one thing for them to be broken, but then a "bedridden" man had suddenly jumped up and taken the opportunity to escape, and the manager had only just figured it out. Even worse, not long after this cook disappeared, there had been a bloody massacre in which almost a hundred citizens of the capital had lost their lives—

If the emperor were to take a closer look at this, who would he blame?

None other than Murong Lian.

Despite himself, a red flush stained Murong Lian's pale face. He felt nearly faint. "Gu Mang...Gu Mang..." he raged. "Once again it's all your fault!" He turned on his heel. "Go get that cook's file and bring it to me to examine! Where did he come from?! How old is he, what's his life history? I need to know every detail, down to how many women he's bedded! Hurry up!"

"Yes! Yes!" Staggering to her feet, the madam mounted her horse and galloped away in a panic.

Shaking out his sleeves, Murong Lian returned to the Mansion of Beauties in an anxious fury. He tilted his head and stared, panting, at the words written on the wall: *This humble one is lonely; sincerely seeking wives.*

One of Murong Lian's personal attendants found himself compelled to offer a suggestion. "My lord..."

"What do you want?!" Murong Lian snapped, irascible as ever.

"This isn't right."

Mind a jumble, Murong Lian was briefly bewildered. "What's not right?"

"Gu Mang injured that cook a month ago, and now Gu Mang's gone berserk and the cook took the chance to escape..." The attendant's voice lowered as he glanced cautiously at Murong Lian. "Don't you think it's a little too much of a coincidence?"

Murong Lian considered this, narrowing his eyes. "You're saying that the cook planned this? That he made use of Gu Mang?"

"Or...what if Gu Mang wasn't the one being used? If you look at all the evidence, my lord, should we not imagine the worst? Is it not possible that Gu Mang and that cook planned all this together?"

Murong Lian's heart tightened. "What country was that injured cook captured from?"

The attendant had been worried for precisely this reason. He lowered his head. "The Liao Kingdom."

So that cook was another dog-bastard from the Liao Kingdom?! Murong Lian's back was drenched in cold sweat. At this moment... at this moment, Gu Mang was still in the palace!

It was better to be safe than sorry. If Gu Mang really had devised some unknown scheme with that cook, and if the two of them were working together to create a diversion and lure the tiger from the mountain, then...

The blood drained from Murong Lian's face. After a breath, he strode out into the snow. "Summon my golden-winged snow pegasus! I must go to the palace at once to see His Imperial Majesty!"

24
Flower-Pluckers Are Human Too

MURONG LIAN RACED to the palace, but the emperor met this revelation with an attitude of pure nonchalance. As he teased the two golden beasts by the brazier—listening to them sing his praises in alternating duets of, "His Imperial Majesty is handsome and carefree," and, "His Imperial Majesty is gloriously majestic"—he reassured Murong Lian with a few careless platitudes, then told him to focus on cracking the case instead of worrying over other matters.

"The imperial palace is closely guarded. Even if Gu Mang did collude with that cook, what could he do? Pull down the sky?"

"Your Imperial Majesty must remain vigilant," Murong Lian said anxiously. "In the end, this incident is the result of this subject's neglect. If Your Imperial Majesty were to come to harm..."

The emperor stopped fiddling with his golden incense chopsticks and put them down. "Enough. You think we don't know you? Gu Mang escaped from your pavilion. You're only so anxious because you're afraid we'll be angry and hold you responsible." He shot a glance at Murong Lian with a smile that didn't reach his eyes. "Oh, A-Lian, you're our brother by blood. Be at ease. Would we punish you for something like this?"

Once the emperor ascended the throne, according to custom, he was to address his siblings and cousins by their official titles.

However, in private, he still sometimes called Murong Lian "A-Lian"—when he needed to reassure him, the closeness of familial bonds had to be emphasized.

"As for Gu Mang, if you still feel uneasy, we'll send him to the prison. It would be a trial for him to escape that even if he grew wings."

With great effort, Murong Lian calmed himself and acquiesced. "Your Imperial Majesty, might this subject receive permission to perform an interrogation, should the case require it?"

"Go ahead. Why wouldn't you be allowed to interrogate someone?"

"Then this subject's use of torture—"

The emperor glanced at him, smiling, then snorted. "They say it's Xihe the Ruthless and Wangshu the Cruel. We see that this is true indeed. Is it that you can't get people to tell the truth *without* torture?"

Murong Lian cleared his throat. "Gu Mang is a special case, of course."

"Enough. Interrogate him however you like, but don't overdo it. We think Xihe-jun retains some kind of obsession with him. We found it amusing the first time you two bickered in the hall, but we'll be annoyed by a second round."

The emperor played with the jade beads in his hand and continued, lightly, "Keep yourself under control. Don't let us hear a formal indictment against you." He rolled his eyes. "One of you is an important military official and the other an imperial scion, yet for the sake of your personal grudges, you act like three-year-olds squabbling over a toy. Do you really think we can't tell?"

Murong Lian found himself unable to reply.

The rising sun emerged in the east. As the light of day pierced the darkness, the citizens awakened and rose from their beds, chattering and gossiping. News of the murders in the Mansion of Beauties the previous night was immediately leaked and swiftly spread across the imperial capital until it became the hottest topic of conversation for all the capital's citizens.

Somehow everyone, from the old and gray to children and youths, had a pithy comment to share.

"Almost everyone in the brothel was killed overnight! How tragic!"

"Aiya, aiya! Good heavens! Has the killer been caught?"

"He's long since escaped! Before escaping, he even left writing on the walls: 'Gold and treasure are a plentiful sight, but rare are the men who can last all night'!"

"The version I heard was, 'This humble one is lonely; sincerely seeking wives.'"

"Um… Who can say! In any case, the Mansion of Beauties is all sealed up now. No one can go in other than the officials investigating the case. But in my opinion, no matter if it was 'gold and treasure are a plentiful sight,' or 'this humble one is lonely,' it sounds like a case of seizing women rather than riches."

"Could it be a flower-plucking rapist with a penchant for murder?"

The more the story spread, the more ludicrous it became, and in the end, a certain storyteller came up with this tale: "There was so much unclean qi at the Mansion of Beauties that it attracted a lecherous vengeful ghost. On a dark and moonless night, he stole into the mansion—heh heh—and killed the men before defiling them, then defiled the women before killing them! That vengeful ghost was unnaturally virile. He defiled and killed more than seventy people in the Mansion of Beauties before the sun rose, and so indiscriminately that he even claimed elderly Official Yu!"

The tea-drinking customers were wide-eyed and speechless.

"Isn't that kind of insane?" One of the customers couldn't hold back and burst into raucous laughter.

"Young Yue-gongzi? Wh-what's brought this on?"

"Ha ha ha ha!" The one who had doubled over with laughter was Yue Chenqing, who was so idle that he had nothing better to do than collect rumors. He chuckled, "I've heard so many versions, but yours is definitely the funniest. Defiling and killing more than seventy people in one night! Bro, I'm afraid that rapist isn't virile—he's a two-pump chump!"

This shattered the atmosphere of terror. Everyone laughed and shook their heads. Even the maidens covered their mouths and giggled in secret. The storyteller was terribly embarrassed, but when he realized his heckler was the young master of the Yue Clan, he couldn't exactly chase him away in a huff. He could only smile along and say, "Yes, yes, Yue-gongzi is right."

And so, the tale of *Virile Rapist Mounts Seventy in One Night* was revised by the singular Yue Chenqing into *Two-Pump Flower-Plucker Kills Brothel-Goers in Furious Rampage.*

Probably the only people in the city who weren't in the mood to listen to this chatter were the friends and families of the murdered clients, the harried imperial guards, everyone at Shennong Terrace, and the two noble masters Xihe and Wangshu.

Within Wangshu Manor, an attendant spoke with their head lowered. "My lord. The servant you wanted from Luomei Pavilion is here."

Murong Lian had just smoked two pipes worth of ephemera. He was in a good mood indeed. "All right, let him in."

The servant hurriedly entered the hall, kneeling in front of Murong Lian to give his report. "This slave greets Wangshu-shenjun, may he receive ten thousand blessings—"

"Enough, enough, save your breath. You shared a room with that escaped cook, correct?"

"Yes."

"Come, tell me about him. What kind of person is he?"

"Um...he was brought to Luomei Pavilion five years ago," the servant replied. "Doesn't like to talk much, bit of a creep, often alone."

"Did anything happen that might have made him develop a grudge against brothel girls?" Murong Lian asked.

"Nothing like that, not exactly," the servant responded. "But I heard he was a lecher in the Liao Kingdom who always wanted to take pretty girls for himself. Apparently, he even slept with his sworn brother's wife."

Murong Lian sighed. "So he's a pervert."

He thought to himself that the rumors spreading among the people might not be too far off. The cook might indeed be a lecherous rapist with some kind of insane craving. Why else would he keep those five women by his side?

"What about him and Gu Mang?" Murong Lian asked. "Did they interact?"

"I don't think they were ever close."

Murong Lian murmured under his breath, then said, "I understand, you may withdraw."

After the servant left, Murong Lian spoke to the attendant. "Bring me my silver fox fur coat, the warmest one. I'm going to the prison to interrogate Gu Mang."

If Murong Lian was focusing on "interrogation," then Mo Xi was thoroughly intent on "investigation." He was analyzing every detail of the crime scene.

This Mansion of Beauties case was seriously bizarre. If the culprit was a vengeful ghost, how had it written anything? If they were a living person, why had they bothered digging out their victims' hearts?

Mo Xi ordered Shennong Terrace to continue examining the wounds on the dead in hopes of finding more clues. After examining each corpse one by one, the healers discovered traces of concealed sword-inflicted injuries. But those marks were quite peculiar as well, which only made the entire case all the more confusing.

"What's strange about the wounds?"

The healer hesitated before replying. "The Water-Parting Sword."

Mo Xi immediately looked up. "The Water-Parting Sword, Li Qingqian?"

"Exactly so."

"How could it be...?" Mo Xi murmured.

The swordsman zongshi[23] Li Qingqian was a cultivator who had been born in Lichun.

He had been poor in coin and kind of heart. He'd roamed the lands for more than a decade, exorcising and defeating countless demons, but had also been helplessly naive. Oftentimes, he'd been the one risking his life to stave off calamity, but ill-intentioned cultivators had always ended up stealing his glory. Thus, even after ten years of hard work, he'd labored in obscurity.

Until the year he fought the battle of Maiden's Lament Mountain.

Maiden's Lament Mountain was in the Liao Kingdom's territory. It had once been known as Phoenix Feather Mountain, but the Liao Kingdom military had at one point gathered some hundred women from who knows where, dressed them all in crimson wedding robes, and buried them alive amid the sounds of their anguished wails.

---

23 *Honorific term for a master cultivator of particularly outstanding skill.*

The explanation given by the Liao Kingdom's guoshi[24] had been: "The stars say that this mountain god requires sacrifices."

After those aggrieved women were buried, their hatred soared relentlessly up toward the heavens. Many roaming cultivators had come forward to try to exorcise them, but they had all died at the hands of the maiden ghosts. Therefore, the terrified local villagers below Phoenix Feather Mountain had renamed it "Maiden's Lament Mountain."

The mountain bride, all night she cried;
First she hates her helpless fate,
Second hates her ill-starred face,
Third their parting does she hate, a lost love left too late.

Garbed in scarlet, crowned in gold;
Once she laughs, face warped by hate;
Twice she laughs, blood streaks her face;
Thrice she laughs, and with that last, forever seals your fate.

These verses told of the corpses of the countless beauties who had been buried alive on the mountain. Any crossing had to be completed within a single day when yang energy was at its peak, and the party could include no women, children, sick, or elderly. To do anything else would agitate the hundreds of vengeful ghosts upon the mountain. With the sound of three laughs, the ghosts would appear behind their victims, and all the travelers would perish on the mountainside.

After Li Qingqian heard of this, he went to Maiden's Lament Mountain to suppress the ghosts. At the time, even though he had

24 *Powerful imperial official who served as an advisor to the emperor.*

defeated countless demons, he had never cared to build up his reputation, so not many people knew his name.

When the magistrate saw this young cultivator in patched-up clothes, looking like some nobody, he couldn't stand idly by. "Even though the bounty's high, there're hundreds of ghosts on that mountain, every one of them a terrible fiend. Xianzhang,[25] don't put your life at risk."

But Li Qingqian only replied that he wasn't seeking riches. Then he walked up the mountain accompanied by nothing more than the sword at his side.

His trip lasted three days. Just as everyone began to sigh that another cultivator had died on the mountainside, the anguished howling of hundreds of women burst out of Maiden's Lament Mountain, along with a beam of jade-colored light that could be seen from miles away.

Later, when people described that sword, their expressions would grow dreamy and they would sigh, mesmerized by the past. "The Water-Parting Sword forms," they would say, "can reach as far as the eye can see, even piercing the Nine Heavens."

All that glitters is not gold, but true gold always shines. Li Qingqian had been buried in obscurity for many years, but this battle finally brought him fame. To this day, countless storytellers still passionately recounted his austere strength of character—those jade-green robes fluttering in the wind, a sword in one hand and a soul lantern in the other as he floated down from the mountain path.

What's more, Li Qingqian had sealed hundreds of vengeful ghosts' souls during this battle. These souls couldn't have been better suited for refining weapons—any artificer would pay such a high

---

25 *A polite term of address for a cultivator.*

price for them that Li Qingqian would never have to worry about food or clothing for the rest of his life.

But Li Qingqian didn't have the heart to sell them.

"Every one of them is a maiden from a pitiful family, buried alive as a sacrifice to the mountain at such a young age and made into a vengeful ghost to do harm. This was not their intent. It would be far too cruel to refine them into magical tools; they'd never be able to reincarnate."

So, Li Qingqian resolved to travel to an island with potent spiritual energy in the eastern sea and help these hundreds of souls pass on. Because their hatred was so deep and their number so great, it was entirely possible that it would take more than a decade to complete the task. Before Li Qingqian left, he passed his *Water-Parting Sword Manual* to his younger brother, reminding the young man to work hard in cultivating and to use these sword techniques to do good as much as he could.

As for himself, Li Qingqian vanished without a trace into the vast mortal world.

The healer from Shennong Terrace spoke cautiously. "Even though Li-zongshi is said to be righteous, these corpses bear the marks of the Water-Parting Sword. Could it be that the rumors are false?"

"Impossible." Mo Xi closed his eyes. "Before Li Qingqian became famous, I had the good fortune to meet him. He was indeed a righteous man; he would never do such a despicable thing."

"Then could it be his younger brother?"

Mo Xi shook his head. "The Water-Parting Sword is very difficult to cultivate. It would be impossible to use without ten, even twenty years of arduous work, and Li Houde has only possessed his elder brother's sword manual for a few short years. The timeline doesn't add up."

After the healer from Shennong Terrace completed their report, Mo Xi sat in the courtyard, eyes closed and brow knitted, carefully thinking through the connections between these events.

Li Wei asked curiously, "My lord, everyone at the street stalls is saying the culprit is a rapist. Some strange fixation made him kill a bunch of the people in a brothel, but he kept five beauties to carry off. Is that not how you see it?"

"It isn't."

Li Wei hadn't expected Mo Xi to so directly refute the city's hottest theory. He blinked, taken aback. "Wh-why?"

Mo Xi unrolled a scroll of spirit jade on the table. The names and appearances of the deceased, as well those of the five missing women, materialized on its surface.

"Come look at this."

Li Wei drew closer and looked at it intently for a good long time. He couldn't find any problems and so replied obsequiously, "This subordinate is too dull to perceive the workings of heaven."

"Pick out the best-looking five," Mo Xi said.

Li Wei loved doing things like comparing and ranking people, so he pointed at a few of the brothel's beauties with all due speed. "Her, and her...ah, nope, she isn't as pretty as the one next to her..."

As he happily made his selection, Xihe-jun said, "Have you noticed that not a single one of the maidens you've chosen was taken by this 'rapist'?"

"Huh..." Li Wei was stumped for a second, and his eyes widened. "It's just as you say..."

"He ignored the star songstress and beheaded many of the most beautiful courtesans to keep these five." Mo Xi looked at the little portraits on the jade scroll and crossed his arms as he murmured as if he were explaining himself to Li Wei, or as if he were sinking back into his thoughts. "He did not do this for women. 'This humble one is lonely; sincerely seeking wives,' likely doesn't reflect his true intentions."

At that moment, a servant of Xihe Manor hurried over. "My lord, my lord—"

"What is it?" Mo Xi turned, frowning. "Has something happened?"

"You had Xiao-Lizi keep an eye on Gu Mang's movements in the prison. Just now, Xiao-Lizi sent a message: Wangshu-jun suspects that Gu Mang had something to do with the Mansion of Beauties murder case, s-so..."

Mo Xi's expression instantly shifted. "So?"

"So he went to interrogate Gu Mang alone in the Chamber of Ice. That room—that room has no windows, so Xiao-Lizi had no idea what was happening within, and he didn't dare alert you without reason, so he waited until Wangshu-jun came out... But then he saw... Gu Mang was already...he was already..."

He pathetically swallowed, mustering the courage to continue.

But Mo Xi didn't wait for him to finish. He'd already thrown down the jade scrolls and rushed straight for the prison without a backward glance.

25

I Want a Home

THE CHAMBER OF ICE in the prison was lightless, airless. Its interior was no larger than a cowshed, but the walls were a foot thick, and it was barred with three layers of gates. Every serious case involving the imprisonment and interrogation of unforgivable criminals was conducted within its walls.

No gods above, no escape below. A bleak prison cell filled with the midnight wailing of ten thousand ghosts.

Who knew how many prisoners had died upon the bone-chilling stone bed in the Chamber of Ice, and how many years' worth of coagulated blood had seeped into the cracks of the heavy, ice-rimmed bricks.

"Treat him quickly. Stop the bleeding. It is His Imperial Majesty's command that this person does not die."

In the dim prison, the warden irritably gave directions. The healers who answered to him rushed back and forth in the cell, scrambling for spiritual medicines and magical implements, while younger disciples rushed to pour out the bloody water wiped from the wounds.

The warden clapped a hand over his forehead, sighing. "My god, Wangshu-jun was too vicious. What even happened here...?"

In their frazzled haste, they suddenly heard someone announce from outside, "Xihe-jun has arrived!"

The warden nearly bit off his own tongue.

Wangshu comes, Wangshu goes, Xihe comes after Wangshu goes; were they the sun and the moon, taking turns to rise in the east and set in the west, not stopping until they had killed Gu Mang?

If he were merely some traitor, they could kill him and no one would care. How many people had ever left an interrogation in the Chamber of Ice alive? But His Imperial Majesty insisted that this person was to remain alive, so if these two noble masters kept having their fun, the sucker who'd have to mop up afterward would be him!

Cursing inwardly, the warden nevertheless put on a warm and enthusiastic smile to greet his visitor. "Aiyo, Xihe-jun's here. This subordinate was too busy to welcome you. I am remiss, and I ask Xihe-jun to forgive me, and not to find fault with someone as—"

—low as this subordinate didn't leave his mouth before Mo Xi lifted a hand to cut him off. He didn't spare the warden a single glance as he headed straight into the Chamber of Ice.

The warden rushed after him. "Xihe-jun, you can't. Gu Mang is covered in wounds—he's not even conscious. Even if you wanted to interrogate him—"

"I wish to see him."

"But Xihe-jun..."

"I said I wish to see him," Mo Xi said angrily. "Do you not understand?!"

The warden was stunned.

"Move aside!"

How would the warden dare to stop him? He swiftly turned to let Mo Xi pass, then followed right behind.

The Chamber of Ice was suffused with a bitter cold. The only source of light was a faint blue flame lapping in a skull-shaped lamp. Gu Mang lay on a stone bed, his white prisoner's garb dyed scarlet, crimson water dripping from the blood grooves in the stone. His face was terrifyingly pale, his eyes wide and unseeing.

Mo Xi walked to his side in silence, betraying no perceptible reaction.

"Wangshu-jun suspected that he had something to do with the Mansion of Beauties murders," the warden cautiously explained. "So he used the Draught of Confession on Gu Mang and tried the Soul-Recording Spell to dig memories from his head, but nothing worked."

Mo Xi made no sound. He gazed at the body on the stone bed. The surrounding healers were hurriedly treating the curse wounds on his body, but Gu Mang's injuries were numerous and deep. As it stood, they couldn't even slow the bleeding...

"See, Xihe-jun?" The warden grimaced. "As I said, he's close to death. Even if you wanted to interrogate him right now, he wouldn't be able to answer a single question. Earlier, Wangshu-jun used all sorts of methods and still left infuriated, so he likely didn't succeed either. Why don't you return another day...?"

"Get out."

The warden blinked.

"Get out!"

The warden scrambled toward the door, his face contorted. He watched Mo Xi drive off the healers one after another, and it took all his courage to shout at Mo Xi's retreating back. "Xihe-jun, His Imperial Majesty wants Gu Mang alive! Remember to have some mercy!"

Xihe-jun had already lowered all three gates with a wave of his hand.

The warden suppressed the urge to weep as he gave instructions to his disciples. "Um, go get that Divine Tincture of Life I keep at the bottom of that one chest. Once Xihe-jun comes out, I suspect only Divine Tincture of Life will keep that little traitor alive...”

The room was now empty save for two. This narrow, sealed world was just as the folk songs said: no gods above, no escape below. The walls were a foot thick, separating those within from the rest of the world—leaving only Gu Mang and Mo Xi.

Mo Xi walked to the side of the bed, lowering his lashes to look at Gu Mang’s face. After a few moments of stillness, he abruptly reached out and lifted him to sitting.

“Gu Mang.” Mo Xi’s mouth opened and closed slightly. His face was still as stagnant water, but his hands were trembling. “You’d better wake up.”

Gu Mang’s only response was to stare from those unfocused eyes.

Both the Draught of Confession and the Soul-Recording Spell devastated their target’s mind. It wasn’t so bad if they obediently confessed, but if they happened to resist, they would feel as if their organs were burning and their innards were tearing apart. Many strong, unyielding individuals might withstand beating and torture, but these two truth-compelling techniques would still drive them crazy.

Furthermore, Mo Xi knew that the Liao Kingdom often cast forbidden secret-keeping spells on the bodies of their soldiers and generals to keep military secrets from being divulged. If such forbidden Liao techniques had clashed with Murong Lian’s Soul-Recording Spell, they would doubtless result in double the agony.

Mo Xi swallowed thickly. This was the first time he had seen what an interrogation did to Gu Mang with his own eyes.

It hurt. It hurt *so much*.

Gu Mang had betrayed him, had tried to kill him. His hands were stained with blood, and his crimes could never be pardoned. But...

This was also the man who had once abandoned everything before the throne, caring nothing for his life, his rank, or his future prospects as he fearlessly shouted at the emperor merely so his soldiers could be properly buried.

This was also the man who had once kept Mo Xi company by a bonfire, roasting meat and chatting with him, smiling at and teasing him, as Mo Xi sat, wordless, by his side.

This was also the man who had once, in bed, murmured to Mo Xi that he loved him.

That spirited, valiant war god's body had seemed as if it would never cool. That youthful, brilliant young man had seemed as if he would blaze passionately all his life. Yet all that remained was this scarred and wounded ruin in front of Mo Xi's eyes...

At that, a thought occurred to Mo Xi, clear as day. He had been away from the capital for a full two years. In that time, how many interrogations of this sort had taken place? So many people wanted to pry words from Gu Mang's mouth and obtain the secrets of the Liao Kingdom. Exactly how many times had he been brutalized beyond the pains of death? How many times had Gu Mang's agonized howling gone unheard?

As Mo Xi's pain deepened, his reason was swiftly disappearing.

The two of us will always be together; no matter how hard, I will endure until the end.

Shidi...

Mo Xi squeezed his eyes shut, suddenly no longer able to bear it. Clenching his jaw, he pulled Gu Mang into his arms. Radiance gathered in his hands as he pressed them against Gu Mang's back and passed the purest, most potent spiritual energy he possessed into that bloodstained body.

Mo Xi knew he shouldn't do it—he would be discovered, and

he had no way to explain why he'd rushed in to personally heal Gu Mang's wounds.

He understood that he should give Gu Mang over to the prison's healers. These people wouldn't defy the emperor's orders and let Gu Mang come to further harm, and Murong Lian's work might not have been fatal.

But...Mo Xi couldn't hold back. His heart seemed to have been snatched away and torn apart, tormented as it had been by more than a decade of love and hatred, unanswered yearning and stubborn attachment.

It was as though if he didn't take hold of this body before him—if he didn't personally pass him spiritual energy—he would be the one to die in this Chamber of Ice.

Most of the wounds on Gu Mang's body had come from Murong Lian's holy weapon, and they healed with awful slowness. In the process of stopping the bleeding and treating Gu Mang's injuries, Mo Xi's military robes were almost entirely soaked. As Gu Mang's limbs gradually began to recover, he unconsciously began to shudder, his bloody hands quivering incessantly.

After a long while, Gu Mang started to mumble. "I...don't know... I don't know...anything..."

Mo Xi had been silent this whole time, not saying a single word as he held Gu Mang. He didn't dare be too intimate, as if any closeness were a colossal sin. But he refused to let go; he felt his own heart would stop if he did. He closed his eyes, slowly sending vigorous spiritual energy into Gu Mang's body.

Other than Gu Mang's half-conscious mumbling, there were no other sounds in the Chamber of Ice. Eventually, amid this hush, Mo Xi heard him mutter something new:

"I...want, I want...a..."

Mo Xi was stunned. "What?"

Gu Mang's voice softened further, almost as faint as a mosquito's buzz. Tearful, trembling, shaking: "home..."

This final word drifted down, soft as willow fluff, but it exploded in Mo Xi's ears like a clap of thunder.

Mo Xi stared down at Gu Mang's face and found that his eyes were tightly closed. His long, dark lashes, laid over the purplish shadows below his eyes, were wet. Gu Mang had choked out those words in a dream.

Many years ago, Mo Xi had once kissed Gu Mang's fingers in the throes of love and desire and said earnestly, "I've been named Xihe-jun by the emperor. In the future, I'll never need to bow to my uncle's whims again. No one can make me do anything. No one can stop me from doing anything. I will achieve everything that I promised you. Wait for me. I mean it."

Before this moment, Mo Xi had never dared to speak of "meaning it" or "the future" to Gu Mang—because Gu Mang had always looked as if he didn't care, and like he didn't believe him.

But on that day, Mo Xi became Xihe-jun. He was no longer merely the young Mo-gongzi under the thumb of his uncle. He finally had the courage to promise a future to his beloved, as if he'd saved up long enough to afford a presentable treasure, and was carefully and cautiously offering it to the one he loved with wholehearted delight in hopes it would be accepted.

Mo Xi wanted to carve out his entire heart. He wanted to swear all the oaths in the world, just for a word of acknowledgment from Gu Mang.

Mo Xi had said so many things that day in their bed. Gu Mang had smiled as he patted Mo Xi's hair, and let Mo Xi fuck him relentlessly, unstoppably. He seemed to listen to and understand everything, yet he also seemed to find his little shidi merely adorable—a little dummy. No matter how fierce Mo Xi became, no matter if he was or wasn't Xihe-jun, his Gu Mang-gege would cherish and indulge him for a lifetime.

"What do you like? What do you want?" Mo Xi asked.

Gu Mang didn't say anything, didn't ask for anything. In the end, after the point Mo Xi couldn't count how many times he'd come inside Gu Mang, after he'd fucked Gu Mang into tearful delirium, Gu Mang spoke. Whether because his thoughts were scattered, or because he was completely spent, Gu Mang tilted his head back to gaze at the inky swirls of the hui-patterned canopy and mumbled, "I... I want...a home..."

Mo Xi was stunned. He suspected he would never in his life forget Gu Mang's expression when he said these words. Gu Mang had always been such a smiling, carefree man, but when he said this, he didn't dare to look Mo Xi in the eye. He was such a confident person, but in that moment, only hesitance and fear remained.

It was as if Gu Mang was begging for something unspeakably precious, pleading for a fantasy he could never hope to attain.

After saying this, Gu Mang closed his eyes, tears rolling down from their reddened rims. Mo Xi wasn't quite sure whether they were the tears Gu Mang usually shed when they went to bed.

Mo Xi realized then with impossible clarity that the invincible General Gu was, in the end, still an orphaned slave. He had been beaten and cursed at for more than twenty years, without a true home that he could call his own, without a single person he could call family.

Mo Xi felt a painful pressure in his heart, an unbearable ache. He leaned down, pressing his lips to Gu Mang's wet and trembling mouth. In the spaces between their gasping breaths, he stroked Gu Mang's hair and whispered, "Okay. I'll give it to you."

I will give it to you. I will give you a home.

This is the first time you've asked me for anything. Even if it's a joke, even if it's nonsense, I'll take it seriously.

I know your life's been horribly hard. So many people have bullied you, toyed with you...so you don't dare accept what others give you. You don't dare believe what others promise you. But I would never lie to you. Wait for me.

Wait for me. I'll do my best—upon battlefields of blood, I'll make my name, I'll use all my war-won merits for the right to be with you. Wait for me.

I will give you a home.

Mo Xi's past self had fervently—naively—made this promise in his heart.

It won't take too many years; it won't be too long. I will give you a home. I want to stay with you, always.

Heartsore, the young Mo Xi had stroked his Gu Mang-gege's face, begging him with such imploring need.

Gu Mang, wait a little longer for me...won't you...?

26

Secretly Watching Over You

WHEN MO XI exited the Chamber of Ice, the warden felt his soul was about to evaporate.

After Wangshu-jun the Cruel had come to interrogate Gu Mang earlier, he'd come out wearing a set of pristine, sapphire-blue robes. Even the moonstone pendant at his chest had been perfectly straight. But once the warden had gone in to look, good heavens, Gu Mang had been drenched in blood.

Wangshu-jun had left Gu Mang in that terrible state without getting a drop of gore on himself, so if Xihe-jun's martial robes were completely soaked through, then didn't that mean that Gu Mang was—

At this thought, the warden's knees went weak, and he nearly fell to the floor. Fortunately, a nearby disciple stepped up to support him in time, so he managed to remain upright, if barely, as he shakily bowed to Mo Xi. "Xihe-jun, safe travels."

Mo Xi stalked wordlessly out of that cold and ghastly prison corridor, his face ashen, lips pursed. He didn't look back. Those military boots, inlaid with iron plating, clicked crisply against the icy brick.

"Divine Tincture of Life, Divine Tincture of Life! Hurry up, hurry up, hurry up!"

The warden's hands shook as he grasped this spiritual medicine that could regrow flesh and reverse necrosis. Leading a dense flock of healers, he rushed into the Chamber of Ice. Before he could get his bearings, he stopped short, shocked.

Gu Mang lay on the stone bed, covered by a warm black-and-gold fur coat. The thin face visible within the depths of the fur...was clean.

The disciple was shocked. "Shifu, wh-what happened...?"

The warden swept a glance over the coat, and his gaze landed on the intricate golden snake totem on its sleeves. His heart pounded. Wasn't that the insignia of the Northern Frontier Army?

Come to think of it, Mo Xi had plainly worn a warm greatcoat when he entered the prison, but when he left, he had been wearing a practical set of fitted black robes. So was it possible that this coat... was...

Swallowing, the warden took a few steps forward and timidly lifted a corner of the coat. Gu Mang was curled up asleep underneath, his breathing even and his wounds no longer bleeding. The warden was astonished. He had a faint feeling that something wasn't quite right...

But when he thought of Mo Xi's usual countenance of icy pride, and then of how Gu Mang had once mercilessly stabbed Mo Xi, this brazen conjecture was rapidly extinguished.

The disciple craned his neck for a better look. After staring for several seconds, he jerked back in surprise. "Aiya! Isn't that Xihe-jun's outer robe?"

The warden didn't immediately respond.

"Shifu, Shifu, don't they say Xihe-jun is a clean freak? That he never lets anyone touch his belongings?"

The warden turned, rather speechless. "Don't tell me you think he wants this coat back?"

"Oh..." The disciple scratched his head in embarrassment. "Of course not." After a second, his curiosity got the better of him once again. "But didn't Xihe-jun come to interrogate Gu Mang? Why would he treat a prisoner so well?"

"It's not like he's an official with a penchant for torture." Although the warden was still apprehensive, he had a keen understanding of what should and shouldn't be speculated on. Patting the little disciple's shoulder, he said meaningfully, "Not everyone is as fond of bloodshed as Wangshu-jun."

"Oh..."

The warden turned to give instructions to the rest. "With regard to what transpired today: You must all be careful; don't spread word of it to outsiders." He shot another glance at the flying snake flashing gold on the fur coat and lowered his voice. "Remember, too much talk brings trouble."

Mo Xi walked along the snowy main road. The west wind whipped across his face. He didn't have a coat, but somehow he didn't feel chilled. His penetrating gaze was all ablaze, and his heart thundered like a drum as Gu Mang's low murmur reverberated endlessly in his ears.

I want...a home...

A spark seemed to have landed on the mess of kindling that was his heart. The flames roared up from his chest and burned so fiercely that even the rims of his eyes reddened slightly.

Mo Xi's belief that Gu Mang's mind might not have been damaged rooted ever deeper. Why else would he mumble *those* words in his delirium?

The flames dancing in his chest were both torment and hope. He was so caught up in his thoughts that he didn't notice his blood-soaked clothes attracting the furtive glances of passersby.

The snow fell faster, but the light in Mo Xi's eyes only grew brighter. He decided that no matter what, once this case concluded, he *had* to wrest Gu Mang from Murong Lian. Only then could he observe Gu Mang from dawn till dusk; only then could he determine if Gu Mang truly was faking stupidity or whether he was genuinely insane.

As he walked, consumed by these thoughts, a sudden shrill scream rose in the distance.

Mo Xi stopped and looked up, searching for the source of the sound.

The capital was in a state of high alert, so he hastened in the direction of the scream. It was a tavern. The chairs and tables were splintered and broken, and a good number of the wine jugs piled in the corner were smashed. Aged pear-blossom white wine seeped into the floor, and the sharp scent of alcohol pervaded the room.

The customers were pushing and shoving one another to run out. Only a few cultivators, who'd happened to be drinking there, were still on the premises. They were in a private room on the second floor, and their number included Yue Chenqing.

Yue Chenqing had a hand pressed over a still-bleeding wound on his arm, and he was cursing furiously. This was a true rarity; he had a good temper and wasn't easily angered. But at the moment, Yue Chenqing was fair smoking with rage, his mouth full of frustrations. "Scaredy-cat! Little turtle! No friend at all!"

Being a simple and cheerful person who so rarely cursed at people, he repeated the only swear words he knew over and over again, among which even "little turtle" counted as profanity.

"Good heavens it hurts!"

Mo Xi reached the second floor with all speed, where he bumped straight into Yue Chenqing, who was still shouting with anger. "Big bad dog!"

When the young man raised his head, he found he had happened to curse directly at Mo Xi.

Mo Xi stared at him.

Yue Chenqing was startled, his round eyes growing even wider. "Xihe-jun? How come you're here? Um, I wasn't referring to *you*..."

"What happened?" Mo Xi's gaze swept over Yue Chenqing. "You're injured?"

"Yes, yes! There was a formidable man in black here a second ago who flipped in through the window to kidnap the tavern's Xiao-Cui-jiejie," Yue Chenqing spoke in a rush. "Xiao-Cui-jiejie is always so cute; every time we buy wine, she gives the bros extra. Sometimes she even gives us peanuts and kidney-bean cakes, even though kidney-bean cakes aren't that tasty, but still—"

"Get to the point."

"Oh, right, the point." Yue Chenqing mulled it over, still steaming mad. "The point is, as soon as I noticed things weren't right, I rushed up to stop the man in black with a few of my friends. But that ruffian used some kind of strange demonic techniques—I couldn't even touch his sleeve before he slashed me with his sword. Some friends I've got! As soon as they saw me injured, they all ran off! Can you believe it? They're all little turtles!"

The more he spoke, the angrier he got, until he looked as though he was about to spit blood.

"It turns out the Chonghua Youth Society is a gang of phonies—seriously, they're so shallow!"

Mo Xi was speechless.

The Chonghua Youth Society was a little group that consisted of Yue Chenqing and a crowd of young juniors—a crowd of gongzi bros whose hobbies were social climbing and putting on airs, and who spent their days parading themselves around together. They even secretly gave themselves jianghu sobriquets, things like "Proud Dragon" and "Brocade Tiger."

Mo Xi had always felt that this was very stupid, and upon hearing Yue Chenqing decry them, he naturally added his own stern rebuke. "I told you not to mess around with those people, but you wouldn't listen. Is your wound serious?"

"It's fine, it's fine." Yue Chenqing wore a lifeless expression. "It's just that I feel such bitter disappointment over my brothers' betrayal. Now I can finally experience what you felt, Xihe-jun, back when you..."

He realized mid-sentence that he was headed in a dangerous direction and hastily shut his mouth, peering wide-eyed at Mo Xi.

Mo Xi considered for a moment, then asked, "Where did the man in black go?"

"I don't know. He moved too quickly. He didn't even seem human. There was just a *whoosh*, and even his shadow had disappeared. Oh, my poor Xiao-Cui-jiejie... Xihe-jun, do you think he was that two-pump chump guy...?"

Mo Xi frowned. "What?"

Only then did Yue Chenqing realize that given how busy Mo Xi had been, he definitely hadn't heard that particular storyteller's embellished version of the brothel murder case. "I meant that Mansion of Beauties murderer," he explained.

"Let me take a look at your wound."

Feeling sorry for himself, Yue Chenqing showed him.

Mo Xi examined Yue Chenqing's injury, his sharp brows furrowing deeper. "It's the Water-Parting Sword..."

Yue Chenqing started. "The Water-Parting Sword zongshi, Li Qingqian?" he asked in astonishment.

Mo Xi shook his head, neither confirming nor denying. All he said was, "Go home for now. The capital has been especially chaotic recently. Unless you have an urgent matter to attend to, don't go running around outside."

"My dad went to Rongliu Mountain to cultivate in seclusion, and my fourth uncle is so aloof he ignores me completely. I can't stay in that manor alone."

"Then go to your brother's."

Yue Chenqing hesitated, then mumbled, "He's not my brother..."

Yue Chenqing had been influenced by the Yue Clan since he was young, so his impression of Jiang Yexue wasn't particularly good. He thought of him as a good-for-nothing who'd brought shame to the Yue Clan. But he couldn't say as much in front of Mo Xi, so he was compelled to change the subject. "Right, Xihe-jun, where did you come from? Why are your clothes all bloody?"

Mo Xi looked down. After a long while, he said, "I dealt with someone."

"D-dealt with someone?" Judging by those red-soaked robes, Xihe-jun might've beaten that person to death.

"No more questions," Mo Xi said. "Can you draw a portrait of the girl who was taken, that Miss Xiao-Cui?"

"Yes, let me give it a try!"

Yue Chenqing asked the tavern's proprietress for paper and a brush. At once, a youthful girl's features appeared in vivid detail on the paper. Mo Xi watched from the side, but even up until the last brushstroke, he couldn't identify what was special about this maiden. Just as he was planning to ask the proprietress about her background, Yue Chenqing seized the brush he had set down.

"Wait a minute! Something's missing!" He hastily added a mole at the end of Xiao-Cui's eye. Only then did he pronounce himself satisfied. "Right, now it's perfect."

Mo Xi widened his eyes slightly. "She has an eye mole too?"

"Huh? What do you mean *too*? Who else has one?"

"Of the five escorts taken from the Mansion of Beauties," said Mo Xi, "one of them had a similar mole."

As he explained to Yue Chenqing, a thought occurred to him: as far as the "rapist" was concerned, this eye mole might be an extremely important attribute. It might have even bought that prostitute's survival.

He was still considering this when he heard Yue Chenqing speak up hesitantly once more. "Actually, Xihe-jun, there's something else I wanted to tell you."

"Speak."

"Well...um, I might be mistaken, but when I was crossing blows with the man in black, I couldn't see his face, but I kept feeling that he had a certain odor, something I'm very familiar with."

"What odor?" Mo Xi asked. "Where did you smell it before?"

"It's not quite an *odor*. It's more a type of...uh...I don't know how to describe it. A type of aura. I felt like I'd experienced it somewhere before, but I was fighting too intently, and he left too quickly, so I didn't have time to carefully analyze it before he disappeared." Yue Chenqing sighed. "Xihe-jun, do you think he really is that Mansion of Beauties murderer?"

"I can't be sure." Mo Xi thought about it further and said, "How about this: Yue Chenqing, go to Shennong Terrace to get your wounds treated, then stop by the Bureau of Public Safety and pass on a message."

"What message?"

"If my guess is correct, that rapist is looking for women with certain characteristics," Mo Xi said, studying Xiao-Cui's portrait. "The eye mole ought to be one of them. Have the Bureau of Public Safety inform the city and ask maidens who share those characteristics to go to the bureau for temporary protection."

"Oh, okay, okay." Yue Chenqing agreed. He was about to leave when he thought of something and turned on his heel. "Right, Xihe-jun, I heard Murong-dage received His Imperial Majesty's authorization to interrogate Gu Mang whenever he wanted. Did you know about this?"

"...Mn."

"It seems like Gu Mang is still useful to you, Xihe-jun, but if Murong-dage goes to interrogate him, I'm afraid he'll interrogate him half to death. Do you want to..."

"It's of no consequence." Mo Xi shook his head, unconsciously caressing a black silver thumb ring as his eyes slowly darkened.

When he had treated Gu Mang's wounds just now, he had planted a tracking talisman exclusive to the Mo Clan within his body. So long as it was active, whenever anything unusual happened to Gu Mang, this silver ring would heat up and tell Mo Xi where Gu Mang was, as well as his condition.

He very truly had no wish to see Gu Mang in the aftermath of such torture again.

"I've already made my preparations," Mo Xi said. "Whatever Murong Lian does next, I'll know about it. You needn't worry."

After leaving Yue Chenqing, Mo Xi returned to his manor, where he again took out the jade scroll with the likenesses of those five prostitutes. He placed Xiao-Cui's portrait next to the songstress with an eye mole and stared at the other four faces.

None of the other four had any noteworthy features. There was no way to discern further details from these paintings.

But that didn't remain the case for long. As the number of missing women in the city steadily increased, Xihe Manor received more and more portraits. Once they were sorted, their similarities became apparent—for example, their lips had the same shape, or their noses were identical.

Based on these patterns, Mo Xi had the imperial guards invite every woman with these attributes to the Bureau of Public Safety for protection.

Soon after, women stopped going missing. Only a few maidens who hadn't yet been taken into custody by the bureau were kidnapped by the "rapist" now and again. Instead, it was the cultivators who started to worry.

"If Chengtian Terrace's Elder Yu was no match for that scoundrel, what would we do if he tried to carve out our hearts?"

"Ah, I've become too scared to cultivate alone in the woods."

As the year came to an end, the usual hustle and bustle of Chonghua City ground to a halt. People went out only in groups and rushed back home before night fell, and the Yue Clan's barrier talismans sold faster than ever. Many of those who failed to snag a talisman in time refused to sleep apart from their weapons.

As for those who couldn't afford the talismans, they could only cry and shout and beg at the gates of Yue Manor for mercy, to let them buy on credit and pay them back later.

Yue Chenqing wasn't entitled to make decisions regarding such things. His father was away, so his paternal uncle came out to furiously shoo off all the penniless little cultivators. "The hell is all this?!" he cursed at them. "Who do you think you are, behaving like this before an elite cultivator's manor? Yue Manor's talismans are unbreakable. They're worth what we charge and no less! Can't afford it? Go borrow money from your brothers and friends!"

The storytellers were too afraid to tell stories anymore. Besides, the situation was getting worse and worse, so who would dare come to listen and laugh?

The red paste paper outside Yuelai Teahouse that said *Enraged Brothel Guest Kills Seventy* gradually disintegrated in the wind and snow. Rainwater soaked into the brushstrokes, rendering the words forever illegible...

Then one night, it stopped snowing. The capital was an expanse of pure moonlight.

Mo Xi sat in Xihe Manor's courtyard, reading the intelligence reports that had accumulated in the past few days as he unconsciously spun and caressed the silver soaring snake ring on his thumb.

He had often found himself doing this of late. The tracking ring felt like a secret, selfish tie linking him to Gu Mang, and he was only at ease when it was safe.

However, on that silent night, just as he was about to roll up a scroll and retire, the ring burned with searing heat.

Mo Xi immediately looked down to see the snake insignia on the ring begin to twist and turn, slowly transforming into an arrow that pointed toward the southwest of the capital. The silver snake's body began to change color, flickering and gleaming until every one of its scales finally flashed jade green.

The scales turning green meant the one being tracked had been drugged. This wasn't unexpected; Murong Lian often gave the prisoners he interrogated a variety of illusion-inducing medicines.

The issue lay in the direction. The prison was not in the southwest of the capital; rather, that was where the resting place of Chonghua's heroes lay: Warrior Soul Mountain.

Why would Gu Mang be taken from the prison and be sent toward Warrior Soul Mountain?

Practically simultaneous to this thought, Mo Xi saw golden light burst from every guard barrier in the capital as the warning bell in the imperial city rang out. *Clang, clang, clang.* One chime after another, thirteen in total before it stilled.

A dangerous criminal had broken out of prison.

Gu Mang had escaped?!

27

Dream of Longing

THE SITUATION WAS too urgent for Mo Xi to personally inform the emperor. He sent a messenger butterfly winging to the palace and took the initiative to rush to the foot of Warrior Soul Mountain.

At the entrance, he found that the two cultivators guarding the mountain were already dead. Their eyeballs had been gouged out, and their hearts taken as well.

They had died in the same way as Elder Yu.

The ring on Mo Xi's hand grew hotter and hotter, and it pointed straight at that blood-splattered mountain path. Mo Xi stared at the ring for a moment, gritting his teeth. "Gu Mang...is it really you?"

He swept straight up the mountain, blood running cold.

The terrain of Warrior Soul Mountain was difficult to traverse. Its cloud-encircled peak was the resting place for generations and dynasties of Chonghua's heroes. It was said that, in the dead of night, the whinnying of warhorses and the clanging of copper bells still sounded from the mountain, as if to lend credence to the legend that so long as the fires of war burned across the Nine Provinces, the souls of Chonghua's heroes would know no peace.

Many magical navigation devices were befuddled by the mountain's flow of spiritual energy and would fail to point in the correct direction. Even Mo Xi's silver ring was affected, recalibrating many times before it spun once more.

Mo Xi arrived at the foothills of Warrior Soul Mountain and stopped, staring at the faint mist that suffused the dense forest. "Dream of Longing..." he murmured.

Indeed, this was no ordinary mountain mist, but rather the Dream of Longing technique, which only elite Liao Kingdom cultivators could use.

This illusion could transform one's true surroundings into an entirely new world. If the technique detected your desires and you sunk within them, your mind would be left vulnerable to destruction. Mo Xi, however, had fought many Liao Kingdom spellcasters who used Dream of Longing on the battlefields; resisting it wasn't particularly arduous for him.

The needle tip of the ring was pointing right into the thick of it, which could only mean that Gu Mang was currently within that illusory mist from Dream of Longing.

Mo Xi had to enter. He pondered this for a spell before lifting his head and gravely intoning, "Illusion Butterfly."

A messenger butterfly materialized in response to his summons.

"Report the location and situation to His Imperial Majesty," Mo Xi said. "I will go forth to investigate. Have him send assistance."

The butterfly fluttered its wings, and in a blink, it disappeared into the depths of the mountain forest. Mo Xi stepped into the dense, unrelenting fog.

He was surrounded by a white haze so thick it was difficult to see his own fingers.

"Gu Mang!" he shouted. "Gu Mang, come out!"

Mo Xi's voice echoed in the mist.

After a moment, soft laughter floated out from the damp, chilly murk. "Xihe-jun?" The speaker was not Gu Mang. He sighed. "Ah, how interesting. I did sense a foreign spiritual flow in my captive Beast of the Altar. It seems you've put a tracking talisman on him."

"Who are you, good sir?" Mo Xi asked carefully.

"Xihe-jun's been investigating the brothel case for so long. Doesn't he have an inkling as to who I am?" That shadowy figure was vague in the mist, appearing for a flash, then disappearing immediately thereafter.

But in that brief flash, Mo Xi had struck. A barrage of blazing fireballs hurtled forward with a resounding *boom*.

"Aiyo." A hum came from the thick mist. After another few moments, the voice sighed. "Xihe-jun, the ruthless god of war...truly lives up to his name." He let out an eerie, ominous laugh. "You really do have a terrible temper."

A muscle in Mo Xi's jaw jumped. "Where's Gu Mang? What is your relationship with him?!"

"I don't have any relationship with him. As for who I am, aren't all those tales being spread in Chonghua City?" The person spoke with relish, as if describing something he found incomparably interesting. "They say I rape brothel girls, or that I'm a runaway cook from Luomei Pavilion..." He laughed loudly, the sound reverberating in mist that grew thicker and thicker. "They're really so fascinating. I heard a great many—and I even told one myself."

He'd told one himself?!

"That's right," the man continued with an indolent lilt, as if he could see Mo Xi's slightly widened eyes. "I was bored of lazing around, so I dressed up as a storyteller and slipped into a teahouse to tell tales. I said I'd mounted seventy victims in one night, but that friend of yours, young Yue-gongzi, didn't enjoy my performance at all. He wanted to gossip about a *two-pump chump*. What a naughty child."

"So you were actually... Then the real storyteller..."

"I killed him, of course," the man said carelessly. "I think I threw him into a dry well afterward? Or maybe a burial mound? Sorry, I've killed so many people. It's a bit of a blur."

He laughed again. "Speaking of, you're certainly more reliable than that Wangshu-jun. All he knows is how to let his imagination run wild. Once he came up with his own conclusion, he tripped over himself rushing to pry proof of it from the prisoner's mouth. You knew better—you properly analyzed those few sword marks I left on the bodies."

The man paused, then asked, nigh delighted, "So, did you figure it out?"

"Are you really Li Qingqian?" Mo Xi's voice was low and fiery.

The man was still for a few moments, the thick fog roiling, before he unexpectedly burst into giggles. His laughter grew louder and eerier, resounding endlessly around them, its source impossible to pin down.

"Li Qingqian...Li Qingqian, ha ha, ha ha ha ha..." This name seemed to have pricked a sore spot in his heart. The laughter wrenched from his throat was like wheeling vultures, circling without cease.

"I'm not!" His voice suddenly tightened, sharp amid the lingering echoes. "The first chapter of the *Water-Parting Sword Manual* says, 'The benevolent blade parts water, the righteous blade cuts sorrow; compassion despite lowliness, resilience against a thousand hardships...' How ridiculous, how wretched, how pathetic! 'Li-zongshi' who? He's nothing more than a penniless miser, a useless good-for-nothing, a pathetic pedant!"

He continued to curse and rage for a long while until he gradually calmed down. In the freezing, silent mist, he snapped, "I'm so sick of you hypocrites. You're unquestionably tainted by all three poisons—greed, wrath, and ignorance, but you remain trapped by cowardly indecision, all for the sake of your precious reputation."

Danger had filled his voice.

Mo Xi could not have been more sensitive to killing intent, and his eyes were instantly wary. "Shuairan! Come!"

A beam of red light flashed, and the holy snake whip hissed into his hand.

"Oh, Shuairan." The man snorted. "So strong. Its power is earth-shattering. Unfortunately, I think you won't need it here."

Mo Xi said nothing.

"I can't defeat you in a fight, so I won't bother trying. However, I've had the luck to overhear some of your secrets. I've no shortage of ways to trap you. For example..." The man paused, then asked in a tone filled with curiosity, "Back when Gu Mang was locked up at Luomei Pavilion, did you or did you not tell him...that the lotus tattoo on his neck...was your doing?"

Mo Xi's blood ran cold. He ground his teeth. "What exactly are you?!"

"Don't be in such a rush to ask that. Why don't I ask you first?" The voice still spoke with interest. "Let me ask you a question—the finest general of Chonghua, the pristine Xihe-jun, distant from all others, self-restrained and self-possessed for thirty years. A man so callous even Princess Mengze's attentive care can't thaw him."

The man's voice rose and fell, moving suddenly close and suddenly far. This time, it seemed to press right up next to Mo Xi's ear, breath humid.

"You and that General Gu—what relationship do you share?"

With a whistle, Shuairan struck, fiery rage making sparks burst from the whip.

The phantom seemed to have expected this. He wasn't hit and dispersed to who knew where.

"You're so mean, Officer. Looks like my guess wasn't far off the mark?"

Mo Xi didn't answer. "Hand over Gu Mang!" he snapped.

"Hand him over? I'm not stupid. He used to be the fiercest general of the Liao Kingdom. Even though his core's been broken, I still have methods by which to control him and revive his battle strength." That phantom was smiling. "Why would I hand over such a strong soldier?"

He paused, and his smile grew broader. "In all of Chonghua, you're the only person who can face him one-on-one, Xihe-jun. As long as I have him to guard me, no one else who comes here could hope to be a match for him. As for you, Xihe-jun..."

The suggestive lilt in that voice grew more pronounced.

"I have other plans."

As the man spoke, the lingering sound drifted into the distance, as if it were about to fade away entirely.

"Since you had the courage to come alone and enter this dreamscape for his sake, I must of course be a good host and let him serve you properly." He laughed softly. "Xihe-jun, pleasant times with your lover are ever brief, so enjoy them while you can."

"You—!"

As if in answer to his wishes, a burst of red lit up in front of him, accompanied by a high, wavering voice. Someone was singing.

"Rain falls soft over Yuchi Pavilion; sun shines down on Jinni Hall. Let wine and music flow for all; mean although their lives may seem, matters of ants are not so small..."

Mo Xi knew that as soon as one entered the Dream of Longing's vision, it could not be broken from within. He would have to wait for the emperor's reinforcements to arrive. Until then, he would be unable to avoid whatever illusory scenes unfolded before him. However, so long as he could maintain clarity of mind, it would be no trial to withstand.

But at that very moment, the phantom's voice slithered once more from the depths of the dreamscape: "Xihe-jun, I know what you're thinking. You mean to endure by means of sheer willpower, don't you?" He snickered. "Too bad. Even if *you* can endure, Gu Mang might not manage."

Mo Xi tensed. "What do you mean?"

"Everyone says Xihe-jun possesses astonishing self-restraint, that his focus never wavers. Naturally, I wouldn't be so stupid as to rely on brute force. But now that Gu Mang's lost his souls, he's nothing more than a pitiful, mentally fragile creature—of course it's easier for me to make use of him." His words were faint, slow. "When that ring of yours pointed the way for you, did it tell you that he'd been drugged?"

Cold shot through Mo Xi's blood. "You're—!" he snarled.

"I'm what? I'm despicable?" The phantom smiled. "I only gave him some medicine to awaken his strength so he could better guard me. Good gentleman Xihe-jun, what were *you* thinking?" The phantom's voice was once more filled with delight. "But you're not off the mark—I truly am shameless. Because the next drug I give him...will be something else."

Mo Xi said nothing.

"You're not the only one I've tossed into this illusion. He's here too." The phantom's voice was unctuous. "*You* can endure with your noble self-control, but can you bear to see him... Heh heh, that's enough, that's enough."

Mo Xi was so furious he wanted to let out a stream of curses.

Who was this rapist in truth? Li Qingqian? The Liao Kingdom cook? Or some deranged vengeful ghost?

"Humans are no more than desires given flesh. Some people indulge in sensual delights, others pursue the heights of reputation. But aren't the desires of passion and the desires of reputation both *desire*?" The phantom laughed softly. "What difference is there?"

Mo Xi made no reply.

"Go on. Your Gu Mang-gege...awaits."

The phantom's voice disappeared, while the sounds of music grew louder and louder. The opera singer's trilling voice was about to reach the clouds, winding like a venomous snake.

"In that shade will a kingdom rise, a lifetime's work etched in his eyes. Qi Xuan's teachings only partly gleaned; when will the east wind wake me from this dream—!"

With that final syllable, the fog surrounding Mo Xi dispersed. He discovered that he was standing amid an expanse of brilliant lanterns. It was evening, and people came and went, passing back and forth like a weaving shuttle through the dazzling nightless dark.

Two guards stood before the extravagant whitewashed, black-tiled doors in front of him, wearing blue spellcasters' robes with storm patterns and golden trim. Eight brilliant lanterns illuminated the path into the manor, the blue bat totem above the doorway glimmering brightly with spiritual energy.

The insignia of Murong Lian's clan.

Why was he at...Wangshu Manor?

The illusory world created by Dream of Longing was usually linked to memories with which one didn't wish to part.

Gu Mang was also in the dreamscape with Mo Xi. It was probable that this scene was born not of Mo Xi's inner demons, but rather those of the other man in the dream—the one who'd been fed hallucinatory drugs...

Gu Mang.

Even though Gu Mang's memories weren't whole, the illusion could draw from any fixation in his heart. But why would they manifest Wangshu Manor?

Wangshu Manor. Drugs. Desire. Past. These words floated through Mo Xi's mind. When he thought about it again, he remembered something, and his elegant face instantly paled.

Was it possible that the dreamscape had absorbed that particular part of Gu Mang's past?

Mo Xi cursed inwardly. His shadow swept over the arcing eaves, toward a certain corner of Wangshu Manor.

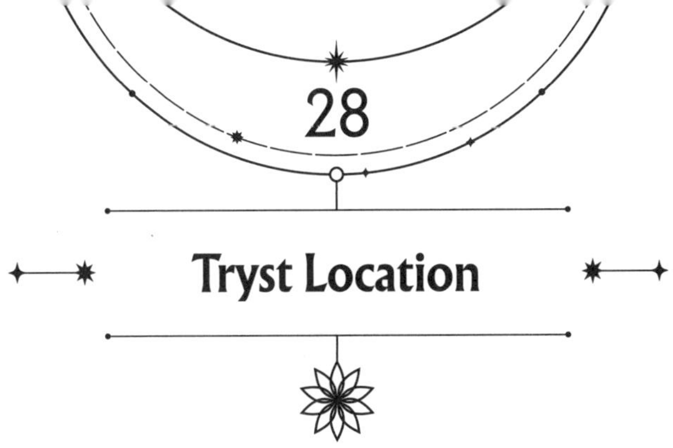

28

Tryst Location

THIS WAS INDEED the right direction. The silver needle gleamed brighter with every step Mo Xi took.

Mo Xi stopped before a servant's cramped quarters and slowed his quickened breath. He lifted pale and slender fingers and found that the ring's needle had reverted once again to the soaring snake pattern. Gu Mang was inside.

If Gu Mang was drugged, then the strongest urge in his heart right now would, inevitably, be lust, and this room...

Mo Xi swallowed. This room...was where he and Gu Mang had shared most of their trysts.

In those days, Murong Lian had been shamelessly despicable. After their first great battle, he claimed credit for all of Gu Mang's battlefield achievements, and the emperor had lavished rewards upon him while Gu Mang remained a nameless little slave in Wangshu Manor.

Given the sprawling vastness of the noble estates, Mo Xi and Gu Mang hadn't been able to meet once since returning from the battlefield. Mo Xi held back and endured quietly as one month passed, then two... Until finally, he could endure no longer. It seemed that Gu Mang couldn't come visit him, so Mo-gongzi donned a grim expression and deigned to pay Wangshu Manor a visit.

At first, he intended to use the excuse of discussing military matters with Murong Lian to catch a glimpse of Gu Mang. However, the housekeeper said that Murong Lian was cultivating in seclusion at the practice field; he wouldn't emerge for a while yet.

"If Mo-gongzi doesn't mind, why not take a stroll in the back gardens? We can arrange for an attendant to come with you."

"Then please ask Gu Mang to come along," Mo Xi replied with complete poise. "We're more or less acquaintances."

This request was not an unreasonable one. Gu Mang happened to be free, so the housekeeper sent for him. When Gu Mang entered the great hall and laid eyes on Mo Xi, he was struck somewhat dumb.

Mo-gongzi and Murong-gongzi mixed as poorly as water with fire. Mo Xi gracing Wangshu Manor with his presence was more shocking than a visit from His Elderliness the emperor himself.

"Shaozhu won't come out for another two hours yet. You must accompany Mo-gongzi on a stroll through the manor grounds," the housekeeper instructed Gu Mang.

A pause. "Of course..." he replied.

Mo Xi glanced at him, then lightly looked away.

Wangshu Manor consisted of seven compounds; the first five bustled with activity, while the last two were reserved for gardening and the cultivation of spiritual herbs. Rarely did any servants go back there.

Gu Mang followed Mo Xi as they walked from the front courtyard to the back. Along the way, he played tour guide for Wangshu Manor's scenery and described the layout of the grounds.

They acted overly distant and courteous with each other, to the point that no guards or servants who passed noticed anything unusual about their conduct. Only Mo Xi knew his own impatience.

He wanted very much to talk to Gu Mang alone. He wanted to look into his eyes and devour this man—who still belonged to Murong Lian—with his bare hands, without leaving a drop of blood or scrap of bone.

But he had to hold on.

"To the left is the qin room, where the young master plays in his leisure hours. There's a five-stringed jiaowei qin made from the wood of a foxglove tree, left by the old master..."

As they walked ever farther into the gardens and the passersby grew ever rarer, Mo Xi's heart began burning hotter, as if even his blood had been set aflame.

When they stepped into a medicine garden, they were finally entirely alone.

"There are seven hundred and sixty-five types of medicinal herbs in the garden," Gu Mang said, "including—"

What they included would remain a mystery, because the Young Master Mo in front of Gu Mang suddenly stopped in his tracks. Gu Mang didn't notice and kept walking, bumping straight into his broad back.

Mo Xi turned to gaze wordlessly at him.

"What's up?" Gu Mang asked hesitantly.

"Don't you..." Mo Xi's expression was wooden. Clearly, he craved and adored Gu Mang beyond measure, but when Mo Xi stood before Gu Mang and his nonchalant gaze, he found himself woefully unsure. Unable to take the hit to his pride, he stiffly finished, "Don't you have anything to say to me?"

Gu Mang muttered something to himself, then rubbed his nose and smiled. "Long time no see, Gongzi?"

Mo Xi said nothing.

"Hey, don't glare at me. You know I'm pretty busy. I have to wipe tables, chop firewood, and catch garden pests. All of those things are super important..."

The expression on Mo Xi's face worsened; he looked as if he'd been poisoned by his own rage.

But at the time, Gu Mang hadn't confirmed they were in any kind of real relationship. In the field, Gu Mang had shamelessly said that this kind of thing was normal—as young men, they shouldn't take sleeping together too seriously.

Now this young man's heart was about to give out thanks to this old scoundrel. And somehow, that scoundrel was still rambling here and chattering there about his "important responsibilities" at Wangshu Manor—as if his lordship the young master of the Mo Clan was less significant than one of Murong-gongzi's damn tables. It made Mo Xi want to hurl a fireball into Murong Lian's desk. Then they'd see what Gu Mang could wipe!

Gu Mang went on and on about Murong-gongzi's high standards for his desk—how you had to be able to see your reflection in the sandalwood surface. Halfway through his next sentence, the world spun, and by the time he came back to his senses, Mo Xi had pinned him to the wall.

"You..." Gu Mang began.

You what? Gu Mang didn't get to finish. Mo Xi kept him trapped with his body, that cool, elegant face tilting closer as one of his hands curled around Gu Mang's waist and the other lifted to press against the wall by his face. Mo Xi dipped his head and firmly sealed Gu Mang's rambling mouth with his own.

Mo Xi kissed Gu Mang forcefully, as if he wanted to bring all his desire crashing down upon the man in his arms, as if he wanted to devour and possess Gu Mang from head to toe. His every movement betrayed an unnerving thirst for domination and control.

His breaths were uncommonly ragged, his tongue unspeakably passionate, as though the aloof Mo-gongzi from a moment ago had been a different person altogether.

"You're crazy...this is *Wangshu Manor*..." Amid their entwining kisses, Gu Mang came back to his senses. He tore himself violently out of Mo Xi's hold as his wet lips opened and closed. "Someone will see!"

Gu Mang pulled with too much strength, and Mo Xi made no attempt to defend himself. With a muffled sound, his arm was dislocated.

"Holy shit." Gu Mang hadn't expected that Mo Xi wouldn't resist, nor that he would emerge the dubious victor in this scuffle. He was instantly mortified, and he swallowed hard. "All right, all right, all right, you're crazy, I admit defeat. I was in the wrong, all right? I'll help you pop that joint back in."

Gu Mang reached out, wanting to help Mo Xi realign his shoulder, but the young master ducked away and refused his touch. He only continued to stare at him fiercely.

"Dage," Gu Mang wheedled, "I'm begging you, let me pop it back into place, okay? Otherwise, when Shaozhu comes out and sees that his guest's been injured, and he asks me how it happened, what am I supposed to say?"

Gu Mang stuck to his act. This rascal who was invincible amid the smoke of war was even more incandescently infuriating off the battlefield. "It's not like I can say I did it, can I?"

Mo Xi made no sound. His face was still icy-aloof, but upon closer inspection, though he was as yet still in control, a dangerous emotion was surging in the depths of his eyes. After maintaining his rigidity for a long moment, he abruptly, stiffly asked once more, "Don't you have anything to say to me?"

"...I do, actually."

"Speak."

"Have you been cursed to repeat yourself?" Gu Mang hastily smiled at Mo Xi's answering expression. "Hey, hey, hey! I'm sorry, I swear!"

"Don't touch me! I can do it myself!" Mo Xi said angrily.

"You can't! You suck at healing magic *and* healing techniques!"

Mo Xi's expression darkened further.

But Gu Mang stopped him, grinning, his smile filled with the smug delight of getting away with a prank. Then he darted close and kissed Mo Xi's cheek.

Mo Xi didn't move.

"How come my princess isn't reacting?" Gu Mang murmured, stroking Mo Xi's chin. "Another kiss, then."

Only after he'd paid for his mischief with many more kisses did Mo-gongzi finally, and very unwillingly, let Gu Mang realign the joint. It plainly didn't hurt very much when it popped back into place, but the glare Mo Xi leveled at him was teary and a touch red.

"Huh? You..." Gu Mang wanted to take a closer look, but Mo-gongzi's palm landed square on that face that was as thick as a city wall, pushing him back. Mo Xi tore his gaze away, refusing to let him see.

After a stretch of silence, Mo Xi said, his face still turned, "I haven't seen you in two months."

"No. Still twelve days to go."

Mo Xi's head snapped around, shooting Gu Mang another fierce glare.

Arms crossed, Gu Mang leaned leisurely against that whitewashed wall. He looked at Mo Xi with a smile, chin slightly raised.

At length, the young master spoke, expression flat: "Take us somewhere no one will see."

In truth, after they'd been apart for so long, Mo Xi wasn't the only one unable to hold back. It was just that Mo Xi disguised his need with cool arrogance, while Gu Mang used breezy nonchalance.

But once they were holding and grinding against each other, both youths burned with torment. In the end, Gu Mang led Mo Xi to an unassuming little room. As hints went, this was way too obvious, and almost as soon as they entered, Gu Mang was shoved hard against the wall. The dark, windowless little room was soon filled with their low panting and the sound of soft kisses.

Just as Mo Xi was biting and sucking on the side of his neck, Gu Mang opened his eyes. Even as the tide of desire rose, he still remembered to gasp, "Don't kiss so high. Sh-shaozhu will notice..."

Mentioning Murong Lian at this moment was clearly not a wise decision. Mo Xi stilled, as if powerfully restraining some terrifying impulse. Gu Mang panted beneath him, and after these few beats of stillness, he was roughly turned around, his belt pulled free...

Mo Xi seemed to be wrestling with some colossal grievance as he pressed Gu Mang against the wall to furtively kiss his cheek, his nape, and eventually that slave collar with which Murong Lian had bound him.

That ice-cold black hoop seemed to stab into Mo Xi, reminding him that no matter how he yearned—to the point of pain, to the point that his heart was about to tear itself apart—the person in his arms still belonged to Murong Lian.

Murong Lian could summon Gu Mang whenever he wanted, torture him however he pleased. It was for him to say whether Gu Mang lived or died, whether he received praise or shame—one iron collar, digging into his spirit, and the lifetime of control it entailed.

Mo Xi was holding someone who belonged to Murong Lian.

Jealousy burned the rims of Mo Xi's eyes. He wrenched Gu Mang's face closer as his control eroded, compelling Gu Mang to twist around and take his kiss while still pressed against the door. Darkness made the wildfire in Mo Xi's heart blaze so searingly. How could their mouths entwine so passionately, so wetly?

Mo Xi made short work of Gu Mang's clothes, but his own weren't yet in disarray. Likely because he could feel the condition of the person behind him, Gu Mang said with petulant amusement, "You're so prim and proper every time you fuck me, but in reality..."

The rest of the sentence turned into a muted groan.

"Shaozhu will be out in two hours. You...you need to be quick..."

Mo Xi pulled out his wet fingers and took hold of Gu Mang's hips. His hot, thick cock rubbed between Gu Mang's legs before suddenly thrusting in.

"*Ah...*" Gu Mang cried out, instantly going limp. He barely managed to stay on his feet by gripping the door. He could vividly feel the heat and girth of Mo Xi's cock throbbing within him, as if it were about to burn him from the inside out.

Panting in low rasps, Mo Xi grabbed Gu Mang's hips and began to fuck him standing there against the door. Even though Gu Mang lived in a remote courtyard, there was no guarantee that no one would pass by. The door was thin, so Gu Mang had to tightly bite his lips, not daring to make a sound. Mo Xi thrust into him in this way for some time before he turned Gu Mang's face to capture his wet lips. Only when Gu Mang opened his mouth did his gasps leak out. Those sounds seemed to provoke Mo Xi further, and the movements from behind him grew more urgent, pounding audibly against his ass. Every one of Mo Xi's thrusts seemed to reach the deepest part of Gu Mang, as if he were fervently trying to press his entirety into him. Amid this brutal pounding, Gu Mang couldn't stop himself from panting out loud.

He struggled, trying to stop Mo Xi, doing his best to turn around, to say something to him. Yet Mo Xi only allowed Gu Mang the slightest space to turn before he pressed him down again without giving him the chance to speak. He lifted Gu Mang's legs from the front and, as if unwilling to wait a moment longer, rubbed his burning cockhead against his still gaping hole before driving aggressively back in.

"*Aahh...ah...* Too deep, it's too deep... Mo Xi... M-Mo Xi... Ah..."

With his legs held up like this, Gu Mang was viciously yet silently fucked by this young man, who usually looked devoid of all desire. His earlier coarse breathing and muted groans soon gave way to incoherency as he felt that his stomach was about to be pierced through. Even Gu Mang's toes, hanging suspended in the air, had curled against his will.

Mo Xi didn't like to speak much during sex, but that primitive, fiery, feral instinct and that deep gaze—that seemed to want to devour Gu Mang whole—was more than enough to make one's heart quiver. Not to mention how ruthlessly and frantically he pounded into Gu Mang, each thrust driving into the deepest recesses of his body, urgent and wild.

Perhaps the door's violent shaking finally brought Gu Mang back to his senses. In the end, he managed to pant in a low voice, "Not—not here. Go inside... There's... There's a bed inside......"

Bed? More like a kennel.

Gu Mang was the only person in the world who was capable of coaxing the overly fastidious Young Master Mo to lie on a battered and broken-down little wooden bed.

"Why not here?"

"S-someone will...ah..." Gu Mang had never possessed a sense of shame, nor was he well-read. Whenever he was distraught, he spoke with mortifying plainness. Arching his neck, he gasped violently. "Someone will hear you fucking me...ah..."

"Does that scare you?"

"B-bullshit! I still gotta live off Shaozhu's money... Ahh... What are you doing?! Not so fast... That's too—too fast... Ah..."

"It'll be best if he kicks you out. You can live off me," Mo Xi bit out.

Despite his words, he knew that if their tryst were to be discovered, getting kicked out would be the least of Gu Mang's worries; it was equally as possible that he'd be drawn and quartered. So he picked up Gu Mang, driving his cock so deep into him that he almost cried out loud, and carried him into the room.

Mo Xi's arms were strong and sturdy, and Gu Mang was not weak. As the two of them walked, Gu Mang's legs tightly wrapped around Mo Xi's waist, his cock never slipped out, and it rubbed repeatedly against Gu Mang's inner walls. The movements were neither quick nor slow, but rather the height of torment.

By the time Mo Xi dropped Gu Mang onto the bed, Gu Mang couldn't hold back anymore. When Mo Xi pressed him down with his vigorous, searing-hot body, lifted his legs, and began to once again fiercely and rapidly fuck him, he panted through muffled moans. "Ah...ah... *Ah,* Shidi... Shidi...fuck me there...*ngh*... Right there... Harder... *Aahhh...*"

This was Gu Mang's way, never bothering to hide anything. Or perhaps it was precisely because he wanted to hide something that he always acted shamelessly, saying things like, *Never mind, never mind, you're young—I respect the elderly and cherish the youth, so I'll let you top. Between us guys, whatever goes as long as we both feel good.*

But Gu Mang's body couldn't bear this kind of stimulation. He had a naturally high tolerance for pain and was unaffected by injuries on the battlefield, but he couldn't bear the pleasure of being fucked. In the end, he always started to cry—but despite his tears, he still threw himself into entangling with Mo Xi.

It was often like this when they made love—Mo Xi wasn't very talkative, but Gu Mang brazenly said things that drove him out of his mind.

You're so big, you're fucking me too hard, get deeper inside me, you're gonna break me, why are you so hot, why haven't you come yet... How... how much longer are you going to take...

This provocation, annoyance, and teasing was too much for Mo Xi, but he couldn't do anything about it.

Gu Mang was a shameless ruffian—he was given to spouting such nonsense. Gu Mang was also a lowly slave, so perhaps, when he slept with Mo-gongzi, even if he did bottom, he had no hang-ups to overcome. He even allowed Mo Xi to...

Mo Xi wasn't sure if he was mistaken, but Gu Mang seemed to *like* it when Mo Xi came inside him. Mo Xi had once asked him about this, his question full of hidden meaning.

Gu Mang had smiled and confessed everything: "Yes, it feels *so* good. Those moments feel amazing—do you want to try? How about I do it next time—"

Mo Xi didn't let him finish, capturing that mouth in sore need of a lesson in a kiss. He buried his hips between Gu Mang's spread legs and pistoned back and forth swiftly and ferociously, reducing Gu Mang's banter to disjointed moans.

Mo Xi was a prudent and decorous person. But unexpectedly, he loved hearing Gu Mang's almost incoherent and wanton noises. He just never admitted it out loud.

In the end, after both of them had come, Gu Mang was practically limp with exhaustion as he lay beneath Mo Xi, soaked in sweat. His hole was still clenched around Mo Xi's cock, which plugged the come inside him as Gu Mang's sturdy chest rose and fell. Who could have guessed that such a powerful, well-muscled male body was currently pumped full of another man's come?

Gu Mang stared into space, dazed, for a while. As Mo Xi kissed him tenderly, he suddenly laughed. "Why'd you come to see Shaozhu?"

Mo Xi was silent for several heartbeats. With rare humility, he mumbled, "I missed you."

Gu Mang laughed harder. "What a righteous gentleman you are," he said to the youth on top of him. "Why didn't you think of climbing over the wall to see me instead?"

Mo Xi stared at him blankly. The idea truly hadn't occurred to him. Upon careful consideration, it seemed like Gu Mang's suggestion was eminently sensible... How hadn't he thought of it before?

As he pondered this, the slave collar around Gu Mang's neck lit up.

"Shaozhu is looking for me," Gu Mang said after a moment. "It's time for you to go too. I'm supposed to be taking a stroll with you, not sleeping with you."

For a period of time after this tryst, until they again received orders to go to battle, Mo Xi often visited Gu Mang. Although Wangshu Manor was shielded by barrier spells, they posed no trouble for Mo Xi.

In those times of impassioned rutting, occasionally, when Mo Xi had fucked Gu Mang out of his mind, Murong Lian would for some reason want a servant. As the slave collar tightened around his neck, Gu Mang would be almost breathless between two forms of torment—choking as he came and reducing the sheets to a sodden mess.

Murong Lian had an irritable temperament and was unwilling to wait long after summoning someone. Often, Gu Mang didn't have time to clean himself and rushed over as soon as he was properly dressed. Sometimes, even as he knelt before Murong-gongzi, Mo-gongzi's come would still be inside him...

Those days had been thoroughly absurd. Thinking back to it now, even Mo Xi was stunned at his youthful recklessness.

There had been no promises between them, no foreseeable future. But his heart had never cooled, as if he meant to be caught up in Gu Mang for a lifetime. They had nothing. They could only turn their love, control, and possessiveness into this intense and yearning entanglement.

One was a pristine young master held above all, while the other was a Wangshu Manor slave, low to the bones.

It was the most shocking of scandals, but it was also the most heartwarming of young loves.

Such were the golden days of their youth.

Now, within the dreamscape, Gu Mang had been sent to this place once again. Dream of Longing had manifested the hidden desires in his heart. In that case, what would Mo Xi see when he opened the door?

Gritting his teeth, Mo Xi stared at that door he had seen countless times before.

At this juncture, he couldn't back out, but he also had no way of breaking through. Nowadays, he was too level-headed and powerful to ever again be that youth who had been unable to distinguish between the waking world and dreams. But the old Gu-shixiong, who had once himself been the one to pull them out of an illusion, had also long since changed.

This time, Gu Mang was the one ensnared in Dream of Longing while Mo Xi was powerless to act. The phantom had correctly identified the nature of their relationship, thereby revealing Mo Xi's greatest vulnerability.

Under these circumstances, if he reacted to Gu Mang and Gu Mang's thoughts were stirred, then Dream of Longing would become more powerful and drag Gu Mang even deeper within it.

But if Mo Xi didn't react at all, Gu Mang would, in all likelihood, still be tormented out of his mind. The phantom had drugged him, and Mo Xi knew what that medicine would do if Gu Mang wasn't granted relief or antidote in time.

So. Before the emperor's reinforcements came, all he could do was his best. He would stall for time and try to keep Gu Mang lucid.

Mo Xi thought this over briefly, then lifted a hand, pushing the door open.

At almost the same moment, the person on the other side grabbed him and pushed him against the wall. In the darkness, helpless, impatient blue eyes met his. Before Mo Xi had a chance to say anything, his lips were caught against a trembling mouth.

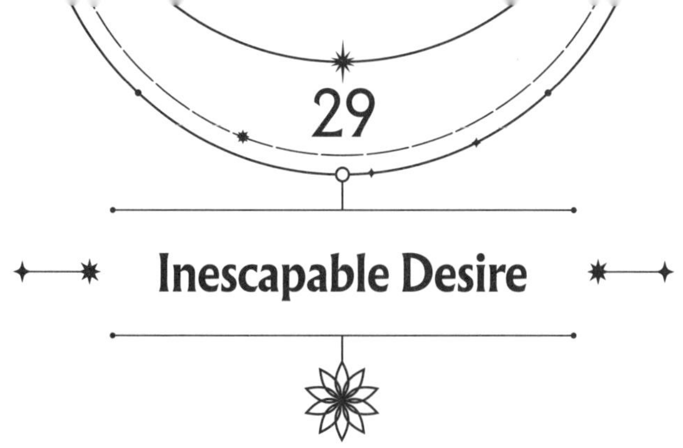

29

Inescapable Desire

EVERYONE USED TO SAY that Gu Mang had the ferocity of an alpha wolf when he fought: he was fierce, sharp, and strong, with a powerful and commanding air. He was the untouchable war general of the empire of Chonghua, positioned so high above others that he seemed to stand upon a holy altar. That was why he had received the title "Beast of the Altar."

But the rest of the world didn't know of his other feral traits.

Only Mo Xi knew what Gu Mang was like in bed. His limbs were taut and muscular, his waist sharply defined, and his body seemed full of tension when they lay entwined. When they had been inseparably tangled together, he had moved to kiss Mo Xi countless times, trapping Mo Xi deep within that wet warmth.

But it was different now.

Too much time had passed, and they were separated by betrayal, death, the nation's need for vengeance, Mo Xi's own hatred. Upon suddenly being pinned and forcibly kissed, a spark landed on Mo Xi's heart and burned up into desire. The final emotion that flickered there, however, was fury.

Mo Xi brusquely grabbed Gu Mang, burying his fingers firmly in the man's hair-knot. The scent of blood came from between their mouths. "Snap out of it."

A fireball ignited in his hand, illuminating the room. It was still just as Mo Xi remembered: a tiny, windowless nook that belonged to a slave, with everything in disarray. A waist-high pickling jar by the bed served as a makeshift bedside table, and a rounded bottle filled with wildflowers was placed on top.

"Bear with it—it'll be over soon."

Gu Mang's mind seemed to have already been completely overrun by the illusion. He gazed blankly yet hungrily at Mo Xi for a stretch, as if he couldn't understand a single word Mo Xi had said. Then he leaned in once more, wanting to kiss those pale, thin lips. What kind of goddamn medicine had that phantom given Gu Mang? Physically, he had recovered so well that if Mo Xi let his guard down even the slightest bit, Gu Mang would break free.

They fought so fiercely that in a moment's carelessness, Gu Mang tripped, falling onto the bed and dragging Mo Xi with him. The little wooden bed creaked dangerously as Mo Xi landed on top of him. Drugged with aphrodisiac, Gu Mang's body was searing, and his blue eyes burned with wet light. It was as if a flame had been ignited over a river's surface and was about to devour his mind and soul.

That fervid and familiar body trembled under Mo Xi. The act of rubbing against another man made Gu Mang's eyes even wilder, to say nothing of how Mo Xi's body had already reacted in the first place. Only by firmly suppressing his own desire could Mo Xi avoid crossing a line.

But he couldn't control his own breathing. It roughened, low and hot. As he commanded Gu Mang not to move, the brush of his breath against the shell of Gu Mang's ear made him shiver.

Gu Mang swallowed thickly, gazing at Mo Xi through eyes full of tears. "It hurts..." he rasped. "So...hot..."

You're not the only one who's hot. But there was no way Mo Xi would say such words aloud. He pinned Gu Mang down with his arms, but Gu Mang continued to struggle and squirm beneath him. How could Mo Xi maintain his control during this back and forth? Between their entwined limbs, Mo Xi angrily shouted, "Stay still!"

But Gu Mang could feel Mo Xi pressing into him, stiff and hard through their clothes. It was merely one accidental brush, but that hardness seemed to summon a memory buried deep in his mind. Gu Mang shivered all over, letting out a low moan.

At this soft noise, the pure and austere Xihe-jun felt painfully hard, frantically swollen. It was unbearable... Not to mention, Gu Mang was lying on the bed with his clothing in disarray, his eyes glazed as his chest heaved.

His expression was wholly pained, as if to reproach Mo Xi for being unwilling to touch him, or as if he only felt agony and emptiness.

Mo Xi couldn't respond and thereby strengthen the illusion. Nor could he extinguish the aphrodisiac within Gu Mang.

His forehead was covered in a sheen of sweat. Amid the chaos, as Mo Xi glimpsed his own reflection in Gu Mang's eyes, he suddenly thought that if...if he could render Gu Mang temporarily unconscious, he might be able to buy more time.

With this thought, he inhaled and got to his feet, his hand striking the back of Gu Mang's neck. Gu Mang fainted.

Mo Xi hadn't known if it would work, but it'd been worth a try. It wasn't like things could get worse.

"Shuairan!" Mo Xi snapped. "Come!"

Answering his summons, the supple whip materialized. Mo Xi had the holy weapon bind Gu Mang to prevent him from doing anything unexpected once he woke. At that moment, he heard footsteps outside the door.

The steps halted. The door opened.

Under the moonlight, a figure gripping a dagger stood in the doorway, the pristine light illuminating his face.

"Gu Mang?!"

Then the man on the bed...

Black smoke rose. The Gu Mang on the bed abruptly dissolved into ash, and Shuairan fell limp like the shed skin of a snake.

"He was an illusion of your own creation." With a cackle, the phantom's voice came again. It seemed omnipresent, issuing from no discernible source. "You're the one who listened to me as I guided you into thinking that Gu Mang had been drugged with an aphrodisiac. You imagined Wangshu Manor, and you imagined him... Xihe-jun, you've only ever experienced Dream of Longing as cast by common cultivators of the Liao Kingdom. You've never entered a dreamscape as powerful as mine! Did you think it would be enough to simply maintain composure? Did you think you were invincible so long as you refused to believe what you saw?"

The laughter echoed ghoulishly around them.

"How naive! Come now, look at the Gu Mang before you. He's going to kill you soon. Is he an illusion or is he real? Can you tell?" The phantom's shrieking laugh was filled with the sadistic delight of toying with a victim. "Do you decide he's an illusion and shatter him? Or do you decide to show mercy?"

He laughed harder. "True masters of Dream of Longing force you to guess. You'll live if you're right, die if you're wrong... Come, aren't you going to strike?"

Gu Mang's dagger met Shuairan in a blaze of red-gold sparks.

"Oh, by the way, Xihe-jun, did you know? Your old paramour cultivated with the methods of the Liao Kingdom and took my demon-strengthening pill. Despite his useless spiritual core, he can fight with malevolent qi."

As the phantom's words echoed in his ears, Mo Xi exchanged more than ten fearsome blows with Gu Mang. Gu Mang's face was devoid of emotion, his expression ice-cold—just like it had been after he defected, when he appeared astride his horse as the Liao Kingdom's commander before the armies of Chonghua. Absent any bygone affection.

"The longer you stall, the more strength he'll regain." The apparition snickered. "Xihe-jun, this passive approach of yours is hopeless. He's the Beast of the Altar, not the Runt of Chonghua."

Shuairan wound around the black blade of the dagger—but with a flick of the blade's tip, its flow of spiritual energy was cut off. The blade flipped to stab at Mo Xi. The light of the dagger illuminated Gu Mang's face, like a silk ribbon flashing past his eyes.

Mo Xi cursed inwardly, leaping backward. "Blade transformation!"

Shuairan whipped back into his palms. In a flash of red light, it became a longsword the color of blood and met the dagger once more with a *clang*.

Mo Xi gritted his teeth. Over the clashing of dagger and sword, he gazed at the emotionless face mere inches away. Was it an illusion from Dream of Longing? Or was it the real Gu Mang sent to meet him...

The phantom laughed wildly. "Come on, with your ability, you could easily kill him for real. Stab him in the chest, why don't you?" He cackled. "Why don't you stab him?! If he's real, he'll die—wouldn't that be just what you wanted? A traitor, a turncoat... Come, Xihe-jun, what are you waiting for? Kill him! Ha ha ha!'"

Yes, Gu Mang was a traitor. He had killed so many civilians and slaughtered so many soldiers; he had made those who had believed in him fall to the deepest depths. He had defected from his motherland and surrendered to the Liao Kingdom.

But hadn't he also been the commander who elevated what was now the foremost imperial army of Chonghua? With his own blood and tears, with his very life...he had led them scrabbling out of the hellish smoke of war.

It was Gu Mang who had brought his brothers crawling back, who had returned the bodies of the dead. He'd seen hope, he'd seen the future, and so he had roared, enduring it all to say: *Come, everything's okay. You've named me General Gu, so I'll bring you home no matter what. I'll bring you home...*

A crowd of dirty cultivators, a slew of orphaned slaves—with his loyalty and devotion, Gu Mang had hoped to grant his dead comrades and brothers an honorable and respectable burial, securing them gravestones inscribed with their names.

But Chonghua had refused.

The old nobles had refused.

Gu Mang's soldiers had entered hell for the people of Chonghua and staggered out half dead, dragging corpses behind them. But the attitude of the person on the throne seemed to say:

Hm? Shouldn't you all have died in hell? Why'd you come back? Where does that leave me? You're an army composed of slaves and led by a slave. Surely Chonghua can't bury your dead on Warrior Soul Mountain, much less reward the living with rank and riches equal to the nobility, can it?

Bastards should go home to hell. Desolate burial mounds will do. What need have you for tombstones? Why didn't you all just die?

So Gu Mang had defected; so Gu Mang had left. It wasn't like Mo Xi couldn't understand or forgive that.

But why had he chosen the Liao Kingdom?

It was the Liao Kingdom that had killed Mo Xi's father! The cannibalistic Liao Kingdom that relied on gruesome techniques to murder and terrorize all in their path! Why?! Nearly all the people of the Liao Kingdom were insane. Every time they conquered a country, a massacre ensued. They ate their victims and drank their blood… They were infatuated with tyranny and willing to ruin all that was good in their nation. Why did he insist on choosing the *Liao Kingdom*?

For revenge? For hatred?

Or was it because the Liao Kingdom was one of the few great nations able to rival Chonghua? Had Gu Mang thought that only by entering that nest of demons, stripping away all his kindness, and sacrificing his loyalty could there come a day when soldiers surrounded Chonghua's city walls—when he could at last tear out the emperor's heart and trample the heads of these disdainful pure-blooded nobles into bloody gore under his feet?!

As Mo Xi's thoughts raced, Gu Mang struck down the Shuairan sword he held.

The dagger flew to a stop, its point against Mo Xi's chest.

Gu Mang made no sound, nor did he make his next move. He only gazed at him apathetically and said, "You've lost."

Mo Xi didn't respond. The phantom, on the other hand, laughed, almost sighing. "I did warn you, Xihe-jun, but you still didn't have the heart to fight him seriously."

Mo Xi remained silent.

"In honor of your infatuation, I'll tell you the truth." The phantom paused dramatically, then resumed with delight. "The Gu Mang in front of you is real.

"This is all thanks to your unwillingness to harm him. Otherwise, I'm sure he'd be no match for you. But…" He laughed again. "You're still attached while he's indifferent. Right now, Gu Mang is under the control of his malevolent qi and only listens to me. If I wanted him to kill you, he wouldn't hesitate."

His voice meandered, unhurried. "Blurring the line between true and false, forcing you to make difficult choices—this is the true use of Dream of Longing. Have you figured it out yet? Unfortunately, even if you have, it's already too late." The phantom delivered his final command with a smile: "Go on, kill him."

Gu Mang's azure-blue eyes darkened, and he brandished his blade—

But at this crucial moment, the red lotus sigil on Mo Xi's neck glowed, and a dozen red sword glares exploded from his body.

Caught off guard, Gu Mang turned to dodge and shattered a good few of the swords flying at him. But in the instant he used his full concentration to avoid the sword array, Shuairan's rope form bound him, snaking up from beneath his feet. Thrown off balance, Gu Mang staggered and fell to his knees, bracing himself with one hand on the floor. He raised his head to level a baleful glare at Mo Xi.

"You were...pretending," he said.

Mo Xi dispersed the sword array, his expression rather complicated. He stepped in front of Gu Mang, spiritual energy flowing in his palm, and made Shuairan tie Gu Mang tighter. Then, with two fingers, he tilted Gu Mang's jaw up and plucked the demonic weapon from his shaking hands.

Mo Xi stared into his clear blue eyes, face dark and voice like ice. "Of course. If I were so easily captured, wouldn't I have wasted all the effort Shixiong put into teaching me?"

Gu Mang's face was expressionless, as if he couldn't understand a single word Mo Xi said.

Mo Xi looked up. "Have any more schemes, good sir? Why not try one of those next?"

That phantom sneered. "Of course I—"

Before he could finish, the surrounding dreamscape shook.

The phantom was clearly shocked. Mo Xi heard low cursing reverberate throughout the illusion, but it continued to dissolve.

"Mo Xi, the victor is yet to be determined," the phantom hissed. "You can't hope to catch me—don't celebrate too soon!"

Mo Xi looked unworried. It seemed that the emperor's reinforcements had finally arrived.

Within the illusion, bricks and tiles began tumbling down one after another, but they didn't hurt Mo Xi. Once someone attacked the Dream of Longing from the outside, it could no longer be maintained. The vision before them twisted and warped. With a crash, Wangshu Manor shattered into thousands of pieces, and the scene disappeared without a trace.

"Xihe-jun! Xihe-jun!" A pair of reinforcements had indeed come and shattered the barrier from outside, and one was none other than Yue Chenqing. After hastily bounding over, he let out a sigh of relief upon seeing Mo Xi—though he started when he saw Gu Mang.

"Are you...uh, are you two okay?"

Mo Xi had returned to the foothills of Warrior Soul Mountain, his hand still buried in Gu Mang's hair-knot, keeping him still. Meanwhile, the red lotus sigil on his neck was fading. Soon, it vanished completely.

Before Mo Xi could reply, the other reinforcement spoke—the emperor had sent who else but Murong Lian. He was leaning against a tree, looking so lazy it seemed as if he were saying, *I don't care if you live or die. If you're alive, I'll go report back; if you're dead, then I'll set off firecrackers and return with your corpse.* He was even holding his pipe, taking a leisurely puff of ephemera and exhaling diaphanous smoke.

"Why wouldn't they be okay?" he asked. "Aren't they dawdling around right here in front of you?"

Yue Chenqing wanted to say something, but Murong Lian beat him to it. "This traitor is so very talented," he said as he sneered at Gu Mang. "I tortured him until he was on the verge of death, yet now he's somehow lively enough to escape prison."

No one said a word.

"Ah, Xihe-jun, this lord can't help but feel suspicious. Given how quickly he healed, could it be that you've been taking care of him in secret?" Murong Lian asked sarcastically.

Mo Xi had no desire to speak to this lunatic. He turned to ask Yue Chenqing, "Why're you here as well?"

"His Imperial Majesty said since I've been your deputy general for two years, I should at least have some experience with Liao Kingdom techniques, so he made me come." Yue Chenqing's eyes widened. "Xihe-jun, have you already found that rapist?"

Mo Xi glanced in front of them. There was a cave up ahead. Casting Dream of Longing required potent spiritual energy, and it couldn't be deployed too far from the spellcaster.

"Right in there," he said.

There was no time to lose, so the three of them ventured into the cave. Yue Chenqing glanced at Gu Mang several times and finally said, "Xihe-jun, you're using Shuairan to bind him—when we meet that rapist later, what will you fight with?"

"Shuairan is not my only weapon."

"But Shuairan is your favorite. How about this—why don't I find you something else to bind him with?" Yue Chenqing scratched his head, digging around in his qiankun pouch and producing a flashy gold immobility talisman. "Use this! It's made by the Yue Clan, and it can—"

"If it's from your dad, put it back," Mo Xi said. "The spiritual energy of those talismans is unmanageable; using them is a headache."

Yue Chenqing hesitated. "My fourth uncle made it, not my dad."

Seeing that Mo Xi said nothing further, Yue Chenqing cupped the immobility talisman in his hands like a jewel and skipped happily toward Gu Mang.

Gu Mang stared at him.

"Aiyo, I'm a little scared. They really do look like wolf eyes." Yue Chenqing rubbed the back of his neck, too afraid to make direct eye contact with Gu Mang. He clasped his hands together twice in greeting. "Wolf-dage, my apologies."

Gu Mang glared viciously at him, his eyes darting back and forth as if to say, *You dare?!*

Yue Chenqing's courage outweighed his skill. With a slap, he stuck his fourth uncle's talisman right onto Gu Mang's forehead.

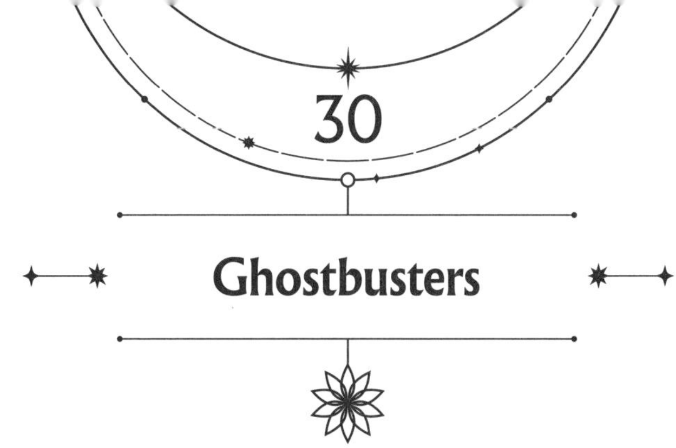

30

Ghostbusters

GU MANG instantly froze.

"Ha ha ha!" Yue Chenqing started laughing. "It really worked! Fourth Uncle is the best."

"The hell do you mean?" Murong Lian asked impatiently. "Now he can't move. Are you going to leave him here? Or are you going to pick him up and carry him inside?"

"It's fine, we can leave him here," Yue Chenqing said. "This immobility talisman is enchanted with a Heavenly Thunder Shield. It would take someone a long time to break it, no matter how strong they are. No one can do anything to him."

"We can't leave him out here alone," Mo Xi said.

"The Heavenly Thunder spell is super strong. Other people can't—"

"Nothing is infallible." said Mo Xi. "Do you have any other magical devices? Anything that can move him along?"

Yue Chenqing thought for a moment, then exclaimed, "I do, I do! Wait a minute!" He dug around in his qiankun pouch once more. After looking for a bit, he took out a small bamboo figurine.

"Isn't that one of those cheap trinkets that children on the street spar with?" Murong Lian said.

"It's the same concept, but this one is enchanted." Yue Chenqing placed the palm-sized bamboo figurine on the ground and rattled off a series of incantations.

Absolutely nothing happened.

"Um, I might've recited it wrong. Let me try again. Murong-dage, Xihe-jun, don't worry." Yue Chenqing anxiously repeated the incantations in a few more variations. Just as Murong Lian was about to irascibly cut this exercise short, golden light flashed, and the bamboo figurine sprang up from the ground. The palm-sized puppet toy had become a bamboo warrior the size of a grown man.

Yue Chenqing beamed. "There we go!" He hefted the immobile Gu Mang, then stared wide-eyed at Mo Xi and Murong Lian. "Lend me a hand?"

Murong Lian gave him a fake smile. "I won't touch him. Too dirty."

Mo Xi had been standing to the side with his arms crossed, but now he stepped forward and asked expressionlessly, "What do you need?"

"We gotta attach his limbs to the bamboo warrior's. There are fastening mechanisms on the warrior, you see?"

Mo Xi did as instructed.

Gu Mang was restrained by the immobility talisman and rendered mute and motionless, but he knew well what was happening around him. He glared at the two people moving his arms and legs, his eyes flashing back and forth between Mo Xi and Yue Chenqing.

The pair tied Gu Mang to the bamboo warrior. To finish it off, Yue Chenqing took the rope around the warrior's torso and wound it several times around Gu Mang's waist. Then he whistled and said, "All right. Let's try taking a few steps."

The bamboo warrior began walking, *clack clack clack*, arms and legs moving in sync. Since Gu Mang was fixed to it, he was also brought clack-clack-clacking along.

This magical device was both wholly marvelous and terribly interesting. Anyone else would have praised Yue Chenqing to the skies, but the two people presently by his side were the deathly stuffy Xihe-jun and the deathly picky Wangshu-jun.

Xihe-jun only watched with his arms crossed, saying nothing. Wangshu-jun snorted.

"Just one of Yue Manor's party tricks." He took two drags of ephemera, exhaled, then pointed the pipe at Gu Mang. "What can it do other than walk?"

"Fight. It can perform all the usual dodging maneuvers." Yue Chenqing took no offense, still pleased with himself. "It can even dance."

Murong Lian bit his pipe, his eyes half-lidded as he mulled this over. "Then why not make him dance?"

Yue Chenqing whistled again. In response, the bamboo warrior began lurching to the left, then to the right, forcing Gu Mang to sway along, this way and that. Even though the movement was silly and cute, those lupine blue eyes glared daggers at them. If Gu Mang could have moved, he definitely would have bitten them to death and torn every one of them apart.

"It can even do the Sogdian Whirl![26] All you need is—"

"Enough." Mo Xi cut him off. "Let's go." After a pause, he added, "Order the bamboo warrior to follow at the back."

The cave where the phantom was hiding was dim and awfully deep. There were multiple branching points inside the great mountain cavern, which split off into many smaller caves. The three of them—plus Gu Mang tied to the bamboo warrior, so the four of them—slowly walked inside. The empty cave echoed with the clicking of Mo Xi's steel-toed military boots, the padding of Yue Chenqing's footsteps, and the creaking of the bamboo warrior's joints.

---

26 *A popular dance during the Tang dynasty named for its originators, the Sogdians, an ancient Iranian civilization that traded extensively with the Tang Empire.*

Only Murong Lian walked without a sound. His gait was light and graceful, and his shoes were made of the highest quality heavenly silk—his steps were completely silent.

Murong Lian was quite pleased with himself. "Forget the rapist, even a toddler would realize we're coming with the noise you two are making."

"I'll walk more softly," said Yue Chenqing, obedient as ever.

Mo Xi, on the other hand, retorted frostily, "Do you think he doesn't know we've entered the cave? There are no other exits, and this is his territory. He's obviously hiding and replenishing his spiritual energy as he waits for us to arrive."

"Then I'll walk more loudly," said Yue Chenqing, easily swayed as ever.

The bamboo warrior creaked in reply.

Mo Xi was right—those who cast Dream of Longing could only do so with great amounts of spiritual energy; the phantom was hiding in one of these caves to gather his strength. As they walked deeper into the bowels of the cavern, they discovered more and more signs that he had holed up within it.

There were dried bloodstains on the central path, and here and there, scraps of clothing dangled from protruding stalagmites. These had unmistakably been left by murdered cultivators and kidnapped maidens who had struggled as they were dragged inside. In one stone crevice, Yue Chenqing even spied a brocade shoe.

In a bid to stall for time, the rapist had cast a great many spells within the cave. However, the emperor had sent three particular individuals: Mo Xi, whose martial power was formidable and who possessed a commander's capabilities; Yue Chenqing, who was born of an aristocratic line of artificers and who carried numerous unexpected magical trinkets at all times; and Murong Lian, who excelled at illusion techniques and was well-versed in healing spells. Thus, the rapist's mysterious traps posed no threat. The trio swiftly arrived at a long karst bridge.

"It should be up ahead." Mo Xi glanced toward the end of the limestone bridge. There seemed to be an expansive cave on the other end, which shone faintly with the indistinct jade-green light of magic.

This "bridge" was a natural formation of the karst cave—it did span from one side to the other, but it was entirely comprised of spirit stones that protruded from the depths of the underground lake below. The stones varied in size and distance, and were perilously slippery withal.

Mo Xi glanced beneath the bridge. The soaring stone pillars were at least a hundred yards tall, with a rushing river beneath. A short span like this was no issue for this group, it was only... He turned to Yue Chenqing. "Is the bamboo warrior skilled at qinggong?"[27]

Yue Chenqing shook his head.

Mo Xi frowned and gazed at Gu Mang, who was still tied to the bamboo warrior, looking murderous.

"But I think I can order it to jump like a jiangshi.[28] It can probably hop across the gaps between the pillars."

Here was a major point of contention during the two years Yue Chenqing and Mo Xi had been stationed together: Deputy General Yue Chenqing liked to use words such as *maybe*, *I think*, and *probably*, while Commander Mo Xi generally only accepted terms such as *certainly*, *definitely*, and *absolutely*.

Consequently, Mo Xi glanced at Yue Chenqing and did not authorize the use of "jump like a jiangshi." He only said, "All of you

---

27 *Literally "lightness technique," the martial arts skill of moving swiftly and lightly through the air.*

28 *The reanimated corpses of dead humans. Their limbs are locked in place due to rigor mortis, meaning they can only move directly forward, hopping with their arms outstretched in front of them.*

follow on your own." Then, with one hand, he grabbed Gu Mang by the lapels and rose into the air, his robes billowing. Mo Xi was extremely strong, and his qinggong foundation was outstanding as well. Before the echoes of his instructions had died, he had already swept far into the distance, fluttering like a black kite.

Yue Chenqing was stupefied. "Wow... So skilled..."

Murong Lian scoffed. "What's so impressive about that?"

In this way, the four of them crossed the hundred-yard-long karst bridge. When they looked back the way they came, all they could see was a distant shadow. Mo Xi set the bamboo warrior on the ground without a glance at Gu Mang. "Let's go," he said to the others.

As expected, this was the deepest cave in the entire system, filled with stalactites and stalagmites. The jade-green light of magic they'd seen was coming from a cluster of rock formations in the center of the cavern.

Just as they were about to enter, Yue Chenqing, who was always peering around, shouted in alarm. "Look! There're words over there!"

A fireball lit up in Mo Xi's palm. With a wave of his hand, the flame flitted up to hover above the lofty cave wall at which Yue Chenqing pointed. Illuminated by firelight were several rows of crooked handwriting, scrawled on the cave wall in muddy red ink that looked like blood.

The mountain bride, all night she cried;
First she hates her helpless fate,
Second hates her ill-starred face,
Third their parting does she hate, a lost love left too late.

Garbed in scarlet, crowned in gold;
Once she laughs, face warped by hate;

Twice she laughs, blood streaks her face;
Thrice she laughs, and with that last, forever seals your fate.

Yue Chenqing mumbled each word aloud. Just as he finished reading and opened his mouth to call to the others, he heard a soft giggle from behind him. "*Hee.*"

He whipped around. Without the slightest warning, the tip of his nose bumped into a ghastly pale face.

"Aaahhh!" Yue Chenqing screamed, leaping high into the air and scrabbling backward.

His vision cleared. At some point, a dozen female corpses garbed in red robes and crowned in gold had slunk out of the shadows between the stalagmites. He'd been standing in front of one of them, so he'd come face-to-face with it as soon as he turned.

"G-G-General Mo—! H-help! *Aaahhhh!*"

Yue Chenqing was a cultivator, but he'd developed an abnormal fear of ghosts after listening to too many horror stories. He shrieked miserably on and on, trying to move his legs and run away, but because he was terrified, he fell to the ground with a crash. With his bugged-out eyes and sunken cheeks, he resembled nothing quite so much as a screaming gopher.

The corpse gazed at him, equally motionless. Robes embroidered with golden phoenixes and butterflies fluttered in the chill wind of the cave.

Yue Chenqing swallowed several times. A realization dawned upon his numbed mind. "Aren't—aren't you...C-Cui-zizi from the teahouse?" he cried.

Miss Cui was expressionless. The dead woman's face possessed a dull, stiff tranquility. After a moment, she giggled again. "Hee hee." Two lines of bloody tears slid down from her staring eyes.

Once she laughs, face warped by hate; Twice she laughs, blood streaks her face; Thrice she laughs, and with that last, forever seals your fate...

Remembering the words on the stone wall, Yue Chenqing's head rang. He shouted to Mo Xi, who was already fighting the other corpses. "Aahhh! Xihe-jun! Hurry up! Don't let her laugh a third time! Or she'll seal my fate!"

The response he received was Murong Lian's pipe rapping against his head. As it turned out, he was standing close by. Incensed by Yue Chenqing's ear-splitting scream, he remorselessly rapped him many more times and left a pipeful of ashes on the boy's head.

"You blithering idiot! Don't you know how to fight on your own?" he snarled. "It's just a jiangshi!"

"But I-I...I'm afraid of ghosts!" Still wailing, Yue Chenqing wrapped his arms around Murong Lian's thighs without warning.

Murong Lian had no words.

At that moment, Miss Cui drew back her scarlet lips and began her third giggle. "Hee...hee..."

"*Hee* my ass!"

The corpse had no chance to finish her last giggle, because Murong Lian rudely shoved his pipe in her mouth. He looked down at Yue Chenqing clinging tight to his pant leg. "Why are you hugging me? Hurry up and let go!"

31

Don't Touch Him

YUE CHENQING'S SOUL was on the verge of dissolving. Only after Murong Lian gave him a few more kicks did he pathetically release him.

It was exactly like the tales of Li Qingqian's exorcisms at Maiden's Lament Mountain: a crowd of women in dark red robes and golden brocade shoes materialized endlessly out of the shadows, wearing miserable smiles and weeping tears of blood. More and more corpses filled the cave, emerging from the darkness, from behind stalagmites, and even rising from the water's surface.

Mo Xi and Murong Lian each dealt with their respective sides. As Yue Chenqing watched them draw farther and farther away from him, he found himself wanting to cry.

"Xihe-jun, Murong-dage, what should I do?" he asked shakily.

No new corpses were appearing near him, but he was surrounded by jagged and shadowy terrain. What if there were more evil, bloody eyes staring at him from the darkness?

Such is the nature of reality: what you least desire is most likely to occur. The dreaded hypothetical almost always comes true. Accordingly, just as this terrifying thought occurred to Yue Chenqing, he felt hairs rise on the back of his neck. He slowly turned and saw, hidden behind a stone outcropping, half of a deathly pale face with two bloody tear tracks.

The woman was leaning against the stone and staring *right at him*!

Yue Chenqing shuddered; he felt like his thrumming head had exploded. In times of great terror, people often call for the one they trust most. The words that tumbled from his quivering lips were: "Fourth...F-F-F-Fourth Uncle!"

Yue Chenqing's fourth uncle wasn't here. Of course he couldn't save him.

Only after Yue Chenqing had sat quaking for some time did he remember this fact. Even if he kept shouting, "Fourth Uncle, save me!" his only companions in this cavern were the heartless Murong Lian and Mo Xi. He was free to choose either one.

He looked left and right and happened to see Mo Xi's long leg kick out from the left, knocking over a row of corpses. Yue Chenqing felt like a holy deity had descended to the earth and gladly made to rush to his side.

But at that moment, the woman hiding behind the stone grinned much too widely, baring eerily white teeth.

Once she laughs, face warped by hate; Twice she laughs, blood streaks her face.

As she slowly crawled out from the depths of the stone, she let out a third mournful laugh. "Hee..."

Thrice she laughs and forever seals your fate!

Seconds after the third laugh, the corpse's resentment erupted. Her eyes rolled, becoming bloodshot and flashing scarlet, and her fingernails shot out into long claws. She wailed at the sky and rushed Yue Chenqing.

"Ah!" Yue Chenqing hadn't the least idea how to fight back. Female ghosts wearing red robes and brocade shoes terrified him more than anything. As she pounced, all he could do was shriek miserably, close to tears, "Fourth Uncle!"

Suddenly there was a thunderous crash. A bolt of lightning struck right in front of Yue Chenqing, and a series of golden-red beams exploded from the ground and burst into raging flames. A silhouette leapt into the air and descended from the skies. Amid the hissing firelight, it landed firmly in front of Yue Chenqing.

The figure turned. Lit by the crackling flame, his profile was dazzlingly heroic, his pupils filled with icy blue light.

Gu Mang?!

Yue Chenqing was stunned. Only after a beat did he realize that no, it wasn't Gu Mang—it was the bamboo warrior. His uncle's bamboo warrior was here to save him. Gu Mang was merely tied to its bamboo limbs, immobilized. Yue Chenqing's thoughts were interrupted by the bamboo warrior waving its hand to unsheathe a blade of dark steel from its weapon compartment. Then, fierce as lightning, it charged the leering corpse.

Construct and corpse fought fiercely, becoming a blur of furious blows.

Yue Chenqing had finally recovered enough to move. He hastily gathered all his energy to shout, "Go, Fourth Uncle!"

Upon second thought, that didn't feel right, so he tried, "Go, bamboo warrior!"

Soon afterward, he saw the corpse's filthy blood spray Gu Mang's face. Gu Mang's expression was ferocious, as if he, too, would have killed that female corpse, if only he weren't bound. Yue Chenqing shouted, "Go Gu... Um... Go, Gu Mang!"

The bamboo warrior was extraordinarily strong; after the first full-force exchange of blows, it swiftly swept backward. Blade flashing, it soared into the air. A swirling gale rushed past as it threw itself at the corpse, filthy blood spraying out.

The corpse stiffened once more before falling, bisected, to the ground.

"Wah, how gross..." muttered Yue Chenqing.

Corpse defeated, the bamboo warrior hefted its bloody blade as if still unsatisfied and stomped toward Yue Chenqing. With a *whoosh*, the tip came to rest at the hollow of Yue Chenqing's throat.

"Big brother... Wait, no, Fourth Uncle... Um, or Gu Mang?" Yue Chenqing tried a few different forms of address but felt that none of them were quite right, so simply decided against addressing him. He carefully waved his hands. "You're pointing the blade in the wrong direction. I'm not a ghost. Don't stab me..."

Gu Mang's blue eyes lowered to gaze down at him. The bamboo warrior swiveled its sword to the side. With the still-dripping flat of the blade, it clumsily patted Yue Chenqing's face as if to scold a junior.

Right then, a strong wind gusted down from above, and red robes fluttered before their eyes. Yue Chenqing jumped in fright. But before he even had the chance to speak, the bamboo warrior shoved him away.

Yue Chenqing fell to the ground with an undignified plop and avoided the strike. Gu Mang, however, was still tied to the bamboo warrior—the ghost's claws raked across his face.

Gu Mang could neither move nor speak, but his expression made clear that he was enraged. Those eyes of a white wolf flashed with hatred as scarlet dripped from the wound on his cheek.

The ghost whose sneak attack had succeeded was grinning hideously before them, as if overwhelmed with joy by her victory. But seconds later, she seemed to sense something, and lowered her head to stare at her bloodstained left hand in a daze.

In the next instant, her features twisted into a mask of alarm and horror. She cried out, holding her hand and wailing unintelligibly, yet piteously, at Gu Mang.

She seemed to be begging Gu Mang for something.

Yue Chenqing's astonishment hadn't yet sunk in before an even more shocking event occurred. When Gu Mang remained unresponsive, the ghost fell to her knees with a thump. Reaching out with the sharp nails of her right hand, she snapped off her left.

"Oh...my...god..." Yue Chenqing didn't know whether he should be disgusted or bewildered. The pungent stench of rot and blood rushed up into his nose, nearly making him vomit.

The corpse, however, was undeterred. She picked up her severed limb and offered it to Gu Mang with a shaking hand, the very image of someone preemptively punishing themselves in a plea for leniency. All the while, soft sobs of, *"ah, aah,"* issued from her mouth.

Gu Mang's blue eyes moved, fixing upon that bloody limb. Yue Chenqing wasn't sure if it was a trick of the light, but his eyes seemed to become paler.

"Eh? What's with this breeze...?" Yue Chenqing was stunned. "Is it getting windy?"

The wind rippled outward from beneath the bamboo warrior's feet—beneath *Gu Mang's* feet. Despite the malice in Gu Mang's expression, his killing intent wasn't especially potent, so the wind wasn't terribly strong either. Nevertheless, as soon as it blew past them, the corpses were struck dumb. At length, they began screaming and shaking as they knelt unsteadily on the ground with their heads lowered, unmoving.

In the blink of an eye, all the corpses had fallen to their knees, facing Gu Mang.

Yue Chenqing hadn't yet realized what was happening, but Murong Lian's eyes were wide. The color drained from Mo Xi's complexion, but he was looking not at the corpses, but at Gu Mang's face—

Swarming corpses and the like had an extremely strong hierarchical instinct. The only things that could scare them were, by and large, other corpses, vengeful ghosts, or resentful spirits of greater power. Somehow, these women who had died tragic deaths were all submitting to Gu Mang, all wailing in audible pleas for mercy... Why was this so?

Was it merely because Gu Mang harbored such high levels of malevolent qi in his body?

Gu Mang seemed incredibly irritated, his blue eyes darting to and fro. Though he made no sound, the direction of the wind changed. The ghosts emitted ululating shrieks, black qi rising from each of their bodies to coalesce over Gu Mang's heart.

He was absorbing their malevolent qi!

As Gu Mang took in more and more of the qi, the female corpses convulsed like dying fish, quickly crumpling. With the resentment pulled from their bodies, they became ordinary corpses. Some, who had died long ago, rotted and withered upon the loss of their resentment, turning into blackened, putrid piles of bones. Some, who had been murdered recently, retained visible hints of the beauty they had possessed in life.

Yue Chenqing endured his disgust to peek at the corpse nearest him. It seemed to be the woman named Yu-niang, who had gone missing from the first brothel...

When Murong Lian saw what was happening, he strode forward and grabbed Gu Mang by the neck, gnashing his teeth. "I knew it... You liar! You *were* colluding with that man who escaped from Liao! What are you planning?!"

But after swallowing the malevolent qi from all those corpses, Gu Mang was like a wild beast that had eaten its fill. His head slumped, and he closed his eyes and fell asleep on the bamboo warrior, entirely insensible to Murong Lian and his wrath.

"You—!" Murong Lian grew enraged, but as he was about to tighten his grip, a hand stopped him.

He whirled to see Mo Xi's face in the shadows of the dim cave. Mo Xi grasped Murong Lian's wrist, not saying a word as he slowly moved it down.

Mo Xi looked quite courteous and said nothing inappropriate. Only Murong Lian knew the strength he was exerting—practically enough to shatter bones through flesh.

"What are you doing?" Murong Lian asked darkly.

"Let go of him."

Murong Lian's nose wrinkled in rage. "He's an accomplice!"

"He isn't," Mo Xi said.

"*Isn't?!* How isn't he? Didn't you see how a drop of his blood made that corpse snap off her own arm? Didn't you see how a single glance from him made them all kneel?! Didn't you see how he took all their corpse energy for himself with even moving an inch?!"

"If he really knew how to control them," Mo Xi angrily retorted, "and was working with that man from Liao, would you still be standing here, safe and sound?!"

This rendered Murong Lian instantly mute. He still wanted to speak, but he couldn't get a single word out, and his pale face slowly reddened. After a long pause, he smiled mirthlessly. "Very well... Heh, *you're* the reasonable one. *You're* defending him. I think you've wholly forgotten what he's done—how cunning he is, how skilled he is at...at..." Murong Lian spat his last word: "lying!"

"His character," Mo Xi said, "is nothing you need remind me of."

"No need for me to remind you?" Murong Lian burst out laughing. By the end, the expression on his face was distorted. "Even if I reminded you, you wouldn't listen! And you still dare to say you're not harboring any personal motives. What a good Xihe-jun you are. Go ahead and keep protecting him, then... I see you've forgotten how your father died!"

The color drained at once from Mo Xi's pale and elegant face as he glared daggers at Murong Lian.

But Murong Lian was thrilled. No one dared mention this sore spot of Mo Xi's, the reason behind his father's death—except for Murong Lian, the only one who could. He was fully aware that though Mo Xi's temper was usually irritable, at critical junctures, he was more clear-headed than anyone.

So Murong Lian snickered, his predatory peach blossom eyes flicking to Gu Mang before landing back on Mo Xi's handsome face. He lifted his chin and crooned, "Xihe-jun is so righteous, so deeply devoted to brotherhood. May you swiftly follow in your esteemed father's footsteps."

Mo Xi's rage seemed to flare, but just as Murong Lian expected, he wasn't the sort of person who lost sight of his priorities because he was upset. He stared into Murong Lian's eyes for a long moment before pushing him away. With both boots and weapon clanging, he strode deeper into the cave with scarcely a backward glance.

"Murong-dage...you... You..." Yue Chenqing sighed. He was practically speechless after watching this scene unfold. He had no wish to speak to Murong Lian any further, and scampered after Mo Xi's retreating back with the bamboo warrior tottering loudly behind him. "Xihe-jun, wait for me! It's dangerous to go alone..."

The sound of their retreating footsteps echoed within the cave.

Murong Lian remained standing in place, tilting his head back to stare into the endless dark of the cavern before closing his eyes. A cruel and mocking sneer appeared at the corners of his mouth. Then, slowly, he followed after the others.

When they arrived at an area glowing with green light, they came to a stop.

This was the last large cave within the system, hidden behind an expanse of stone formations. The green light flickered bright then dim—it turned out to be a protective barrier placed at the entrance of a cave.

Mo Xi only needed one glance to identify it. "It's the God-Repelling Array."

The upright countries of the Nine Provinces cultivated the righteous immortal path, so they usually named spells things like "Demon-Repelling," "Ghost-Repelling," or "Malevolence-Repelling." Any protective formation described as "God-Repelling" was almost certain to be from the Liao Kingdom.

"Is it hard to break?"

"No," Mo Xi said. "But it takes time."

The release incantation for the God-Repelling Array was extremely long and complicated. Mo Xi lifted his vambraced left hand and closed his eyes, soundlessly reciting the words. Only after a good stretch did the green light gradually dim under his hand as the array slowly retreated...

As the glow dimmed to nothing, soft laughter came from within the cave. That phantom's voice resounded from the deepest recesses. "You broke through my final defense..." Pausing, he continued in an eerie tone. "Then, honored shenjun, welcome in."

32

Sword Spirit

IT WAS TERRIBLY COLD and damp in the cave, the air suffused with the perfume of makeup and the stink of corpse fluids. The ground was littered with scraps of human bone and fabric, and some yet-unconsumed human hearts and eyes were piled on a shallow white plate in the corner. In contrast with this ghastly scene, the center of the cavern held a pile of crimson mats, and upon it a golden bed canopy embroidered with colorful butterflies.

Within the depths of the canopy, a woman in tattered clothes was curled up and wailing piteously. She was delirious and didn't seem to register their arrival.

Yue Chenqing jumped with fear. "How is the rapist a woman?"

No sooner had he spoken than a hand shot out from the pile of red bedding and savagely grabbed the maiden. Before she could so much as scream, that hand dragged her into the billowing red cloth. A pale-skinned man emerged from the bedding and climbed on top of her. As they watched, he fiercely bit the maiden's lips.

Her soul seemed to be sucked out of her in the blink of an eye. Her hands went limp like soft cotton, and her eyes went wide and blank as she died...

After the man took her soul, he turned his head. He had a thin face, with long, slender eyes and slightly sunken cheeks. A few wisps of long black hair dangled at his temples. He was extraordinarily emaciated. This was the true "rapist."

There were a few beats of silence.

"It's you," Mo Xi said.

The man licked his wet lips, then smiled. "Xihe-jun's met me before?"

A pause. "Yes."

They had met before.

Many years ago, on a battlefield of the northern frontier, Mo Xi had been alone and in danger: a pack of demon wolves trained by the Liao Kingdom had surrounded him, leaving him no way out. In the nick of time, a young cultivator clad in green arrived, sword in hand. With sword technique both ethereal and exquisite, he fought alongside Mo Xi—a stranger—and helped him beat back the pack of demon wolves, more than a thousand strong.

Mo Xi had wanted to thank the cultivator before he left, but the man only turned with a smile, his features as gentle as the green ribbon in his hair, fluttering on the breeze.

"It was nothing—I was only passing by." His cheeks were faintly creased with laugh lines. "You need not think on it any further, Officer."

Luminous as the first snow, a righteous and honorable swordsman. That was the Li Qingqian whom Mo Xi had met.

That was also why, even though multiple marks of the Water-Parting Sword had been found on the brothel murder corpses, Mo Xi had been unable to believe it without laying eyes on the man himself.

Murong Lian had seen Li Qingqian's portrait in the records of heroes, and he recognized him now as well. Though briefly stunned, he soon sharply asked, "Why is it *you*?"

"Who else did you think it would be?" Li Qingqian rose, carelessly kicking Miss Lan's limp corpse to the side as he spoke scornfully. "Did you really think I was that runaway cook?" He bared his teeth. "That fool was nothing more than one of my pawns. If he had half my ability, could you have kept him locked up for so many years?"

When it came to sarcasm, Murong Lian never admitted defeat. After his initial shock passed, the corners of his mouth crooked upward in mockery. "Heh heh, how odd. The Water-Parting Sword, Li Qingqian, is a lofty master whose name is known throughout the land. His reputation has ever been clear and honorable. But upon meeting him today, I find that he's no more than a rapist who likes to drink blood, eat flesh, and dig hearts. This has truly broadened this lord's mind—how admirable. How admirable indeed..."

Unexpectedly, before Li Qingqian could respond, Yue Chenqing blurted out, "That can't be right."

"What isn't right?"

"He isn't Li Qingqian, he's—he's clearly a..." Yue Chenqing hesitated for a moment, as if he weren't sure of his judgment. "He's not a living person. He's a sword spirit!"

As soon as these words were uttered, the faint smile on Li Qingqian's face froze. His gaze landed on Yue Chenqing. As yet, his smile hadn't quite disappeared, but the malice in the depths of his eyes was fully hostile.

Yue Chenqing couldn't help flinching, and he shuffled his feet to hide behind Mo Xi.

Li Qingqian bared his teeth in a ghastly grin. "This little brother acts ordinary but is quite the sage. Please enlighten me with your esteemed name."

"M-my name is Yue..."

"Why are you answering him?!" Mo Xi lifted a long leg and gave the boy a hard kick. "Do you think you're still a disciple at the academy, obligated to answer all questions?!"

Yue Chenqing shook his head like a rattle-drum. "My name isn't Yue—" he said hastily.

Li Qingqian threw his head back in raucous laughter, his scarlet lapels opening wide. "Enough. All I needed to know was your surname. Chonghua's Yue Clan is one of the top artificer lines in the Nine Provinces and Twenty-Eight Nations—no wonder a little rascal like you was able to decipher clues that even the two shenjun Xihe and Wangshu could not."

On the battlefield, Yue Chenqing liked to hide in the back. At present, there were only three people and a bamboo warrior in the mountain cavern, and he was suddenly the focus of attention. He was left feeling extremely nervous, cowering like a quail. "I-I-I..."

Though Mo Xi had kicked him a second ago, he pulled Yue Chenqing behind himself. He turned to ask, "He was the one you fought at the tavern?"

"Y-yes..."

"Why couldn't you tell he was a sword spirit then?"

"I only thought his scent was somewhat familiar..." Yue Chenqing mumbled. "Xihe-jun, don't you remember? I told you. In hindsight, that *was* the aura of a sword spirit, but..."

"But I was intentionally suppressing it at the time." Li Qingqian took over with a contemptuous smile. "And this young Yue-gongzi only exchanged a few blows with me. At his age, he likely hasn't yet mastered the artificing and analysis techniques of the Yue Clan. That's why he couldn't identify me straightaway."

He paused, licking the corner of his lip. "But young Yue-gongzi, the most important lesson your family elders ought to impart to you has nothing to do with artificing, but rather something else."

"Huh?" Yue Chenqing was baffled.

"Sometimes, even if you know something, it's best to pretend..." Li Qingqian soared into the air before he finished his sentence, summoning an iron sword and striking at Yue Chenqing as he gritted out his final three words: "that you don't!"

As the sword point rushed toward him, Yue Chenqing shrieked miserably. "Xihe-jun, *help*!"

Mo Xi shoved Yue Chenqing toward Murong Lian and stepped forward to meet the attack. With a flash of red light, Shuairan transformed into a longsword and clashed against Li Qingqian's blade.

Sword spirit... Sword spirit... So that's what it was!

No wonder those wounds had borne the marks of malevolent qi as well as an ordinary weapon. Vengeful ghosts typically didn't use weapons to harm people, nor were they particularly clear-minded, and they couldn't possibly write on walls. But if the culprit was a sword spirit, everything made sense.

In pursuit of an even stronger and more versatile weapon, rather than the usual method of imbuing a sword with a spirit, some artificers of the Nine Provinces sacrificed living people to a blade. However, this method of tempering was unbelievably cruel, and the twenty countries headed by Chonghua had long since banned it. The only nation where this technique remained prevalent was the Liao Kingdom.

After the human soul was imbued in the weapon's blade, their consciousness would either sink into an eternal sleep as the years flowed by, never to wake—or, if they possessed an unresolved obsession, slowly coalesce into human form. Sword spirits who could recover their human shapes were nearly identical to living people in appearance and bearing, but for the intense malevolent qi they emanated. They required large amounts of spiritual energy to maintain their form, so if their own cultivation was insufficient, as Li Qingqian's was, they would need to consume the flesh and hearts of other cultivators in order to absorb the souls of weaker beings and thereby pursue their larger goals.

A corporeal sword spirit was often extremely strong, each move and strike better than the last—but they had a fatal weakness. This was why, upon being exposed by Yue Chenqing, Li Qingqian was livid and moved at once to kill him.

Their true form could not fall into their enemy's hands.

That was to say, if someone obtained the weapon vessel of the sword spirit and either sealed or destroyed it, the sword spirit would be helpless no matter its strength.

Murong Lian had clearly realized the same thing. While Mo Xi engaged the sword spirit, he pulled Yue Chenqing aside. "You said this Li Qingqian is a sword spirit. Do you know how to locate his true form?"

"I'll try!" Yue Chenqing closed his eyes and created an array seal with his hands. After a moment, he blinked his eyes open and stared dazedly at Murong Lian.

"Why are you looking at me like that?" Murong Lian asked, perplexed.

"Murong-dage..." Yue Chenqing said incredulously. "His true form... His true form is on you!"

"What nonsense is this?!" Murong Lian said angrily, loudly rapping Yue Chenqing's head with his pipe. "You dare accuse me of working with Liao Kingdom flunkies?"

"I'm not, I'm not! I just said that his true form is, is—"

"*Not* on me!"

"...Okay."

Murong Lian pressed down on his head in displeasure. "Try again!"

Yue Chenqing was left with no choice but to comply, but after several more attempts, he finally opened his eyes and stared pitifully at Murong Lian without daring to speak.

Murong Lian's face was beginning to turn green. His lips parted—he wanted to take a puff of ephemera to steady his nerves. However, as soon as he remembered that he had stuck his pipe into a corpse's mouth during their grand battle a few minutes ago, he was immediately disgusted. He wiped the pipe back and forth, again and again, on Yue Chenqing's clothes.

As he did so, something occurred to him. His expression grew stiff, and his movements gradually slowed. "Hold it," he muttered. "It might...actually be on me."

He glanced toward Li Qingqian and Mo Xi, who were clashing with sword qi. It would be impossible for Li Qingqian to get past Mo Xi and draw near to them anytime soon, so he hastily pulled Yue Chenqing aside, aiming to find a more secluded spot behind the stalagmites.

Li Qingqian wasn't stupid. He spied their movements out of the corner of his eye, snorted, and turned his blade, planning to give chase.

Yet before he had swept even a few yards in that direction, he heard Mo Xi intone coldly from behind him: "Shuairan, spirit transformation!"

Li Qingqian was startled. He heard an explosion behind his back, and red light lit the stone cave into a sea of flame. A spiritual snake as tall as three men slithered out from the blazing crimson, furiously charging at Li Qingqian and blocking his path.

Li Qingqian turned to bark furiously, "Watch yourself, Mo Xi! Maybe others don't know about the shameful things you've done with that damned Gu Mang, but I know them all too well! I know all about what you said and did with him at Luomei Pavilion upon your return! If you continue to get in my way, I'll destroy your reputation!"

He didn't expect that Mo Xi would do nothing more than shoot him a frosty glance. Holding the leather whip that manifested as Shuairan's physical form, Mo Xi cracked it and uttered a single word: "Go."

Shuairan swooped down toward Li Qingqian.

"Asshole!" Li Qingqian shouted. "Do you really not care about what I could say?!"

"Me, care about what you say?" Mo Xi narrowed his eyes, his expression filled with scorn. "Who would believe you?"

"You—!"

But Li Qingqian knew Mo Xi's words were true. Mo-gongzi had been pristine and proper since youth, and he never behaved outrageously. No matter if he was presented with beautiful men or alluring women, he was completely uninterested. Gu Mang was perhaps the only stain, the only scandal in all the world that could be linked to this man. Li Qingqian was a malevolent spirit, so even if his story was watertight, who would believe it? What could they do even if they did?

He clenched his jaw and turned to fight the Shuairan snake.

The bamboo warrior creaked noisily as it ran back and forth, wanting to help. Mo Xi looked at the sleeping Gu Mang still tied to it. With a wave of his hand, he conjured a protective barrier and enclosed him within it.

The bamboo warrior creaked furiously.

"Stay there and don't move," Mo Xi said.

The warrior seemed dejected by its inability to pull its weight as part of the team. Its head drooped, bringing Gu Mang's head down as well. After a while, it extended its arms, straightened its back in resignation, and stood there like a scarecrow.

Behind the stalagmites, Yue Chenqing knelt on the ground, staring stupefied at a pile of miniature weapons before him. Blades, swords, rods, and whips, all the size of a fingernail, crashed and poured out of Murong Lian's qiankun pouch as he shook it.

"These were all confiscated from the captives of Luomei Pavilion," Murong Lian said. "Even though their owners' spiritual cores were broken, the weapons might not accept a new master so easily. Their resentment is very potent."

"Murong-dage, keeping so many unclaimed holy weapons on you is super dangerous—if they transformed into spirits, it would be a disaster!" Yue Chenqing said, shocked.

Murong Lian rolled his eyes at his concern. "I'm not an idiot. This qiankun pouch was made by your great-grandfather, and emblazoned with his seal. A couple hundred weapons is nothing for it. Even a thousand wouldn't pose a threat. Besides, I had your father extract the spiritual forms of these weapons long ago—they're all suppressed in the Qingquan Pool at Luomei Pavilion. Forty-nine spirit-suppressing carp are kept in that pool, and on top of that, barriers to prevent the escape of malevolent spirits are all around Luomei Pavilion, so usually..."

At this point, he stopped. Then, as if a new thought had occurred to him, his expression slowly fell. "I understand now..."

"Murong-dage, what do you understand?"

"I understand how the sword spirit Li Qingqian escaped from Luomei Pavilion."

33

Want You

MURONG LIAN GRIMACED. "Do you remember when I punished Gu Mang with a month of confinement?"

"I do, but what does it have to do with this?"

"If someone approached Qingquan Pool while they were weak, they might be possessed by malevolent spirits," Murong Lian said. "Gu Mang was hungry, so he knelt by the pool. He even tried to catch those fish with his bare hands."

"Huh? Murong-dage, how come you know about that?"

"I know everything that happens at Luomei Pavilion." Murong Lian cleared his throat. "Gu Mang trying to catch fish attracted the attention of the sword spirit Li Qingqian, who was suppressed inside the pool. So Li Qingqian temporarily took over his body..."

"Ah," Yue Chenqing said. "Then Li Qingqian triggered the malevolent qi in Gu Mang's heart and made him go on a rampage?"

"No," Murong Lian said. "He wasn't able to, at the time. He was extremely weak and couldn't possess Gu Mang for long. The only sort of vessel he could occupy long-term would be feeble, on the brink of death; Gu Mang was merely hungry." His gaze was sharp. "So Li Qingqian used the limited time he had to do one thing."

"What thing?"

"He severely injured someone."

"Oh, that cook!"

"Exactly," Murong Lian said, his voice chill and eerie. "Li Qingqian took control of Gu Mang, then used that sword array to injure the Liao Kingdom cook without killing him. In this way, he created a target suitable for long-term possession. Then he waited for the right opportunity to trigger the malevolent qi in Gu Mang's heart, making him go berserk and break the barrier. In the chaos, Li Qingqian used the cook's body to escape."

"If he understands Gu Mang so well and was even able to trigger Gu Mang's malevolent qi, he has to be from the Liao Kingdom!" Yue Chenqing said.

"Li Qingqian wasn't from Liao, but now that he's somehow become a sword spirit, it does sound like he was a Liao cultivator's weapon." Murong Lian considered for a moment, then added, "And it would have been an elite cultivator's weapon."

He lowered his head, using his pipe to poke incautiously at those miniaturized weapons. "Look, can you tell which one is its true form?"

This wasn't difficult; it was more or less a foundational skill taught by the Yue Clan. Yue Chenqing closed his eyes and studied the flow of spiritual energy for a bit. Then his eyes flew open again as he reached out to pick up a very small, shrunken sword. "It's this one!"

"Good." Murong Lian picked up the bean-sized sword, placed it in his palm, and noiselessly recited an incantation. A brilliant light burst from his hand, and the bean-sized blade became a slim, light sword with a taotie[29] pattern on its hilt, every inch gleaming with jade-green light. The words *Hong Shao: Red Peony* were carved on the blade in seal script.

"Eh? This sword obviously has a jade-colored hilt, so why is it named Red Peony?" Yue Chenqing asked, perplexed. "These two

---

29 *A bilaterally symmetric decorative pattern consisting of the face of a taotie, a mythical beast.*

words were obviously branded by the sword spirit itself after someone was sacrificed to the blade. Li Qingqian died for the sword, but it's not called Qingqian Sword or the Water-Parting Sword. Why is it called the Hong Shao Sword?"

"Don't worry about why," Murong Lian said. "Destroy the blade first."

"D-d-destroy it?" Yue Chenqing sputtered and shook his head. "No, that's too hard! Breaking weapons imbued with spirits is a high-level Yue Clan technique—I can't do it!"

Murong Lian swore under his breath. "How long would it take you to go back to Yue Manor and find someone who can?"

"There isn't anyone else!" Yue Chenqing said. "That technique is too dangerous, so my dad doesn't pass it on to just anyone, and he isn't even in the capital right now..."

"Then what about your bofu?"[30]

"He doesn't know how!"

"What about your fourth uncle?!"

Yue Chenqing felt wronged. "You know what he's like! He never pays any attention to me. Even if he were in the capital, I wouldn't know where to find him..."

"On and on with all these excuses!" Murong Lian said angrily. "All this whining and we're still stuck with you, however rubbish you are! You're up!"

Only when one requires knowledge in real life does one regret their previous lack of learning. As of now, Li Qingqian had been identified as a sword spirit, but whether he would let them leave alive was still up for debate. Even if they managed to escape, it would be for naught if they couldn't then destroy this Hong Shao Sword.

---

30 *Father's elder brother.*

Yue Chenqing could only grimace. "Okay, then I'll try. But in case I fail, could you..."

"Don't worry. I'll definitely disembowel you if you fail," Murong Lian said darkly.

Yue Chenqing went quiet.

It was just as Yue Chenqing said: destroying an ordinary weapon wasn't difficult—find a strong man who could break boulders over his chest and have him bend it in half, and that would be the end of it. Destroying a weapon imbued with a spirit was far more onerous.

Yue Chenqing bit his fingertip hard enough to draw blood, put Hong Shao on the ground, and began to draw a talisman around it. The talisman was terribly complicated, and he didn't remember it with that much clarity to begin with, which meant he had to fix it again and again. Watching this, Murong Lian grew profoundly impatient.

"Are you done yet?"

"Don't rush me. The more you rush me, the more mistakes I'll make."

"Hurry up! I want to go home and smoke!"

Now that Murong Lian was craving ephemera, his expression became more and more unsightly, the rims of his eyes faintly reddening as a sickly flush suffused his pale face. He lowered his head to look at his pipe only to see another filthy jiangshi bloodstain he hadn't wiped clean. He found himself feeling even more disgusted as he closed his eyes and leaned to the side.

"I'm done, I'm done! I'm done drawing! I've finally got it!" Yue Chenqing cried at last. Hastily sitting with crossed legs, he closed his eyes and formed a seal in front of the blood array.

Murong Lian endured the irritation surging in his chest and glared through narrowed eyes at this youth, who earnestly began to chant the incantation and perform the spell. As Yue Chenqing recited, the array on the ground glowed with gentle white light, as if wisps of immortal qi were enclosing Hong Shao.

"Thy blood fills the furnace, thy bones become the blade."

The glow grew steadily brighter, and Hong Shao emitted a sharp shriek from within the array and shuddered slightly.

"This sword of water's gleam was once a yearning dream."

Li Qingqian obviously felt something strange happening from his end of the cave. He spun around, his face a rictus of fury as he gnashed his teeth. "That rascal from the Yue Clan! Ruining my work!"

He made to fly over and attack, but was stopped by Mo Xi's sword. Li Qingqian grew even more furious. "Move aside or else!"

His Water-Parting Sword maneuvers were so fast they merged into a ghostly blur, but nevertheless, he could not escape. The clanging of metal and the flying of sparks filled the dim cave.

In desperation, Li Qingqian threw his head back and shrieked, a massive cloud of black miasma exploding from his chest. The black qi coalesced into a hissing spiritual talisman in his palm and shot toward Gu Mang.

This was the highest-level Demon-Summoning Talisman of the Liao Kingdom. No more than ten people in all of Liao were versed in its use. The talisman burst in midair to become hundreds of flying arrows wreathed in plumes of demonic qi. They flew hissing in Gu Mang's direction. Just as they were about to pierce the barrier around him, Mo Xi leapt through the air to land in front of Gu Mang. Holding the Shuairan sword straight up in front of him, he twisted the blade, light illuminating his features.

"Lotus Snake Formation, open!" Mo Xi bellowed.

Shuairan's sword form shattered into thousands of motes of red light in his hands, blossoming like lush lotus flowers. Each fragment of the sword landed in the form of a snake with gleaming scales, which launched into the air and tore Li Qingqian's talisman apart.

Yet at that moment, Li Qingqian jumped behind Gu Mang, concentrating the sword qi around him to blast a hole through the protective barrier. Mo Xi whipped around and kicked Li Qingqian square in the chest. Li Qingqian spit out a mouthful of filthy blood, but at the last second, he used what remained of his strength to mercilessly implant the Demon-Summoning Talisman within Gu Mang's chest.

Gu Mang's clear blue eyes snapped open. The malevolent qi in his body immediately and explosively increased.

Mo Xi tensed. "Gu Mang..."

"Thy blood fills the furnace, thy bones become the blade. This sword of water's gleam was once a yearning dream..."

On the other side of the cave, Yue Chenqing's incantation was like a curse encircling Li Qingqian.

Panting, Li Qingqian's face paled further, but he staggered to his feet with a hand pressed to his heart. He threw his head back in laughter.

"No matter how you try to suppress him," Li Qingqian panted, "you're no match for the control that the Liao Kingdom's Demon-Summoning Talisman exerts!" He swallowed a mouthful of bloody spittle, eyes crimson. "Gu Mang, come!"

Greenish tendons protruded from Gu Mang's wrists. With an explosive *boom*, he burst free from the bamboo warrior's immortal-binding ropes. In the next breath, a wisp of black qi flew out from his forehead and reduced Yue Chenqing's immobility talisman to ashes.

Gu Mang looked up through those blue, lupine eyes and tore apart the last and thickest loop of immortal-binding rope, which had been wound around his waist. He strode toward Li Qingqian and knelt before him. "Awaiting orders."

Li Qingqian clenched his jaw and pointed at Mo Xi. "Kill him!"

"Understood."

The Demon-Summoning Talisman demanded a terrifying quantity of spiritual energy from its caster, so in controlling Gu Mang thus far, Li Qingqian had used only ordinary techniques to awaken Gu Mang's demonic qi. The rest would hang on this moment. No matter how high the cost, Li Qingqian had to rely on Gu Mang for this final salvo.

Malevolent qi swirled around Gu Mang's body, the blue of his eyes so bright they glowed nearly white. A colossal blaze in the shape of a wolf's head flared to life behind him.

The bamboo warrior creaked as it readied.

Gu Mang lifted a hand and, without so much as a twitch of his finger, sent the bamboo warrior that had sought to launch a sneak attack flying into the wall of stone.

Those blue eyes reflected Mo Xi's black figure. Pausing, he dully repeated his orders: "Kill you."

He shot forward to attack.

While Mo Xi had his hands full fending off Gu Mang, Li Qingqian seized his chance to leap behind a stone formation. His expression was livid; he looked like he wanted to wring Yue Chenqing's neck into a fountain of blood.

Murong Lian had, of course, noticed this series of events. Even though Li Qingqian's abilities outclassed his own, the sword spirit had expended too much energy and was faltering like an arrow at the end of its flight. Facing him wouldn't be out of the question.

"Hurry up, I'll stall him!" Murong Lian said to Yue Chenqing.

He flitted behind the stalagmite and flung out a Water Demon talisman that transformed instantaneously into its eponymous demons. They rose from the ground one after another to tear into Li Qingqian.

"The sword subsumes thy soul, my bidding lights thy way."

Yue Chenqing had reached the end of his incantation. Black water spilled forth from Hong Shao's blade to pool around the blood array.

On the other side of the rocks, Li Qingqian swept away the charging horde of demons with a flick of his sword and leapt toward Murong Lian. His sword technique had once been terrifyingly powerful—but at this precise moment, a shudder ran through him. Shuairan's tip struck Li Qingqian's wrist, and his blade fell clanging to the ground.

If a sword spirit's true form was destroyed, they were instantly annihilated no matter how strong they had been. Li Qingqian was certainly aware of this crucial fact; the only reason he had eaten the hearts of cultivators to supplement his cultivation and remained in Chonghua all this time had been to find a way to reclaim his true form from Murong Lian. But Murong Lian had been too well-guarded; Li Qingqian had been utterly unable to get close to him. On top of that, no matter how many people he'd eaten or souls he'd absorbed, the seal on the Hong Shao Sword prevented him from merging with the blade and accessing his true powers.

That was why he had used demonic curses to lure Gu Mang out of his prison—he'd wanted to use him to steal back Hong Shao.

But who could've known...

Li Qingqian had prepared for thousands of contingencies, but he'd never anticipated that Xihe-jun would leave a tracker on Gu Mang that would allow him to chase him down so quickly...

Li Qingqian's eyes were scarlet, and his chest heaved as he howled in outrage. "I can't die, and no one can stop me! It's no use!"

He shouted this over and over, but his spirit form could hold on no longer. He fell to his knees, his hands bracing him over the ground.

Fucking hell. Among his three pursuers, why did one of them have to be a descendant of an aristocratic artificer clan? This was truly...truly...

As Li Qingqian thought, wild laughter bubbled up from his throat, the sound indescribably distorted and hateful.

Come to think of it, no matter whether he'd fought for good or for evil, whether he'd persevered along the righteous path or fallen into a den of demons, the heavens had never once treated him with mercy. And what of that saying, "I decide my fate, not the heavens"? For all his desperate struggling, what had he managed to achieve? How laughable! How very laughable!

Li Qingqian watched as, in the distance, Yue Chenqing's work made Hong Shao shake miserably. His heart seized with hatred. His struggle and descent into depravity over the past few years, the blood that had soaked him through... The memories came back against his will, one after another.

Li Qingqian was filled with a sudden dogged refusal to accept this outcome. "Gu Mang!" he shouted. "Come, take the sword!"

Gu Mang was fighting intensely with Mo Xi nearby. As this shout resonated throughout the entire cave, his blue eyes shifted. He turned to rush toward Li Qingqian, but Mo Xi grabbed his shoulder and held him.

Gu Mang looked back at him. "I'm taking the sword," he said coldly. "I don't want *you*."

What he meant was that his current mission had become taking the sword rather than killing Mo Xi.

Mo Xi still didn't let go, and Gu Mang's eyes narrowed further as his tone grew more clipped. "*I don't want you.*"

Those blue eyes, paired with the way he bit his lip in frustration as he said something so suggestive and willful—*I don't want you*—

Mo Xi knew that Gu Mang didn't mean anything by it, but a fire blazed to life in his chest nonetheless. He threw up a hand to cover Gu Mang's face, refusing to even look at him. "Is it your choice to want me or not?!"

"Let go."

"You want to take the sword and not me, right?"

"Yes," Gu Mang said.

His firm and ringing words made Mo Xi's rage burn only more fiercely. "Wasn't the order to kill me?" he snapped. "You can't take the sword before you do that!"

Those blue eyes glazed over. That sounded...about right?

Although a person controlled by the Demon-Summoning Talisman could follow orders well enough, rarely could they think for themselves. This was why the Liao Kingdom cultivators who employed this technique usually expressed their orders very explicitly, precisely marking out the start and end of each command. It was obvious that Li Qingqian had learned the technique in secret, and that he therefore didn't know the proper method by which to control a subject.

Thus, even though Gu Mang was strong, he was confused.

Those lupine eyes swept back and forth over Mo Xi again and again, as if assessing whether what Mo Xi said was true, or weighing whether the person in front of him was worth biting.

Then he made his decision. "All right. I want you first. Then the sword."

"Gege wants you. How could I not want you?" Once, those black eyes had smiled and shone as Gu Mang gazed at Mo Xi in the night, his expression lazy and carefree. Strong arms had pulled Mo Xi close—his shidi and comrade, his lover and young master.

In the forest near the battlefield, Gu Mang had pressed in and kissed Mo Xi—first tenderly, then with blazing passion.

The *want you* from back then had been answered with a moment of stolen pleasure.

The *want you* of now was followed not by tenderness, but by the unsheathing of a demonic blade that struck at Mo Xi, fierce and sharp. The legs that had once trembled around Mo Xi's waist were now both vicious and well-aimed, lifting high and kicking hard.

No matter how much malevolent qi Gu Mang absorbed, his core was broken. Though he was exceptionally strong, he was no match for the pure-blooded descendant of gods, Mo Xi. And that was to say nothing of how well Mo Xi knew Gu Mang's fighting style—each move, every strike...

When Gu Mang turned to kick, he met only empty air. Mo Xi turned to grab his ankle and glanced at him sidelong before offhandedly catching the flying blade Gu Mang threw. Spiritual energy blazed, and the thin blade in his hand splintered into shards.

"What a coincidence." Mo Xi paused for a second before speaking, his tone like ice. "I want you as well."

Gu Mang had no chance to respond before the world spun before his eyes as Mo Xi threw him to the ground. Mo Xi's strong frame pinned him down in a manner almost brutally dominant, forcing him to the cave floor with his knees at Gu Mang's hips, one hand around his wrists and the other gripping him by the jaw.

In all of Chonghua, none knew the Liao Kingdom better than Mo Xi. Other than Medicine Master Jiang, he was perhaps the only other individual who could lift the Demon-Summoning Curse.

He held the violently squirming and resisting Gu Mang still and stared down into those blue eyes that darted around with unease.

"Want you."

Gu Mang's face was flushed in Mo Xi's grip, but he ground out his insistence through gritted teeth.

Yes, this was the order he'd been given, but the way it sounded...

Mo Xi's heart flared with searing heat. He looked at Gu Mang struggling underneath him, staring up at him fiercely, helplessly. Like a spark landing in a pile of firewood, an urge rushed through Mo Xi's mind—an urge to tear Gu Mang to shreds, to hurt him in the most intimate of ways, to make him *regret*, to make him beg for mercy.

At that moment, Mo Xi found himself with second thoughts about uttering words so coarse and simple as "I want you as well." Had he chosen this phrasing to help Gu Mang more easily understand him—or had the years of hunger piled up in his heart seized this opportunity to spill forth?

This self-doubt frightened Mo Xi. At the same time, Gu Mang's eyes welled up in discomfort beneath him, his blue irises hazy with a sheen of involuntary tears. He panted, lips parting as he tried to speak again.

To stop himself from thinking any more terrifying thoughts, Mo Xi covered Gu Mang's mouth. "Behave," he ground out. "I'm lifting the curse for you."

Gu Mang made furious noises of displeasure beneath him, and even tried to bite Mo Xi's fingers.

"It'll hurt." Mo Xi's hot exhales sank down. He stared into Gu Mang's eyes, their faces so close. "Bear with it."

34

Bite Me

JUST AS MO XI promised, being freed from the Demon-Summoning Talisman was extremely painful—like having thousands of thorny brambles pulled from one's flesh.

Gu Mang tried to bear it silently at first, but by the time Mo Xi had recited half the incantation, he could no longer endure. His tense form went lax beneath Mo Xi as he shivered and convulsed, until finally, great tears spilled from the corners of his eyes to trail shakily to his temples.

His eyes were red from crying, but Mo Xi kept a hand over his mouth, blocking all sound. Gu Mang's clothes were soon soaked in sweat, gaze unfocused and eyes blank as they reflected Mo Xi's face. His reflection fractured with a blink, becoming the tears in Gu Mang's stinging eyes.

Mo Xi had to exert all his strength to keep Gu Mang pinned, to stop him from going berserk.

It hurt. It hurt so *much*, a pain deeper than bone and marrow...

Mo Xi found the sight of Gu Mang's quivering lashes so difficult to bear that it frightened him. Against his will, his grip loosened a touch.

In that momentary slack, Gu Mang struggled away from the hand muzzling him. He turned his head and gasped for breath, crying out desperately in a voice both hoarse and pitiful. Unlike his powerful body, his voice when he whimpered was as delicate as spring leaves.

In truth, Gu Mang had cried like this before—but no one else knew when. Only Mo Xi had heard it, in their bed.

"Bite me," Mo Xi murmured.

Gu Mang didn't understand. He was deaf to anything Mo Xi said. Mo Xi took a deep breath, pushing aside his unease, and bent down.

At this angle, he knew Gu Mang would reflexively bite his shoulder.

Gu Mang's canines were terribly sharp. They'd broken skin many times in the past, to the point where the scars he'd left still hadn't faded and might not ever. *Same old spot. Go ahead and bite,* thought Mo Xi.

Ruthlessly, he continued to chant.

This short respite followed by even worse pain made Gu Mang flinch, body going taut as he gasped hoarsely once more... Caught between maddening frustration and breaking down completely, he instinctively opened his mouth and sank his teeth into Mo Xi's shoulder.

His entire body was soaked in sweat. He spasmed and shook in Mo Xi's arms...

The closer the incantation came to completion, the more unbearable the pain became. By the end, Gu Mang could no longer keep his jaw clamped down on Mo Xi's shoulder. He abruptly let go and tilted his face away, gasping raggedly. Sweat beaded his skin, his eyes so teary they resembled storm-swept seas. He finally spoke. "It hurts..."

This was the first time since Mo Xi's return to Chonghua, the first time since their reunion, that Gu Mang had expressed himself with such undisguised emotion.

"I...hurt..."

Mo Xi's chest tightened. That heart, once stabbed and never the same, throbbed and ached violently within his ribs.

He gazed into Gu Mang's eyes. Gu Mang had collapsed, limp in his arms.

Mo Xi had a sudden irrepressible urge to press his head to Gu Mang's clammy forehead, like he had long ago, before anything had broken beyond repair. To caress Gu Mang's sweat-soaked brow and tell him, *Don't worry, you'll be all right once the curse is broken, I'll stay with you...*

I'll stay with you.

But as Mo Xi lowered his face, as he drew close, he at once remembered all that had happened—all that could never be undone.

He remembered that Murong Lian and the others were separated from them by merely a stone wall. If he didn't quickly release Gu Mang from the Demon-Summoning Talisman, this mess would become even harder to resolve.

Jerking himself awake, Mo Xi turned away and blinked his eyes a few times, continuing to chant.

It was the last piece...only the last piece...

He felt a sudden pain at his neck. It was Gu Mang, so weak he could no longer bite into Mo Xi's shoulder, longingly opening his mouth to sink his teeth into something softer instead. He was biting into the side of Mo Xi's neck.

Or, not so much biting, since he was already so weak, but mouthing. Beneath those wet lips, only the sharpest canine could still hurt Mo Xi. The others barely touched him.

The final walls in his heart came crumbling down. Mo Xi closed his eyes. *Just this once...only this once.*

Heedless of whoever might see them, uncaring of what they would think, unbothered, even, by all that had happened between himself and Gu Mang—their deep and bloody hatred—Mo Xi lifted his hand to cradle the back of Gu Mang's head and let him bite.

He stroked Gu Mang's hair, softly coaxing him, "It's okay, it's okay... It's all over now...all over now..."

The pain was over.

If only their debts and hatred could be so easily cast away. If only the chasm between them could be closed as quickly as the end of this agony. If only.

He held and comforted the trembling man in his arms. No one saw; even Mo Xi himself was unwilling to bear witness, closing his eyes before gently laying a kiss at the top of Gu Mang's head.

If only all the suffering in the world could end too. If only.

Released from the curse, Gu Mang drifted into slumber. Mo Xi rose and summoned the bamboo warrior, commanding it to take care of him. Then he transformed Shuairan into a spiritual snake once again and left it to stand guard, while he went around the stone wall to help Murong Lian and Yue Chenqing bring this difficult battle to a close.

But by the looks of it, they didn't need his help.

Yue Chenqing's spiritual power wasn't particularly potent; he had to recite each line of the sword-destroying incantation some thirty times. But with each repetition, Li Qingqian's energy weakened. By now, Yue Chenqing was almost at the final round, and Li Qingqian was no longer much of a match for Murong Lian.

"Thy blood fills the furnace, thy bones become the blade..."

These incantations had morphed into hazy plumes of white smoke that wound around Li Qingqian.

"This sword of water's gleam was once a yearning dream..."

Li Qingqian was a force to be reckoned with. His form had already dissipated to a significant extent, but, face pale, he continued to exchange unsteady blows with Murong Lian. Murong Lian grew more relaxed the longer they fought, knocking his opponent to the ground again and again. He watched Li Qingqian stagger up with blood leaking from the corners of his mouth, clothes askew.

Murong Lian scoffed. "Why are you still struggling? Defeat is inevitable, yet you insist on this pathetic display. Do you enjoy getting kicked?"

Li Qingqian did not speak. He simply laughed maniacally, his lips parting to spit up a fountain of blood. His eyes flashed with a mad perseverance, difficult to describe, as though there was something for which he must survive at all costs. He couldn't dissipate until he achieved that goal, nor could he merely look on as Yue Chenqing destroyed the Hong Shao Sword.

That glint in his eyes wasn't saying, "I decide my fate, not the heavens," but rather, "I cannot defeat the heavens, but no matter what, I will do as I ought. Even if I lose, even if I die, even if I'm reduced to windblown ash—I will never bow to fate."

I will not bow.

Crazed, he laughed again, and Murong Lian sent another brutal kick at his face with his slippered foot. Again Li Qingqian crawled to his feet, inching toward Yue Chenqing.

"Ha ha ha, ha ha ha ha—"

"Li-zongshi."

Mo Xi's address made the wildly laughing Li Qingqian shudder. His red eyes swiveled to stare unsparingly into Mo Xi's, his expression both unsettling and bewildered.

"You disappeared after the ordeal at the Maiden's Lament Mountain. What happened afterward?"

Mo Xi had asked on a gamble, but as this question hung in the air, he was certain he'd struck true. Li Qingqian's eyes had narrowed slightly, that crazed smile beginning to distort.

The Hong Shao Sword, the writing on the wall, the maidens

kidnapped for their similar faces, the extravagantly dressed ghost brides in the cave...

First she hates her helpless fate; Second hates her ill-starred face; Third their parting does she hate, a lost love left too late.

All this seemed to point to the involvement of an unknown woman. But why? What had happened at Maiden's Lament Mountain? What had made that swordsman clad in fluttering green become a vengeful sword spirit—an unrecognizable evil ghost?

Mo Xi gazed at him. "Who forged you into the sword? Who did you come to Chonghua to seek?"

Li Qingqian wanted to laugh again, but after a hard swallow, only a pathetic rasp escaped his lips. "Who's Li-zongshi? Not me! I'm not him! That idiot Li Qingqian is dead! He should've died even sooner! It's all because he lived too long, and was too delusional, too desperate for fame, that he was able to hurt others, hurt himself, and end up like he did! He has no one to blame but himself!"

These words were viciously spat.

"He deserved it!" The sword spirit shrieked unsteadily, malevolently. "Who am I looking for? Those girls! Ha ha ha! I'm here for vengeance! I'm here to kill! I'm going to kill!"

Li Qingqian's screams grew more hateful, but glimmering light rose from the surface of his body—with Yue Chenqing's last chant, he would become but ashes on the wind, together with his secrets.

"Rest not in this holy sword, return thyself to the earthly world," Yue Chenqing finished.

Hong Shao jerked, a jade-green light shining from the blade.

Yue Chenqing's eyes snapped open.

Murong Lian, leaning against a stone pillar, realized at once that something had gone wrong. "What happened? What's with that damn sword?"

Yue Chenqing had never been in this kind of situation before and anxiously chanted again. "Rest not in this holy sword, return thyself to the earthly—ah!"

Hong Shao suddenly stopped shaking, and the pool of black water surrounding it rushed back into the blade at frightening speed.

"No!" Yue Chenqing cried. "It's going to break free!"

He was still speaking when he heard the *boom* of an explosion, and his vision went dark. The waves of qi sent up by the blast flung him violently away. Yue Chenqing smashed into a stone wall and spit up a mouthful of blood.

Yue Chenqing looked up in panic only to see that Hong Shao had flown straight up into the middle of the bloody fight. It emitted a dazzling green light from within a cloud of black smoke, illuminating Yue Chenqing and Murong Lian's pallid faces.

Murong Lian clung to the wall for balance, grinding his teeth. "This is..."

Yue Chenqing cried out, his voice breaking. "The sword-destroying incantation backfired; it broke the seal! Murong-dage, come quick! Come stop it!"

Was there any need for Yue Chenqing to say it? Murong Lian swept over and attempted to use his qiankun pouch to contain it again, but Yue Chenqing's final mistake had freed Hong Shao of its restraints. This time, its strength and resentment were formidably strong. It sent out a burst of sharp sword energy that struck down Murong Lian before flying into Li Qingqian's hand.

"Yue Chenqing!" Murong Lian opened his mouth and spat, "You useless fool!"

"Didn't I already say I was useless?! That I didn't know how to do it?!" Yue Chenqing wailed dejectedly. "You're the one who made me try!"

"What mistake did you make on the last line?!" Murong Lian was so furious his face could have frozen in a scowl.

"I didn't make a mistake!" Yue Chenqing insisted. "*Rest not in this holy sword, return thyself to the earthly world.* How could I have recited that wrong? It must be—it must be something I don't understand! Or maybe I drew the array wrong at the beginning. I..."

There was no point in explaining further. Li Qingqian was clutching the glowing Hong Shao Sword—the sword spirit was fusing with its vessel.

When Mo Xi saw the cloud of light burst forth, he shouted, "Tuntian Barrier!"

A beam of golden light sprang from his palms and morphed into a massive whale. Whistling, it swept aside all the rock debris and completely enveloped his allies under its halo.

On the other side of the whale's barrier, Li Qingqian, having recovered his sword, was seething with terrifying evil energy. Floating in midair and surrounded by bluish streaks of power from the blade, he slammed against the Tuntian Barrier and released a fearsome flow of spiritual energy.

Li Qingqian lowered his head and watched the wounds on his arms and palms heal. He straightened his clothes, a sinister smile creeping over his pale face. After a long moment, he turned around with smiling eyes, looking askance at Yue Chenqing below.

"Yue-gongzi is yet unpracticed." His expression was horribly unsightly. The pain of nearly having his soul dissipated would not be so easily forgotten, but the discomfort was nothing now that his strength had exponentially increased. "Many thanks for your unintended support."

Murong Lian watched as this situation—which was still intimately connected to his responsibilities over Luomei Pavilion—continued to deteriorate. Profoundly discomfited, he turned to Mo Xi. "Why aren't you fighting him? How is it that you can't even defeat a sword spirit?"

"If I fight him, will you maintain the protective barrier?" Mo Xi snapped.

"I—" Murong Lian choked. "Don't you still have Shuairan? Let Shuairan take him down in snake form!"

"Shuairan is guarding Gu Mang!"

Murong Lian pounced, as if he had found an incredible piece of leverage against Mo Xi. He refused to put aside petty differences even before the enemy. "Very well, so you really *are*—"

"If he goes berserk again, are *you* going to stop him?" Mo Xi angrily interrupted.

"You—!"

"Murong-dage, it's useless." Yue Chenqing said, his little face stark white. "If a sword of that caliber fuses with the sword spirit, they're close to invincible. Only an artificer zongshi could hope to defeat him." He was near tears. "I messed up..."

Li Qingqian, now delivered from danger, had no plans to tangle any further with these three. He was determined to swiftly break away in order to complete his unknown mission. Raising his hand, he cast a powerful sword glare barrier, separating himself from Mo Xi and his allies, then lifted Hong Shao to fly out of the cave.

"Quick, after him!" Murong Lian said.

"What use would it be to go after him?" Yue Chenqing cried. "I just said he's more or less invincible right now, only the most powerful artificer zongshi could—"

Before he could finish, a beam of blinding white light streaked toward Li Qingqian's back. The bamboo warrior had flown up into the air, uninhibited by Li Qingqian's barrier. With a single flip, it landed before Li Qingqian and unsheathed its saber with a *shing* to bar Li Qingqian's way.

Li Qingqian wasn't the only one who was shocked; even Yue Chenqing was dumbfounded.

Had he not said a fused sword spirit was close to invincible, and that only an artificer zongshi with skills on par with his father could defeat it?

Who was this zongshi? The bamboo warrior? That was beyond ridiculous!

Yue Chenqing's brain was a buzzing mess—until he heard the bright sound of a sword behind them. He turned to see a man soaring toward them from the cave entrance, his white robes fluttering as he rode the winds.

The man's white robe was of light and graceful make, and the silver trim at his sleeves gleamed faintly. His long hair was bound by a tall jade crown, fastened with a pin overlaid with a ribbon, the snowy silk fluttering in tandem with his sleeves.

All his flowing sleeves and silks gave him a strikingly immortal aura. Though this man possessed extremely delicate features, the delicacy of his face couldn't diminish his imposing presence—an apathetic coldness was visible in his eyes, such that his spartan elegance was not one softly tender but rather piercingly frosty and indifferent.

The white-robed cultivator briskly steered his sword to alight upon the ground, expressionlessly lifting his refined face.

Those severe sword brows and majestic phoenix eyes swept across the battlefield. When his gaze landed on the bedraggled Yue Chenqing, he let out a dismissive snort. He stepped forward with a wave of his sleeves, horsetail whisk resting in the crook of his arm.

Here was the "Ignorance" of Chonghua's three poisons—master of the bamboo warrior, Murong Chuyi.

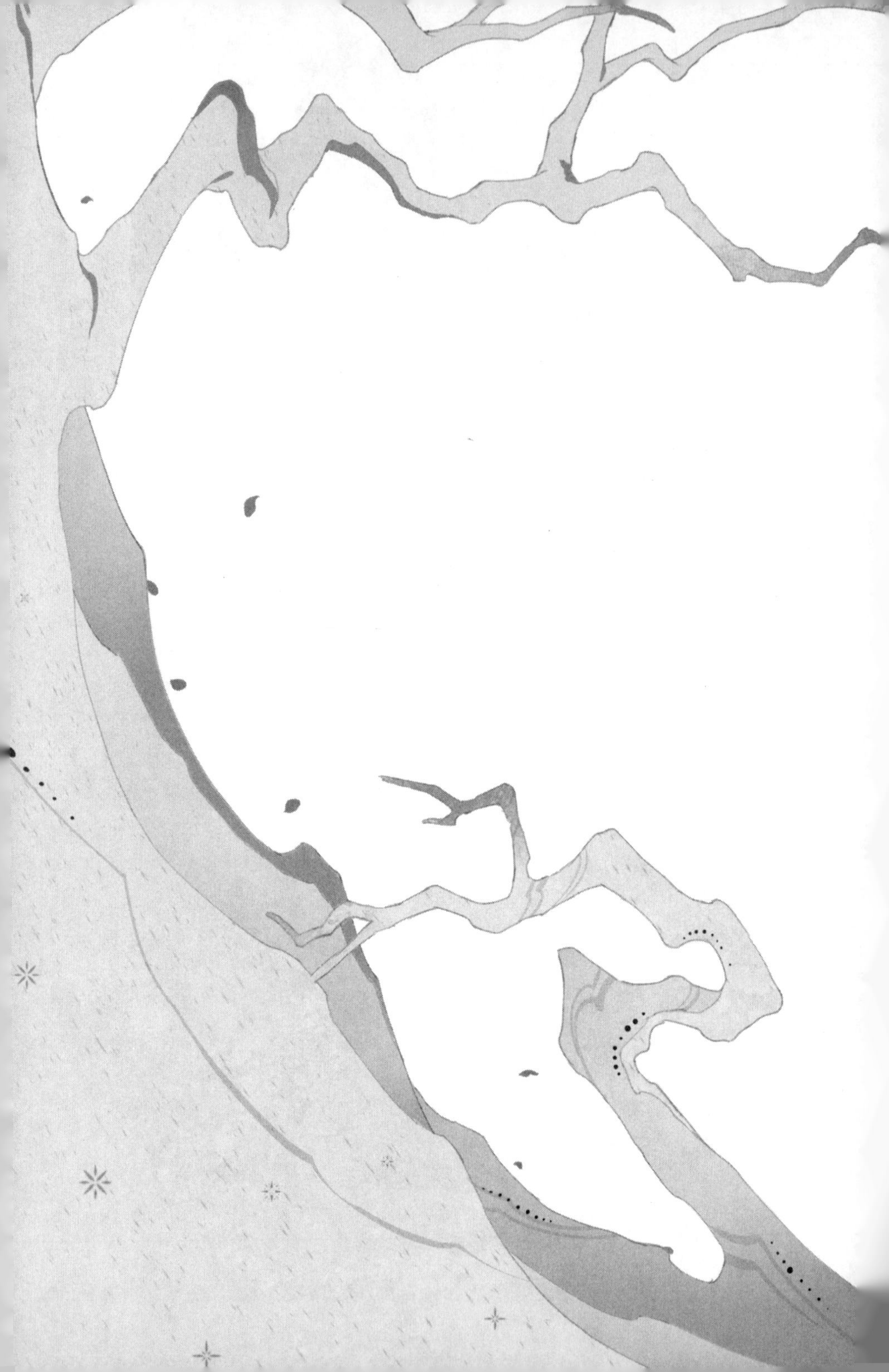

THE STORY CONTINUES IN

Remnants of Filth

VOLUME 2

APPENDIX

Characters, Names, and Locations

Characters

Mo Xi

墨熄 SURNAME MO; GIVEN NAME XI, "EXTINGUISH"

TITLES: Xihe-jun (羲和君 / "sun," literary), General Mo

WEAPONS:

Shuairan (率然 / a mythical snake): A whip that can transform into a sword as needed. Named after a snake from Chinese mythology, said to respond so quickly an attack to any part of its body would be met immediately with its fangs or tail (or both). First mentioned in Sun Tzu's *The Art of War* as an ideal for commanders to follow when training their armies.

Tuntian (吞天 / "Skyswallower"): A scepter cast with the essence of a whale spirit.

The commander of the Northern Frontier Army, Mo Xi is the only living descendant of the illustrious Mo Clan. Granted the title Xihe-jun by the late emperor, he possesses extraordinary innate spiritual abilities and has a reputation for being coldly ruthless.

Gu Mang

顾茫 SURNAME GU, "TO LOOK"; GIVEN NAME MANG, "BEWILDERMENT"

TITLES: Beast of the Altar, General Gu

WEAPON:

Yongye (永夜 / "Evernight"): A demonic dagger from the Liao Kingdom.

Once the dazzling shixiong of the cultivation academy, Murong Lian's slave, and war general to the empire of Chonghua, Gu Mang fell from grace and turned traitor, defecting to the enemy Liao Kingdom. Years later, he was sent back to Chonghua as a prisoner of war. His name comes from the line "I unsheathe my sword and look around bewildered" in the first of three poems in the collection "Arduous Journey" by Li Bai.

Murong Lian
慕容怜 SURNAME MURONG; GIVEN NAME LIAN, "MERCY"

TITLE: Wangshu-jun (望舒君 / "moon," literary)

WEAPON:

Water Demon Talisman (水鬼符): A talisman that becomes a horde of water demons to attack its target.

Gu Mang's former master and cousin to the current emperor, Murong Lian is the current lord of Wangshu Manor and the owner of Luomei Pavilion. He is known as the "Greed" of Chonghua's three poisons.

The Emperor
君上

TITLE: His Imperial Majesty, "junshang"

Eccentric ruler of the empire of Chonghua. Due to the cultural taboo against using the emperor's given name in any context, he is only ever addressed and referred to as "His Imperial Majesty."

Jiang Yexue
江夜雪 SURNAME JIANG; GIVEN NAME YEXUE, "EVENING SNOW"

TITLE: Qingxu Elder (清旭长老 / "clear dawn")

Disowned son of the Yue Clan, Yue Chenqing's older brother, and Mo Xi's old friend, Jiang Yexue is a gentleman to the core.

Yue Chenqing

岳辰晴 SURNAME YUE; GIVEN NAME CHENQING, "MORNING SUN"

TITLE: Deputy General Yue

Young master of the Yue Clan and Murong Chuyi's nephew, Yue Chenqing is a happy-go-lucky child with a penchant for getting into trouble.

Murong Chuyi

慕容楚衣 SURNAME MURONG; GIVEN NAME CHUYI, SURNAME CHU, "CLOTHES"

Yue Chenqing's Fourth Uncle, Chonghua's "Ignorance," and all-around enigma, Murong Chuyi is a master artificer whose true motivations remain unknown.

Li Wei

李微 SURNAME LI; GIVEN NAME WEI, "SLIGHT"

The competent, if harried, head housekeeper of Xihe Manor.

Li Qingqian

李清浅 SURNAME LI; GIVEN NAME QINGQIAN, "CLEAR AND SHALLOW"

Once the honorable zongshi of the Water-Parting Sword.

Jiang Fuli

姜拂黎 SURNAME JIANG; GIVEN NAME FULI, "TO BRUSH AWAY, MULTITUDES"

Also known by his title of Medicine Master, Jiang Fuli is the finest healer in Chonghua, dubbed the "Wrath" of Chonghua's three poisons.

Murong Mengze
慕容梦泽 SURNAME MURONG; GIVEN NAME MENGZE, "YUNMENG LAKE"

A master healer and the "Virtue" of Chonghua's three gentlemen, Princess Mengze's frail constitution and graceful, refined manner are known to all.

Locations

Dongting Lake
洞庭湖

A real lake in northeastern Hunan, named "Grotto Court Lake" for the dragon court that was said to reside in its depths.

Luomei Pavilion
落梅别苑 "GARDENS OF FALLEN PLUM BLOSSOMS"

A house of pleasure where the nobility of Chonghua can have their pick of captives from enemy nations.

Feiyao Terrace
飞瑶台 "FLYING JADE"

A terrace in the imperial palace.

Chengtian Terrace
承天台 "HEAVENLY WORSHIP"

Not much is known about this ministry, aside from their unfortunate leader Elder Yu.

Mansion of Beauties
红颜楼

A pleasure house in the capital of Chonghua.

Qingquan Pool
清泉池 "CLEAR SPRING"

A pool in the back courtyard of Luomei Pavilion, stocked with forty-nine spirit-suppressing carp in order to control the spiritual forms of various weapons kept within.

Shennong Terrace
神农台

The healers' ministry of Chonghua. Shennong is the deity and mythological ruler said to have taught agriculture and herbal medicine to the ancient Chinese people.

Warrior Soul Mountain
战魂山

Where the heroes of Chonghua are laid to rest.

Maiden's Lament Mountain
女哭山

Once Phoenix Feather Mountain, this peak was renamed due to the vengeful spirits of the maidens buried alive upon it.

Yuelai Teahouse
悦来茶馆 "INVITE JOY"

A teahouse in the capital.

Name Guide

Diminutives, nicknames, and name tags

A-: Friendly diminutive. Always a prefix. Usually for monosyllabic names, or one syllable out of a two-syllable name.

DOUBLING: Doubling a syllable of a person's name can be a nickname, e.g., "Mangmang"; it has childish or cutesy connotations.

XIAO-: A diminutive meaning "little." Always a prefix.

-ER: An affectionate diminutive added to names, literally "son" or "child." Always a suffix.

Family

DI/DIDI: Younger brother or a younger male friend.

GE/GEGE/DAGE: Older brother or an older male friend.

JIE/JIEJIE/ZIZI: Older sister or an older female friend.

Cultivation

SHIFU: Teacher or master.

SHIXIONG: Older martial brother, used for older disciples or classmates.

SHIDI: Younger martial brother, used for younger disciples or classmates.

DAOZHANG/XIANJUN/XIANZHANG/SHENJUN: Polite terms of address for cultivators. Can be used alone as a title or attached to someone's family name.

ZONGSHI: A title or suffix for a person of particularly outstanding skill; largely only applied to cultivators.

Other

GONGZI: Young man from an affluent household.

SHAOZHU: Young master and direct heir of a household.

-NIANG: Suffix for a young lady, similar to "Miss."

-JUN: A term of respect, often used as a suffix after a title.

Pronunciation Guide

Mandarin Chinese is the official state language of mainland China, and pinyin is the official system of romanization in which it is written. As Mandarin is a tonal language, pinyin uses diacritical marks (e.g., ā, á, ǎ, à) to indicate these tonal inflections. Most words use one of four tones, though some (as in "de" in the title below) are a neutral tone. Furthermore, regional variance can change the way native Chinese speakers pronounce the same word. For those reasons and more, please consider the guide below a simplified introduction to pronunciation of select character names and sounds from the world of *Remnants of Filth*.

More resources are available at sevenseasdanmei.com

NAMES

Yú Wū

Yú: Y as in you, ú as in "u" in the French "tu"

Wū as in **woo**

Mò Xī

Mò as in **mo**urning

Xī as in **chic**

Gù Máng

Gù as in **goo**p

Máng as in **mong**rel

Mùróng Lián

Mù as in **moo**n

Róng as in **wrong** / **crone**

Lián as in batta**lion**

Yuè Chénqíng

Yuè: Y as in **y**ammer, uè as in **whe**lp

Chén as in ki**tchen**

Qíng as in ma**tching**

GENERAL CONSONANTS

Some Mandarin Chinese consonants sound very similar, such as z/c/s and zh/ch/sh. Audio samples will provide the best opportunity to learn the difference between them.

X: somewhere between the **sh** in **sh**eep and **s** in **s**ilk

Q: a very aspirated **ch** as in **ch**arm

C: **ts** as in pan**ts**

Z: **z** as in **z**oom

S: **s** as in **s**ilk

CH: **ch** as in **ch**arm

ZH: **dg** as in do**dg**e

SH: **sh** as in **sh**ave

G: hard **g** as in **g**raphic

GENERAL VOWELS

The pronunciation of a vowel may depend on its preceding consonant. For example, the "i" in "shi" is distinct from the "i" in "di." Vowel pronunciation may also change depending on where the vowel appears in a word, for example the "i" in "shi" versus the "i" in "ting." Finally, compound vowels are often—though not always—pronounced as conjoined but separate vowels. You'll find a few of the trickier compounds below.

IU: as in **ewe**

IE: **ye** as in **yes**

UO: **war** as in **warm**

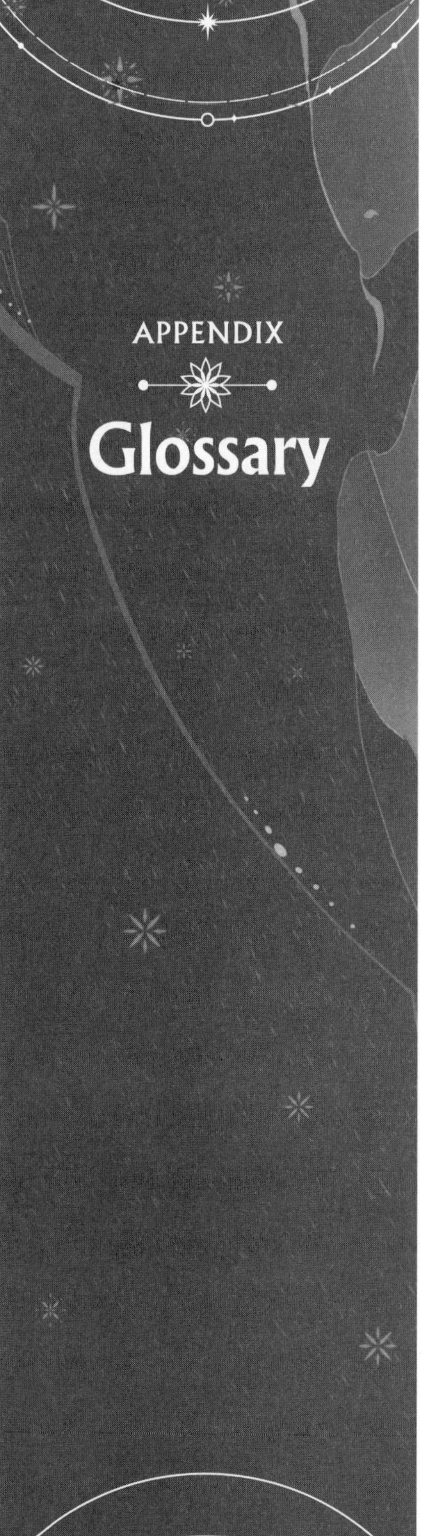

APPENDIX

Glossary

Glossary

While not required reading, this glossary is intended to offer further context for the many concepts and terms utilized throughout this novel as well as provide a starting point for learning more about the rich culture from which these stories were written.

GENRES

Danmei

Danmei (耽美 / "indulgence in beauty") is a Chinese fiction genre focused on romanticized tales of love and attraction between men. It is analogous to the BL (boys' love) genre in Japanese media and is better understood as a genre of plot than a genre of setting. For example, though many danmei novels feature wuxia or xianxia settings, others are better understood as tales of sci-fi, fantasy, or horror.

Wuxia

Wuxia (武侠 / "martial heroes") is one of the oldest Chinese literary genres. Most wuxia stories are set in ancient China and feature protagonists that practice martial arts and seek to redress wrongs. Although characters may possess seemingly superhuman abilities, they are typically mastered through practice instead of supernatural or magical means. Plots tend to focus on human relationships and power struggles between various sects and alliances. To Western moviegoers, a well-known example of the genre is *Crouching Tiger, Hidden Dragon*.

Xianxia

Xianxia (仙侠 / "immortal heroes") is a genre related to wuxia that places more emphasis on the supernatural. Some xianxia works focus on immortal beings such as gods or demons, whereas others (such as *Remnants of Filth*) are concerned with the conflicts of mortals who practice cultivation. In the latter case, characters strive to become stronger by harnessing their spiritual powers, with some aiming to extend their lifespan or achieve immortality.

TERMINOLOGY

COWRIE SHELLS: Cowrie shells were the earliest form of currency used in central China.

CULTIVATION/CULTIVATORS: Cultivation is the means by which mortals with spiritual aptitude develop and harness supernatural abilities. The practitioners of these methods are called cultivators. The path of one's cultivation is a concept that draws heavily from Daoist traditions. Generally, it comprises innate spiritual development (i.e., formation of a spiritual core) as well as spells, talismans, tools, and weapons with specific functions.

DI AND SHU HIERARCHY: Upper-class men in ancient China often took multiple wives, though only one would be the official or "di" wife, and her sons would take precedence over the sons of the "shu" wives. "Di" sons were prioritized in matters of inheritance.

EPHEMERA: In the world of *Remnants of Filth*, a drug from the Liao Kingdom. Its name is likely a reference to the line, "Life is like a dream ephemeral, how short our joys can be," from "A Party Amidst Brothers in the Peach Blossom Garden" by Tang dynasty poet Li Bai.

EYES: Descriptions like "phoenix eyes" or "peach-blossom eyes" refer to eye shape. Phoenix eyes have an upturned sweep at their far corners, whereas peach-blossom eyes have a rounded upper lid and are often considered particularly alluring.

FACE: Mianzi (面子), generally translated as "face," is an important concept in Chinese society. It is a metaphor for a person's reputation and can be extended to further descriptive metaphors. "Thin face" refers to someone easily embarrassed or prone to offense at perceived slights. Conversely, "thick face" refers to someone who acts brazenly and without shame.

FOXGLOVE TREE: The foxglove tree (泡桐树), scientific name *Paulownia tomentosa*, is endemic to China. In flower language, the foxglove tree symbolizes "eternal waiting," specifically that of a secret admirer.

GENTLEMAN: The term junzi (君子) is used to refer to someone of noble character. Historically, it was typically reserved for men.

GUOSHI: A powerful imperial official who served as an advisor to the emperor. Sometimes translated as "state preceptor," this was a post with considerable authority in some historical regimes.

HORSETAIL WHISK: Consisting of a long wooden handle with horsehair bound to one end, the horsetail whisk (拂尘 / "brushing off dust") symbolizes cleanliness and the sweeping away of mortal concerns in Buddhist and Daoist traditions. It is usually carried in the crook of one's arm.

IMMORTAL-BINDING ROPES OR CABLES: A staple of xianxia, immortal-binding cables are ropes, nets, and other restraints enchanted to withstand the power of an immortal or god. They can only be cut by high-powered spiritual items or weapons and often limit the abilities of those trapped by them.

INCENSE TIME: A measure of time in ancient China, referring to how long it takes for a single incense stick to burn. Inexact by nature, an incense time is commonly assumed to be about thirty minutes, though it can be anywhere from five minutes to an hour.

JADE: Jade is a semi-precious mineral with a long history of ornamental and functional usage in China. The word "jade" can refer to two distinct minerals, nephrite and jadeite, which both range in color from white to gray to a wide spectrum of greens.

JIANGHU: A staple of wuxia and xianxia, the jianghu (江湖, "rivers and lakes") describes an underground society of martial artists, monks, rogues, artisans, and merchants who settle disputes between themselves per their own moral codes.

LOTUS: This flower symbolizes purity of the heart and mind, as lotuses rise untainted from muddy waters. It also signifies the holy seat of the Buddha.

LIULI: Colorful glazed glass. When used as a descriptor for eye color, it refers to a bright brown.

MERIDIANS: The means by which qi travels through the body, like a magical bloodstream. Medical and combat techniques that focus on redirecting, manipulating, or halting qi circulation focus on targeting the meridians at specific points on the body, known as acupoints. Techniques that can manipulate or block qi prevent a cultivator from using magical techniques until the qi block is lifted.

MYTHICAL CREATURES: Chinese mythology boasts numerous mythological creatures, several of which make appearances in *Remnants of Filth*, including:

GUHUO NIAO: A mythical bird created by the grief of women who died in childbirth; their song mimics the sound of babies crying as the bird seeks to steal chicks and human infants for itself.

ZHEN NIAO: Also known as the poison-feather bird, this mythical creature is said to be so poisonous its feathers were used in assassinations, as dipping one in wine would make it a lethal and undetectable poison.

TENGSHE, OR SOARING SNAKE: A mythical serpent that can fly.

TAOTIE: A mythical beast that represents greed, as it is composed of only a head and a mouth and eats everything in sight until its death. Taotie designs are symmetrical down their zoomorphic faces and most commonly seen on bronzeware from the Shang dynasty.

NINE PROVINCES: A symbolic term for China as a whole.

QI: Qi (气) is the energy in all living things. Cultivators strive to manipulate qi through various techniques and tools, such as weapons, talismans, and magical objects. Different paths of cultivation provide control over specific types of qi. For example, in *Remnants of Filth*, the Liao Kingdom's techniques allow cultivators to harness demonic qi, in contrast to Chonghua's righteous methods, which cultivate the immortal path. In naturally occurring contexts, immortal qi may have nourishing or purifying properties, whereas malevolent qi (often refined via evil means such as murder) can poison an individual's mind or body.

QIANKUN POUCH: A common item in wuxia and xianxia settings, a qiankun pouch contains an extradimensional space within it, to which its name (乾坤, "universe") alludes. It is capable of holding far more than its physical exterior dimensions would suggest.

QIN: Traditional plucked stringed instrument in the zither family, usually played with the body placed flat on a low table. This was the favored instrument of scholars and the aristocracy.

QINGGONG: Literally "lightness technique," qinggong (轻功) refers to the martial arts skill of moving swiftly and lightly through the air. In wuxia and xianxia settings, characters use qinggong to leap great distances and heights.

SEAL SCRIPT: Ancient style of Chinese writing developed during the Qin dynasty, named for its usage in seals, engravings, and other inscriptions.

SHICHEN: Days were split into twelve intervals of two hours apiece called shichen (时辰 / "time"). Each of these shichen has an associated term. Prior to the Han dynasty, semi-descriptive terms were used. Post-Han dynasty, the shichen were renamed to correspond to the twelve zodiac animals.

HOUR OF ZI, MIDNIGHT: 11 p.m.–1 a.m.
HOUR OF CHOU: 1–3 a.m.
HOUR OF YIN: 3–5 a.m.
HOUR OF MAO, SUNRISE: 5–7 a.m.
HOUR OF CHEN: 7–9 a.m.
HOUR OF SI: 9–11 a.m.
HOUR OF WU, NOON: 11 a.m.–1 p.m.
HOUR OF WEI: 1–3 p.m.

HOUR OF SHEN: 3–5 p.m.
HOUR OF YOU, SUNSET: 5–7 p.m.
HOUR OF XU, DUSK: 7–9 p.m.
HOUR OF HAI: 9–11 p.m.

SOULS: According to Chinese philosophy and religion, every human had three ethereal souls (hun / 魂) which would leave the body after death, and seven corporeal souls (po / 魄) that remained with the corpse. Each soul governed different aspects of a person's being, ranging from consciousness and memory, to physical function and sensation.

SPIRITUAL CORE: A spiritual core (灵核) is the foundation of a cultivator's power. It is typically formed only after ten years of hard work and study. If broken or damaged, the cultivator's abilities are compromised or even destroyed.

SUONA: A traditional Chinese double-reeded wind instrument with a distinct and high-pitched sound, most often used for celebrations of the living and the dead (such as weddings and funerals). Said to herald either great joy or devastating grief.

SWORD GLARE: Jianguang (剑光 / "sword light"), an energy attack released from a sword's edge, often seen in xianxia stories.

A TALE OF NANKE: An opera by Tang Xianzu that details a dream had by disillusioned official Chunyu Fen, highlighting the ephemerality of the mortal world and the illusory nature of wealth and grandeur.

TALISMANS: Strips of paper with written incantations, often in cinnabar ink or blood. They can serve as seals or be used as one-time spells.

THREE DISCIPLINES AND THREE POISONS: Also known as the threefold path in Buddhist traditions, the three disciplines are virtue, mind, and wisdom. Conversely, the three poisons (also known as the three defilements) refer to the three Buddhist roots of suffering: greed, wrath, ignorance.

WANGSHU: In Chinese mythology, Wangshu (望舒) is a lunar goddess often used in literary reference to the moon.

XIHE: In Chinese mythology, Xihe (羲和) is a solar goddess often used in literary reference to the sun.

XUN: A traditional Chinese vessel flute similar to the ocarina, often made of clay.

YIN ENERGY AND YANG ENERGY: Yin and yang is a concept in Chinese philosophy which describes the complementary interdependence of opposite/contrary forces. It can be applied to all forms of change and differences. Yang represents the sun, masculinity, and the living, while yin represents the shadows, femininity, and the dead, including spirits and ghosts. In fiction, imbalances between yin and yang energy may do serious harm to the body or act as the driving force for malevolent spirits seeking to replenish themselves of whichever energy they lack.

ZIWEI STAR: A star known to western astronomers as the North Star or Polaris. As the other stars seemed to revolve around it, the Ziwei Star is considered the celestial equivalent of the emperor. Its stationary position in the sky makes it key to Zi Wei Dou Shu, the form of astrology that the ancient Chinese used to divine mortal destinies.

ABOUT THE AUTHOR

Rou Bao Bu Chi Rou ("Meatbun Doesn't Eat Meat") was a low-level soldier who served in Gu Mang's army as a cook. Meatbun's cooking was so good that, after Gu Mang turned traitor, the spirit beast Cai Bao ("Veggiebun") swooped in to rescue Meatbun as it passed by. Thus, Meatbun escaped interrogation in Chonghua and became a lucky survivor. In order to repay the big orange cat Veggiebun, Meatbun not only cooked three square meals a day but also told the tale of Mo Xi and Gu Mang as a nightly bedtime story to coax the spirit beast Veggiebun to sleep. Once the saga came to an end, it was compiled into *Remnants of Filth*.

The Emperor Reborn and His Dearest Enemy

Cruel tyrant Taxian-jun killed his way to the throne and now reigns as the first ever emperor of the mortal realm. Yet somehow, he is unsatisfied. Left cold and bereft, abandoned by all he held dear, he takes his own life...only to be reborn anew.

Awakening in the body of his younger self—Mo Ran, a disciple of the cultivation sect Sisheng Peak—he discovers the chance to relive his life. This time, he vows to attain the gratification that once eluded him: all who defied him will fall, and never again will they treat him like a dog. His greatest fury is reserved for Chu Wanning, the coldly beautiful and aloofly catlike cultivation teacher who betrayed and thwarted Mo Ran time and again in their last life.

Yet as Mo Ran shamelessly pursues his own goals in this life he thought lost, he begins to wonder if there might be more to his teacher—and his own feelings—than he ever realized.

Available now in print & digital!

耽美Danmei

Seven Seas Entertainment

sevenseasdanmei.com

From *New York Times* Bestselling Author

ROU BAO BU CHI ROU

The HUSKY & His WHITE CAT SHIZUN

ERHA HE TA DE BAI MAO SHIZUN

© 肉包不吃肉 (Rou Bao Bu Chi Rou) / JJWXC / Seven Seas Entertainment